continued . . .

"Absolutely fabulous! . . . I was blown away by this latest release. The action and romance were evenly matched and the flow of the book kept me glued until the last page . . . Paranormal fans will be raving over this one!"   —*The Romance Readers Connection*

"Ashley has created a riveting tale that . . . explores different interpretations of human and nonhuman interaction."

—*Fresh Fiction*

"A very promising start to what should be a fresh take on a well-worn idea . . . A clever, quick book with some interesting twists that has whetted my appetite for more."

—*The Good, The Bad and The Unread*

THE MANY SINS OF LORD CAMERON

"Big, arrogant, sexy highlanders—Jennifer Ashley writes the kinds of heroes I crave!"

—Elizabeth Hoyt, *New York Times* bestselling author

"A sexy, passion-filled romance that will keep you reading until dawn."   —Julianne MacLean, *USA Today* bestselling author

LADY ISABELLA'S SCANDALOUS MARRIAGE

"I adore this novel: It's heartrending, funny, honest, and true. I want to know the hero—no, I want to *marry* the hero!"

—Eloisa James, *New York Times* bestselling author

"Readers rejoice! The Mackenzie brothers return as Ashley works her magic to create a unique love story brimming over with depth of emotion, unforgettable characters, sizzling passion, mystery, and a story that reaches out and grabs your heart. Brava!"

—*RT Book Reviews* (Top Pick)

"A heartfelt, emotional historical romance with danger and intrigue around every corner . . . A great read!"   —*Fresh Fiction*

"A wonderful novel, filled with sweet, tender love that has long been denied, fiery passion, and a good dash of witty humor . . . For a rollicking good time, sexy Highland heroes, and touching romances, you just can't beat Jennifer Ashley's novels!"

—*Night Owl Reviews*

THE MADNESS OF LORD IAN MACKENZIE

"Ever-versatile Ashley begins her new Victorian Highland Pleasures series with a deliciously dark and delectably sexy story of love and romantic redemption that will captivate readers with its complex characters and suspenseful plot."   —*Booklist*

"Mysterious, heartfelt, sensitive, and sensual . . . Two big thumbs up."   —*Publishers Weekly*, "Beyond Her Book"

"A story full of mystery and intrigue with two wonderful, bright characters . . . I look forward to more from Jennifer Ashley, an extremely gifted author."   · —*Fresh Fiction*

"Brimming with mystery, suspense, an intriguing plot, villains, romance, a tormented hero, and a feisty heroine, this book is a winner. I recommend *The Madness of Lord Ian Mackenzie* to anyone looking for a great read."   —*Romance Junkies*

"Wow! All I can say is *The Madness of Lord Ian Mackenzie* is one of the best books that I have ever read. [It] gets the highest recommendation that I can give. It is a truly wonderful book."
                    —*Once Upon A Romance*

"When you're reading a book that is a step or two—or six or seven—above the norm, you know it almost immediately. Such is the case with *The Madness of Lord Ian Mackenzie*. The characters here are so complex and so real that I was fascinated by their journey . . . [and] this story is as flat-out romantic as any I've read in a while . . . This is a series I am certainly looking forward to following."   —*All About Romance*

"A unique twist on the troubled hero . . . Fresh and interesting."
                    —*Night Owl Reviews* (Top Pick)

"A welcome addition to the genre."   —*Dear Author*

"Intriguing . . . Unique . . . Terrific."   —*Midwest Book Review*

Berkley Sensation Titles by Jennifer Ashley

THE MADNESS OF LORD IAN MACKENZIE
LADY ISABELLA'S SCANDALOUS MARRIAGE
THE MANY SINS OF LORD CAMERON
THE DUKE'S PERFECT WIFE

PRIDE MATES
PRIMAL BONDS
WILD CAT
MATE CLAIMED

MATE CLAIMED

JENNIFER ASHLEY

BERKLEY SENSATION, NEW YORK

THE BERKLEY PUBLISHING GROUP
Published by the Penguin Group
Penguin Group (USA) Inc.
375 Hudson Street, New York, New York 10014, USA
Penguin Group (Canada), 90 Eglinton Avenue East, Suite 700, Toronto, Ontario M4P 2Y3, Canada
(a division of Pearson Penguin Canada Inc.) • Penguin Books Ltd., 80 Strand, London WC2R 0RL,
England • Penguin Group Ireland, 25 St. Stephen's Green, Dublin 2, Ireland (a division of Penguin
Books Ltd.) • Penguin Group (Australia), 250 Camberwell Road, Camberwell, Victoria 3124, Australia
(a division of Pearson Australia Group Pty. Ltd.) • Penguin Books India Pvt. Ltd., 11 Community
Centre, Panchsheel Park, New Delhi—110 017, India • Penguin Group (NZ), 67 Apollo Drive,
Rosedale, Auckland 0632, New Zealand (a division of Pearson New Zealand Ltd.) • Penguin Books
(South Africa) (Pty.) Ltd., 24 Sturdee Avenue, Rosebank, Johannesburg 2196, South Africa

Penguin Books Ltd., Registered Offices: 80 Strand, London WC2R 0RL, England

This is a work of fiction. Names, characters, places, and incidents either are the product of the author's
imagination or are used fictitiously, and any resemblance to actual persons, living or dead, business
establishments, events, or locales is entirely coincidental. The publisher does not have any control over
and does not assume any responsibility for author or third-party websites or their content.

MATE CLAIMED

A Berkley Sensation Book / published by arrangement with the author

PUBLISHING HISTORY
Berkley Sensation mass-market / October 2012

Copyright © 2012 by Jennifer Ashley.
Excerpt from *Tiger Magic* by Jennifer Ashley copyright © 2012 by Jennifer Ashley.
Cover art by Don Sipley. Hand lettering by Ron Zinn.
Cover design by George Long.
Interior text design by Laura K. Corless.

ISBN: 978-0-425-25101-0

BERKLEY SENSATION®
Berkley Sensation Books are published by The Berkley Publishing Group,
a division of Penguin Group (USA) Inc.,
375 Hudson Street, New York, New York 10014.
BERKLEY SENSATION® is a registered trademark of Penguin Group (USA) Inc.
The "B" design is a trademark of Penguin Group (USA) Inc.

PRINTED IN THE UNITED STATES OF AMERICA

10 9 8 7 6 5 4 3 2

CHAPTER ONE

Iona smelled him long before she saw him—Eric Warden, the alpha Feline who ran the local Shiftertown, who'd decided to make half Shifter Iona Duncan's life hell.

She loped down the desert canyon, rock grating on her paws. The Nevada night was warm though it was early winter, the sky a riot of stars, the glow of the city far behind. Out here, Iona could be what she was meant to be—a wildcat, a Feline Shifter, running free.

For some reason, Eric wanted to end that.

Catch me if you can, Feline.

Last night, after her half sister's bridal shower, Iona had stayed out until dawn with Nicole and about twenty friends—all human. They'd gone to a human bar, no Shifters allowed, thank God. They'd liberated the bar of plenty of margaritas before limping home in the light of early morning. Iona had snatched a couple hours of sleep before she'd dragged herself to work.

The frenzy of the night out followed by the hangover of the day triggered Iona's need to shift. After work, Iona had driven her red pickup out to her favorite spot in the middle of the desert, off-roading half an hour to get there. She'd barely shed her clothes before her wildcat had taken over.

And now Eric was following her.

He pounded behind her, a powerhouse Shifter, his wildcat more snow leopard than anything else. Sleek, strong, cunning. Feline Shifters were a mixture of all wildcats—lion, leopard, jaguar, cheetah, tiger, and others—but most Shifters tended toward a certain type.

Iona was mostly panther, with black fur to match the hair she had while human. Her panther was long-legged, sure-footed, and a good jumper. This was her territory, and she laughed with glee as she left Eric far behind.

She dodged across a dry wash, kicking up dust, and scrambled into the rocky crevices on the other side. She knew by scent how far she was from Area 51, a place guarded by men with SUVs and rifles. Shifters could escape detection if they wanted to, but heading the other direction, east and a little north of here, was safer. Iona hopped from one sandstone ledge to the next, her paws scrabbling a little in the gravel.

She loved this. The joy of being in wild country nearly impossible for humans to reach was heady. *This is what I'm meant to be.*

Damned if Eric didn't follow right after her, faster than she'd thought he would. Iona crested the ridge at the top of the canyon and kept going.

She ran along a ledge and dropped down the other side of the ridge. Before she got to the bottom, she slunk into a shallow cave she knew was there from previous exploration. Anyone watching from the top would see only that she'd vanished.

Eric wouldn't need to see her to find her though. He'd scent her, but why make it easy for him?

Ever since Eric had spotted her in Coolers last spring, one of the few clubs that allowed in Shifters, he'd tracked her. *Stalked her*, Iona corrected.

Damned stubborn, hotter-than-hell Shifter with the green eyes—he followed her when she went out at night, sometimes showing up at her house or coming after her on her runs. She'd spot him here and there throughout the day, when she went to work or ran errands or drove out to a building site. Protecting her, Eric said. Driving her insane, was more like it.

The fact that Iona was half-Shifter was a deep, dark secret

her mother and half sister had kept for thirty-two years. Eric's interest in her was dangerous, could expose her as Shifter, and once that happened, her happy life would be over.

But Eric's scent had triggered something in Iona from the moment he'd sat down next to her in the club's dark corner and told her he knew what Iona was. He'd smelled of sweat and the night, and a musk that had made everything in her alert and aware.

His scent was stronger now, overlaid with that of his wildcat. He was coming.

Iona flattened herself into the black shadows at the back of the cave, but Eric was at the entrance, his leopard filling the opening. She faced him, ears flat against her head, her fur rising on her neck.

Eric didn't move. Dominants didn't need to show teeth or make any noise to tell another Shifter who was in charge. You knew.

He was far larger and more powerful than a natural snow leopard, his pelt creamy white and branded with a black jagged pattern. His eyes, fixed on her, were jade green.

Iona's wildcat was more slender than Eric's but no smaller, though it would be an interesting contest to see whether she matched him in strength. The biggest difference between them, though, was that Eric wore a silver and black Collar, and Iona did not.

Eric rose on his hind legs until his head nearly touched the roof of the cave. At the same time, his fur and cat limbs flowed into human bones and flesh. In a few seconds, a man stood in the leopard's place, a tall, muscular, naked male who made Iona's heart pound.

His face was hard and square, his chocolate brown hair cut short. A black tattoo swirled around his large shoulder and trailed down his arm in a jagged line. The tattoo wasn't magical—Shifters didn't need tatts. Eric just liked it.

His green eyes saw everything. There was no escaping that gaze once it fixed on you, even across a packed dance floor in a Las Vegas club. Iona still remembered the burn of his stare across the room; Eric, the first person in Iona's life outside her family who'd looked at her and recognized her as Shifter.

Even through her worry and anger, Iona had to concede

that Eric was delectable. He put to shame all the guys who'd tried last night to get her to dance with them.

What was between Eric's legs put them to shame too. The man was *hung*.

"You can't keep this up," Eric said. His voice, deep and fine, with the barest touch of Scots, had lately started invading her dreams.

Iona gave him a snarl to let him know he didn't worry her. Which was bullshit. He could take her in a heartbeat and both of them knew it.

Eric took one step forward. She crouched, waiting, letting him take another step, and another.

Once he'd cleared the entrance to the cave, Iona leapt up and sprang past him. His leopard she couldn't outrun, but she could outrun him in her animal form while he remained human. She barreled out of the cave and onto the rocks . . .

And found two hundred pounds of leopard on top of her, pinning her to the ledge.

How the hell did he shift that fast? Shifting took a while for Iona, and it could be painful. Eric flowed into his wildcat so smoothly it made her sick.

His growl became bad tempered as Iona struggled. His ears went flat, and he locked his teeth around her throat.

Fur protected Iona from the prick of his fangs, but she panicked. He could kill her right now, rip out her throat or slice open her belly. The panther sensed his strength—a fight with him would be tough. She couldn't get away—he was too fast.

Iona shifted. She didn't want to, but some instinct told her he wouldn't hurt her if she became a human. She felt her claws change to fingers and toes, her pelt fade and withdraw to become human flesh.

Eric lifted his long teeth from her throat, but he didn't do anything to stop her shifting. He waited and watched until Iona became a human woman, one with a large, soft-furred snow leopard draped over her bare body.

That large, soft-furred snow leopard suddenly became a man. One minute Iona had a big kitty lying on her, the next, a strong, naked human male pinned her to the ground.

She struggled, but Eric trapped her wrists and held them against the cold gravel. He wanted her to look away as he stared her down, but she refused to. Somehow Iona knew that if she ever did look away, she'd lose—not only now, but always.

"I told you to call me when you needed to go running," he growled.

"You follow me anyway. Why should I bother?"

"I scented you fighting the shift even as you drove away. It's getting harder, isn't it?"

Iona tried to ignore the stab of fear his words gave her. "Why can't you leave me alone? If anyone finds out I'm Shifter . . ."

She knew exactly what they'd do. The human Shifter bureau would slap a Collar on her without listening to her protests, strip Iona of all her rights, and keep her in quarantine before releasing her to whatever Shifter they assigned to keep her under control. Three guesses as to who that Shifter would be.

And who the hell knew what they'd do to Iona's mother, who'd kept the fact that Iona was half-Shifter quiet all this time.

"I can't leave you alone. You're in my jurisdiction, my responsibility. And you're losing control, aren't you?"

Iona shivered with more than anger. His long body was hard on hers, muscles gleaming with sweat in the moonlight. Eric's living strength made the wild thing in her want to respond.

"I was hung over," she said. "I'm not like this every day."

Eric lowered his head and inhaled, his nose touching her throat. "You will be soon. Your mating need is high and getting stronger."

That need pounded through her, tried to make Iona's body rise to his. *A male, ready for you—take him!*

"What I do is none of your business," Iona managed to say. "Leave me the hell alone. My life has been fine so far without you in it."

"But I'm in it now." His voice was deep and rumbling, almost a purr. The tattoo that wound down his arm kept drawing her gaze, and she so much wanted to touch it . . .

For Eric's part, he was barely holding on to his self-control. Iona's scent was that of a female Feline who'd reached her fertile years, a little over thirty by human standards, a few years past cub by Shifter.

This female Feline didn't know how to control her pheromones, didn't realize she was broadcasting her availability to every Shifter male far and wide. She might as well hold up a flashing sign.

Good thing Eric was so disciplined, still mourning his mate lost long ago, so uninterested in mating. Right?

Or he'd be hard as a rock, wanting to say *to hell with it* and take her. They were alone in the middle of nowhere, and Eric was within his rights to take whatever stray adult female wandered into his territory.

He didn't necessarily have to mate-claim her. As clan leader as well as pride leader, he could father cubs on a lone female belonging to no pride or clan if he wanted to. For the good of the clan, for the strength of his pride. So he could say.

But those had been the rules in the wild. Shifters were tamer now, civilized. Living together in a community, in harmony. *And all that crap.*

Eric's instincts said, *Screw the rules. She's unmated and unclaimed. By rights, she's fair game, and I found her. That makes her mine.*

Wouldn't that be sweet? Iona Duncan had a face that was pure Celtic, her hair black as the night sky, her eyes the light ice blue of her ancestors. Shifters had been created about the time the Nordic invaders would have been subduing Celts in northern Scotland, and some of that mixture had gotten into Iona.

Now her soft but strong body was under his, and her blue eyes held longing, oceans of it.

"Does it hurt?" Eric asked in a gentler tone.

"Having a big Shifter male resting his weight on my wrists? I'd say yes."

Eric wanted to laugh. He liked the challenge in her, liked that she wasn't cringing, timid, and submissive. Untrained, yes; terrified, no.

"I mean the mating need," Eric said. "It's rising in you, and you can't stop it. That's why you're out here, why you've been running around like a crazy thing. You want to be wild, to taste the wind. To hunt. To feel the fear in you flow to the innocent creatures out there, to make them fear *you*."

Iona stopped squirming, her eyes going still. Eric read the hunger in her, the need to find a male, to mate in wild frenzy for days. Iona wasn't stopped by a Collar. Her instincts would flow like fire. Untamed.

Eric's own need rose in response. He wanted to kiss that fire, to taste the freedom in her that was now only a memory to him.

He nuzzled the line of her hair, already knowing her scent, already familiar with it.

"I'll take care of you," he said. "You'll become part of my pride, and I'll look after you. Me and my sister and my son. We'll take care of you from now on."

Iona's glare returned. "I don't *want* to be part of your pride. They'd put that Collar on me." Her frenzied gaze went to the chain fused to Eric's neck, the Celtic knot resting on his throat. "It's painful, isn't it? When the Collar goes on?"

"Yes." Eric couldn't lie. He remembered the agony when the Collar had locked around his throat, every second of it, though it had been twenty years ago now. The Collars hurt anew whenever a Shifter's violent nature rose within him— the Collar shocked so hard it knocked said Shifter flat on his ass for a while.

"Why would you want me to experience that?" Iona asked. "You say you want to take care of me, but you want me to go through taking the Collar?"

"No, I don't." And if Eric did things right, she wouldn't have to wear a Collar, ever.

The urge to take Iona far away, to hide her somewhere from prying eyes, to protect her from the world was making him crazy. *Protect the mate* was the instinct that drove all males.

Eric caressed her wrists where he held them down. "If you don't acknowledge the Shifter, if you don't learn how to control what's going on inside you, you're going to go feral."

"Feral?" Her sable brows drew down. "What the hell does that mean?"

"It means what it sounds like. The beast in you takes over,

and you forget what it is to be human, even in your human form. You'll live only to kill and to mate. You'll start resenting your family for trying to keep you home. You'll try to get away from them. You might even hurt them."

Iona looked stunned. "I'd never do that."

"You won't mean to, but you will. You can keep them safe if you learn how to be Shifter and live with Shifters. I won't let humans know anything about you until the Collar is on you and you're ready."

"My point is that humans should never have to *know* I'm Shifter. No one's ever suspected, but they will if an asshole Shifter keeps following me around."

Eric clamped down on her wrists, at the end of his patience. "If you go feral, they might not bother Collaring you. They'll just shoot you like an animal, and your mother will go to prison for not reporting your existence. Is that really what you want?"

He felt her fear reaction, but Iona kept up her glare. "I'm half-human. Won't that keep me from going feral?"

"Not necessarily. Sometimes the human side helps. Sometimes it doesn't."

"I'm not giving up my entire life to live with you in a ghetto because you say I *might* go crazy," Iona said. "I'll risk it."

Eric growled. "I can't let you go on living without protection."

Her eyes widened. "How do you plan to protect me? Abduct me and lock me in your house? What would the human police say to that?"

Taking her home and keeping her there was exactly what Eric wanted to do. At any other time, he'd simply do it. Iona was getting out of control, and she needed help.

But Shiftertown might not be the safest place for her at the moment, now that the idiot human government had decided— to save money—to shut down a northern Nevada Shiftertown and relocate all those Shifters to Eric's Shiftertown. The humans, in their ignorance, had decided that the new Shifters would simply be absorbed under Eric's leadership.

What the humans didn't understand—in spite of Eric talking himself blue to explain—was that Shifters of both Shiftertowns were used to a certain hierarchy and couldn't change it overnight. The other Shiftertown leader was being forced to step down a few rungs under Eric, which wasn't going over well, especially since that leader was a Feline-hating Lupine.

Eric at least had persuaded the humans to let him meet the other leader, Graham McNeil, face-to-face before the new Shifters moved down here. Eric had found McNeil to be a disgruntled, old-fashioned Shifter, furious that the humans were forcing him to submit to Eric's rule.

McNeil was going to be trouble. He already had been, demanding more meetings with humans without Eric, insisting that Eric's Shifters got turned out of their houses and crammed in with others so McNeil's Shifters wouldn't have to wait for the new housing to be built.

McNeil was going to challenge for leadership—Eric had known that before the man opened his mouth. McNeil's Shiftertown had been all Lupine, and his Lupines were less than thrilled to learn that they had to adapt to living with bears and Felines.

And in the middle of all this, a young, fertile female with the rising need to mate was running around loose and unprotected.

Iona struggled to sit up again. It went against Eric's every instinct to lift himself from the cushion of her body, but he did it.

She leaned against the rock wall and scraped her hair back from her face. Goddess, she was sexy, bare breasted in the moonlight, lifting midnight hair from her sharp-boned face.

Naked and beautiful, filling Eric's brain with wanting. *And* if he did this right, she might provide the answer to some of his Shiftertown problems.

"I was coming to see you tonight for a reason," Eric said. "Not just to track you down. I came to ask you to have Duncan Construction bid on the housing project to expand Shiftertown."

Iona stared at him in surprise, letting go of the hair she'd been smoothing. "Why would I want to do that?"

"Because I need someone I can trust to build these houses. Shifter houses aren't just places for Shifters to live.

I need them constructed in a way that's best for Shifters. It's important."

She looked curious in spite of her caution. "What do you mean, in a way that's best for Shifters?"

Eric couldn't explain—yet. He'd have to wait before he revealed to her that Shifter houses didn't simply hold Shifter families. They held secrets of Shifter clans that humans could never know about.

Even McNeil would need to protect the secrets of his pack; probably why the man wanted to move into the existing Shifter houses—they already had the necessary spaces. Eric had planned to modify the new houses the same way he and his Shifters had modified the old houses, a little bit, over time, so the humans never realized they were doing it. But Graham's Shifters didn't have the patience, and it would be smarter to do it right away. Using Iona's company and guiding her through the process could get it done quicker, and help both her and Shiftertown.

"I can't tell you until you win the contract," Eric said. He met her gaze, not disguising anything in his. "Please."

CHAPTER TWO

Iona blinked, for the first time looking at him in more than frustration, anger, or crazed need. "Are you saying you need my help?"

"Yes." He said it simply, no shame attached.

"And what do I get in return? You leave me alone?"

Eric felt his grin spread across his face. "I can't leave you alone, love. You're unmated and unclaimed, in my territory. I need to look after you. But I think we can come up with an agreement."

"Oh really? The moment I enter your Shiftertown, all the Shifters there will know what I am. How will that help me?"

"Your sister or your mother can be the on-site manager. You never have to leave your office if you don't want to."

Iona wrapped her arms around her knees, gathering herself in. "Never leave my office? Never go to Shiftertown? Seriously?"

"Seriously. I'd come to you."

"Huh. I'll think about it."

Eric moved to her side again but kept himself from touching her. "I really do need you. And you need me. Think of it as an opportunity to better understand your Shifter side."

"I don't think I *want* to understand my Shifter side."

"Yes, you do. You're going wild, and you need to learn how to contain it."

Iona shivered, looking away, and Eric's protective need sprang to life again. He wanted to fold her in his arms, take her home, keep her safe.

When Iona looked up again, the fear in her eyes was stark. "What do I do?"

Eric leaned into her, inhaling her ripe, sensual scent. "I'll help you through this. But you have to trust me."

Iona went still, though he sensed her body reacting to his. She wanted him, and everything in Eric knew it, and responded.

"You have to give me reason to trust you," she said.

"No, sweetheart. *Trust* means believing in me even when you don't understand."

Eric nuzzled her again, and Iona let him, not pulling away. He'd scent-marked her the night he'd met her, but a scent marking was not the same as a mate-claim. Eric could scent-mark his children, his siblings, and anyone else he needed to, and it meant that Iona was under Eric's protection.

Any Shifter coming across her would scent Eric and know he'd need to deal with the Shiftertown leader if he messed with her. Even Graham would understand that, though whether Graham would leave her alone was another question.

Eric breathed his scent onto her again as he brushed the line of her neck, renewing the mark. Goddess, she was sweet. She smelled clean like a mountain meadow, and her underlying scent was warm with wanting.

He made himself sit up and push away from her, rising in one move. Before Iona could scramble to her feet, he reached down, took her by the arms, and hauled her up next to him.

His human side was fully aware of her nudity and the petal-soft feel of her skin. Her breasts were full, the tips dusky, and the twist of hair between her legs black. Beautiful.

"You need me, Iona."

Iona took a step back, breaking the contact. "You need *me*, you mean."

"In theory."

"Chew on this theory, Eric. I'm not one of your mate-claimed females, or whatever you call them. I'll give you what you need to build your Shiftertown houses, and you'll leave me the hell alone. Bargain?" She stuck out her hand.

Eric looked at the hand, Iona offering a handshake in the human way. He didn't bother to take it. "No bargains, love. We do what's necessary."

Iona was gorgeous when she was fired up, blue eyes hot, her stance challenging. Eric's reaction to her was obvious, even in the dark.

Her gaze dropped down his body, stopping at his very erect . . . erection. She put one hand on her bare hip and kept her voice light. "So what is that? An extension of your tail?"

Eric shrugged, unembarrassed. "I'm a male Shifter at the prime of life, and you're a female entering her hottest mating years. What do you think it is?"

Iona's eyes flickered, her need strong. Her pheromones filled the air until Eric could taste them. "Damn it," she whispered.

She shifted to her wildcat. She couldn't shift as swiftly as Eric could, and Eric saw that it was painful for her. His hard-on faded as he watched her struggle, but his wanting for her didn't die. Iona was beautiful and wild, and he wanted her to be free. And safe.

Iona bounded past him. Her wildcat was sure-footed and fast, her pelt beautifully dark, her eyes as ice blue as her human eyes.

Eric watched in pure enjoyment before he fluidly shifted and ran after her.

Graham McNeil watched the humans shrink back in a satisfying way as he walked into the meeting room at the courthouse. They tried not to react to him, pretending they had all the power, but Graham knew he'd rule this room.

The only person who didn't look intimidated was Eric Warden, the leader of the Vegas Shiftertown. Not leader for long, if Graham had anything to say about it.

The humans didn't like Graham's buzz of black hair, the fiery tatts down his arms, and his motorcycle vest. Eric had a tatt as well, jagged lines that started somewhere under his short-sleeved black T-shirt and wove down one arm.

Eric was going to be a problem. He was a strong alpha and had been leader of his Shiftertown for more than twenty years. As soon as Graham walked in, Eric's jade green gaze fixed on him and stayed there.

The shithead wanted Graham to look away. To acknowledge that Graham was going to be second, maybe way less than that. Pussy.

Graham wasn't about to look away. Neither was Eric. Graham felt his hackles rise, the wolf in him ready to shift. Eric's eyes flicked to his cat's, slitted and very light green.

They'd have stared each other down across the room for hours if a clueless human male, with no idea that a dominance fight was in progress, hadn't walked between them.

"Mr. McNeil," the man said. "Sit down, please."

"Graham's fine." He'd rather remain standing, a better position for facing an enemy, but humans had a thing for chairs.

They wanted Graham to sit next to Eric. Idiots. Eric proved he wasn't stupid by walking to the other end of the table and planting himself in a chair, leaving Graham to sit at the opposite end.

What did the humans expect Graham to do? Shake Eric's hand, give him a big hug, wait for Eric to say, *Welcome to my territory, let's be friends*?

They did, the morons. Amazing.

Graham's Shiftertown had been tucked inside a mountain range south of Elko, a long way from anywhere, and he and his people had done pretty much what they wanted. A man with a check sheet came around every once in a while to make sure Shifters were behaving themselves and not eating people or whatever they thought Shifters did, and then he'd go.

But then someone in an office way back east, who'd never been to a Shiftertown in his life, had decided that times were tough, budgets had to be cut, and there was no reason to have two Shiftertowns in Nevada. So why not shove all the Shifters into one? The Shifter bureau could keep a better eye on them all that way.

Graham was used to the vast emptiness of rural Nevada, a

place where a wolf could shift and run and run, never see a human for months if he didn't want to. In this effing city, there were humans everywhere. They smelled like shit. Even Eric smelled wrong.

Graham had seen, on his way to the meeting, a sign on the top of a taxi advertising Shifter women dancing nude in clubs just off the Strip. Shifter females, taking off their clothes for human males. And Warden sat back and let it happen. That needed to stop.

He felt Eric's eyes on him again. Graham returned the look with as much determination. *You're going down.*

The trouble was, Graham was getting the same message back from Eric. This was going to be a long, bloody fight. The humans in this room had no idea what they'd started.

Eric took the seat on the opposite end of the table from Graham, not only to keep himself from ripping out Graham's throat, but also to prevent Graham smelling Iona on him. It had been two days and many scrubbings since Eric had chased Iona in the wild land north of town, but he didn't need Graham to catch any lingering scent.

Her sexy scent. Eric had dreamed of her for the last two nights, the dreams so vivid that he woke up surprised he was alone in his bed. He woke up hard and sweating, groaning as the sheets brushed his aching cock. He was like a Shifter in mating frenzy, but Eric had conquered that a long time ago, right?

Iona was made for mating frenzy. He thought of her with her long limbs curled around herself as she'd gazed at him in the moonlight outside the cave.

Eric needed to protect her, yes, but he also wanted to go to her, wrap himself around her, declare her his mate, keep her away from all others. A Shifter's primal need was to hole up with a female for weeks at a time, keeping her safe while they sexed themselves mindless, nature's way of ensuring that cubs came.

Times were more civilized now. Females could reject the mate-claim, and they all lived in peace and harmony.

Bullshit. Whenever Eric looked at Iona, or scented her, or felt her warmth, civilization went to hell. He wanted Iona, wanted to be naked with her, nothing more.

Those thoughts were dangerous while Graham McNeil watched him from the other end of the table, but he couldn't stop them coming.

One of the humans cleared his throat, calling the meeting to order.

The humans in the room were nervous. The smell of fear was rank, and Graham didn't hide his disgust. But at least their fear scent would cover any residual one of Iona's.

The talk moved instantly to housing, a bone of contention.

"Every effort is being made, Mr. McNeil," the leader of the bunch said, a shit of a man called Frank Kellerman.

Kellerman was the head of the Shifter liaison committee, and the only one of the humans who wasn't sweating hard in his suit. The rest eyed Graham in outright fear if they could bring themselves to look at him at all.

Kellerman went on, "The housing being built will equal that which is already in Shiftertown. For now, your families will have to adapt to boarding with others."

Graham balled his hands on the table. "I'm not putting my wolves in houses with a bunch of fucking Felines or bears. *His* Shifters can double up. We'll take the houses they empty."

"I agree," Eric said. All gazes shot to him now, including Graham's. "Shifters have a tough time living with strangers," Eric went on. "The Elko Shifters should occupy houses together, and our Shifters will move in with their own clan members."

Kellerman gave Eric his smooth smile. "The point is that the Elko Shifters and the Las Vegas Shifters need to integrate as quickly as possible. Bunking together will induce camaraderie and make the transition painless."

What an idiot. Eric kept his face straight, but Graham rolled his eyes. When strange Shifters found themselves thrown together in a tight space, the natural instinct was to go into a dominance battle.

Who controlled each house was as important as who controlled Shiftertown. Members of the same clan or same community already knew who was dominant. There would still be conflict, but exponentially less.

Eric said, "You shove us together without letting us get used to each other first, and there'll be a bloodbath."

"But you have Collars," the nervous man who'd called the meeting to order said. "Shifters can no longer fight one another."

"Then you'll have a crapload of Collar-shocked Shifters all over the place," Graham said from his end of the table. "We'll fight for dominance, Kellerman. It's instinctive, and it won't be pretty."

Eric stared down the table at Graham, willing the guy to shut up. Graham wasn't used to dealing with humans. Eric had learned to let the humans understand just enough Shifter business to keep them happy, and how much to keep from them.

Graham met Eric's gaze, but instead of subsiding, he sat up straighter, meeting the challenge. Dumb-ass. Challenging for leadership in this room would only get them both arrested.

"An even better solution," Eric said, still looking at Graham, "would be to get the houses built before the wolves transfer down."

"We can't wait that long," Kellerman said. "Though the houses will be started soon. We formally accepted a bid from a construction company this morning."

Eric kept his gaze from moving. He hadn't heard from Iona since their encounter, and he didn't know whether she'd had her company make the bid. His Guardian, Neal Ingram, good at getting info Shifters weren't supposed to have, said he hadn't seen a bid come forward from Duncan Construction in the Shifter council's records. It must have been sent at the last minute, right before this meeting, in fact.

Graham's gaze sharpened as he watched Eric, catching Eric's subtlest reaction. The Lupine was good.

"What construction company?" Graham asked without looking away from Eric.

Kellerman consulted his notes. "A small, local company who does quality work. They put in a decent bid, and we accepted it." He closed the file, but Eric couldn't see it anyway from his vantage point. "Their architects are already drawing up plans. Within a month, you'll have new places to live."

Eric didn't let his expression change. The players in the poker tournaments downtown would have envied his blank face. Graham kept his gaze hard on Eric for a few moments before switching it to Kellerman.

Graham turning away didn't mean Graham was giving up. He'd sent Eric a signal that he knew there was something going on, and he was going to find out what.

After the meeting ended—with nothing resolved—Graham fell into step with Eric as they headed for the parking garage and their separate vehicles. "Why so interested in the construction company, Warden?"

Eric didn't bother looking at him. "You aren't?"

Graham stopped. They were relatively alone, the upper floors of the parking garage sparse at the human lunch hour. "What are you up to?"

"You know we have to alter the houses," Eric said. "Be good to know what kind of plans these architects are coming up with. Better still to have the plans changed to fit our needs."

Graham's wolf gray eyes narrowed, but he gave Eric a conceding nod. "I get that. But how would they make plans to *our* specs? Without us giving away anything?"

"Agree to let me take care of that. Your idea of liaising is intimidation and fear. There's an easier way."

"No, there isn't," Graham said. "Terrify the humans, and they do what you want. Works like a dream."

"In a place where Shifters outnumber humans, sure. Look around you." Eric jerked his chin at the streets and buildings below them. "Humans everywhere. Trust me, subtlety works."

"Yeah, look where subtlety's got you. You didn't argue with them very much in there, and you tried to shut me down when I did."

"Because I don't need humans knowing our business." The more humans believed that the Collars controlled the Shifters, the better.

"I'm not crawling and hiding from humans," Graham said.

"Keeping your hole shut about Shifter secrets is not the same as crawling and hiding. There's too much at stake."

Graham's scowl would have sent most of the Shifters in Eric's Shiftertown running for cover, but Eric met him stare for stare. Graham was going to be hard to tame.

Graham finally shrugged. "All right—I'll keep my mouth shut around humans. Because I'm not talking to them anymore. You *liaise*, if that's what you like. When you fail, tell me, and I'll scare the shit out of them and get a few things done."

With a final glare, Graham turned his back and walked away. If they'd been in animal form, Graham might have sprayed behind him or done something equally disgusting to show Eric his contempt.

Eric turned away himself, so that if Graham glanced behind him to see how Eric had taken the insult, he'd see nothing but Eric walking uncaringly toward his motorcycle.

He knew Graham wouldn't look back, though. Eric unstrapped his helmet and heard Graham start up his own bike. Graham was dominant enough to know his gestures made the right implications, without having to double-check.

Eric waited until Graham had ridden out, watching the man drive through the streets toward Charleston and North Las Vegas, before he started his bike and departed the other direction, heading for Duncan Construction's office on the west side of town.

I ona dropped her sandwich and jumped to her feet when she sensed Eric outside the door to the office. It was a terrific sandwich from a little deli down the street, and now it was a mess of roast beef, honey mustard, lettuce, and fresh bread all over her desk.

Eric walked in, bringing with him a wave of November chill, but Iona broke into a sweat.

He wore a short-sleeved black T-shirt under his leather jacket, one that showed the tatt sliding down his arm when he took off the jacket. He removed his sunglasses, giving her the full flash of his jade green eyes.

She'd tried to forget his tall, strong body over hers when he'd cornered her like prey in the canyons, or at least pretended to forget. Now with Eric in front of her, she shivered all the way down, the sensation of him stretched out on top of her as vivid as when it'd happened.

That had been in his territory. This was hers. Iona gathered up the mess of her sandwich, dropped it back on the paper it had come in, wrapped it up, and wiped her hands on paper napkins.

Eric let the door close behind him. Her office was a trailer on the site where they stored their equipment and supplies and sold building goods on the side. At least it was lunchtime— her mother and sister were off doing wedding shopping, the guys lunching wherever they liked to lunch.

Iona was relatively alone here, but . . .

"What the hell are you doing, Eric?" she said, making her voice not shake. "How is a Shifter coming openly to my office going to keep me safe?"

CHAPTER THREE

Eric gave her his stare, not smiling or saying hello, nothing a normal person would do. He showed up, sliding into her life again, and that was that.

His Collar glinted above the line of his T-shirt, proclaiming what he was—not human, a wild thing someone had tried to cage. His look said that, though humans might try for centuries, he'd never be tamed, though he might pretend he was for his own reasons.

He asked her, "Did Duncan Construction win the bid?"

No apologies, no embarrassment. Not even glee. Eric leaned against the desk and looked at her, and it was all Iona could do to not react. In any way.

"Yes," she said.

Eric's eyes softened the slightest bit. "Good girl."

Why did that little morsel of praise warm her all over? "You couldn't have called to ask me that? I know Shifters have phones. Or did you forget how to use yours? You push the numbers on the little buttons . . ."

"Cute." Eric leaned toward her and brushed his fingertips over her chin.

She should jerk away, break the contact, but Iona couldn't move. He was an alpha male, and she was . . .

She didn't know. She'd avoided Shifters all her life, so Iona had no idea if she was dominant or submissive or what either of those really meant.

She knew only that when Eric looked at her, her thoughts shot back to the night they'd stood together behind the Forum Shops, and he'd fed her sweet chocolate with his fingers. She remembered every taste of that chocolate, every flavor passing her lips, and best of all, Eric's mouth following it.

"I thought you wanted to protect me," she said. "Coming openly to my office isn't the way to do it."

Eric straightened up, removing his mesmerizing touch. "No one's here, and no one noticed me. I need to see the architect's plans for the Shifter houses."

That was the reason he'd come? Why did she feel disappointed? "I won't have them for a while. It takes time to get blueprints, even on a rush job."

"I need to see them as soon as you have them."

Iona thought about what he'd said up in the cave when he talked about the houses—*I need them constructed in a way that's best for Shifters.* She still didn't know what that meant.

"Ask the Shifter council to show you a copy when they're finished," she said.

Eric leaned across the desk, right over her rewrapped sandwich. "Much more fun to come here and demand them from you."

Why did she want to agree? "You might be the leader of Shiftertown, but this is my office, and here, I'm the boss."

Something hot flickered in his eyes, and his lips twitched. "Never try to out-alpha an alpha, sweetheart. You'll lose."

His stance said, though, that he liked her sass. This man wasn't one for timidity. To a Shifter, she'd heard, being timid meant being submissive, and the alpha would take full advantage. She couldn't afford to be timid with Eric.

Eric brushed his thumb over the corner of her mouth, where she realized that some honey mustard lingered. "What am I going to do with you, Iona?"

"Don't buy me any more chocolate."

She hadn't been able to look at the chocolate box he'd bought her without remembering Eric's fingers at her lips, his mouth on hers. She hadn't been able to resist taking out a piece at a time, in the privacy of her bedroom, savoring it, and pretending Eric was there to feed it to her.

"You like the ones with the chiles the best," Eric said softly. "I remember."

His finger moved on her mouth, then he leaned forward and inhaled, his nose nearly touching her hair.

Eric thought he could drown in her scent. Cinnamon and spice, overlaid with her musk, a heady combination that filled his dreams. She was a woman in her prime calling out to a male, and Eric was losing control.

Iona's blue eyes were close, her breath warm on his skin. "Why do you do that?" she asked.

"Do what?"

"Smell me like that?" Her voice was sultry, like a caress.

Because I could lie down and bathe in your warmth, and nothing else on this earth would matter.

"Scent is a powerful way to communicate. From scent alone I can tell you've been here awhile, working intently on something, and when I came in, I shook you out of that."

"You can tell all that by sniffing me?"

"Plus I see notes all over your desk, computer files open, and you eating here instead of going out with your family."

"Had something I wanted to get done."

"What?" Eric drew blueprints out from under the remains of her sandwich. The careful lines and neat letters and numbers didn't mean anything to him. "What is this?"

Iona's slight relaxation told him she cared about this project but didn't fear him knowing about it. "An extension to my sister's house. My mom and I decided to put in a couple bedrooms and a rec room for her as a surprise while she and Tyler are on their honeymoon in Hawaii. We won't finish by the time they get back, but everything will be well under way."

"I like the way you think." Eric did, because if Iona could plan a covert extension to her own sister's house, she'd be able to keep quiet on the work Eric wanted done. He traced the dimension marks on the blueprints. "You understand what all these mean?"

"Of course I do. It's kind of my job."

Eric looked around the small but warm office. "Three females running a construction company."

"Yes." Iona's eyes held a challenge. "What about it?"

Eric wanted to relax, to laugh with her, to casually sit down behind her desk and draw her onto his lap while they talked. *Soon.* "You know, I still have to smack some of my males around to get them to let their mates or daughters have jobs or go to college. McNeil's Shifters are even more old-fashioned. When I bring you in, you'll be a good influence on the others."

Iona's eyes glinted. "*If* you bring me in, you mean."

"You know I have to." He said it quietly, trying to keep the arrogance out, and the triumph. Eric wanted her in his fold, to be able to put his arm around her and tell all other Shifters, *Back off. She's mine.*

"Then I can say good-bye to everything I've worked for," Iona said. "My mom and sister can too. My dad—my stepdad, I mean—built this company from the ground up. I'm not about to do anything to let them lose it."

Eric didn't answer. She was right that here lay the problem. If Eric took Iona to Shiftertown—to keep her safe—her family would suffer repercussions for hiding her all this time. He had ideas on how to get around that, but he'd need Iona's cooperation.

But Iona couldn't deny her Shifter side all her life. The half human, half Shifters Eric had known who'd tried to shut out their Shifter side had died. They'd gone feral and had either been killed by other Shifters or human hunters, or they'd killed themselves.

Eric couldn't let that happen to Iona, no matter what he had to do. No matter that he might have to put her in restraints and haul her in, keeping her sequestered in his house while she got used to the idea of being his captive.

And why did that thought beat excitement through him? Iona in bonds, glaring at him with her beautiful blue eyes . . . Being Shifter, she'd be able to get out of any mundane restraints, but it would be fun for a while.

Eric opened the wrapper on her desk and looked at the mess inside. "Is this what you're eating?"

"I was."

"What did you do, sit on it?"

Iona slammed the paper back over the sandwich. "Will you go before someone sees you?"

"Come with me. I'll buy you lunch."

Iona's eyes flared hunger. That hunger touched Eric like a flame.

"Can't. Too busy here, and we'd have to find someplace where no one knew me. Plus, you're obviously a Shifter."

Eric shrugged. "I go where I want."

"No, you don't. Plenty of places don't allow Shifters."

"You allow them."

She made a noise of exasperation. "No, I don't. One just keeps barging in."

He held back his laugh. "Why don't you throw me out, then? You could call your security guards or the police. Why haven't you?"

He saw the catch in her breath, the tightening of her eyes. "I can handle you myself."

"Sure about that?" Eric leaned to her again.

"Will you stop *smelling* me? It's just weird."

"Have you closed yourself off to using your scent-sense? That's dangerous, love."

"I had to. It was driving me crazy."

Eric had some sympathy. Scent could be powerful, triggering emotions and sense memory, as well as physical hunger and mating need. The smell of burned matches took him back to the Second World War when he and his sister Cassidy had slunk through the night carrying explosives to sabotage the German army. The smell of strawberries transported him to the happy days when he'd first met Kirsten, his mate, passed long ago now. Iona, untrained and trying to deny her natural instincts, must be going insane.

"That roast beef smells good, even all squashed, doesn't it?" Eric asked, glancing at the wrapped sandwich. "If you were in your panther form, you wouldn't worry. You'd gulp it down and spit out the paper."

Iona's hunger came to him again. "That's why I have to ignore scents when I'm in my human form. I'd make a complete idiot of myself."

"Don't ignore them. Control it." Eric spread his hands on

the desk. "Starting now. Use your nose on me and tell me what it tells you."

Iona stared at him, her fear as palpable as her hunger. Then she swallowed, her slender throat moving, and she leaned to him.

Eric held himself still as her nose brushed the line of his hair. His impulse was to grab her, shove the sandwich remains and blueprints from the desk, and lay her across its top, spreading her and letting his body and hers do what both truly wanted. The coupling would be good. Intense. Memorable.

Instead, he made himself stand still as she roved his face to his neck, breasts lifting as she inhaled.

"You had eggs for breakfast," she said. "You've been riding around on your motorcycle, farther than just between here and Shiftertown, and you've been very close to at least one other Shifter. You were also extremely angry this morning." Iona lifted her head, puzzlement in her eyes. "Angry about what?"

"Not angry," Eric said. "Frustrated. What kind of Shifter?"

"How am I supposed to know that?"

"You'll know. Come on. Give it your best shot."

Iona leaned closer, her eyes closing as she drew in a long breath. Her hair brushed his cheek, and Eric's body tightened.

"Felines," Iona said, opening her eyes and drawing back. "And another kind, but I don't recognize it. I'm only familiar with Felines."

"Lupine," Eric said. "The Felines were my sister and son at breakfast. I hugged them both before I left. The Lupine is Graham McNeil, the asshole who's being shoved into my Shiftertown. Which is why we need the new houses."

"Which you want constructed to your specifications."

"Without mentioning it to anyone," he said.

Iona drew back. "How am I supposed to have my crew build houses without them noticing what they're building?"

"You're having your sister's house remodeled without telling her."

"Only until she and her husband get back from their trip. I think she'll notice the guys hammering and sawing and putting up walls then. It can't be done."

He liked the way she stood and glared at him, not bowing her head and meekly promising him whatever he wanted. She was strong, this lady. A survivor.

"Find a way," he said. "I'll keep my Shifters from you, and the humans from finding out about you, and you alter the plans to my specs without telling anyone. All right?"

"And if I refuse? You'll expose me?"

"You think I'm threatening you?" Eric came out of his nonchalant, Eric-is-everyone's-friend stance, and leaned over the desk to her again, not stopping the predator. Iona stood her ground, but her eyes widened, and her wild scent washed over him.

"I don't need to make deals with you, Iona. You're an unmated, unprotected female in my territory. I could make you mine right here in this office, carry you home, and sequester you, and you couldn't do anything to stop me. Could you? You'd fight, but in the end I'd win."

He leaned closer, the desk no barrier, and she stepped back, catching herself on the chair behind her. Her eyes flickered, and he smelled her fear, but she wouldn't look away.

She wet her lips, which made them red and sultry. "Is this how you romance all the girls?"

The little bit of defiance kicked hot need through Eric's body. Having her was going to be good, so good.

"Sweetheart, an unprotected female raises the capture instinct in all unmated males, and most aren't strong enough to control it. McNeil's Shifters are just this side of wild, and they're not about to control anything. Females protected by a clan or family are safe, but someone like you . . ." Eric reached across the desk and touched her cheek. "When Shifters see you, alone and unmated, their beasts will come out. The wild things we once were just *want*." His touch grew firmer. "And they take."

She drew a quick breath. "But you control your beast?"

"Barely." Eric brushed her skin with his fingertips, liking how her cheek flushed. "I can keep it together, but whenever I see you, it's one hell of a struggle."

"But you hold it in. Is that why you're the alpha?"

"One of the reasons."

Eric felt his eyes change to Shifter, and Iona's flicked to

Shifter in response. He smelled her desires, the wild frenzy in her fighting to take over. She tried to tamp it down, but Eric's own frenzy was responding.

He could do it. He could pull her across the desk to him, strip her down, make her his in the most inescapable way. It wouldn't take long.

Eric leaned closer and licked across her lips.

Iona jumped, but she didn't back off. He felt her body shaking, sensed her rise in temperature, tasted the mustard from her sandwich that lingered at the corner of her mouth.

He licked her again, and this time, Iona's tongue came out to meet his.

Eric slid his hand to the back of her neck and gripped her while he played, licked, and nipped, chasing her tongue, her hot breath tangling his. Iona licked the pad of his lip, then the tip of his tongue, their mouths meeting and parting, soft sounds in the quiet.

The thick, female scent of her made him growl. Need and frenzy, long buried, rushed to the surface. Iona would be his, and no other Shifter would touch her, ever. She was *his*.

Eric dragged her closer, the desk still between them. He felt her nipples tight behind her thin blouse and bra, heard the little noise she made in her throat. He remembered her naked up in the cave, firm breasts pale in the moonlight, dark tips beckoning his tongue. He wanted to rip open the blouse, sending buttons flying through the room, to bend her backward and fasten his mouth on her. He would do it, taste every inch of her, lick up every bit of goodness. She was made for tasting.

Iona seemed fascinated by the Collar. As they kissed, she glided her fingertips around it to the Celtic knot fused at his throat—the "eternal" knot, the Fae thinking to make Shifters slaves eternally. Fools. The eternal knot meant two hearts bound together forever, and that's what would free the Shifters in the end. Their strength and love.

Eric would make Iona understand this, *after* he took her in every position known to humans and some they didn't know.

Iona slid her fingers down to find the smooth line of his tatt. She swirled her touch around and around the tattoo, moving her tongue in his mouth in the same rhythm. She probably didn't even know she was doing it, but Eric's hard-on was about to dig through the desk.

He felt a sudden draft of air behind him, smelled the strong scent of human, then heard a gasp. "Iona?"

Iona jerked away, her face flushed, her eyes still her wildcat's—blue, slit-pupilled, almost luminescent. She backed away from the desk, her arms coming up as though to hide herself.

"Mom," she said breathlessly.

CHAPTER FOUR

Iona tried to make her eyes return to human, to the unscary daughter she tried to be. Wasn't working. Eric's mouth, his touch, his scent, had her wild side wide awake.

She wanted him. She needed to feel his body heavy on top of hers, Eric holding her down.

No, no, no, no. Eric was hot, and what woman wouldn't fantasize about him? But if Iona succumbed to her need, that would be the end of her.

Sex with Eric would be more than scratching an itch, and she knew it. Sex with Eric would have a deep meaning, some Shifter connection, a mating thing she didn't understand.

Iona's brain told her that, while her body shrieked at the interruption.

"Mom," she said again. "This is—"

"I know who he is," Penny Duncan said crisply. Iona's mother had dark hair pulled back into a sleek ponytail, a short but sturdy body, and dark blue eyes. Iona's black hair and Celtic coloring came from her Shifter father, but she'd never known him. Penny and Howard, Iona's stepfather, were the ones who'd taken care of her, kissed her skinned knees better, and protected her at night. "Eric Warden, Shiftertown leader,"

Penny went on, her gaze on Eric, not Iona. "What is he doing here?"

Iona's words felt heavy in her mouth. "He came to talk about the plans for the new houses in Shiftertown."

"Is *that* why he was trying to put his tongue down your throat?"

"Mom."

"Honey, I know all about alpha male Shifters and what they do. They work their way into your life, seducing you with their charm and their protectiveness, their out-and-out attraction. And then . . . it's too late. You can't get away if you try."

"You're talking about Iona's father," Eric said. "Who was he?"

Watching, Iona realized she'd been sidelined. This conversation was between Eric, used to being in charge of everyone around him, and her mother, whose heart had been broken by an alpha Shifter male.

"Oh, a charmer, like you," Penny said. "I was nineteen and spending the summer at my grandparents' house up in Fallon. He came out of the night and found me on the porch, where I was looking at the stars. I wasn't used to being out in the country, and I wasn't used to talking to panthers who'd become human. Next thing I know, I'm sneaking up to his cabin to be with him, and then not much wanting to leave. He gave me Iona, and I'm forever grateful for that, but he tricked me good, Shifter."

"Times change," Eric said. "What happened to him?"

"Hell if I know," Penny answered. "He disappeared one night, and I never saw him again. When Shifters were revealed and took the Collar, I was scared he'd come and find Iona. But he never did."

"I could look for him," Eric said. "Find out what happened to him for you."

Penny stilled a moment, a sudden longing in her eyes, then she resumed her neutral expression. "Like you said, times change. I don't care what happened to him."

Iona did, and she'd seen, in that flash, that her mother did too.

"It's unusual for a Shifter to abandon his cubs," Eric said. "I'm guessing he never knew about Iona."

"I raised Iona to be human. I've kept her away from Shifters, and I'd like that to continue. You understand, don't you?"

"It's easier to hide them when they're cubs," Eric said. "I grant that. But Iona's made her Transition now, entered her mating years. She's losing control, and it's only a matter of time before another Shifter sniffs her out."

"Transition?" Iona broke in. "What are you talking about? What *transition*?"

When Eric turned his green eyes to her, he'd gone from the teasing, hot, tattooed man who'd been kissing her to the wise leader of Shiftertown, who'd been alive far longer than Iona or her mother. "The Transition from cub to adulthood. It's your body telling you it's ready for you to find your place in the pride, to start looking for a mate."

"Oh." Iona flashed back to a few years ago, when she'd thought she was going insane. She'd hurt all over and wanted to fight everyone all the time, for any reason. She'd go up to their cabin in the mountains, trying to stay as far away from her mother and sister—from everyone—as possible, and let herself shift and run. And run. But no matter how far or fast she went, she couldn't run from the fires burning her from the inside out. "Is *that* what that was?"

"All Shifters go through it," Eric said. "You must be very strong to have made it through alone." He sounded admiring.

"I thought I was going to die."

"During *my* Transition I wanted to fight and challenge anyone—everyone. My sister had to hit me with a frying pan, those big cast-iron ones we had a hundred years ago. Several times."

Iona suddenly wanted to meet this sister. "You obviously got through it."

"Because I had help, had a family and a clan."

"And a sister not afraid to smack you down."

"That too. But you have no protection—no clan, no pride. That why I'm extending mine."

"But who protects her from you?" Penny asked him.

Another stare down between Eric and Iona's mother. Iona broke it by walking around the desk and planting herself between them.

"Both of you, stop it. Mom, I'm not you, and I'm not nineteen.

Eric, I'll send you the blueprints when they're ready. But if you want to protect me so much—*stay away from me*."

Eric looked Iona up and down and spoke around her to Penny. "She's feisty. I like that."

"You heard her," Penny said. "Get out, Shifter."

"I'm going." But only because he chose to. Iona saw that. He could have done whatever the hell he wanted, including carrying Iona off over his shoulder back to Shiftertown. The reason Eric had told her about the Shifters' instinct to capture her was so she'd understand that Eric wanted to do that himself.

Eric went to Iona and pulled her into a warm, tight embrace. His breath tickled inside her ear. "The Goddess go with you, Iona."

He nipped her earlobe, then he released her, gave Penny a nod, grabbed his jacket, and walked out of the office.

They heard the rumble of his motorcycle starting up, the powerful throb as the engine revved. Iona went to the window as Eric lifted his feet and glided the bike out of the parking lot, sunlight gleaming on his dark hair and the jacket he'd resumed. He slid into the street and away, and the engine sound faded into the traffic.

Iona blew out her breath, moved back to her office chair, and sat heavily on it. The roast beef sandwich started to stink, and she shoved it away from her.

Her mother remained standing in the middle of the office, as though she couldn't decide what to do now. "Iona."

"Mom, I really don't want to talk about it."

Penny wasn't put off. "Why didn't you tell *me* that the leader of Shiftertown knows you're Shifter? How long has this been going on?"

Iona heaved another sigh. "He saw me at a club last spring." Iona remembered her shock when Eric dropped into the chair next to hers, asked who she was, and announced that he knew good and well that she was Shifter. "He just knew."

"Of course he did. They can smell you. But why didn't you tell me?"

"Why did you just tell Eric more about my real father than you ever told me?"

Penny sighed, looking suddenly older. "I don't know. I

really don't know. I guess maybe I didn't tell you much about your father because I was ashamed I fell in love with him. But I wanted Eric to understand that I knew what Shifters did."

If Iona's father had been anything like Eric—strong, compelling, pinning others with that Shifter gaze—Iona understood her mother's feelings toward him. But Iona probably wouldn't have understood, she realized, before she'd met Eric.

"Why should you be ashamed?" Iona said, a little more sharply than she meant to. "It wasn't your fault."

"Yes, it was. I went to him, I knew what he was, and I didn't care."

"He was Shifter. I bet he made you do things you had no intention of doing until it was too late."

Penny came alert. "Is that what Eric is doing with you?"

Iona shook her head. "I don't think so. I'm Shifter too, so maybe he can't compel me the same as if I were human."

"Don't count on that, Iona. You'd be amazed at what they can do. Why do you think I've protected you from them all this time?"

"I can't hide what I am, Mom. Eric proved that when he saw me in the club." *And I'm proving that by wanting to run wild all the time—with him.*

Penny glanced out the window. "The guys are coming back to work. We'll talk about this later." She snatched up the tote she'd dropped and banged back outside without another word.

Iona dropped into the desk chair and put her face in her hands. Emotions poured through her—anger at her mother, anger at Eric, fear of her own reaction to him.

Even more powerful was her need to see Eric again, to go after him, to bask in his circle of warmth, even if they argued.

The scent of ruined roast beef sandwich was strong in the room, but stronger to her was Eric's scent overlaid with the scent of her mother's stark fear.

Eric rode his motorcycle far out into the desert, shifted, and went for a run. He ran to work off his frustration at being so near Iona and not being able to have her and also to cover

Iona's scent with his own. If he ran long enough under the warming sun, he'd get pretty smelly.

He rode back into Shiftertown later that afternoon and drew his Harley up in front of his house in time to see a Shifter fight in his next-door neighbor's yard.

He was off the bike and into the yard before the motor died. He grabbed Shane, his bear Shifter next-door neighbor, and hauled him off the half-shifted wolf he was pummeling.

Shane was a giant, but his Collar was sparking like crazy, reacting to Shane's attack to drive pain and shocks through him. Eric peeled Shane out of the fight and shoved him away. Shane landed, panting, against the pickup with its hood up in his driveway, his eyes wild, but he stayed put.

The wolf, one of Graham's, was in his half-shifted state, upright, covered with fur, eyes red with rage, mouth full of sharp teeth. He should have recognized Eric as alpha and dropped immediately, apologetically, to wait for Eric to decide what to do. But the wolf, crazed with fury and pain from his own sparking Collar, charged Eric.

Eric spread his arms and growled, feeling himself half shift, his clothes and jacket ripping as his half-Shifter body broke through. The wolf slammed into Eric full force, and Eric caught him in his arms.

The wolf clawed and fought as the two went down. The wolf's Collar arced blue, the snakes of electricity slapping Eric's skin. Eric's Collar remained silent; Eric had learned how to control his Collar's reaction somewhat. For now. Payback would come later.

The wolf ripped claws into Eric's chest, and blood ran down Eric's fur-covered skin. Eric snarled as he fought, the two rolling over each other, dust and gravel rising. Eric heard other Shifters coming out of houses, running to see the fight, sensed their anger and bloodlust rising. This needed to end. Now.

Though a good fighter, the wolf was young and inexperienced. Eric waited for his opening, then he plunged his mouth over the wolf's throat and sank his teeth in, just enough.

Eric tasted blood, hot and satisfying. The wild thing inside him, harder to control in the half state, urged him to make the kill. The wolf had been fighting one of Eric's Shifters, and Eric had the right to retaliate.

The tiny part of Eric that was still Eric, the coolheaded Shiftertown leader, knew that killing the wolf would bring down a firestorm from the humans, not to mention from Graham. Graham wouldn't hesitate to kill.

But the beast in Eric didn't care. It wanted the blood of his enemy, wanted to roar his victory with the ripped-up body of this wolf at his feet.

"Back off!"

The wolf went suddenly quiet under Eric's teeth. Eric knew who stood beside them without looking—Nell, Shane's mother, a formidable grizzly and the alpha bear of Shiftertown.

"Mom, put down the gun," Shane said.

Eric put his half-shifted paw on the wolf's chest, unlocked his teeth from his throat, and carefully looked up. Nell stood a foot away from them, a double-barreled shotgun aimed at the wolf's head.

CHAPTER FIVE

"I'll put down the gun when this stupid-ass wolf learns who he's not supposed to fight," Nell said.

The wolf snarled. Shane stood with hands on hips, face and arms covered with bloody scratches. Nell stood straight and unwavering, the large woman's stare hard over the shotgun.

Eric stood up and planted his foot, still in his motorcycle boot, on the wolf's chest. As he eased back to human form, he heard and smelled Graham coming up behind him.

"Put it down, bitch," Graham growled.

Nell didn't move. Eric kept his boot on the wolf and wiped blood out of his eyes. The wolf's Collar still sparked but was fading, the wolf giving up the fight.

"Nell, put that fucking gun away," Eric snapped.

Nell was high in the Shiftertown hierarchy, but she knew just how far she could push Eric. She lowered the shotgun.

Graham strode past Shane and Nell without looking at them, broadcasting that they didn't matter to him. His gaze fixed on Eric, the only Shifter Graham considered any kind of equal. "Get your foot off my wolf, Warden."

"After I kick his ass," Eric said calmly. "He attacked my tracker and didn't stand down when I told him to."

"And your she-bear was ready to blow his head off!"

"To protect her cub and her alpha. That's her right. But by Shifter rights, the kill is mine."

"He's *my* wolf."

Eric met Graham's ice gray gaze. "This is my Shiftertown, and you didn't keep him under control."

"Territory fights are natural," Graham said, unflinching. "If that means one of your bears has to go down, they do."

Nell growled. "Anyone who touches my cub gets lead in their ass."

"Mom," Shane, her seven-foot-tall cub, said.

"Looks like *you* can't control your females," Graham said to Eric without looking at Nell. "What kind of alpha lets women carry weapons and strip themselves for humans? How'd you stay alive this long?"

Eric took his foot off the wolf. The Lupine's limbs flowed back to human—he was a youngish Shifter, little more than a cub, about the same age as Eric's son, Jace. He didn't look up at the other Shifters but lay quietly, breathing hard, his neck a mess of blood. He was naked, which meant he'd charged in fully shifted before Shane and he had even started to fight.

"Who is he?" Eric asked Graham.

"One of my nephews. Name's Dougal."

Eric took another step back, indicating he relinquished the disciplining to the culprit's clan leader. As Shiftertown leader, Eric liked to let each clan take care of their own, intervening only when needed. Whether or not Graham appreciated that, Eric didn't know or care.

"Take him home," Eric said. "If he attacks one of mine again, he answers to me."

"If one of *yours* attacks one of *mine* again, I'm taking him out." Graham shot a glare at Shane before lifting Dougal to his feet by the nape of his neck. "You only have your tracker's word that my nephew attacked him."

Shane started to speak, but Eric signaled him quiet. Graham gave Eric one last hard stare before he shoved Dougal, still gripping him by the neck, out of the yard and back down the street.

Neither wolf looked back, but Eric heard Graham growling, "You'd better have good reason for this shit . . ." before they turned the corner out of sight.

Eric drew a long breath, feeling the twinge of pain around his neck that told him his payback was on its way.

The Collars were part technology, part Fae magic that sent deep pain through a Shifter's nervous system whenever he or she got violent. Eric had been learning how to suppress the Collar's reaction, a technique Jace had learned from the Austin Shiftertown leader and had taught to him. Once Eric had it mastered, he planned to teach it to others. He wasn't as good as Jace yet, though he could stave off the pain long enough to finish a fight.

His shirt was ripped and bloody, his jeans and jacket as well. Only his boots had survived his half shift, because his cat feet weren't as big as his human's.

Shane looked contrite, but defiance glinted in his eyes. Nell still scowled, the shotgun hanging loosely over her forearm.

"Where the hell did you get that?" Eric asked her.

Shifters weren't allowed firearms of any kind. Most Shifters didn't like them anyway, finding teeth and claws more handy. Besides, guns took the challenge out of fighting and hunting—a naturally made kill was much more satisfying.

"Xavier lent it to me," Nell said. "He's teaching me how to shoot."

"He's an ex-cop," Eric said. "He knows the laws—is he crazy?"

"Xavier is discreet, and he trusts me." Nell slid the cartridges out of the gun and put them into her pocket. "Good thing I stopped the fight, because you were about to kill that wolf, and the dominance war would have started. It's going to be bloody when it comes, but we're not ready yet."

Eric's short temper didn't want to hear Nell being right. Eric killing Graham's nephew would have been unforgivable.

"And what if Graham decides that since you have a gun, he'll arm his own Shifters? Give the damn thing back to Xavier and tell him to keep it out of Shiftertown."

Nell's scowl deepened. "Whatever you say."

"Shane."

Shane raised his large hands. "Don't look at me, Eric. The little shit came running in here and decided it would be funny to attack me. I was working on Brody's truck, bent over the engine . . ."

If Eric hadn't been so wound up from the fight, he'd laugh. "He's not much more than a cub. Why didn't you stop him?"

"I tried, and then it got out of hand. These wolves are barely shy of feral, Eric. They're used to living rough."

Which was going to become an even bigger problem when the bulk of Graham's Shifters arrived. Graham had moved down here with a handful of Shifters, leaving his second in charge back in Elko until the mass exodus of his Shifters to Las Vegas. Like Graham, they were arrogant, impatient, and this side of feral.

"Let it go, Shane," Eric said. "If any more of Graham's Shifters come over, sit on them and call me. We have bigger things to worry about."

"Sorry," Shane said.

Eric's anger boiled. The incident hadn't been Shane's fault, and now the bear felt like he had to apologize to his alpha. Graham would probably demand an apology too, from both Nell and Shane. What a waste of time.

"Don't worry about it, Shane. Just don't do it again." Eric surveyed his ruined clothes as another twinge of pain raced around his neck and down his spine. "Damn it."

"You going to be okay?" Shane asked worriedly.

"Yeah. I'm fine."

A lie, but they accepted it. Without another word, Eric walked back to his house.

He didn't need to say anything more. Nell and Shane would know he didn't blame them entirely, and that it was over. That was the point of forgiveness by the alpha—the subordinates could go on to the next thing without fearing retaliation.

Other Shifters who'd come out to watch the confrontation drifted back inside, understanding what had happened and taking the warning, even though they didn't like it.

Eric entered his house, which was silent, warm, and dim after the bright afternoon. He knew without looking around that no one was home. The house felt empty, smelled empty, and besides, his family would have been the first outside for the fight they'd have stopped it before Eric even got home.

Diego, his brother-in-law, was at work, and Eric's sister, Cassidy, along with Jace, would be working at their ongoing task of helping the near-feral females Cassidy had rescued this spring adjust to life in Shiftertown. The arrival of Graham and his wolves wasn't helping with that.

No air moved in the still house, the sun warming it as only the sun in Nevada, even in November, could. Eric turned on the window air conditioner in the living room, stripped off his ripped clothes, and stood naked in front of the cold stream of air.

Didn't help. The heat that beat at him wasn't from the sun but from the adrenaline of the fight, coupled with the frenzy that being near Iona always aroused.

He closed his eyes and thought about facing her over the desk, about the sweet tang of the honey mustard he'd licked from her lips. He again saw her hugging her naked limbs up at the cave, remembered the taste of her when he'd fed her the chocolates last spring, kissing her as she ate them. He'd have to buy her some more of those chocolates.

The first wrench of pain dragged a groan from deep within him. Eric took a long breath, trying the calming meditations Jace had taught him. But another sharp pain sliced through his abdomen, and he balled his fists against his stomach.

More pain came, hard and fast, and this time, Eric was aware of something different. He'd faced Collar payback before, but the agony that tore through him now was ten times worse. His arms and legs felt like someone was trying to yank them off. What the fuck? He hadn't fought the Lupine that hard.

The intensity of the pain drained him of strength and sent him to his knees. Eric dug fists into his temples and suppressed the roar he wanted to let out. If he made noise, his neighbors would come running to see what was wrong, and some part of him knew he couldn't let them see him like this—their leader beaten and weak.

What the hell was the matter with him? He wanted to vomit, to scream, to dig at the floor with his fingers.

His fingers turned to claws as he raked them across the tile, leaving gouges Cassidy would yell at him about. He willed his hands to return to human, but the claws remained, and his teeth elongated to fangs.

Goddess, make it stop!

Eric drew shuddering breath after shuddering breath, meditation forgotten. This wasn't his Collar. This was something else, maybe something planted a long time ago finally working its way to the surface. Maybe him trying to learn to suppress the Collar had triggered it . . .

Maybe he didn't know what the hell he was talking about.

The pain eased off the slightest bit. Eric drew a long breath and forced himself to his feet, sick and shaking.

The flow from the AC was like ice on his skin. Eric shut it off with a shaking hand as his claws receded, grabbed his shredded clothes, and limped to his bedroom. His was the smallest one, narrow, with a bed, a closet, and not much else.

He pried his cell phone out of his now cracked belt, dropped the clothes, and fell onto the bed in another spasm of pain. He couldn't stifle the moan that came out this time.

Eric punched buttons with his thumb, swallowing bile as he held the phone to his ear.

She answered. A part of Eric unclenched when he heard Iona's dusky tones saying, "Hello?"

"Iona."

"Eric?" She sounded startled, then a note of concern entered her voice. "You sound awful. Are you all right?"

"Talk to me."

"What?"

"I said talk to me." Eric closed his eyes, letting his body fold up into a fetal position. "About anything. Just talk."

"Why? Eric, what happened? What's wrong?"

She must be alone in her office, thank the Goddess, because Iona would never have said his name like that if someone had been there with her.

"Please, just talk. About anything. Tell me about the houses, how you'll get them built, what materials you'll use. Whatever you want."

"Eric . . ." It was almost a whisper.

"I need to hear your voice."

Iona went silent a moment, and then she began to talk. What she said was innocuous, about load bearing walls, roughing in plumbing, the problem of basements in the desert. Eric only half heard it. The music of her voice, the dulcet syllables, floated through him and eased the pain that continued to beat at him.

Talking to her through a cell phone was nowhere near as good as having her next to him, where he'd be able to inhale her clear scent, to cover himself with her warmth.

Eric listened until the pain began to recede. When it finally faded enough for him to take a regular breath, he thanked her quietly and hung up the phone.

Iona stared at the phone a long time after Eric clicked off. His voice had been so weak when she'd answered. He'd sounded almost panicked.

She'd never seen Eric anything but strong and certain, but he'd been rasping, barely able to talk. Had he lost a fight, had another Shifter hurt him? The Collars were supposed to keep Shifters in check, but Iona had seen firsthand how "tamed" they really were.

Iona hit the Callback button on her phone. Eric's rang on the other end. And rang and rang. No voice mail, no Eric picking up. Damn it.

Why should she be so worried about him? Eric drove her crazy. He was pretty much stalking her, talking about bringing her in and slapping a Collar on her, scent-marking her, mate-claiming her, whatever that entailed. Iona should not only be glad he didn't pick up the phone, she shouldn't call him at all.

If only he hadn't sounded so broken . . .

Going out to Shiftertown herself to see if he was all right wasn't an option. The Shifters would smell her a mile away.

Call the cops? No, that would bring trouble to Shiftertown, and maybe Eric was only exhausted from a hard day of being Shiftertown leader.

Cops. Hadn't Eric's sister married a cop? Eric hadn't given Iona the details, but Iona had read a newspaper story about Diego Escobar, a cop who'd quit his job and started a private security company after he'd moved to Shiftertown to live with his Shifter mate.

A computer search now led Iona to a Diego Escobar in Las Vegas running a private security firm with his brother, cryptically called DX Security. Their website had nothing but a banner and a phone number on it.

Iona dialed the number.

"DX Security," a male voice answered. He sounded tough, deep-voiced, exactly the kind of person you'd want if you needed someone or something protected.

"Can I speak to Diego Escobar?"

A hesitation. He must be looking at the caller ID, which would show her personal number and no name. She'd known better than to use a company phone.

The man spoke again. "What do you need, Ms. Duncan?"

Iona jumped. All right, so they were good. "To speak to Mr. Escobar."

"Is this about the housing?"

Word traveled fast. Duncan Construction had been granted the contract for the Shifter housing only this morning.

"No. It's not." *And I'm not about to explain to a complete stranger who I am and why I'm calling.*

Iona was about to hang up, deciding this a bad idea, when the man said, "Hold on."

The next voice she heard was smooth and rich. "Ms. Duncan? I'm Diego Escobar. What can I do for you?"

"Check on your brother-in-law," Iona said.

"What?" Diego came alert, curiosity giving way to wariness.

"I just talked to Eric," she said. "He sounded bad, and now he won't answer his phone."

Silence. Oh, for a webcam. She'd love to know whether he stared into space or was busily looking up information about Iona Duncan of Duncan Construction.

"Sounded bad, how?" Diego's voice betrayed no worry, but then, he wouldn't be good as head of a security company if he let himself sound anxious.

"Weak, tired. Not like himself."

More silence. Iona wished she could see what he was doing on the other end of the line.

"Ms. Duncan?"

"Still here."

"Thanks for calling," Diego said. "I'll take care of this."

"Good. Thanks. I just wanted to . . ."

"Yeah?" He sounded impatient, ready to go.

"Nothing. Thanks, I hope he's all right."

"I'm sure he's fine. Good-bye, Ms. Duncan."

She echoed his good-bye and hung up.

There. She'd done something about it. Diego Escobar was Eric's family, and he'd make sure all was well.

But Iona was restless. She told herself it was none of her business whether Eric was running around, healthy and fine, or passed out in his bed. The only thing she should be concerned about was having to work with him to build the houses.

So why did she itch to jump in her truck and charge to Shiftertown to see if he was all right?

Iona tried to get back to work. She had accounts to go over and bills to pay, but she found herself sitting at her desk with her fingers unmoving on the keyboard, staring at the numbers on the screen without seeing them.

"Iona, I found the shoes." Nicole breezed in with a big shopping bag, talking before she even got inside the door. Nicole was a younger version of their mother, with her same dark brown hair, blue eyes, compact body, and round face. "I was going to get the ones we saw at the bridal store, but then I walked by this boutique, and they had the *perfect* shoes in the window. They're not really wedding shoes, but I don't care. I fell in love with them."

Iona got up and walked around the desk, forcing herself to pay attention. "Doesn't matter. For your wedding, you should have what you love."

The shoes were gorgeous, high-heeled white Mary Jane's with tiny pink rosettes across the straps, the exact color of the flowers Nicole had chosen. Nicole held up one shoe, cradling it in her hands.

Any other time, Iona would be all over them, but worry about Eric was distracting her. "Nice," she said.

Nicole's face fell. "You don't like them. I knew I should have bought the satin ones. I don't know what I was thinking. I'll take them back . . ."

"Nicole. Nikki." Iona stepped in front of her sister and rubbed her shoulders. "Stop it. I love the shoes. Really. They're great."

"That's not what your face said." Nicole dropped the bag and the shoe. "Iona, I'm so scared I'm going to screw something up. This is supposed to be the happiest time of my life, and I keep changing my mind about everything and wanting to break down and cry every five minutes."

"Nicole, you're getting married and planning a big wedding. Give yourself a break."

"I run a business with you and mom, a man's business. I know all about stress. Why am I getting so crazy?"

"Come here." Iona opened her arms and pulled her sister close. Nicole rested her head on Iona's shoulder, letting out a little sigh.

Iona had always found great comfort in embracing her mother and sister. *The calming power of the hug*, she'd always said. Whenever Eric hugged her, though, Iona found herself torn between drinking in the comfort and wanting to jump his bones.

Eric had nudged Iona's Shifter sense of smell awake this afternoon. She hadn't been able to shut it off since, and so as she hugged Nicole, she scented, loud and clear, that Nicole hadn't only gone shopping on her lunch hour. Her very long lunch hour.

Iona smelled Tyler, Nicole's fiancé, along with the sticky sweet smell that came with sex. She wanted to smile. Nicole and Tyler had met for a nooner.

She also scented something else. She didn't exactly recognize it, but the panther instinctively knew what it was. Maybe she sensed a shift in Nicole's hormones, maybe she could already scent the second life inside her sister, or maybe this came from Iona's mating instincts ready to come out and play.

Whatever it was, Iona knew that her sister's urge to cry came from more than stress.

"Nicole," she said carefully. "Maybe you should have a checkup before the wedding."

Nicole's head popped off Iona's shoulder. "Why? You think there's something wrong with me?"

"No, no," Iona said quickly. "But I think you should."

Nicole took a step back. "What's wrong? Your eyes have gone all . . . Shifter."

Iona blinked, trying to make her eyes behave. Any trigger of adrenaline and her pupils would become catlike, slits of black in light blue irises.

"Nothing's wrong," she said. "I promise. Everything's right."

"Iona, when you get weird like this, you scare me. Tell me what's wrong."

Her sister's distress poured off her in waves. She cried out for reassurance, the scent of that stirring Iona's protective instincts even more.

Iona put her hands on Nicole's shoulders again. "You're pregnant."

Nicole stared in shock. "What are you talking about? I am not."

"Yes, you are. Don't ask me how I know. I just . . . *know.*"

"You have to be wrong. Tyler and I agreed to wait to have kids."

Iona grinned. "Well, the kid didn't wait to have you. Go get a checkup. If I'm wrong, I'm wrong." But Iona wasn't. She knew it in her bones.

"How can you possibly tell?" Now Nicole looked angry.

"I told you, don't ask me. But kids are what happens when you have sex. It's kind of the whole reason sex was invented."

"But we're being so careful . . ." Nicole nearly wailed.

Iona hugged her sister again. "Tell Tyler to check his condoms for holes. Don't be so upset. This is a wonderful thing."

"I still think you're wrong."

"Doesn't matter what I think. Go have the damn checkup."

Nicole burst out laughing. She picked up the shoe she'd dropped and put it back into the bag. "Okay, I'll call my doctor. I think you have no idea what you're talking about, but you're right. Better to make sure before I drink all that champagne at the wedding."

"Not to mention the shots at your bachelorette party."

"Good point." Nicole picked up the shopping bag and peered again at Iona. "You'd better go home if you can't keep your eyes under control."

"I'll think about it. I have a lot of work to do."

"I'll do the work. Get out of here."

Iona saw that her sister wasn't going to budge. *Protect Iona* had been the watchwords in the family since she could remember.

No one in the world had known about Iona's Shifter side but Penny, Nicole, and Howard, Iona's stepfather. They'd understood why they needed to keep the secret, and they'd done it. But keeping the secret sometimes entailed making sure Iona was out of sight.

"Fine. Want me to take the shoes and drop them off at your house?"

"No, I want to show Mom. Go on, before someone comes in."

Iona went. She hugged Nicole again, giving her a kiss on her cheek, then put on her sunglasses as she stepped outside, in case her eyes didn't change back.

She started her red pickup, then ended up with her hands on the wheel, dragging in deep breaths. The wild thing inside was clawing its way up, wanting out, needing release.

Iona still worried about Eric. Diego would look in on him, she tried to reassure herself, but Eric's voice, his distress, pulled at her. She needed to see him.

No, she needed to stay away from Shiftertown.

But she needed to see him.

Iona clenched the wheel. Her hands sprouted claws, black fur rippling down her fingers. *Damn it.*

She forced her claws to be fingers again, put the truck in gear, and backed out of her place. She sped out into thick traffic, the commuters from Las Vegas heading home to Henderson and outlying areas.

Iona strove to drive carefully, but every time someone cut her off or tried to shove her out of her lane, the beast in her snarled.

This wasn't road rage—she wanted to *kill*. She could taste it, felt the need to have hot blood filling her mouth.

Her hands changed to panther again, and Iona lost hold of the wheel. Shit. Iona grabbed it again, willing her hands to change back to human.

Hold it together, hold it together.

Eric's visit had roused the Shifter in her. Iona had tried to keep the Shifter side of her quiet and out of sight all her life, suppressing the animal so she could live in peace and safety. Eric was goading that animal to become part of her everyday life, whether Iona liked it or not.

He'd showed her how to open herself to her sensitive sense of smell. Now scents poured in at her so thick and fast she couldn't process them. Iona glanced at the man in the car next to her, and knew that, if she decided to, she could break through his window, grab him, and rip out his throat.

Just get home.

Iona drew a breath, slid her pickup into the quieter side streets of her neighborhood, and made it to her driveway. She shut off her engine, peeled her fingers from the wheel, and let out a long sigh.

Home. Safety.

Her next-door neighbor's cat bounded over, a sleek black-and-white with a black patch over one eye. He jumped onto the hood of Iona's truck and let out a meow.

Iona slid out of the truck and reached out to give Pirate a stroke as she went by. He liked Iona—most cats did.

Pirate drew back in alarm, flattened his ears, and hissed, before leaping down from the truck and running back home.

Hissing was defensive behavior, what a cat did when it perceived a threat. Pirate had seen the aggressor in Iona, even though she'd meant to caress, and had decided to get the hell out of there.

Iona hurried inside the house, shutting the door firmly and locking it with shaking fingers. She pulled out a bottle of merlot and poured a tall glass while she tried to think of something for an early dinner.

Except she wanted only meat, cooked rare if at all. Or maybe fish. She found herself diving through her freezer, searching frantically for something to satisfy her hunger, finding nothing.

"Fresh vegetables," she said, pulling out bags from her crisper drawer. "Just why?"

Takeout. She could get takeout. But she didn't trust herself to drive somewhere and pick up the food. She grabbed the

phone and called her favorite pizza place, ordering three of
the all-meat specials. "Having a party, Ms. Duncan?" the
order taker asked.

She practically knew the kid, since she ordered from there
all the time. "Yes," she lied. "Can you rush those?"

"Sure thing."

The pizza took twenty minutes, fast for delivery pizza.
Even so, Iona nearly ripped open the door when the car
arrived, remembering at the last minute to shove on her sunglasses. She grabbed the pizzas and threw money at the guy,
too much, but he deserved a big tip. She slammed the door on
his startled expression, and ran back into the kitchen.

"I'm just hungry," Iona said out loud. "Eric ruined my
lunch."

Eric.

The thought of him brought new hunger, a rising frenzy
that wanted her to take Eric by the neck and pull him down to
her, to let his body cover hers, to feel his sweat on her skin, his
mouth on hers.

"Eat," she said to the empty kitchen.

The pizzas were slathered with hamburger, sausage, pep-
peroni, and Canadian bacon. It should have been called The
Carnivore Special.

Penny had taught Iona how to eat healthy, nutritious meals.
Right now, Iona could care less.

Eric had said, *If you were in your panther form, you
wouldn't worry. You'd gulp it down and spit out the paper.*

Substitute *pizza boxes*, and he was right.

Iona got out a plate and napkins before she dumped the
pizza onto the plate. She could be civilized.

She growled. The mirror in her dining area told her that
her eyes were still Shifter. She moved quickly through the
house, closing all the blinds, then tossed off her clothes and
let her panther take over.

Much better. Iona padded back into the kitchen, put her
paws on the counter, and gulped down the pizzas. All three of
them, all that meat and cheese going down fast. The tomato
sauce and the crust tasted a little weird to her, but it was a
small price to pay for the greasy, hot, spicy *meat*.

When the boxes were empty, her panther tongue licking up

the last bit of cheese clinging to the cardboard, Iona burped. Then she sat down and started washing her whiskers.

The pizza filled her up and made her sleepy. Iona didn't generally remain in her shifted form long, in case someone came over to catch her, but right now, all she wanted to do was curl up on her sofa and sleep. She went slowly to her living room, climbed onto the nice cushy sofa, and let her body go limp.

I ona jumped awake to find everything dark. She lifted her head, startled to find herself still panther. Her claws had dug a deep gouge in her sofa, she saw with her cat vision. Crap.

She stepped down from the sofa and stretched. She was supposed to feel better—fed, rested, the worry of the day behind her.

Instead, she was restless, pacing, growling to herself. She needed to shift back to human.

And found she didn't want to. She wanted to run, to hunt, to *kill*. She *needed* to.

She remembered the scent of lovemaking on Nicole, the heightened warmth of the baby inside her, and started to wind up again. Iona needed that, the smell of sex, the heat of a male body on hers, wanted to press her hand to her own abdomen and know that life was growing there.

She needed it *now*.

Iona forced herself back to human. The shift took a long time, and hurt, more so than usual, her panther reluctant to let go.

She stood in the middle of the hallway between living room and kitchen, shaking. The mirror there showed her black hair a mess, her eyes enormous and still Shifter.

Iona snatched up her phone and started punching numbers. He answered this time. Thank God.

"Eric," she said frantically. "Eric, I need you."

CHAPTER SIX

Eric killed his motorcycle's engine before he reached Iona's house, and coasted the dark bike up into the driveway, parking it in the shadows. Iona opened the door for him as he approached, but Eric pushed her back into the house.

Iona smelled of wild female, full of need. Eric wanted to grab her by the nape of the neck, haul her up the stairs to her bedroom, shut the door behind them, and not come out for a week.

Iona had put on sweatpants as Eric had told her to on the phone, and she wore a cropped sports shirt that doubled as a bra, its collar hugging her throat.

The honed body the small shirt revealed didn't help Eric's frenzy. They might not even make it to the bedroom.

"Ready?" he asked.

Iona nodded. She clenched her teeth, her eyes definitely Shifter.

They quietly left the house again, Eric leading her to his bike.

Iona took the helmet he handed her but didn't put it on. "I've never ridden a motorcycle before."

"You'll get it. Helmet first, then hold on to me when you're on."

He straddled the seat and held the bike steady so Iona could mount behind him. Even with her helmet, she looked sexy as hell, felt sexy as hell cuddled up to the back of him.

Iona figured out how to rest her feet, then wrapped her arms around Eric.

The night suddenly got warmer. Eric coasted the bike down the driveway, starting it up when they swung out into the street.

Eric took them north, out of the city, back to the empty country. Feeling Iona's lithe body against his loosened something inside him, dissolving the last of the pain that had debilitated him this afternoon.

He opened up the bike once they cleared the suburbs, racing it down the highway under the stars. Iona's arms tightened around his middle, her strength making him stronger.

Eric took them well off the road, down dirt trails only he knew, the bike's light slicing through absolute darkness. The eyes of startled animals glittered in the sudden glow, then faded back out of the way.

The trail ended in a wash. Here, Eric killed the engine. Iona slid off, hopping a little until she got her leg over the seat, then she ripped off the helmet.

She was smiling. "Is that what it's always like?"

"Nothing's better than a Harley when you can let it rip," he said as he dismounted. "Now, strip."

He could tell Iona was far gone in frenzy, because she didn't even blink. She started shedding clothes, and once she was free of them, she shifted.

Though it took her a couple of minutes, this shift was easier for her than the last time Eric had seen her do it. Maybe because her frenzy was strong tonight, maybe because her wildcat was dangerously close to taking over.

As soon as she was panther, Iona hit the ground running. Eric quickly got out of his clothes, flowed into his leopard shape, and bounded after her.

Though the panther was fast, Eric's snow leopard caught up to her quickly. They ran side by side through a wide, sandy wash and then turned and loped along its far bank, dodging brush, rocks, and soft patches of dirt.

Eric sensed the terror of smaller creatures among the

creosote and sage. The animals were picking up on Iona's need to hunt, to chase, to feed.

Iona ran and leapt and scrambled, climbing up a hill, gravel scattering. Eric was at her heels.

The last time he'd chased her, she'd run in fear and anger. This time, he could tell, she ran for the enjoyment of it.

And for her wild need. Iona's voice when she'd called him tonight had been half-crazed, Iona barely containing herself. A run might settle her tonight, but her mating hunger wouldn't stop until it was satisfied. Or it killed her.

Iona made it to the top of a ridge and raced along it, never minding the sharp stones and prickly weeds. Eric bounded after her, shouldering his way in to run beside her on the edge of the cliff. His need to protect her was powerful, and one missed footfall could mean her death.

Iona growled and sprinted past him, leaving him in the dust.

Eric doubled his speed. Iona's tail whipped across her back in annoyance, then she picked up the pace even more, running recklessly along the top of the ridge.

As soon as they hit a wide enough stretch, Eric leapt, landed on Iona, and took her down.

Iona snarled and fought, ears back, teeth snapping. Panther limbs writhed under Eric's, Iona's pelt foamy with sweat.

Eric closed his mouth over her throat, the alpha subduing a pride mate. He held hard without his teeth penetrating, his body weight stopping her struggling. He needed to teach her that he wouldn't hurt her but that he wouldn't let her get away either.

Iona shifted. Soft human flesh replaced fur, scrabbling claws became clutching fingers. Eric found himself with his leopard's mouth on her warm throat, her pulse pounding beneath the prick of his teeth.

"Get off me, you big . . . cat," she said, pushing at him.

Eric grunted as he eased away, but he remained leopard. Iona rolled away and to her feet, then she stretched, arms above her head.

Her body almost glowed in the moonlight, her black hair sleek and beautiful, matching the midnight hair at the join of her legs. Her breasts were round and full, the tips dusky.

Even in his wildcat form, Eric appreciated the beauty of her. Her body was strong but curved, hips rounding from her waist, her navel a shadowed indent in her belly. He wanted to lick her skin, revel in the silk of it, let his tongue find the sweet honey he knew waited for him between her thighs.

Iona stood above him without shame, a woman enjoying the freedom of being bare under the starlight. She laughed, then she spun away from Eric, shifted again, and ran.

Little shit. Eric growled and was after her.

Iona heard Eric snarling as he chased her, but she didn't care. He was trying to subdue her, make her obey, and Iona wasn't about to obey.

The human part of her laughed as her panther paws connected with the earth, her wildcat fast and strong.

Eric, though, was faster. In about ten strides, he was on her again, taking her down to the packed earth.

Iona landed on her side but instinctively rolled onto her back, feet coming up to fend him off. Eric locked his jaw around her throat again, keeping her from biting him, his teeth sharp in her fur.

She struggled against him, even that making her want to laugh. Eric thought he'd bested her. Well, he could try.

But she couldn't get away. Eric's leopard body pinned her to the ground, his paws heavy, his mouth unyielding.

Only one thing she could do. Iona shifted again, the shift a little more difficult this time. Once she became human, she wrapped her arms around several hundred pounds of leopard fur.

"Eric," she said.

He shifted. In a few seconds, Iona found herself hugging not a soft leopard, but a large, well-muscled man with jade green eyes and strength she couldn't match. He grabbed her wrists, pinned them over her head, and gave her a raw, brutal kiss on the mouth.

Iona struggled, but his strength excited her. She drew her foot up the length of his leg at the same time she parted her lips and let him inside.

Eric had kissed her like this when he'd fed her the chocolate.

He glided his tongue over her lips, dipped between them, tasted her entire mouth. His weight held her down, his body and hers slick with sweat.

His breath was warm, fingers tight on her wrists, the rigid length of his cock against her abdomen, Eric not disguising what he wanted. His kiss opened her mouth, the taste of him like sharp spice.

Iona lifted her head to get more of him. His tongue tangled hers, fierce friction, lips mastering.

She curled her hands into fists, her struggles against him slowing. Eric's touch gentled as he lowered her to the ground, his mouth becoming tender. He licked over the lips he'd kissed so roughly, then lightly caressed them, ending with little kisses to the corners of her mouth.

He raised his head, starlight glistening on his Collar, his throat damp with sweat. "Iona . . ."

"What?" she whispered, her body heavy with wanting.

Eric's next kiss was savage but brief. "If I take you out here, you'll belong to me, and me alone."

"I don't belong to anyone," she said, still defiant.

His hands tightened on her wrists. "The mate-claim means you go to no other Shifter but me. It means I protect and take care of you, no matter what, no matter how much you fight me."

Iona slanted him a smile. "And if I fight you?"

"You can if you want to." He growled. "I told you, we like the chase."

Iona liked it too, and she really shouldn't. Eric's heartbeat thudded against her chest, his skin so hot.

"You scared me earlier, when you called me," she said, remembering her worry. "You sounded . . ." Weak, exhausted. Everything Eric Warden was not.

"I was in pain." He kissed her again, this kiss gentle, followed by a light flick of tongue. "Your voice soothed me."

"How? I didn't say anything much."

Eric nuzzled her. "The sound of the mate's voice—her touch, her scent—calms and heals. Better if you're in the same room with me, but I took what I could."

"But I'm not your mate."

"Not yet."

Iona decided to deal with that later. "Why were you in pain? What happened?"

Eric shrugged, which moved his body deliciously against hers. "I had to pull one of McNeil's wolves off one of my Shifters and thump him hard. Even then the wolf didn't want to yield to me. That's going to be a problem."

"Did the wolf hurt you?" Iona managed to slide one hand out from under Eric's—because he let her. She traced his shoulder and the tattoo hugging it, finding his skin hot, smooth, the muscle beneath it solid.

"He didn't. My Collar did." Eric frowned as he spoke, as though uncertain about something.

Iona let her fingers drift to the Celtic knot at his throat. The Collar was dormant, warm from his skin. "This went off?"

"Sparked, yep."

Iona studied the pain that lingered in his eyes, matching the bleakness she'd heard in his voice on the other end of the phone. She brushed fingers over his face, wanting to erase every last vestige of hurt.

"And my touch helps?"

"Yes."

She traced his cheek again, his unshaved whiskers sandpapery under her fingertips. "Part of me tells me to fight you with everything I have," she said, her voice softening. "But part of me wants to help you, to make sure you're all right."

"At least part of you wants that," Eric said, voice going low. "Let me work on the other part."

He kissed her again. He didn't trap her hands this time, and she shivered as she slid her palms across his shoulders and down his back as he kissed her. Eric's mouth opened hers, the brush of his whiskers rough on her skin, the taste of them sharp.

Her need was driving her crazy. Iona ran her bare foot up his leg again, letting her toes caress his thigh.

Eric was a beautiful man, and he lay on top of her, ready for her. The space between her legs was wet, and she knew that if she moved her hips just right, his hard cock would slide right into her.

That thought brought the beast back to life. Wanting raged. Never mind how rocky the ground was under her back, never mind she didn't want to be trapped by this man.

She wanted his seed. Inside her. Now.

Iona bit his shoulder, not gently. Eric rumbled, "Easy."

"I can't." Iona nibbled his neck above his Collar, licking where she bit. "I can't . . . I want . . ."

"Yes, you can." Eric grabbed her wrists again, trapping them against the ground. His eyes had gone Shifter, the wild-cat pupils slitted. "Control the hunger, love. Don't let it take over."

"You want me. You're hard as a rock. What's stopping you?"

Eric put his face close to hers. "You're frenzied. I don't want mating with regrets."

"But you want me. I'm going *insane* . . ."

Eric's hands shoved hers into the dirt, his weight heavy on her. "You're right, I damn well want you," he said, the words a snarl. "I want you so much, it's killing me. I want to pump myself inside you until we're so spent we can't get up for days. I want you here and now, all night, who cares if the sun comes up and roasts us alive? I'll keep going, and so will you. We'll screw so hard and be so mindless that we'll probably die, but we won't give a shit."

"Die?"

"If we give in to the mating frenzy that's crawling through me and you, we won't notice. We'll fuck for days, never mind about eating or drinking or even getting up off this ground."

Iona started to smile. "That doesn't sound so bad."

She wanted it. Wanted *him*. She fought to get her hands free, to *touch* him. She needed so much to touch him. She raised her head and licked his throat.

"I know it doesn't sound bad," he said. "It sounds damn good. But I don't want to kill you, Iona. I want you alive, and with me."

"Then why are you naked on top of me?"

"That's *my* frenzy talking. And I'm naked on top of you because I didn't want my leopard hurting you. Humans are fragile, and you're only half-Shifter."

"All right, so let me go. Let me run."

He growled again, the rumble vibrating her and making her warm. "You're out of control. You're running like a wild thing. You have to learn to control it."

"I have. I've controlled it all my life."

"No, you suppressed and ignored it. Not the same thing. You have to let it out, love, but you need to be in charge."

"Like you are?"

Eric licked her lips again. "I have iron control. I never came close to losing it until I met you." Another lick. "I'll help you through it."

"And then you'll boff me?"

His growl turned to a chuckle. "When we make love, it will be like the world exploded."

Iona wanted it to be like that now. A tiny part of her mind was waving at her, telling her that if she did go into frenzy with him now, she'd hate herself later. She'd be angry, resentful, both at him and herself.

Or would she? Eric's body on hers felt so right, as though she'd been waiting all her life for him. How would she know what she felt if she didn't give in and let him take her now?

"Eric, I——"

Eric put his fingers to her lips. "We'll run some more. I'll wear you out with running, and then I'll take you home."

Disappointment bit her. Iona felt her fingers become claws, heard the snarl in her throat. Her panther was pissed off.

Eric unclasped his fingers from around her wrists, letting her go, and as smoothly climbed to his feet.

Iona remained on the ground and gazed up at his tall body above hers, the strength of him obvious. He was erect, the firm length of him beautiful to see. Shifter cocks were longer and bigger than humans', Iona's friends who were excited about Shifters had told her. Lying here with the evidence above her, Iona believed them.

The female in her made her want to rise to her knees, fit her mouth around the tip of that cock, and draw it into her. She wanted to feel how heavy it would be against her tongue, find out whether it tasted as good as had the skin on his neck and shoulders.

Eric's gaze on her told her he knew where her thoughts were going, and that he had the same thoughts.

Unembarrassed, he reached down and helped her to her feet. Iona landed against him, and he lightly kissed her lips as she tried to catch her breath.

"There's something I want to check out," Eric said.

Iona blinked at him, half startled out of her arousal. "Check out?"

"Something my trackers told me about this evening. I brought us out here, figuring we can take a look while we're running things out of our systems."

"Oh, right. Sure." She stared at him, bewildered by the abrupt way he could change from seduction to being Shifter-town leader again.

Eric kissed her one more time, the warm, easy kiss of a man with a woman he liked. "Ready?"

Without waiting for her answer, Eric shifted back into his leopard. He stood against her a moment, his hot leopard breath fanning down her abdomen to her too-sensitive female places.

He made a low sound in his throat that Iona swore was a laugh before he turned and sauntered away.

Iona's shift this time hurt, the stiffness from lying on the ground not helping. She shook herself once she became panther, and trotted off to catch up to him.

CHAPTER SEVEN

Eric led her down the ridge, across a valley cut by another deep wash, and up another hill. At the top of this, Eric moved along a saddle between two boulder-strewn ridges, then climbed even higher to the top of the highest ridge.

When he reached the summit, he crouched low and moved in a wildcat slink that Iona hadn't yet perfected. His belly nearly touched the ground, paws moving automatically to find the best purchase and balance his weight.

Iona copied his movements as best she could, her limbs stiff and sore. At last, Eric dropped all the way to his stomach and looked down the hill.

Sounds came to Iona from what must have been a half mile away, but her wildcat easily caught them.

People talking. Men, two of them, she heard distinctly. They weren't saying anything important, just general conversation.

"Warm tonight."

"Yeah, hear it's going to be in the nineties tomorrow. Where's winter?"

Hunters? Campers? There were no marked campgrounds out this way, Iona knew, but that didn't mean hikers didn't walk out and set up tents.

Drug dealers, maybe? But they sounded relaxed and ordinary, not worried about anything. As though they had every right to be out here in the middle of the desert in the vast darkness.

Eric sniffed the wind, making a soft sound in his throat. Iona sniffed too, and caught the scent. Humans. How many, she couldn't tell, but not a lot of them. A crowd of humans smelled far different from one or two.

Eric dropped even lower. The light from the waning moon dappled both his fur and the ground around him, making the snow leopard almost impossible to spot.

Iona puffed a little as she moved closer to him, trusting her black fur to blend into the shadows.

Eric didn't look at her. His gaze was riveted to what was below, and when Iona saw, she stilled as well.

Three rows of one-story buildings were strung along the desert floor, each about a hundred feet long but not more than about ten feet wide. Doors entered these at intervals, but there were no windows.

Square bulks of air conditioners that doubled as heat pumps squatted on the roofs. The three buildings were surrounded by a chain-link fence topped with barbed wire.

Few lights illuminated the place, only one on either end, each near a gate. The men they'd heard were two guards, standing together, smoking cigarettes, automatic rifles slung over their shoulders.

Iona tried to do what Eric had taught her this morning—reach inside and open up her scent ability. She widened her cat nostrils and drank in the wind.

She smelled very little out of the ordinary. The two men, the dust and creosote, the scent of coyotes, rabbits, birds, and reptiles that lay hidden in the brush. From the buildings, nothing. A bit of Freon from the air conditioners, but the units were silent.

Eric's nose was twitching too, his sides moving as he sniffed and sniffed.

Finally he turned to Iona, his gaze unmistakably telling her it was time to leave. Iona let him lead the way, but as she followed, her foot caught on gravel, the stones grating. The trickle of pebbles didn't fall over the edge of the ridge, but the rattle was loud and startling, sound carrying a long way out here.

"What was that?" one of the men said.

The other didn't seem worried. "Probably a coyote. Or a snake. This place is crawling with snakes."

"Yeah, no one's stupid enough to come out here," the first one said. "Except us."

The second chuckled, Iona heard the flick of a lighter, and then she crept away after Eric.

Iona made no more noise as she picked her way down the ridge, back the way they'd come. When Eric reached the bottom, he broke into a run, leading her across the valley and back to the hill where they'd lain. Iona pounded behind him.

Eric didn't stop, didn't shift, but loped on, never doubting she'd follow, all the way back to where they'd left the bike and their clothes.

The leopard stretched when they reached the motorcycle, bending his front almost to the ground to unkink his fore-legs, then lengthening to stretch hind. As Eric rose from the stretch, his body changed back into that of a delectable, naked man, his tattoo black in the faint moonlight.

Iona shook herself out, trying to dislodge gravel, stickers, and creosote leaves from her fur, while Eric watched her. He made no move to dress, but waited until she'd slowly and painfully changed back to human.

Not until Iona was standing on her human feet, rubbing her aching arms, did he reach to the ground for his clothes. Iona enjoyed watching him a moment before she slipped on her underwear, sweatpants, and sport top, a bit disappointed that they were getting ready to head home.

But the stealthy move to the top of the hill and the equally careful one down had taken the edge off Iona's frenzy. Eric had been smart to include her in his reconnaissance.

"What was that place?" she asked as Eric settled his black T-shirt over his body.

"No idea. What did you get from it?"

"You mean the scents? Nothing. I mean, apart from the guys and the usual smell of desert and buildings. But I'm not very good at scenting, I told you."

Eric buckled his belt. "I didn't smell anything either. It was neutral."

"Maybe the buildings are airtight."

He shook his head as he leaned on his motorcycle's seat and pulled on his boots. "No building's that airtight, unless it's underground or something. These are crappy buildings on temporary foundations. I should be able to smell what's inside them."

"Unless the buildings are empty."

"Then why the AC units, and why the barbed wire and guards? Very weird." Eric took the helmet from the back of the bike and handed it to her. "I'll send my trackers back out to have another look around."

"Trackers?"

"Trackers are my eyes and ears. Brody, who lives next door to me, is one, a couple of wolves, my son, and Neal, our Guardian."

Iona didn't know what a Guardian was either, but she wasn't in the mood for lessons on Shifters at the moment. The men on the other side of the ridge made her nervous.

"Your son," she repeated. Iona had looked up information on Eric after she'd met him and knew he'd had a wife—a *mate*—who'd given him a son. But Eric, so far, had never spoken about him.

Now he grinned. "Jace. You'd like him. He's nicer than me."

"Most people are."

Eric was across the few feet of gravel, his hand gripping the back of her neck before Iona registered he'd moved. He held her solidly, his eyes glittering in the moonlight, gaze fixing hers and not letting her look away.

"I can't be *nice* and be leader," he said, all smiles gone. "My Shifters have to be ready to obey me in an instant, or everyone is in danger. That doesn't leave me much room for being *nice*."

Iona stilled as her mating heat started to rise again. Why did him touching her with so much strength make her want him?

She looked steadily back at him, knowing he could scent her fear as well as her excitement and need. "I was joking," she said.

"You have a sassy mouth. I like it." Eric licked swiftly across her parted lips, then released her.

He walked to the bike, straddled it, and started it. He didn't look at Iona as she quickly jammed on the helmet and swung on behind him, but he waited until she'd wrapped her arms around his waist before he lifted his feet and guided the motorcycle back down the narrow dirt trail.

E ric arrived home to a full house. He was restless as he dismounted and put away the bike, the run with Iona not having calmed him. Even the long ride he'd taken after he'd dropped her off, to get her smell off him, hadn't helped either.

Having her under him, ripe and ready, still had his body roaring. He could have taken her, fallen back on what Shifters did in the wild, forced the mate-claim on the female and dragged her home. She'd been ready, her mating need high.

If Eric had been younger, he might have done it. He'd chased Kirsten hard, and she'd played just coy enough to make him crazy.

When Kirsten had finally let him catch her, and they'd mated, it had been fast and frantic. Eric had shut her with him into the half of the house he'd shared with Cassidy in Scotland, and they'd not come out for days.

Since Kirsten's death, Eric hadn't bothered to pursue females. He had enough casual encounters to keep his libido under control, he already had a son, and besides, he missed Kirsten. Females were scarce among Shifters, and he'd decided to leave the females in their fertile years to younger males who hadn't yet produced cubs.

He knew that what he should do with Iona was bring her into Shiftertown and give the younger males first chance with her. Neal, their Guardian, still needed a mate, as did several other males, including Shane and Brody.

But every time Eric thought about stepping aside and letting another Shifter have her, sharp, red rage boiled through him. Eric had seen her first. Iona was *his*.

Cassidy was in the kitchen, leaning on the breakfast bar to watch her husband cook. What Diego was mixing up in that cast-iron pan—strips of steak that smelled like they'd been marinated with spices and jalapeños—made Eric's mouth water and stomach growl. He was *hungry*.

Cassidy drank water, her stomach distended with the cub she carried, while Diego had a beer. At Eric's appearance, Diego, without a word, fetched another beer from the refrigerator and handed it to him.

Eric opened the bottle but didn't drink, his adrenaline still too high. Beer would calm him down, but he didn't really want to calm down.

Cassidy's pregnancy looked good on her. She wore a knit shirt that clung to the bump that was Eric's nephew or niece, the rest of her as long and lean as ever. It would be cliché to say that Cassidy glowed, but in Eric's opinion, she truly did. Her face was rosy, her eyes bright, her pale hair sleek, her smile wide. Her love for Diego was plain to see, as was Diego's for her.

"You look good, Cass," Eric said.

He put his arm around his sister and leaned to press a kiss to her neck. Cassidy returned the embrace, ruffling Eric's hair.

Diego watched them, the man used by now to the way Shifter families needed constant touch for reassurance. Diego was all for embracing and touching Cassidy, but he wasn't as comfortable hugging Eric or Jace, even after living with them for most of a year. How humans had survived this long without curling close to their loved ones was beyond Eric's understanding.

Eric could never resist goading Diego a little, though. Even now, when he was still wound up from Iona, he walked around the counter to Diego and wrapped both arms around his brother-in-law.

"Eric," Diego said carefully. Eric suppressed a laugh as he squeezed Diego and nuzzled his hair. Diego didn't move, though Eric felt the man's fighting instincts rise.

Eric relented, released Diego, and clapped him on both shoulders. Human men were much happier when they were hitting each other, for some reason.

Eric picked up his beer again and leaned back on the counter, finally tipping the cold liquid into his mouth. "Smells good."

"Carne asada." Diego flipped the nearly smoking meat in the pan.

"Diego's teaching me to cook like his mother," Cassidy said.

"Cassidy is *watching* me cook like my mother," Diego said. "Has been all week."

Cassidy winked.

"You feeling better?" Diego flashed Eric a dark-eyed look. Diego was what humans called Latino, meaning his origins were a combination of Latin American Indian and Spanish European, mixed hundreds of years ago.

Diego had black brown hair, light brown skin, and dark eyes that held intelligence and passion—at least, passion for Cassidy. He'd grown up hard but had turned his life around, taking care of his mother and brother at huge cost to himself. He'd never been submissive to Eric, no matter that he was human, and he was a good match for Cassidy. He took care of her and made her happy.

Diego had come home early today, startling Eric, who'd been leaning against the wall in the shower, letting cold water beat down on him. Iona had called Diego, concerned about Eric, which once Eric had taken his hand from Diego's throat after Diego surprised him—had made Eric warm all over.

Diego, who didn't know about Iona, had tried to question him. Eric had put him off, going next door to see Brody, who'd called while Eric had still been lying in bed recovering, wanting to talk about the buildings in the desert.

"Sure," Eric said, answering him. "I went for a run. Checked out something Brody told me about."

Eric described the guarded buildings sitting empty in the desert behind the fences topped with barbed wire. Both Cassidy and Diego looked interested and agreed that the compound warranted a closer look.

"I can do some research for you," Diego said. "Xav is good on computers. He can find the place on a satellite map, figure out who built it and what it's for."

"Could be some secret human government place," Cassidy said. "You know, like Area Fifty-one. You were close to that. Maybe it's some new weapon-testing site. Humans like to build weapons."

"Possibly."

Eric knew Cassidy was likely right—it would turn out to be a human facility built for whatever weird purpose the humans thought important at the moment. The compound would stay there until funding ran out and no one could remember what the weird purpose was. Then they'd abandon the buildings or tear them down and cart out the pieces, moving on to some other project equally as bizarre.

"I'd be interested to see what Xav can find out," Eric said.

"Me too," Cassidy said. "Now, who is Iona Duncan, and why was she so worried about you today?"

Eric jolted, and a small amount of beer spilled to his shirt. "Shit, Cass."

Cassidy didn't look sympathetic. "A woman calls Diego out of the blue and says you're here alone, and you sound weak and hurt. Diego rushes home and finds you dealing with the aftereffects of your Collar. How did she know? Is she psychic or something?"

"No, I was talking to her on the phone when it happened."

Cassidy just looked at him, and so did Diego. Eric glanced at the pan. "You're going to burn that."

Diego stirred the contents. "No, I won't. Been making this since I was ten. Iona Duncan is the daughter of the woman who owns Duncan Construction, the company that's building the new Shifter houses. That was easy to find out."

"I've been talking to her about the plans," Eric said. "I need to find out if I can trust her."

His sister and brother-in-law both gave him an *oh-sure* look. Cassidy smiled as she took a sip of water. "You can tell us, Eric. Is she hot?"

Eric hesitated, but he knew he couldn't lie to Cassidy. She'd smell a lie on him a mile away. "Black hair, blue eyes, body like a goddess."

Diego's face split with a grin. "Good for you."

"Is she the woman I saw you with at Coolers last spring?" Cassidy asked.

Damn Cassidy's terrific memory. When Eric had first spied Iona in the Shifter bar, he'd gotten her out of there before any of the other Shifters could scent what she was. Iona had been passing for human—still was—but Eric had sensed something different about her when he saw her, and scented her easily when he'd gotten close. Eric hadn't thought anyone else had noticed him walk her out of the bar.

Cassidy, of course, had an eye on everything Eric did. Eric loved the connection he had to his sister, but the close bond could be inconvenient at times.

"Yes, that was her," Eric said. "And, yes, I found out all about her and who she was. So, when we needed the new houses, I asked her to try to get the bid."

"And you've kept quiet about her all this time," Diego said.

Eric took another sip of beer, hearing the implied *why?* in Diego's voice. "Stop being a detective, Diego. I'm Shiftertown leader. If I start a relationship with a woman, it's talked about all over Shiftertown. Shifters debate whether she's good for them, how alpha she is, and all that crap. I'm trying to keep it casual, to ease her in gradually."

A half-truth. Eric would bring Iona in eventually, and when he revealed that she was half-Shifter, the shit was going to hit the fan. He needed to make sure Iona was completely safe first.

"Don't mention this to anyone." Eric fixed Cassidy and Diego, in turn, with his alpha stare.

Which they both completely ignored. "We don't talk about your private life," Diego said.

"Except to each other," Cassidy said, her smile teasing. "And to bug you with questions about it."

At least they were joking, thinking Eric had the hots for a human woman he'd met in a Shifter bar. He'd tell them soon.

Some part of Eric, though, wanted to keep Iona private. Shifters had sequestered their females in the old days—they had to, to keep other males from challenging for them or outright stealing them.

Times were changing, Shifters lived in relative safety now, and they were one big happy family. Right?

Cassidy became serious. "What *are* you going to do about the modifications to the houses?" she asked. "Can she keep it quiet?"

"I think so. But I'll make sure before I tell her anything."

"Modifications?" Diego asked. "You mean your secret hideaways?"

Diego, once he'd become Cassidy's mate, had been taken downstairs to the hidden rooms all Shifter houses had. In them, Shifters could take refuge or hide the wealth they'd accumulated over the years, safe from humans or other Shifters.

Go to ground wasn't just a saying among Shifters. No one outside each Shifter clan was allowed into the spaces—even different prides of the same clan could keep each other out if they chose.

No human knew of these things, and no human, except a mate of the pride or pack, could ever know.

Eric was relieved of having to explain more about Iona by the arrival of Jace. "Hey, Dad," he said, breezing in. "Graham wants to talk to you."

Eric didn't hear him for a second, struck, as always, by how much Jace looked like Kirsten. He had her look, the shape of her face and nose, the quirk of the head she'd had. It hurt, but at the same time, Eric felt a wash of love.

Eric went to Jace and pulled him into an embrace, holding his son hard for a moment or two. Jace returned the embrace, then Eric let him go and ruffled his dark hair, still amazed that Jace, his unruly little cub, had grown into such a power-ful man.

"What does he want now?" Eric asked.

"He wasn't about to tell me," Jace said. His eyes were green, like Eric's. "I said I wasn't his messenger service, but I thought you'd like to know."

Nor could Eric run to Graham's side the instant Graham wanted to talk. Graham wanted that—to make it look as though Eric had answered his summons.

Damn the wolf. Everything Graham did and said was cal-culated, the Lupine determined to take over. He'd do it subtly at first and then overtly.

Cassidy smiled a predatory smile. "Want me to talk to him, Eric?"

"I want you as far away from him as you can be," Eric growled. "Understand?"

"I'm your second," Cassidy went on in a reasonable voice. "I'm supposed to take care of things you decide don't need your firsthand attention. You sending me to meet him will underscore that he's not your top priority."

"You're female," Eric said. "And pregnant. He hates females in authority."

Cassidy brightened. "Even more insulting, then."

"No, Cass," Diego said before Eric could answer. Diego's voice was hard, and he gave the meat a vicious stir, dark eyes on Cassidy.

Cassidy looked at her mate, mouth open to say more, then she closed it, went to Diego, and snuggled up against his side. "Thank you," she said.

"I agree with Diego," Eric said. "It's tempting to rub McNeil's face in it, but, no. We can't predict what he'd do. I'll meet him—I want to know what he's up to."

First, though, Eric had to make sure Iona's scent was completely off him.

A female heavy with child would have the strongest scent, so Eric went to Cassidy, peeled her away from Diego, and pulled her into another hug.

Then again, he just loved his sister. They'd been through so much together—hardship and good times, joy and grief, always there for each other. Eric held Cassidy for a long time, rubbing her back and kissing her hair, while she hugged him in return without question.

Eric released Cassidy and hugged Jace again, his love for his son pouring through him.

Jace returned the hug but looked at Eric in puzzlement when they drew apart. "Love you too, Dad. What's up?"

"Nothing. Just wanting time with my family." Eric grinned at his brother-in-law and spread his arms. "Diego."

Diego brought up his cooking fork. "Back off, Eric."

Eric did, still chuckling, and he left the house to find Graham.

Graham McNeil approached the meeting place in the common ground that ran between Shifter backyards, knowing damn well that Warden would never agree to talk to him anywhere but there.

An old picnic table with one bench sat in a weedy spot out in the open, away from the mesquites that lined the long open space. Graham knew why Eric had chosen it—the table could be watched by any number of Shifters out their back windows, even in the moonlight.

Eric's Shifters, that is. If Graham so much as raised his voice to Eric, those Shifters would come out in force. Which was why Graham always stationed a few of the wolves he'd been allowed to bring from Elko at certain intervals, watching for trouble.

By the time Graham approached the meeting place, Eric was already there, his ass planted on top of the picnic table, moonlight picking out his black tattoo. As always, the man sat stone still, watching Graham with the confidence of a predator who knew he ruled this patch.

Let Warden pin him with his stare all he wanted. When Graham challenged for leadership and won, he'd gouge out those weird green eyes and play marbles with them.

Graham stopped about two yards from the picnic table, out of Eric's reach, Eric out of his. No challenges tonight.

Eric stank of his sister and her unborn cub—the Shifter-town leader was ecstatic about his sister giving birth to a half human, half Shifter. He had to be out of his mind.

Warden didn't ask what Graham wanted. That would acknowledge that Eric had come because he wanted to know what Graham had to say.

Graham didn't want to talk about leadership tonight, though. His nephew's behavior this afternoon had reminded him of a need, and also reminded him that this Shiftertown provided him a good opportunity to fill it.

"My nephew's an idiot," Graham said without greeting. "I disciplined him for the attack on your bear."

If Eric was surprised, he hid it well. He acknowledged the apology with a nod.

"But his asshole-ness brought home to me how much I need an heir," Graham said. "A son. And for that I need a mate. So I want you to provide me one."

CHAPTER EIGHT

Eric didn't blink, but Graham scented the amazement that jolted through the Feline's body. He hadn't been expecting that.

After a deliberate silence, Eric asked, "Why can't you mate with someone from your own Shiftertown?"

"Because the only surviving females belong to my clan, too closely related to me. I need fresh blood."

The *fresh blood* pissed Warden off, but too bad. Graham needed a wolf female from a new gene pool to give him strong cubs.

Eric's voice held a warning growl. "I don't tell my Shifters who to mate with."

"That's obvious. You let your own sister mate with a human. How fucked up is that?"

"They share the mate bond."

"A Shifter can't share a mate bond with a human." Everyone knew that. "Your sister's fooling herself if she thinks so."

"You've lived out in the sticks too long. It happens."

"Yeah, I heard the leader of the Austin Shiftertown mated with a human. Dickhead. Just proves that Felines are insane. Doesn't matter. You've got unmated wolves here. Tell them to come see me. I need someone alpha, not bottom of the pack."

"If you want a mate, McNeil, you're on your own. The females here choose for themselves."

What an idiot. "Goddess, what kind of leader are you? I'm offering you the chance to make a good alliance with me. If you do, I might let you survive when I take you down."

"I'm touched," Eric said dryly. "My females are welcome to take your offer or spit on you, as they choose." He paused. "Although, now that I think about it, Nell is getting lonely for a mate."

He knew Eric was trying to be funny, but Graham's irritation rose. "You mean that crazy-ass bear with the shotgun? Bears are even worse than Felines. You need to keep her under control."

"I'll tell her you said 'hi.'" Eric rested his hands on his knees, a posture that said he didn't need to bother being defensive. "Was that it? Because my human brother-in-law is a hell of a chef, and I want a taste of what he's making tonight."

"You've gone soft, living here."

"We've survived, living here," Eric said. "Fewer deaths, more cubs."

"Yeah, yeah, Shiftertown is paradise and all that bullshit. Our houses have to be altered. I have plenty of stuff to move down here, and I don't need the humans finding it."

"I'm taking care of it."

"So you say. I don't trust you."

Eric's green eyes narrowed. "Too damn bad. Are you cleaning up your Shiftertown behind you? I don't want humans raiding here because they found all the hidey-holes you left behind."

"Being taken care of even as we speak. My crew is reliable."

Eric stood up, acting nonchalant, but at the same time maintaining the few feet of distance between them. Warden didn't move his gaze, though. His eyes had been on Graham's the whole time.

"My crew is reliable to get the houses altered," Eric said. "I'll keep you posted. In the meantime, don't harass my wolves. If a female spits in your face after your romantic proposal, suck it up."

Graham gave him the finger. Eric didn't respond, except to casually turn his back and walk away.

Graham let him go. He didn't trust Warden an inch, but Graham had decided to let him know about his mate need as a courtesy. A good leader did that. He didn't trust Eric about the houses either, but when Graham was leader, that wouldn't matter.

Now to do exactly what he'd planned to do, and to hell with Warden.

Three days passed, and Nicole's wedding rushed at Iona with sickening speed. Iona wanted Nicole married and happy, yes, but things would never be the same between them again. Iona was going to miss her little sister.

Iona picked up her bridesmaid's dress from the bridal boutique the day before the wedding and looked it over in her bedroom at home. The gown wasn't too appalling, thank heavens, because Nicole had taste. The skirt was an ankle-length sheath of royal blue, slit to the thigh on one side, the top a satin tank with inch-thick shoulder straps. That was it. No tulle or poofiness anywhere.

Iona hung the gown carefully in her closet so it wouldn't get wrinkled, and changed into a black linen pantsuit with a white sleeveless shirt for the wedding rehearsal. When she and Nicole and friends transitioned to the bachelorette party, here at Iona's house, she could shuck the linen blazer and be comfortable in just the top and pants.

Iona wondered, as she left the house, what Eric would think of her outfit. She knew he'd see it, because while Eric hadn't called Iona or shown up out of the blue in the last few days, he'd been watching her.

He was good at it, never lingering too long in one place, staying in the shadows or melting back into a crowd when she looked for him. He covered his Collar with shirt or jacket and somehow made himself look smaller and more human, so that no one noticed a Shifter hanging out on the streets with them.

But Iona knew he was there. She'd catch a whiff of his scent or see a movement that was unmistakably Eric.

He watched her go to work, appeared at building sites she visited, was there in the evenings when she got into her truck to drive home. Whenever Iona looked out her bedroom window in the middle of the night, she swore she caught a glimpse of Eric in the street below.

Didn't he have better things to do? Like run Shiftertown? Maybe she should call Diego again and tell him to post security on his brother-in-law.

Iona didn't see Eric anywhere nearby when she arrived at the church for the rehearsal. Why did that disappoint her?

Iona entered the church, the last to get there, to find Nicole talking excitedly with her bridesmaids. Tyler, the groom, stood next to Nicole, a stunned look on his face. He'd worn the look ever since Nicole, who'd taken Iona's advice and gone to her doctor, had told him she was pregnant. Happy, but stunned.

"Hey, Tyler," Iona said, giving him a brief hug. "How's Daddy?"

"Fine." Tyler sent her a sheepish smile. "Just fine."

"This wedding stuff will be over soon. And then you'll have Nicole all to yourself."

"Sure," Tyler said. "Over. Right."

Iona rubbed his shoulders. "Don't worry, you can get nice and drunk tonight. Just make sure you can stand up in the morning long enough to say the vows. And don't drop the ring."

"You're all heart, Iona."

Iona gave him a peck on the cheek and turned to embrace her sister. The scent of the child growing inside Nikki had strengthened, even in such a short time. The scent sparked the need Iona had been fighting the last few days, fanning it to life.

She backed off and moved halfway down the aisle, pretending she wanted to sit down. She couldn't trust her eyes to not go Shifter around Nicole, or the mating need not to start making her sprout fur.

Iona breathed a sigh of relief when the rehearsal began. Remembering what she had to do would keep her mind off shifting—and mating—she hoped.

As the maid of honor, Iona had to lead the other brides-maids down the aisle, timing her steps to avoid rushing or going too slowly. She'd stand to the left of her sister and hold the bridal bouquet while Tyler put the ring on Nicole's finger. She'd then wait until everyone went back down the aisle and pair up with Tyler's brother, Clay, the best man, to walk out with him.

Iona liked Clay, but she felt a little uneasy with him. When Tyler and Nicole had first started getting serious, Clay had thought it would be great if he and Iona paired up too. Iona had put him off—she didn't want to tell him that a) she sometimes shifted into a panther, and b) she would probably live twice as long as he would, which is what her research told her half human, half Shifters did. Though she looked the same age as Clay, she was ten years older than he was already. Clay got the hint that Iona wasn't interested, but he still showed hope around her.

After the rehearsal, they all left the church for the rehearsal dinner. Iona didn't see Eric between church and restaurant, nor did she when she returned home to finish prepping for Nicole's party. Nicole and her friends arrived soon after, and the party started to swing.

Well toward midnight, the doorbell rang. Iona pretended to be busy in the kitchen, and Nicole's friends goaded Nicole to answer it.

Nicole screamed with laughter when a fireman sauntered into the house, complete with hose, and started shedding his gear in the living room. The women surrounded him while he danced to a thumping beat, and Iona watched from the doorway with a smile.

The music wound louder. The music, combined with the women's excitement, embraced Iona and made her want to dance too. The living room was dim except for the middle where the stripper gyrated—someone had turned on one of Iona's ceiling spots and killed the rest of the lights. The girls danced with him, Nicole laughing as the man wrapped his hose around her.

Nicole spotted Iona in the doorway. "Come on, Iona," she yelled. "You know you love to dance!"

Iona shouldn't. Too dangerous. But the music called to her, the rhythm synching with some rhythm inside her body. The *thrum, thrum, thrum* was fierce and primal.

The ladies whooped as Iona kicked her shoes off and danced in. The stripper grinned, a good sport, and wrapped the end of his fire hose around her waist.

Iona raised her arms in the dance, her blood getting hot, but not because the guy was attractive. He smelled too much of human sweat and cologne, not a good combination to a Shifter. Eric always smelled clean, like wind and the night.

But Iona was loving the dance, her hips swaying, the beat of the music like the rhythm of sex. The stripper was a good dancer, smoothly pulling Iona into synch with him. He had Iona straddling his knee, locking her in close as they rocked together. The other ladies whooped and screamed.

The noise and heat grew suddenly too intense. The panther inside Iona wanted to tear away from the man who held her, swat him aside, and then run around the room, ripping down decorations like an unruly kitten. Then she'd devour the entire hors d'oeuvre tray, especially all the shrimp cocktail. Yum.

Control, Eric had told her. *You can control it.*

Maybe if she'd grown up Shifter with years of training and discipline, she could have.

The fireman leaned in and tried to kiss her. Iona forced a laugh, though she wanted to bite his face off. She whirled so hard she untangled from the hose and was halfway across the room before he could stop her.

She nearly ran away from him, but two of the other girls instantly took her place, and the fireman turned to them, not minding. Breathing hard, Iona slipped out of the room into the back hall, seeking peace in the relative coolness and darkness.

Two strong arms folded around her from behind. Iona found herself trapped back against a hard male chest, while a grating voice said in her ear, "No, Iona. You belong to *me*."

CHAPTER NINE

"**E**ric, what the hell are you doing here?" Iona asked in a loud whisper.

For answer, Eric turned her around and pressed her into the wall.

His kiss stole her breath, his lips forcing her mouth open, teeth scraping. The thump of the music in the other room pulsed through her, and she curled her fingers on Eric's chest. Fingers became claws, tearing Eric's shirt.

Eric shed the shirt and turned them together so that now *his* back was against the wall. "If you want to feast on someone, you feast on *me*."

I didn't want to, she tried to say, but the words stuck in her throat.

Iona put her nose to the curve of his neck, inhaling his scent as he'd taught her to. Eric smelled of the outdoors and a little wildness, no cologne or too much sweat to cover it up.

She licked him. Eric made a noise in his throat, hand coming up to cradle her head.

Feast on him. Yes. Iona licked again, tasting the salt of his skin. She moved her mouth to the tattoo on his bare shoulder, tongue finding the outlines of the ink. She tasted and licked, more salt and the taste of Eric, then she nibbled his skin. A growl escaped his lips, drowned by the music.

They stood only a few yards from the living room, hidden in the darkness in the narrow passage, while Nicole and her friends laughed and screamed, and the music throbbed.

Iona nipped Eric's throat while he held her against him. She licked her way down to his pecs, fingers playing with the wiry hair dusting his chest.

She moved to his flat nipple, teeth finding the point. Eric jumped. "Sweet girl."

Iona flicked her tongue over his nipple, liking how it tightened under her attention. He tasted darker here, the tip of the nipple smooth under her tongue. Eric's heart pounded, his breath coming fast.

His fingers furrowed her hair, his touch strong. Eric didn't gentle himself, Iona thought with rising excitement, because he knew she could take it.

She wondered what *he* could take. She played her tongue over his nipples a little longer, before she licked her way back to the hollow of his throat.

At the same time, she slid her hand downward, tracing the narrow line of hair that pointed to his belt buckle. Eric moved his legs apart as Iona took her hand past the buckle to the hard ridge that pressed the zipper of his jeans.

Eric's head went back against the wall, eyes half closing. He twitched her hand aside so he could unbuckle and unzip his jeans, shoving them and his underwear down before he guided Iona back to him.

Iona closed fingers around his rigid cock. She thought again of her Shifter-loving friends giggling that Shifters were extra long. Eleven inches was common.

Iona found every inch while Eric leaned back and let her, his eyes green slits in the darkness.

The shaft of his cock was smooth and firm, sleek and hot. Iona slid her hand all the way around him in wonderment, feeling the pulse beat through it in the darkness. She worked her fingers upward to the spongier texture of the tip and ran her thumb back and forth over the head. A bead of moisture slicked the tip, and Eric bit back a groan.

Iona skimmed her hand down again, liking the contrast

between soft head and extra-hard shaft. Eric couldn't stop the next groan when Iona reached the base of his cock, fingers finding and cupping his balls.

"You're going to kill me," he said in a low voice.

Iona stilled. "I can stop."

"No." Eric's grip bit into her wrist. "You can't."

Iona closed her fingers around his shaft again. Eric loosened his hold a little but kept his hand around her wrist while she glided her closed hand up the cock. Eric shuddered, his head moving against the wall.

Iona leaned into him, loving his warmth, loving that she had the powerful Shiftertown leader to herself in her back hall, his jeans and underwear sagging around his ankles. He tugged her into the circle of one strong arm, holding her close as she stroked him.

Her hand slid easily up his shaft, the tip bumping her palm, his tight balls filling her hand when she reached the base again. Eric breathed raggedly as he held her, his fingers still hard on her wrist.

The music and noise went on in the other room, the stripper keeping the ladies' attention. In the darkness of the hall, Iona indulged herself touching this incredible man. Eric's body was tight with the power of him, his broad neck encircled by the Collar that gleamed in the dark.

Tall, sexy, strong Eric. Iona licked the tattoo on his arm as she kept stroking.

Eric tugged her sleeveless top upward, his hand on the warmth of her belly. He slid his fingers to her back and popped open her bra, then moved to cup and hold the warmth of one breast.

Now Iona groaned softly as Eric flicked his thumb over her nipple, bringing her to life as she had him.

This encounter was different from when he'd tackled her up on the ridge, pinning her with his warmth and strength. That had been exciting but playful, Eric teaching Iona that he could take her down anytime he wanted.

This was raw sex, nothing playful about it. Iona's panther watched from within her, bemused by the human need for erotic touch. Iona the woman fastened her teeth on Eric's neck above his Collar and sucked.

Eric's moan was heartfelt. His hand moved hers faster on his cock, his hips pushing from the wall, rocking into her hand.

Iona sucked harder on his neck while she stroked him through her fist, knowing what was coming.

Eric shoved her away suddenly, and she looked up at him, startled, to find herself being flattened against the wall again. He curved over her, naked in her arms, his hips still moving, cock thrusting through her closed fist.

"I want my seed on you," he said savagely. "To mark you as mine. To keep you away from some stupid dancer dressed up like a fireman."

Iona started to laugh. "I wasn't . . ."

He silenced her with a kiss. The kiss was fierce, his mouth brutal, Eric biting her lips until she quieted. At the same time, his hips moved faster and faster, until he broke the kiss, his breathing hoarse.

Eric leaned one arm on the wall behind her, bracing himself to keep his weight from crushing her. His eyes flicked to Shifter as his head rocked back, and his seed shot out to land, scalding, all over Iona's hand and her bared belly.

In the living room, the music cut off abruptly, followed by the women's raucous cheers and laughter. Eric stifled his growls, but barely, as he came and came, holding Iona, his mouth landing on hers again.

Iona caught his tongue with hers, tasting his mouth, letting her teeth scrape his lips as his scraped hers. She held six feet six of shuddering male in her arms, his skin slick with sweat as his hot seed roped over her fingers.

Eric scooped Iona's long hair back from her face, his kisses softening from fierce to tender. Iona's heart ached as he took her lips in slow, openmouthed kisses, his eyes still that of his wildcat.

When the music started again, Eric raised his head, his face relaxed, touch warm. He started to speak, but Iona put her fingers to his lips.

"Let's go upstairs," she whispered.

He gave her a silent nod then rolled away from her to lean against the wall and catch his breath.

Iona almost lost *her* breath. Eric's long, naked body reposed against her hallway wall, the sweat on his sun-bronzed skin glistening in the fingers of light from the living room. His jeans and underwear were crumpled around his ankles; they were the only stitch of clothing he wore.

His tattoo, black and sharp, wound down his arm, his navel a shadowed indentation on his flat stomach. Below his abdomen, his cock hung, long and dark, still half-erect, damp from his coming.

Iona could look at him forever. *Feast on me*, he'd said. She had—with her touch, her tongue, and now her gaze. He'd let her take what she needed of him without asking anything in return.

"Iona!" Nicole shouted from the living room. "Get back in here. You have to *see* this!"

Iona was seeing plenty. She grinned at Eric, who half smiled back.

Eric leaned to grab his shirt from the floor, then used the shirt to wipe Iona's hands and abdomen, then himself. He pulled up, zipped, and buckled his jeans, then he wadded the shirt in his hands.

"Clean up and go back to your sister's party." Eric kissed her, his mouth still hot, then turned to leave.

Iona's heart pounded. "Wait." She went to him where he paused near the back door. "Why have you been following me around?"

"Not following. Watching out for you."

"You have a whole Shiftertown to watch out for."

Eric stroked his hand through her hair, his touch strong. "I have family to help me look after Shiftertown. But I'm the only one who looks after you."

"You don't have to look after me."

Eric kissed the line of her hair, then let her go. "Yes, I do."

He was about to turn around again, walk out the back door, fade into the night. Iona caught his hand, for some reason not wanting him to go. "I was sent a set of the blueprints from the architect late this afternoon. I was going to call you."

Eric stepped closer to her again. "I'll come to your office tomorrow and show you what I need you to do."

"No, you won't. I'll be at a wedding all day."

"Doesn't matter. I'll go to your office and look at them. Leave them out where I can find them."

"Right, a Shifter will go into our locked office the day the company's closed for Nicole's wedding and help himself to blueprints. Security will be all over your butt, and you'll be in jail trying to explain yourself."

He shook his head, the light from the living room glinting on his short, dark hair. "Security will never see me. Give me a key if you want to make it easier, but I'll get in anyway."

"Eric, I see you all the time. You're not that stealthy."

His laughter rumbled as he put his face close to hers. "You see me, because you have a connection to me." Eric traced her cheek. "You're the only one who does."

He laughed again as she stared at him, then he kissed her parted lips and walked out of her house.

The shower was a sweet bite on Eric's sensitive skin. He lifted his face to the water, enjoying its warmth, letting his hands rest on the cool tiled wall.

Sweeter was the memory of Iona's teeth in his neck and her hand stroking his cock. It was already erect for her again.

His life would be so much better if Iona were here in the shower with him, helping him soap off, her hands gliding all over his naked body. He'd return the favor and wash her, and then they could slide against each other, Eric lifting her to make love to her against the tiled wall he and Jace had put in.

Eric needed to mate-claim Iona soon, bring her in, install her in this house, and make her part of himself. No stepping aside so younger males could have their chance with her. Iona was *his.*

He remembered looking into the living room from the back hall and seeing Iona dancing with the stripper. Eric had taken in the smile on her face, her arms raised above her head as she gyrated and slid against the man.

Something primal had ripped through him. Instinct wanted him to grab the stripper away from her and tear his head off. Eric wanted to feel the blood of his rival running down his arms and dripping from his teeth. His brain had switched back to the days when Shifters were wild and untamable, when they'd turned on their Fae masters and left bloody bodies in their wake.

She's *mine*.

Sudden pain sliced through his stomach, robbing him of breath.

Shit, not again. Eric folded his arm over his abdomen, trying to find air. What the hell?

The pain faded, and Eric relaxed. Weird. He hadn't been fighting today, no Collar going off, no practicing the technique to suppress it. He'd gone to DX Security to ask Xavier Escobar to, on the QT, search for Iona Duncan's birth certificate. Xavier had agreed, promising not to mention the search to any Shifter, though he was obviously curious about the order for silence. But Xavier would keep his mouth shut. Eric had learned that he could trust him.

Eric had spent the rest of the day watching Iona. He hadn't meant for her to find him in her house during the party. But when she'd hurried, mussed and sweating, eyes wild, into the back hall, he couldn't resist the opportunity to touch her.

The pain blinked out like a forgotten dream as Eric relived her clawing at his shirt, licking his chest when he bared it for her. She'd tongued his nipples in delight, as though she hadn't realized men were as sensitive as women. Another bite of triumph filled him with the knowledge that Eric was her first.

She hadn't known quite how to stroke him, but he hadn't minded letting her learn on him. Eric's body relaxed even more as he thought of how she'd touched him in wonder, then the erotic pulse of his coming, his basic need to mark her with his seed.

His cock rose with delighted memory, and Eric gave it a calming stroke.

At the same time he tried to cool down. He couldn't walk out of here with an erection, not with Cassidy and his son in the living room. The house was too small. They'd scent his arousal even if he hid it well with his towel. And they'd find it hilarious.

Eric's thoughts drifted back to Iona dancing. Goddess, she was beautiful, taller and fuller figured than her friends and half sister who'd surrounded her, her body graceful as she moved in sinuous rhythm. Eric had wanted to be that stripper, with his thigh planted firmly between Iona's legs . . .

Out of nowhere, pain smacked Eric's entire body, as

though something were trying to twist him in half. A cry escaped his lips as he fell, his knees banging the shower's tile floor.

He clenched his teeth, arms folded over his stomach, every muscle hurting, every nerve burning. His heart pounded with the agony and also with fear.

What the hell was wrong with him? Shifters didn't get the same diseases humans did, their metabolisms not allowing what killed humans to manifest inside them. But Shifters had been living among humans for a while now, breeding with them, eating their food, drinking their water—who knew what had developed?

Or maybe this *was* the residual effects of suppressing his Collar three days ago. Eric wasn't as good at overriding the Collar as Jace was. Jace had been mastering the technique, traveling to Austin every month or so to get instruction from the Shifters there who knew how. Jace was good at it, better than Eric or Cassidy.

Whatever was going on with Eric, it hurt like holy hell. Eric curled up around himself and moaned.

Iona, I need you.

He craved her touch, the sound of her voice. But he was on his ass in the shower, the water beating on him, and he couldn't move to crawl out and find help.

"Dad?" Jace's voice was right next to him. Eric peeled open his eyes to find his son crouched next to the shower stall, staring through the glass at Eric in concern. "Shit, Dad, are you all right?"

"No," Eric croaked.

Jace stood up, opened the shower door, and turned off the water before he grabbed a towel and draped it around Eric's body. "We heard you moaning in here. Cass made me come in and see if you were all right."

Eric shivered under the towel. "I will be."

"Bullshit. Look at you."

"No, thanks." Eric was drained of strength, and he probably looked awful. He started to dry himself off, but his hands shook so much that Jace had to help him.

"You were with a woman tonight," Jace said, still sounding worried.

Damn it. "Can you still scent her on me? Give me the soap."

"No, I can tell because you have love bites up and down your neck."

The clenching pain receded slightly as Eric thought of Iona's mouth on him, her tongue tracing the line of his Collar. He smiled faintly. "She likes to chew on me."

"Was it Iona Duncan?"

Eric lost his smile. "Cass told you."

"Yeah. She also told me to keep it quiet. Like I'd rat out my own father."

Eric grabbed Jace's offered hand and let his son help pull him to his feet. "What would you say if I told you I wanted to take a new mate?" he asked.

Jace rolled his eyes. "I'd say it's about fucking time."

Eric growled a laugh. He caught Jace around the neck and pulled him close for a swift, damp hug. The pain finally dissolved with his son's warmth through the towel.

"That's what I love about you, Jace," Eric said. "You don't hold back."

"Why should I? You're not that scary, Dad."

Eric squeezed Jace again before letting him go. "I'll have to work on that. Go tell Cass I'm okay."

Jace returned the embrace, then dried off his hands on the end of the towel. "Better clean up in here before you let Cassidy in. And when you're done, Shane and I want to talk to you."

"Sure thing."

My son, third in command, is getting stronger. Eric thought it with pride as Jace left the bathroom with one final worried look at Eric.

Eric also sensed the restlessness in Jace, his need to prove himself in the hierarchy. Jace was third automatically, because he was Eric's son, but Jace was getting to the age where he'd need to show he had dominance of his own, unconnected to his father's position in the clan.

That might entail a fight with Eric, or a battle with any number of Shifters, including Graham. Graham's arrival was triggering all kinds of issues.

Eric's strength returned somewhat as he dried himself, got

himself to his room, and dressed again, but the incident in the shower left him shaky. He needed to find someone to talk to about it, but quietly.

No one could know of the alpha's weakness, not if Eric wanted to avoid even *more* dominance fights. And Graham would use the slightest excuse to push Eric out.

Eric kissed the worried Cassidy on the cheek when he emerged from his bedroom, telling her that Jace had made him feel better, then he walked out into the dark backyard to meet with Shane.

Nicole's wedding was a whirlwind of flowers, music, excitement, and—for Iona—sadness. Nicole stood serenely at the altar in her slim ivory satin gown, Iona holding her bouquet of pink roses as Tyler and Nicole exchanged rings.

Tyler was still obviously stunned about being an unexpected father, but the look he gave Nicole when he slid the ring onto her finger was so loving that more eyes than Iona's teared up.

At one point in the service, Iona glanced back over the packed church and faltered when she saw Eric in the last pew on the bride's side. She had no idea when he'd slipped in, but once she spotted him, his presence shouted itself to her.

He wore a button-down shirt and suit coat that hid his Collar, so at first glance he looked like any other man attending the wedding. But the bulk of him filled his corner of the pew, which thankfully was otherwise empty. No one seemed to notice him, thank God.

When Tyler leaned to kiss Nicole, finishing the ceremony, Iona looked again for Eric, but he'd gone.

Her heart fluttered, and the itchy feeling she'd had since her encounter with him last night ignited again. She'd dreamed of Eric all night, waking up hot and sweating, craving him.

Staying awake had been just as bad, because she could remember precisely what his kisses felt like as he pressed her into the wall, the sounds of excitement he made while she stroked him, the exact size and feel of his cock in her hand.

She'd licked the palm that had held him, imagining she

could still taste him on her. The spurt of his come had excited her. Thinking of it, lying alone in her hot bed, made her wet and aching, and she'd slid her hand between her legs to try to suppress it.

That hadn't helped at all, and now, standing at the altar, in a *church*, she still wanted him. All this fertility—Nicole pregnant, the wedding ceremony, the flowers—all the symbols of matrimony and fruitfulness were driving her insane.

Even the fun of dressing up Nicole before the wedding and sharing her excitement hadn't dampened Iona's crazed longing for Eric. She watched the service and spoke the responses as though not really there, everything muted and fuzzy around the edges.

Only when she'd glimpsed Eric in the back had she seen clearly again, every nerve coming alive with the closeness of him.

Eric had said he'd go to the construction office to look at her blueprints. Then why had he come here? For the keys? Or another reason?

The organ started with the recessional, and Iona made herself pay attention. Nicole and Tyler sailed back down the aisle, married, Nicole stopping to kiss their mother, who was openly crying.

Iona waited for her cue to meet up with Tyler's brother, Clay, and hurry out of the church with him. Clay leaned to her. "You look beautiful, Iona."

"Thank you," she said distractedly.

"Best man and maid of honor get to dance, you know."

Iona, scanning the fringes of the crowd for Eric, barely heard him. "Sure," she said.

Clay squeezed her arm. "Looking forward to it."

Crap, what had she just promised? Eric was nowhere in sight, and he wasn't in the crowd in front of the church. The tingling his presence triggered was gone as well.

Everything in Iona wanted her to rush to her red pickup and gun it to the office in hopes of meeting up with Eric there. But this was her sister's wedding, for heaven's sake. Nicole's special day. Iona couldn't just leave.

Iona slid away from Clay and went to Nicole, embracing her. "Congratulations, Nikki. Be happy."

"I am happy." Nicole had a hint of tears in her eyes, but she was mostly smiles. She leaned to Iona and whispered, "And maybe a little bit exhausted from last night. You threw the *best* party."

Nicole didn't know the half of it.

Time for photographs. They took forever, Iona having to stay close to be in her share of them. Then off to the reception for food, drink, cake, toasting the bride and groom, dancing, laughter, and talking. All the while Iona stood by and wanted Eric.

She shouldn't. Eric was dangerous for her. But Iona was being pulled apart by instincts—one telling her to run as far from him as she could, the other telling her to grab him and have sex with him until she couldn't walk.

Penny took Iona aside while everyone piled into cars to go to the reception. "You okay, honey?"

"I'm fine," Iona said, still distracted. "I'm happy for Nicole, that's all."

"I know. I'm so sorry, Iona."

Iona drew back, holding her mother, six inches shorter than her, by the hands. "About what?"

"I know it will be hard for you to find what Nicole has. A boyfriend, a fiancé, a wedding. Normal things."

Worry about whether she'd have a normal wedding was so far from Iona's thoughts that she started to laugh. "I'm fine, Mom, really."

"I've seen you have to stand by while Nicole does everything every other girl does. And I know that if you do choose to marry, you'll find a Shifter."

Iona stared. "Don't write me off yet, Mom. Maybe I don't want to find anyone. I'll run the business with you. I don't mind. I like the work."

Penny smiled. "I don't know a lot about Shifters, but I know what your Shifter father told me. You'll need a . . . mate . . . someday, and you'll want to have children. It's built into Shifters. And I saw how you looked at Eric."

Iona flushed. "Mom."

"It's all right, sweetheart. You can't help what you are. I wish I hadn't fallen for your father, but at the same time, I'm so, so glad I had you." Penny drew Iona close again. "What

I'm trying to say is, if you want to run off to Shiftertown with Eric, I won't blame you."

"Why didn't you?" Iona asked. "Become my father's mate, I mean. Didn't he ask you?"

"Oh, he asked me," Penny said. "I refused. That's why he left one night, and I never saw him again."

CHAPTER TEN

Iona stared at her, this being the first time her mother had talked this much about the Shifter who was Iona's father. "Why did you refuse him? If he was charming and handsome and irresistible, why?"

Penny looked evasive, her gaze straying to the cars filling up to head to the Bellagio for the reception. "It's complicated."

Iona tightened her hold on her mother's hands. "Tell me. Please, Mom. It's important that I know."

Penny heaved a long sigh. "I didn't go with him because I already knew your stepfather. Howard and I had . . . an understanding. We'd planned to finish college and then get married. I never thought I'd meet anyone who would make me betray him, but then I met Ross. I fell hard in love with him. I'd never felt like that before, and to be honest, I never have since."

Iona had always known that Howard Duncan was her stepfather, but she'd grown up calling him *Dad* and loving him as much as she loved her mother. Howard had done all the dad things, like attending Iona's soccer games, and teaching her to drive, and surprising her with a car on her eighteenth birthday. He hadn't minded that Iona wasn't his real daughter and was the child of a shapeshifter.

He'd loved Iona for herself, and that was all there was to it.

Howard had been a wonderful man, and the family's grief at his death had lasted a long time. They still grieved him.

"Mom, you can't stand here and tell me you never loved Dad."

"That's not what I meant." Penny flushed. "Of course I loved Howard. You know I did. What I had with Ross was different. But I knew I couldn't give up my entire safe life to be with him. I was too scared and ashamed. I didn't know at the time that I was pregnant with you. So I told Ross I could never be his mate."

Iona imagined the Feline Shifter asking Penny to be his mate, looking at her like Eric looked at Iona. Intense, protective, compelling—telling her what would happen and willing it to be so.

"What did Ross do?" Iona asked softly.

"He took it hard. But in the end, he understood. He said he'd fooled himself thinking I'd go off with him." Penny shrugged. "And then he disappeared. By the time I knew I was going to have you, I had no idea where to find him."

Iona thought some more, processing this with the knowledge—or half knowledge—she'd grown up believing. "Mom, you didn't marry Dad until I was five."

Penny heaved another sigh, old regret in her eyes. "I know. I told Howard the truth, all of it, when I found out I was pregnant. I couldn't lie to him. He was very, very angry—he had every right to be—and he went away. I thought it was over for good. I had you on my own and didn't meet Howard again until five years after that."

"I remember." Iona recalled with precision, though she'd been such a small child, meeting Howard for the first time. She remembered how his kind eyes had widened when he'd looked at her, how he'd crouched down to hold out his hand to her.

She'd liked his blue eyes and his smile, how gentle he'd been with her. Howard and Penny had sat up well into the middle of the night talking, not only that first night, but many subsequent nights.

Finally, Iona had said, in front of both of them, "Mom, why don't you and Howard get married? He could be my dad, and he wouldn't have to drive home at three o'clock in the morning."

Penny had been embarrassed, but Howard had said that Iona was very smart. A few months later, Penny and Howard had married, and a few years after that, Nicole had come along. They'd been one smiling, happy family.

One smiling, happy family with a daughter who had to turn into a panther every so often or go crazy.

"If you decide to go to Eric," Penny was saying, releasing Iona's hands, "I'll understand."

"I haven't decided anything." Iona took a step back. "I don't want anything about what I am to blow back on you."

"I can take care of myself, Iona." Penny smiled. "Have for years." She glanced again at the line of cars. "Nicole is waiting for you. It's her day—let's be happy for her."

"Iona!" Nicole was shouting from the limousine. "Come on!"

"Go," Penny said sternly.

Iona let out her breath and kissed her mother's cheek, her emotions still swirling, and scurried away to pile into the back of the limo amid satin skirts and too many flowers.

The reception at the Bellagio was in one of the grand ballrooms. The food was good, and Iona caught herself taking helping after helping. Even Clay stared when the tray went by and Iona shoveled another ten canapés onto her plate.

She told herself she was upset by her mother's revelations, trying to reconcile what she'd learned today by stuffing herself. But she knew that wasn't quite true. She'd been hungry like this all week.

Nicole should be the one wanting to eat, with the baby. Iona wasn't anywhere near pregnant, unless Shifters could be impregnated by kissing. And touching. Licking, biting . . .

She shivered and popped a canapé into her mouth, whole. No, Shifters made babies the usual way. She'd been shown that when she'd held Eric last night, the pulses of his seed spilling over her hands.

Shifters made babies—cubs—with sex. The mating frenzy, Eric had told her, shutting themselves away from the world and making love like crazy, not coming out for days.

Then what was the matter with her? Iona's metabolism was burning up, and she was so *hungry*.

She polished off her canapés and grabbed another handful while Clay was giving his best man's speech. After that was dancing. Iona had a tissue at her eyes for Nicole's entire first dance with Tyler. Nicole was so beautiful, so happy. She even smelled happy, the scent of her perfume and excitement overlaid with the scent of her pregnancy.

Iona's skin itched as she cried, and she had to force herself not to scratch. What the hell had Eric done to her?

Dancing helped a little. Iona did her obligatory dance with Clay, then she whirled around the floor with her friends, male and female, working off her restlessness. She hoped to exhaust herself so she could sleep tonight, but it didn't work. She just got more hungry.

Finally, as twilight darkened the wide desert sky, Nicole and Tyler left for their honeymoon. Iona joined the throng behind the hotel, and Nicole threw her bouquet.

The bouquet of roses and baby's breath flew up into the air, tumbled end over end, ribbons streaming, and landed right in Iona's hands. She squeaked, jumped back, and dropped it.

Laughter echoed among her friends. "Don't be afraid of it, Iona," they said. "Take it, girl!" "You're next, you know it."

Iona picked up the bouquet with trembling hands, smoothing the ribbons. "I'll keep this for you, Nikki."

Nicole laughed, kissed Iona's cheek, and waved good-bye. She was going. Off to Hawaii to lie on a beach, while Iona carried on without her.

One of Iona's friends grabbed her hand. "Party time. Let's go out to that Shifter bar, you remember it? The one where the Shifter guy tried to pick you up?"

Iona did remember her utter shock when Eric had sat down next to her that night. His presence had blown her away, and she hadn't been the same since.

Iona disengaged her hand. "No thanks," she said, as politely as she could. "I'm tired, and I need to look in on some work. You all have fun."

They protested and cajoled, but in the end, they gave up. Iona was a pathetic workaholic, in their opinions, but they laughed when they said it. Iona gave the bouquet to the care of her mother, walked away from the celebration, got into her red pickup, and drove to the office.

The gate at the site was locked, but Iona had the keys with her. She unlocked the padlock, being careful about keeping dirt and grease off her pretty satin gown. She drove the truck through the gate, parked, and went back to lock the gate after herself.

The sun had gone, but floodlights lit the back of the site to prevent theft of costly equipment and supplies. The trailer office was dark and looked deserted, but Eric's motorcycle was parked behind it.

Iona's heart beat faster as she climbed the steps and opened the door.

Eric looked up from her desk. He'd taken off his coat and hung it on the chair and rolled up his sleeves, baring sinewy forearms. Iona drank in his male scent, fresh like the night.

The blueprints for the new Shifter houses were spread over the desk in front of him. The lack of light didn't seem to bother him, but Eric was Shifter. He'd be able to see well in the dark.

He got up and came to Iona as she shut the door. Without speaking, Eric put callused hands on her elbows and ran his hands up her bare arms.

The itchiness eased, but a new hunger flared. Eric gathered her to him, tilted her head back, and kissed her. His tongue chased hers, his lips slow, savoring. The frenzy of last night was still there, but not quite the same. Iona tasted something a little different in him, though she wasn't sure what.

Eric pressed his thumbs to the corners of her mouth, opening her to him. This kiss was warm, loving, taking its time. The Shifter called Ross must have kissed her mother like this—leisurely, confident, knowing he'd wooed a woman to him against her better judgment.

When Eric eased the kiss to its end, Iona nestled against his shirt, closing her eyes to hear the rapid beating of his heart.

"Why were you at the wedding?" she asked. "Someone might have seen you."

"I didn't want to miss a family ritual so important to you," he answered, voice rumbling beneath her ear.

Why did that idea please her so much? "I'm happy for Nicole. Sad for me."

"I know, sweetheart." Eric smoothed her hair. "Humans

make weddings about families going their separate ways. Shifter weddings are about drawing new family in."

Drawing family in. That sounded so nice. Throughout Nicole's childhood, Iona had protected her little sister as much as Nicole had protected her. Saying good-bye to Nicole tonight had been hard. No, not hard. Impossible.

But Nicole would be back, and Iona would surprise her with her remodeled house, and they'd visit each other all the time. All was not lost.

Right now, though, the good-bye felt like finality.

She drew back from Eric, liking the comfort of him too much. "How did you get in here? Everything's locked up tight."

"Because I'm good, sweetheart. Let me show you what I want you to do with the plans."

He led her by the hand to the desk and turned on the light—for her benefit—and spread out the blueprints.

The houses the architect had designed were simple, nothing complex for Shifters. The basic house was a long rectangle, with a living room and kitchen taking up one end, and a hall leading to three bedrooms taking up the other. A bathroom nestled between bedrooms one and two. That was it.

"Simple is good," Eric said. "We can do false walls in two of these closets that will open to steps down to the underground rooms."

"Underground rooms? What underground rooms?"

Eric smiled up at her, his flash of teeth predatory. "That's where the real Shifter houses are. Downstairs. We like burrows. Especially the bears. Sometimes, in deep winter, getting Shane and Brody to come out is a hell of a job."

Iona didn't laugh. "I've never heard of this."

"It's not something Shifters share. That's why you tell no one." He pinned her with a stare.

"Not tell my crew why they're digging the foundation so deep? They're not stupid or blind."

"Shifters will do that work," Eric said. "We'll cover it up. We've done this before. Your job is to get an altered set of plans into the hands of your head builder and make him think there's nothing wrong."

He looked up at her, his eyes warming. Iona realized that

she leaned over him, her bare arms and half-bare breasts about an inch from his face. Eric didn't bother pretending not to look, his gaze sinful.

Iona stood up and rubbed her arms, the itch returning. "That's all? Give him altered plans and make him think there's nothing wrong with them?"

"I have Shifters who can redraw them for you. They'll look legit. And the original, real plans will stay with the human committee and be public record."

"The guys we hire aren't stupid," Iona said. "They'll know something's wrong."

"Be persuasive. And their bank accounts will have some nice bonuses in them, far more money than the humans will pay."

Iona thought about her foreman, who'd worked in Las Vegas, a city once run by criminal families, his entire life. If people wanted hidden rooms in their houses or hotels, he probably wouldn't blink, nor would he bother to tell anyone about the sudden influx of money to his checking account.

"*Shifters* are going to come up with this money?" Iona asked. "You all lived in poverty in the wild and aren't allowed to have high-paying jobs, right?"

"You let me worry about that," Eric said.

"You're seriously trusting me."

"I have to. I have no choice." Eric stood up. "Sit here. I'll show you exactly what we need."

Iona's body kept flushing hot, then cold, like she had a fever, and she was hungry again. The finger food from the reception wasn't cutting it. A gallon of beer wouldn't go down too badly either.

Eric leaned over the plans, his torso close enough for her to lick. She wanted to lean into him, fasten her teeth in his shirt, maybe tear it to little shreds with her panther teeth to get to the man inside.

His gaze flicked to hers. "You paying attention?"

"Sure." Iona licked her lips. "Sure."

The hunger, the itching, the heat—she knew what it was. Need for Eric. She didn't want a big, juicy burger; she wanted to devour *him*. If she rubbed herself all over him, that might soothe her burning skin, her boiling blood.

She reached out and covered his big hand with hers. It was so warm, so strong. Iona raised his hand to her lips and kissed his palm.

"Eric," she whispered.

"I know," Eric said, voice low. "I know—"

The door of the office slammed open and a large man Iona had never seen before barreled in. His dark hair was buzzed ultra short, his eyes were gray and glittering, and flame tattoos wound around muscular arms bared by a short-sleeved T-shirt and biker vest. A Collar hugged his neck, but even if he hadn't worn one, everything about him, including his rife scent, screamed Shifter.

Eric was up from the desk and in front of him before Iona could rise or ask what hell he was doing there. The Shifter met Eric face-to-face, not even glancing at Iona.

"What are you doing here, Warden?"

"Get out," Eric said.

"Fuck you. My trackers say you've been coming here and talking to the women who own this company. You sleeping with one of them? All of them, maybe? To get them to do what you want—and to help you screw over me and my wolves?"

Eric tried to force the other Shifter back out the door, but the big man wasn't budging. "Is she one of them? Not bad. I get why—"

McNeil stopped, his eyes fixing on Iona and becoming white gray. He inhaled once, sharply. "Son of a bitch. She's *Shifter.*"

Eric's snarl rumbled through the trailer. He blocked the other Shifter with his body, his teeth becoming Shifter, lips pulling back from fangs.

McNeil's eyes lit with feral fire. "Fair game," he said, triumph in his voice.

Eric swung to Iona. His eyes were shining green, his pupils black slits. "Iona Duncan, I claim you as mate under the Goddess and before a witness." He spoke rapidly, drowning out the growls of Graham McNeil, who was trying to get around him.

"*I Challenge,*" McNeil said.

The two Shifters faced each other again, both bulking large, barely containing their shift. McNeil's hands grew coarse black hair, claws like thick needles sprouting from spread fingers. Both Shifters' eyes were glittering, primal.

They weren't men anymore—they never had been. The beasts of their true selves shone through, uncaring of human rules and restrictions, of anything civilized. They were males confronting each other over a very basic conflict—wanting a female.

Graham spoke, his voice guttural. "Name the time and place, Warden."

"Fight club. Tomorrow night."

"Done."

They remained in place, neither giving way. Graham's Collar sparked once, but Eric's stayed silent.

Though they didn't move, tension crackled between them. At any second, one might strike, and then the fight would be on. To the death.

Iona didn't know how she knew this, but every nerve hummed it. She came around the desk and shoved her way between the two Shifters.

It was a scary place to be, but Iona put her back to Eric and glared up at Graham. "Get out. You're trespassing. Go before I call security."

Graham, as though he just now noticed that Iona stood in front of him, switched his gaze to her.

His eyes were terrible. McNeil's irises had become very light gray, almost white, the red rage of his wolf glowing in the black of his pupils. His lips curled back from fangs, and his stare skewered her like a rabid dog's on a rabbit.

Iona kept her head up and returned his gaze, somehow knowing that if she looked away, he'd crush her, even with Eric standing there. Graham growled low in his throat, and Eric gave him an answering growl.

Finally Graham moved his gaze from Iona to Eric. "Tomorrow night. Then I take her away from you."

Eric said nothing. His enraged snarls filled the room, his body vibrating against Iona's back.

Graham kept his gaze on Eric as he took three steps backward to the door, then he turned, contemptuously, and made his exit, slamming the door behind him. Iona heard his footfalls, the rattle of the fence, then a motorcycle started up and glided away.

Iona swung around. "Eric, what . . . ?"

She stopped, her words dying. She'd never seen Eric like this, his eyes blank with rage, his body so tight that when he moved his head to look down at her, it was like he bent his neck on a stiff hinge.

"Get the blueprints," he said, voice harsh and strange. "We're going."

"Going where?"

"Home," Eric said. "My home. In Shiftertown."

CHAPTER ELEVEN

Eric's entire body hurt as he half dragged Iona in that luscious dress out of the office and toward her red pickup. She had the blueprints in a tube under her arm and was still protesting.

"You said yourself I can't go to Shiftertown," she said. "Shifters will know I'm Shifter, remember?"

"I mate-claimed and scent-marked you. They'll know you're *my* Shifter."

"But you scent-marked me before and still told me to stay away."

Eric yanked the keys out of her hand and unlocked and opened the truck. "That was when no one knew about you but me. Graham won't keep his mouth shut, and he's right. You're fair game."

"You just said all the Shifters will know you mate-claimed me."

Eric stopped and faced her. "Iona, listen to me. You're part of no pride and no clan. You're unprotected, even with the mate-claim. If I'm not constantly with you to support my claim, others can cut you out and steal you away. Remember when I told you Shifters liked the chase and the capture? You're fresh blood, ripe for the plucking. In Shiftertown, you'll stay in my house where you'll be protected by me, my sister, and my son, the three most powerful Shifters in Las Vegas."

Iona started to answer, and Eric all but shoved her into the pickup, telling her to slide over so he could drive. She lost hold of the tubes, and Eric grabbed them and dropped them behind the seat.

The pickup roared to life, Iona frantically tugging at her seat belt before Eric shot out of the gate he'd opened.

Iona protested about leaving the gate open behind them, but Eric didn't slow. He'd send Jace and Shane back to pick up Eric's bike, lock the place up, and go to Iona's house to fetch clothes and whatever for her.

"What about the human side?" Iona said as they raced down the street. "They'll arrest me. They might arrest my mother . . ."

"As far as the humans know, you're human. Graham hates humans more than he hates me, and my Shifters will obey me. We'll say I met you when I came to see you about the Shifter houses. I liked you, invited you to shack up with me in Shifter-town, and you came along. You wouldn't be the first human to do that."

"Shack up with you in Shiftertown," Iona repeated. "Don't make it sound so glamorous."

Eric laughed. His blood was up, his body pulsing with excitement. He'd made the mate-claim, and she was *his*, this glorious, beautiful, lush-bodied woman.

"Only until we get this sorted out," Iona said sternly. "I told you, I'm not giving up my entire life to live in Shifter-town."

She would. But Eric would deal with that later. *My mate. My mate. My mate.*

"What fight club?"

Eric blinked, realizing that Iona was talking to him, and that he'd gone several intersections without noticing. He slowed the truck, trying to calm down.

"Shifters fight each other in organized matches to blow off steam. Humans forbid it; we don't listen. I pretend I don't notice my Shifters slipping off to fight each other illegally. They know I know, but we don't talk about it."

"What will your Shifters do when you show up in their secret club tomorrow to fight this McNeil?"

"They'll live with it. I have to fight him there, because what happens at the fight clubs doesn't count as a dominance change."

"Dominance change? Which means?"

"If I lose the fight, it doesn't mean McNeil gets Shiftertown. Nothing in the hierarchy changes. But I won't lose."

"But if you *do* lose, he thinks he gets *me*?" Iona's glare intensified. "This is the twenty-first century. You don't do battle over a woman, and I'm not meekly submitting to whoever wins."

"*I* will win. And even if I didn't, you could reject his mate-claim."

"Then I reject it now! Take me home."

"You can't reject him until the Challenge is settled, and you still need to be protected. I won't lose, Iona."

"You're saying I'm supposed to sit around and wait while you two fight over me? Forget it. I'm not playing."

"It's not play. It's deadly serious. When I win this fight, the other Shifters will know they'll have to Challenge me for you, and they won't dare."

Eric knew that Graham didn't really want Iona—he'd made it clear he'd mate only with a Lupine and wouldn't taint his line with a Feline. Graham had Challenged for Iona simply because he wanted to take her away from Eric.

A Shifter could mate-claim a female, even officially mate with her under the sun and moon ceremonies, and then never use her to make cubs. Pride and pack leaders of old had kept their packs and prides in line by mate-claiming all females not related to them and doling them out to the other males when they reached their mating years. Graham seemed the type to keep up that old tradition if he could.

Eric tasted the primal excitement of the rivalry. He hadn't felt like this about a female since Kirsten, a need for a mate he thought he'd never experience again. He'd told himself he'd been keeping quiet about Iona all these months to protect her, but in truth, he was as old-fashioned as Graham, sequestering Iona from prying eyes while he worked on winning her. He laughed.

"Eric!"

Eric came out of his reverie to avoid slamming into a truck stopped in front of them.

"Maybe I should drive." Iona was already halfway out of the truck.

"Don't try to run away from me, Iona. I'd just have to catch you again."

No, let her run. Hunt her. Bring her in . . .

Eric shut off the thought.

Iona didn't run anywhere. She came around to the driver's side, and Eric slid over for her. Another driver whistled as Iona climbed into the driver's side, the slit in her bridesmaid's gown riding up her thigh. Eric barely stopped himself from leaping out and ripping out the guy's throat.

Iona put her foot to the gas and glided the truck down the road again. "I'm not going to run away. I like my truck. Besides, the sooner we resolve this, the sooner I can get back to my normal life."

Eric sat close enough to her to touch her, loving the way her body moved beneath the satin gown. "You won't have a normal life ever again. Your mating hunger is calling to you. You can't fight it forever."

"Not the best sales pitch you could make." Iona gripped the wheel and turned through streets without asking directions, heading north to Shiftertown.

Iona had driven past the Las Vegas Shiftertown before, unable to stem her curiosity about it, though she'd never been through its gates. She'd seen that, behind the high chain-link fence, Shiftertown was a grid of streets with small, neat homes.

The fact that the gates were left wide open, the fence not topped with barbed wire or anything, had always made her feel better. The fence and gates were more symbolic than imprisoning.

A number of Shifters seemed to have motorcycles, she saw as she followed Eric's directions down a street a block away from the gates. She also saw that, though it was dark and around dinnertime, Shifters were out and busy, some carrying boxes from house to house, some stacking furniture on front porches.

"They're moving in with their families and neighbors,"

Eric said to her curious glance. "Doubling up because Graham's Shifters get here day after tomorrow. Stupid humans wouldn't wait for the houses to be built."

"We can get them done quickly," Iona said. "But that still means a couple of months." She slowed and turned where Eric indicated. "The new Shifters arrive day after tomorrow? After your fight?"

"Why do you think I picked tomorrow night? Graham and his seconds will have to follow the rules of the Challenge and the fight club, but I wouldn't trust the bulk of his wolves not to do something dumb-ass while he fought me."

Iona was surprised. Eric had been in a flat rage when he'd faced Graham in her office, ready to kill him. He'd made no sign that he'd been coolly calculating the best time for the fight. "Do you always plan everything so carefully?"

"I do, my love. Remember that."

Iona pulled into the driveway of a long, low house with a deep front porch that looked little different from its neighbors—except that the driveway and yard of this house were full of Shifters.

In the center of the driveway, standing in front of Iona's pickup as she halted it, was a tall blond woman who was obviously pregnant. She stood shoulder to shoulder with a Latino human, and another Latino, resembling him, stood next to him. A younger version of Eric stood at the tall woman's other side.

Two enormous men came to flank the truck. They were accompanied by a dark-haired woman who was a bit smaller than them but no less intimidating.

Eric hadn't called anyone after Graham had gone and before they'd left the office. He'd helped Iona roll the blueprints into the tubes, and then he'd hustled her out the door and opened the gates. That meant Graham McNeil must have alerted the Shifters that Iona was on her way.

Iona set the brake, but she didn't turn off the truck's engine. She doubted she'd be able to ram the truck through the surrounding Shifters, but it never hurt to be prepared.

Eric got out, unworried, and came around to the driver's side of the cab. He reached in, shut off the truck, and took the keys, then opened the door and held out his hand to Iona.

Swallowing, Iona got out.

It was dark without the truck's headlights, though a small porch light on this house and the one next door provided some illumination. But Shifters didn't need light—they could see fine in the dark. Iona knew they were all scenting her, knowing she was half-Shifter, knowing she'd been all over Eric, and Eric all over her.

Eric led Iona to the younger man. "Jace," he said. "This is Iona Duncan. Tonight, I mate-claimed her. Iona, Jace Warden, my son."

Jace was no kid—he was a full-grown adult. He had the same hard build and dark brown hair as Eric, and he looked back at her with his father's measuring green stare.

"Iona," Jace said before she could speak. "I acknowledge and respect the claim."

The next thing Iona knew, Jace had opened his arms and folded them tightly around her.

Iona started, but Eric's hand warmed her back. "It's all right. Hug him. You're supposed to."

Tentatively, Iona brought up her arms to return the embrace. Then Jace *really* hugged her, pulling her in so tight that her breath left her. Her nose picked up how similar his scent was to Eric's and yet had a unique character of its own.

Jace was grinning when he released her. "Welcome to the pride, Iona. Dad, I commend your taste."

Eric took Iona by the shoulders and moved her to the pregnant woman, who was regarding Iona with great interest.

"Cassidy Warden," Eric said. "My sister and my second."

"I acknowledge and respect the mate-claim," Cassidy said, sounding delighted.

She pulled Iona to her for a warm, cushy hug, which Iona returned less hesitantly. As with Nicole, Iona breathed in the fragrance of Cassidy's child inside her, and Iona's sharp need to mate rose up to bite her once more.

"You're half-Shifter," Cassidy said as she released Iona but held her by the hands. "Your father?"

"My father was the Shifter, yes. Panther." Somehow, Iona knew Cassidy would want to know that.

The woman's green eyes warmed. "Welcome, Iona. This is my mate, Diego Escobar. You called him the other day, about Eric. For that, I thank you."

Diego was very attractive—okay, he was *hot*—his liquid dark eyes and handsome face complementing his dusk-velvet voice. "We took care of it," Diego said. He glanced at Eric. "Am I supposed to say the thing?"

"Technically," Eric said.

"Then I acknowledge and respect the claim." Diego held out his hand instead of trying to embrace Iona, but he clasped her hand between his strong, warm ones. "From one person who's been sucked in by Shifters to another, welcome to their world. It's a fine place."

The second Latino man shouldered his way forward. "I'm Xavier, Diego's better-looking younger brother. Call me Xav. I acknowledge and respect the claim, and I'm hugging you, because I *like* Shifter ways."

Xavier pulled Iona into a hearty embrace. "Don't worry," he said, when Iona came out of it, breathless. "You get used to it."

Iona thought she possibly might, until she got to the bears.

"This is Shane," Eric said. "Bears don't have last names."

Shane was big, about seven feet tall, broad of chest, thick of muscle. He had black hair flecked with brown that looked shaggy even though he cropped it short, and chocolate brown eyes.

"Welcome to Shiftertown, honey," Shane said. He opened his big arms and scooped up Iona, giving her a . . . bear hug.

Shane lifted Iona off her feet and swung around with her but didn't let go even when he set her down again. "Keep in mind—when things don't work out between you and Eric, come see the grizzly next door."

"There's two grizzlies next door, bro." The second bear shoved his brother aside, and Iona got another enthusiastic and dizzying hug. "I'm Brody. Remember, once you go bear, you never go back."

Eric did and said nothing while the bear brothers hugged her, but he stood close. Very close. Iona bumped into Eric's hard body when Brody finally let her go.

They must have seen something in Eric's face, because Brody lifted his hands in a sign of surrender. "Hey, we acknowledge and respect the claim, oh great leader. No Challenges here."

"But keep your options open," Shane said to Iona.

The large woman pushed herself between them. "Shut up, boys. Don't scare her. I'm Nell, sweetie." Nell was not as tall as the two bear males, but she looked as strong, and she shared the brothers' black and brown mottled hair. She pulled Iona into a somewhat gentler hug. "Half Shifter, and you're just learning how to deal with your Shifter side, aren't you?"

So true. Iona was ready to collapse after her long day, the wedding, her increasing hunger, kissing Eric in her office, Graham's violent interruption, and now this sudden introduction to Shiftertown.

She swallowed. "It's been rough, yeah."

"Well, if it gets too bad, you come and see me. I got these two through their Transitions and their first mating hunger, and don't think *that* wasn't pure hell. Helping you will be a joy, sweetie, compared to hosing down a couple of frenzied grizzlies."

"Mom, come on," Brody said. "You only needed to open the fire hydrant twice."

Nell pulled Iona into another hug, this one warmer. "Really. Don't let Eric intimidate you. If you need help, I'm here. And you can always turn down his mate-claim. Males don't get to have it all their own way."

If Nell and Cassidy were anything to go by, Iona believed that.

Nell let Iona go, but she glared over at Eric. "You making her stay in your house? You don't have to. I have room."

Eric's hand landed on Iona's shoulder again. "I know you do, but I don't trust McNeil to play by the rules. She stays in my house, under my protection."

"In your tiny bedroom?" Jace asked. "You can't turn around in there without bumping into yourself. She can have my room—it's much bigger. Tonight though, me and Shane will stay at Iona's place and make sure Graham doesn't do anything stupid. I'll need keys and directions." He held out his hand to Iona.

"You and Shane?" Iona looked at the grizzly, who grinned at her with a mouthful of pointed teeth.

"Don't worry," Shane said. "We're litter trained. You have cable?"

"Yes."

"Sweet. Let's go, Jace."

Jace took Iona's house keys and gave her another hug. "Welcome to the family," he said. Then he and Shane were gone, Jace behind Shane on a Harley, the bike roaring down the quiet street.

Eric could see that the mating need was getting to Iona as they ate some dinner. The kitchen smelled good, Diego cooking again. He made a mess of burgers slathered in salsa, and Xavier went behind him and fried up a batch of sopapillas dripping with cinnamon and honey.

Iona sat down and ate every morsel, then followed Xavier back to the kitchen to see if she could find more.

Cassidy had been like this when she'd first hit her mating years, Eric recalled, watching Iona and Xavier banter in the kitchen. Cassidy had eaten everything in sight and had been crabby when she couldn't find anything else.

Cassidy's mating need had been high. She'd been on the prowl to get it out of her system, though she hadn't found a mate of her heart until she'd met a Shifter called Donovan, who'd passed the year before she'd met Diego.

Xavier finally went home—actually to his mother's house to help her with something or other. Cassidy offered to lend Iona some clothes, and the two women shut themselves in Cassidy's bedroom so Iona could change. Apparently, this involved a lot of giggling.

Eric looked back from gazing longingly at Cass's bedroom door to find Diego planted on a living room chair next to him. Eric had lounged back on the couch as usual, beer bottle balanced on his stomach, practicing his ability to look completely casual, almost half-asleep, while at the same time being more alert than anyone on the street. But Diego had known Eric long enough not to be fooled.

"She came with you willingly?" Diego asked him.

CHAPTER TWELVE

Eric's human brother-in-law was smart, practical, and not easily intimidated, damn him. "She didn't want to, but Iona understands the danger," Eric answered.

"You had to bring her here? Couldn't you protect her in her own house?"

"The thing is big and has too many entrances, too many windows. No place to hide." Eric took a sip of beer. "I'm surprised you humans have survived this long."

"Humans have alarm systems, big dogs, and hired security to protect them."

"All useless against someone like McNeil." Eric opened his eyes all the way to give Diego a stern look. "Understand something, Diego. McNeil is dangerous. He's exactly like me, except I can be calm because I'm secure in my place as leader. He's not anymore, so he's looking for any way to push me out so he can rule. That means that no one connected with me is safe—not you, not Cass and your unborn cub, not Jace, and now, not Iona. I can protect you best if you're all in one place. If I'm forced to divide my attention all over town, McNeil will slip in somewhere and gouge me, using one of you to do it. You're all fair game to him."

"So you decided to meet him at a fight club?" Diego asked, eyes showing his anger. "What happens if you lose?"

"I won't lose." Eric stopped. "But in case I do, make sure Iona rejects his claim loud and clear, in front of witnesses. Then bring her back here, under Cassidy's and Jace's protection. If I'm badly hurt or killed, Cassidy will become leader, which means McNeil will go after her. You and Jace will have to protect Cass too, with everything you've got. Get Shane and Brody and Nell with you—Nell's pretty much fourth in dominance, or maybe even above Jace, I don't know. But between all of you, you can keep Iona and Cassidy safe."

Eric slumped back into the sofa, the speech tiring him. But he had to say it, and say it quickly, cutting through whatever protests Diego was about to voice.

"All right," Diego said after a time. "Cass and I will look out for Iona if something happens to you. There must be something you can do about Graham, though. You're Shiftertown leader. Arrest him or something."

"It's a tricky situation. It's not Graham's choice to be here, and if I grab him and confine him to a hole—or get the humans to arrest him—his Lupines will never forgive me. There would be retaliation battles for years to come. I need to win in a fair fight against Graham. Leaders don't resort to tricks."

"Sure, Eric," Diego said. "What if he touched Iona?"

"Then I'd kill him."

Diego nodded, knowing Eric wasn't joking. "All right, then. You need a second at this fight? Can a human be second?"

"Yeah, thanks. You and Shane can back me up. I don't want Jace there, in case Graham tries something underhanded. I don't trust *him* to fight fair."

"Done."

Eric had never liked humans before he'd met Diego, but his brother-in-law was proving that humans could be as strong, loyal, and protective as Shifters.

Iona came out of Cassidy's bedroom, and Eric's thoughts about the upcoming fight dissolved. Cassidy had given Iona a cropped top and skirt, Cassidy being too tall to lend Iona any jeans. The skirt bared Iona's athletic legs, and the top showed a slice of slim belly that Eric wanted to lick.

He was up off the couch and at Iona's side before Iona could leave the hall. Cassidy squeezed around them, amused, and headed for Diego, but Eric leaned Iona back against the wall.

"My home is the best place for you," Eric said, liking how she fit inside the curve of him. "Under my protection."

"We'll talk about it," Iona said.

Eric breathed in her scent, something tight inside him loosening. "I'll tell Jace to stop on his way home and buy us some chocolates."

Her eyes went dark, her scent filling with need. "If you want the truth, I can't taste chocolate without thinking of you."

"Good." Eric licked the corner of her mouth. "I only like it when it tastes of you."

"We could find a hose," he heard Cassidy say to Diego.

"You'd just get the hallway all wet," Diego answered.

Iona blushed. Eric touched a kiss to her mouth. "Ignore them. Cass likes to tease." Eric could tell that Cassidy was pleased with Iona though.

Iona shivered and rubbed her arms. "I'm still hungry."

Cassidy rose from the arm of Diego's chair and headed for the kitchen. "Sweetie, when I went through my first mating heat, I wanted to eat everything in sight. Now that I'm pregnant, I want to eat everything in sight *again*. I say we have ice cream."

Eric didn't want to let Iona go. He wanted to lean against her there, in the hall, absorbing her warmth, her smell, the taste of her.

But eating would help her metabolism, which was going crazy, as all females' did when the mating urge first touched them. Soon Iona would want to slake her hunger a different way, and Eric would be right there to help her.

Diego and Eric watched from the living room as Cass and Iona devoured a tub of ice cream at the breakfast bar in the kitchen.

The two women were already getting along, Cassidy talking in her open way, asking Iona about her family, the construction company, and her life growing up as a half Shifter. Iona, who always told Eric to mind his own business, readily answered Cassidy's questions.

Then Cass and Iona put their heads together and started talking softly to each other. Occasionally they'd glance up at the two men in the living room, and snicker.

Females.

After the ice cream, Iona started yawning and declared she'd go to bed. She was exhausted from the wedding, the reception, the mate-claim, meeting all these Shifters . . .

Eric let Iona enter Jace's bedroom alone. He knew that if he followed her in, he wouldn't want to leave. He'd kiss her again, savoring more than he'd been able to in the hall, then he'd take her down to the bed, burrowing under her clothes and completing the mating.

In Iona's current state, she wouldn't fight him. But Eric didn't want only a casual encounter with Iona, she looking to ease her frenzy. When Eric took her, he wanted it to be as full mates. Then he'd make Iona his, forever.

Iona looked a bit surprised that Eric only said good night and watched her walk into Jace's empty bedroom, but she quickly closed the door behind her. And locked it.

A groan in the middle of the night woke Iona from a sound sleep.

Jace's bedroom was the first one in the hall, with Eric's bedroom, a narrow space that looked like a converted closet, next to it. Iona had seen, when she'd followed Cassidy to the bedroom she shared with Diego at the end of the hall, that Eric's room held a bed and that was pretty much it.

The groan had come from Eric's bedroom, through the wall separating Iona from him. A groan of pain.

Iona scrambled out of bed, the hem of her borrowed sleep shirt brushing her thighs. The clock on the nightstand—an old-fashioned folding travel clock, nothing digital—told her it was three thirty.

She stepped into the hall, surprised by how quiet the house was. No sound came from outside—no cars, trucks, motorcycles, or trains, and they were a long way from the airport. A faint breeze blew through the eaves, but that was it.

In the silence, Eric groaned again. She paused to see whether Cassidy or Diego would respond, but she heard no

movement from their bedroom at the end of the hall. Either
they were heavy sleepers or the fairly large bathroom between
them and Eric's room muffled the sound.

Iona walked softly to Eric's door and opened it.

In the near darkness inside, her Shifter sight took in the
bulk of Eric's bed with him on top of it, his naked skin gleaming. The bedcovers lay in a pale heap on the floor beside the
bed, where he'd thrown them off.

"Eric?" Iona whispered.

A stifled groan answered her. Iona quickly crossed the
room to him and touched his shoulder.

She pulled back in alarm. Eric's skin was burning and
drenched in sweat. "Eric, are you all right?"

Eric's hand closed on her wrist, fingers shaking but his
grip strong. "No, I'm bloody well not all right."

"What's the matter?"

"Hell if I know." His words cut off as a spasm wrenched
his body. "I don't know what the fuck this is."

"Your Collar?" Iona touched it, finding the black and silver
band cool, the Celtic knot at his throat quiet. "Is it malfunctioning?"

"Like I said, hell if I know." Eric tried to rise but fell back
to the pillow. "This is killing me."

Iona rubbed his shoulder, wanting to do something, but she
didn't know what. "Let me take you to a hospital. I'll get Cass."

"No." Eric grabbed her again as she started to straighten
up. "A hospital won't know what to do with me, and I don't
want to see knives or needles ever again." He tugged at her.
"Stay with me, Iona. Touch me. You're already helping."

Iona sat on the edge of the bed and put a tentative hand on
his chest. His heart pounded beneath her fingertips, his skin
roasting hot.

"Can you shift?" she asked. "Will that help?"

"I tried. Made it worse."

Iona smoothed her hands across his hard chest, remembering how she'd enjoyed teasing his nipples with her tongue. His
nipples were soft now, Eric nowhere near excited.

She drew her fingers down his abdomen, finding the
smooth indentation of his navel. Farther down to his lower
belly until she touched the cock below it.

"Mmm," Eric said. "Better."

The sweat on his face and his rapid breathing didn't convince her. "Are you sick? Shifter flu?"

Eric shook with silent laughter. "No such thing. I haven't felt like this since . . ." He trailed off, his laughter dying.

Iona lifted her hand from the base of his cock, sensing he didn't need sexual play right now. "Since when? Since your mate died?"

"No, that was different. This was later, when we first took the Collar."

Eric closed his mouth abruptly, as though he didn't want to talk about the Collar. Iona lightly rubbed his stomach. "Tell me about your wife. Mate, I mean. What was she like?"

Eric didn't answer right away. He hesitated so long that Iona thought he wouldn't answer at all, but then he spoke softly.

"Kirsten was—amazing. Hair like sunshine, but her eyes were black. She could run like nothing I'd ever seen before, and she didn't take any shit from me."

"What kind of cat was she?" Iona kept rubbing his abdomen, noting that his nearly frantic breathing had finally slowed.

"Leopard. Not a snow leopard like me and Cass, a gold and black one. Leopards are one of the smallest wildcats, even among Shifters, but they're the most dominant. Kirsten had . . . personality. A lion Shifter was after her once, a huge guy, both in his human and wildcat form. She pretty much told him what to do with himself. That was fun to watch."

"You loved her."

"I did. With everything I had." Eric stilled Iona's hand with his large one. "Why do you want to know this?"

"It tells me what kind of person you are. And it's making you feel better."

Eric drew a breath and relaxed. Then, at the bottom of the breath, his body went rigid with pain, his hand closing hard on hers. "Son of a bitch."

"Let me get Cassidy."

Eric's hold tightened. "Don't leave me. Stay with me. *Please.*"

The grating cry wrenched Iona's heart. She lifted their

joined hands and kissed his fingers. "Keep telling me about Kirsten."

"Can't." Eric's teeth were clenched, eyes tightly closed. "She died. It hurt. It hurt so much."

The grief in his voice was true. "Then tell me about Jace," Iona said quickly. "He looks so much like you."

"He puts up with a lot." Eric tried to smile, lips barely moving. "It's tough, being son of the leader."

"Were you the son of a leader? Was your father leader?"

"Yeah, he was clan leader, but he passed right after Cassidy was born. I was too young to know him."

"What about your mom?"

"Died soon after that. She never got over losing my dad, and she just gave up. It was me and Cass from then on."

"I'm sorry," Iona whispered. She imagined two young Shifters, alone, scared, unsure what to do. "Where did you live?"

"Scotland. In an old, burned-out manor house some Englishman abandoned. The people in the village took care of us. They thought we were demons or Fae or something. We became a local legend—the villagers believed that if they took care of the wild things up at the old house, we'd take care of them. And we did. Cass and I protected them."

"But you still took the Collars."

"Times changed. Superstitions died. The World Wars changed everything. Cass and I went to Norway in the forties to help the underground movements, and when we came back to Scotland, our house had been requisitioned and turned into a hospital. We had to find somewhere else to live. People who remembered the old ways had passed, and new people from the cities moved in. When Shifters were revealed and the locals finally knew what we were, they wanted to kill us. I turned us in to save Jace and my sister."

"And you were relocated here?"

"Hell of a long way from the Scottish Highlands." Eric brushed his fingers across her bare forearm. "You have Scots in you too. It shouts loud and clear, and so does your name."

"My mom's family moved out here about a hundred years ago," Iona said, "From St. Louis. I don't know why my mother named me Iona."

"It's a beautiful name, an island in the Hebrides. I'm thinking she named you to remember your Scottish father."

"Who I've never found out about. My mother has kept a lot from me, but I'm thinking she still never knew very much."

"His name was Ross McRae."

Iona looked down at him, startled. "How do you know that?"

"I have resources." Eric's voice was less pain-filled now. "I have Xavier and his ability to find information on humans. Ross McRae was the name on your birth certificate."

"My mother told me only a little bit," Iona said. "Did Xavier find out anything about him?"

"Not yet. There might not be anything to find," Eric said, his look serious. "If he's still alive, he could have hidden himself well. Shifters can be tricky."

"No kidding."

Eric managed a chuckle. "If we mate, my Iona, under sun and moon, I'll never leave you. We'll be mates for life."

Mates for life. The hunger inside Iona flared, and her stomach rumbled. "I wonder if there's any more ice cream."

"No." Eric reached for her again, the desperate note reentering his voice. "Stay with me."

He didn't mean for sex. Eric was shivering now, his skin cold.

"Let's get you under the covers," Iona said.

She stood up but didn't release Eric's hand as she scooped up the sheets and blanket he'd thrown on the floor. She got into the narrow bed with him and pulled the covers over them both, snuggling down against him.

"You're right," she said. "This is better than ice cream."

Eric smiled again, but he was still shivering. He traced her shoulder, and she nestled her head into his neck, trying to warm him.

He didn't talk anymore. Iona had thought of many more questions to ask him, including making him tell her when he'd last felt this horrible, gut-churning pain, but Eric only kissed her hair and slid his hand up to cup her breast.

He caressed her through the shirt, his touch gentle. Though his caress was nowhere near as erotic as it had been last night in her back hall, Iona's hunger started to calm, thoughts of ice cream fading.

Eric's shivers slowed, then ceased, and Iona drifted to sleep in his warm embrace, comforted by the sound of his breathing.

E ric woke to sunshine pouring through the windows, his pain long gone. His cock was hard, awakened long before Eric, because Iona lay in the curve of his arm, her nose against his chest.

Beautiful. *And all mine.*

"Eric." Cassidy swung the door open, fully dressed in elastic-waisted jeans and a clingy sweater. "I can't find Iona . . . Oh."

CHAPTER THIRTEEN

Eric put his finger to his lips and smiled at his sister. He felt good, happy, energized. Whatever pain had twisted at him last night was gone, not even vestiges lingering to stab at him.

Cassidy did not look displeased to find Iona snoozing in Eric's bed. "Shane is back," she whispered. "He needs to talk to you."

Eric nodded, and Cassidy tiptoed away. Eric kissed Iona's hair again, and Iona came awake with a start.

She blinked at him in confusion, sultry black lashes over lake blue eyes. Then she came fully awake and tried to pull away.

"What am I doing in here? . . . Oh, yeah." Iona's look turned concerned. "Are you all right?"

"Haven't felt this good in a long time." Eric felt his smile stretch his face. "Sleep with a mate is a great cure."

He cupped Iona's cheek and slanted a kiss across her mouth. A deep kiss. He swept his tongue across hers, half rolling onto her to press her lips apart even more.

Iona's fingers bit into his shoulder, nails lightly scratching as she arched up to him, her thin nightshirt a flimsy barrier.

Eric broke the kiss and lowered his head to her breasts, teeth closing around one nipple through the fabric.

Iona's little moan of pleasure almost had him spilling his seed. Eric skimmed the shirt up to bare her abdomen and the blue satin panties she must have picked out to go with the bridesmaid's dress.

He nipped the waistband of the panties, then licked her belly above them as he pushed up the shirt to expose her breasts. Her breasts were pale, lush, and full, as Eric remembered from running with her in the desert, firm globes that fit so nicely into his hands. He ran his tongue around the areola of one nipple and sucked the tip into his mouth.

Iona rose to him, pushing herself farther into his mouth. She parted her legs, her foot coming up to skim his bare thigh, urging him. Eric feasted lovingly on her breasts, first one then the other, reveling in the firm feel of her nipples against his tongue, the soft flesh on his lips.

He licked between her breasts, then slid up her body to kiss her mouth, pressing his aching hard-on over the satin panties.

"Accept my mate-claim, Iona," he whispered. "Join with me under sun and moon, and we'll have a mating frenzy that lasts all year."

Iona ran a hot hand through Eric's short hair. "We'd be tired."

"And hungry. But we wouldn't care."

"Hungry." Iona's eyes gleamed. "Please tell me Shifters eat pancakes."

"Sometimes."

"Do they have breakfast in bed?"

"That can be arranged," Eric said. "Is that what you want? Me, I just want to enjoy the taste of you."

He scented and felt that the satin under his cock had grown damp. He could draw the panties down and lick the nectar of her, and be perfectly sated.

Iona pretended she wasn't as rampant for sex as she was. "I'll pay you back for all the food I ate last night. Or, I'll buy more for you. In fact, I'll go grocery shopping . . . right after breakfast."

She started to sit up, to shove him away to get at her butter and maple syrup. The thought of syrup on Iona made Eric press her back down into the bed.

He opened her mouth with his tongue, licking the moisture behind her lips. He felt her fingers tracing his tattoo, and again the light scratching.

Eric rolled onto his back, pulling her over on top of him. Her nightshirt had slid down again, covering her breasts, but Eric cupped them through the shirt. He positioned her so he could rub against her satin-covered pussy, his cock tingling with the near satisfaction of it.

If he ripped the underwear from her and let himself slide inside now, the two of them wouldn't come out of this bedroom for days. Eric would forfeit the Challenge to Graham by not showing up, but who cared?

Challenges and their rules had been created by Shifters to prevent them from killing each other over scarce females in a free-for-all. Let Graham try to take Iona away and see what happened. Eric would simply kill him, problem solved.

The way Iona made Eric feel was primal, a throwback to the bad old days when Shifters fought to the death over a mate and were happy to do it. The Fae had created Shifters to be fighting beasts, and the beast always lurked close to the surface.

Iona's little growl wasn't helping. Eric smelled the feral being in her, uncontrolled by Shifter rules and a Collar. She was wild, free, and Eric wanted her.

Iona touched kisses to his face, his nose and mouth, her lips featherlight. Her body rubbed against his as she did it, sending Eric's blood searing. He had to have her, had to slake his need on her before he faced the world today.

One burst, that's all it would take. A few quick thrusts inside her, and Eric would be satisfied.

He knew that was a lie. Eric wanted the lovemaking to last. He wanted to lock himself in this room with her and let the world go to hell.

Iona gave him another kiss on the lips, then rolled away from him, so quickly that he lost his hold on her. "I think we should go have the pancakes now."

Eric growled. He grabbed her wrists, came off the bed,

pulled her up with him, and pinned her against the wall. He kissed her hard on the mouth as she ran her hands along his naked body, his erection nowhere near tamed. Her breasts pressed into his chest through the nightshirt, the heat from the join of her thighs caressing his flesh.

"You saved me last night," he said.

"You're all right now?"

He touched his forehead to hers. "Better than ever."

"You look it."

Eric grinned at her. He always wanted to laugh around this wonderful woman.

He released her, his body protesting all the way, and shoved her at the door. "Breakfast. I'll be right there."

Iona stopped before she opened the door, her gaze dropping to his groin. "Looks like you need to take care of something else first."

"Exactly. Get out of here."

Eric laughed softly as Iona opened the door a crack and slipped out, leaving him alone and aching.

Iona heard the shower running for a long time after she'd washed and dressed and made it to the kitchen to join Diego and Cassidy. No pancakes. But Diego was whipping up a batch of eggs, peppers, cheese, and broken fried corn tortillas he called chilaquiles. He'd already made a stack of toast slathered in butter, cinnamon, and honey.

Iona piled her plate high with the toast. She'd make good on her promise to go grocery shopping, because she was eating all the Wardens' food. In spite of Eric's reassurances, she knew that Shifters had little money, and food must be expensive for them.

The way Diego was going through the carton of eggs and mountain of cheese, though, told Iona that he, at least, could afford it. Diego was human and ran his own business, no restrictions on him.

"Where's Jace this morning?" Iona asked as she dug into the steaming chilaquiles Diego dumped onto her plate. She quickly decided that chilaquiles were her new favorite breakfast food. "Still at my place?"

Diego and Cassidy exchanged a glance. "No. He didn't come home," Diego said.

Iona realized then that the shower had stopped running. Eric walked in a few moments later wearing jeans and pulling a black T-shirt over his head, his hair still damp. He radiated cold, which told Iona how he'd dealt with his pesky erection.

"What do you mean, he didn't come home?" Eric asked.

Diego answered, still busy with cooking. "That's why Shane wants to talk to you. Jace is fine, but he went . . . investigating."

"I didn't tell him to." The edge in Eric's voice made Iona lift her gaze from her food. Eric's mouth was turned down, his eyes hard with anger.

"He's not a cub anymore, Eric," Cassidy said. "He acts on what he thinks is best at the time, like I do."

Eric's growl was low but fierce. "Where the hell is Shane?"

"Waiting for you next door," Cassidy said. "Go easy on him. Jace outranks him."

Eric growled again, grabbed a piece of toast from the top of the stack, and munched it as he slammed his way out the back door.

"Does he always wake up this crabby?" Iona asked, sliding her fork through more chilaquiles.

Cassidy shot her a look of amusement as she took a seat at the kitchen table and started in on a plate almost as loaded as Iona's. "That was radiant, for Eric. He's just worried about Jace. Shane brought over a suitcase for you with some clothes from your house."

"He didn't need to. I'll go out and pick up some groceries for you all, then I need to check in with my mother. I can change clothes at home."

Cassidy's smile vanished. "You won't be leaving Shifter-town until the Challenge is over, Iona. Eric's orders."

Iona's fork stopped halfway to her mouth. "Orders?"

Cassidy moved her hand to her abdomen, caressing it, as though she'd felt the baby move. "I agree with him," she said. "Graham is dangerous. By Shifter law, you should be untouchable before the Challenge, but I wouldn't put it past Graham to try to abduct you and use you to hurt Eric somehow. Graham is determined to be leader, and he'll do it any way he can."

"But I can't stay here. I have a business to run—my sister's on her honeymoon, and my mother can't do it all by herself."

"It's Sunday," Diego said. "You're closed anyway, right?"

"We catch up on Sundays. I can't just disappear, no matter what Eric thinks. My mother will get frantic and call the police."

"No harm in telling her where you are," Diego said. "Eric's not trying to keep you prisoner, he's trying to protect you. So am I. Eric's right—you're safest here."

Iona seethed, but even her frustration couldn't keep her from resuming her breakfast. "What is this Challenge anyway? Why are you letting Eric and Graham *fight* over me?"

"It's Shifter tradition," Cassidy said calmly. "The Challenge was created to keep Shifters from arbitrarily stealing one another's mates. Shifters used to be pretty bloodthirsty, and with females scarce, males went all out to fight for them. The Challenge keeps it civilized."

"That explains almost nothing," Iona said.

Diego gave her a nod. "I'm right there with you. But go with it. I'll put it this way—it's better than Graham trying to rip Eric's head off and run away with you slung over his shoulder. Eric knows what he's doing. As far as I understand it, whatever the outcome of the fight, you can still choose whether to accept the mate-claim. Right, Cass?"

"Right. Doesn't mean Eric won't keep trying. He can be persistent."

Iona laid down her fork, but only because her plate was empty. "You two are very sanguine about Eric bringing me home and fighting this guy because of me. You don't know anything about me. Why are you being so accepting?"

Both of them fixed her with stares, Cassidy's green one over her plate, Diego's dark one from the stove. They each seemed to know what the other wanted to say, and Diego got to go first.

"I did some research on you after you called me the other day," he said. "I didn't know about you being part Shifter, but the info about your business and family is there for everyone to see. You work hard, make decent money, and pay your taxes." He gave her a small smile. "Nothing underhanded about you."

"Scent tells me a lot," Cassidy said, still tackling her flavorful eggs and cheese. "You're half-Shifter, unmated, and fairly open and honest. You don't hide anything. And to tell the truth, Eric's lonely. Crazy lonely. He doesn't admit it, but I see it. I think you'd be good for him."

Iona stared at her empty plate. "But will Eric be good for me?"

Cassidy nodded, her expression matter-of-fact. "He's the leader of Shiftertown, which means you'll be the alpha's mate. That's a good place to be."

"I might think that if I'd grown up Shifter," Iona said. "But I grew up human. I have a human life, a house, a career, things I worked very hard for. You and Eric expect me to give it all up without a fight."

"You're also young, for a Shifter." Cassidy's voice gentled, and she laid down her fork. "I'm not. Iona, all those things—the house, the business, whatever place you carved in human society—they don't last. A hundred years go by, the world changes, and Shifters watch it all." She glanced at the sunny backyard, and her hand returned to her abdomen. "This Shiftertown, the restrictive laws humans put on us—they won't last either. Life in Shiftertown has been only a small part of my existence, and it will disappear in time. Humans will get used to Shifters, or figure out they can benefit by using us, or we'll force the situation to change when we're ready. Nothing is fixed and forever. In another hundred years, all this will be gone."

Diego finished at the stove, brought over the rest of the mixture in the frying pan, scraped more onto Iona's plate, then finally filled a plate for himself. He returned the pan to the counter and sat down to start eating.

"It weirds me out to hear her talk like that," Diego said. "I grew up human, like you did. But Cass is right. Everything is mutable, even when it seems like it will last forever. What does last though—and I had to figure this out the hard way—is family. The people who love you and what you feel for them—that never goes away."

"Yes, it does," Iona said, a little less hungry now. "You lose people. I loved my stepfather, and he's gone." She felt a pang, as she always did when she remembered sitting those last days with her stepdad in the hospital.

"I know," Diego said. "I lost my dad when I was a kid. But you still love him, don't you? You still think about him—I bet part of why you work so hard is to keep up the business he built and not let him down. And that's what I meant. They're never really gone. You miss them like hell, but they're still a part of you, part of your life. That's what lasts—not houses, not businesses, not money. All that can change on the spin of a coin."

Iona forked up the last of her eggs and lifted a piece of the sweet toast, trying to push her emotions aside. Emotions made her jumpy, and hungry, moving her again toward frenzy. "You two should be philosophers or something," she said lightly. " 'How to live life, the happy way.' "

Diego laughed, his stern expression softening. "My mom wouldn't think so. I'm mouthing things she said to me growing up, when she needed to get me and Xavier through some tough times. I guess growing up rough makes you philosophical."

"So does growing up Shifter," Cassidy said. "Not to mention fighting Nazis." She winked. "We're not always this serious. You should stay with us, Iona, because we're great at parties. And anyway, there's plenty to do around here, and I could use your help. You like kids?"

"Eric, do not blame this on me. Jace does what he wants." Shane leaned his bulk against a post on his back porch and folded his massive arms. The post, built to withstand bear Shifters, didn't budge.

"Which means you didn't try hard enough to talk him out of it," Eric said severely. "Why did he want to go back out there?"

Jace, according to Shane, had departed Iona's house at four that morning to take his motorcycle out to the desert to again check out the buildings out there. Shane's gaze kept flicking from Eric's, Shane unable to meet Eric's anger.

"He said he wanted to watch them change shifts to see what happens," Shane finished.

"If he left Iona's at four, he's been gone five hours now. You didn't stop him, you didn't call me, and you didn't go with him."

"Because I think he's right." Shane met Eric's glare for a fleeting instant. "He can sneak around out there better than a huge grizzly can. Jace isn't stupid, and I wasn't going to wake you and Cass at four in the morning for no reason. Especially Cass. She needs her sleep these days, and she can be really snarly when she doesn't get it."

"That's my son out there, Shane," Eric said. Shane looked nervous, despite the fact that he was six inches taller than Eric. Height didn't make any difference in dominance. "My only son, and those guys were ready to shoot any stray noise they heard."

"Jace can take care of himself. I know it. I've seen him in action."

Yes, Jace was good at handling himself. But Eric was on edge, the mating need making him squirrelly, the problem of Graham and the Challenge not helping. Eric couldn't call Jace to make sure he was all right without risking that a ringing or even vibrating cell phone wouldn't be heard by one of the guards in the stillness of the desert.

"Where's Reid?" Eric asked, naming the Fae they'd captured earlier this year. The man was now living in Shane's house.

"I don't know. Sleeping? Eating breakfast? Chasing Peigi? I just got home myself."

"Never mind." Eric pushed past Shane and walked into the bear's house by himself.

Nell was in her kitchen making coffee, wearing a big pink bathrobe embroidered with darker pink hearts twined with roses. She gave Eric a black look as he strode into her kitchen.

"Knocking would be good, Eric. Reid went for a walk." Being Shifter, Nell would have heard every word of the conversation on her porch. "I get why you're scared about Jace, but Shane wouldn't have been able to stop him. Jace definitely is your son."

"Jace is my cub," Eric corrected. "When Shane has cubs, he'll understand."

"Granted," Nell said. "You can guess which direction Reid went."

Eric could, and he walked down the common space between backyards toward the house where the female Shifters and cubs they'd rescued last spring had been housed. The bone-thin Reid was there all right, leaning on a low stone wall that marked off the porch, talking to a tall bear Shifter female called Pcigi.

Stuart Reid was a dark Fae—*dokk alfar*, he called himself, which was a different species from the high Fae, the *hoch alfar*, who'd created Shifters. *Dokk alfar* hated the high Fae as much as Shifters did.

Reid had redeemed himself a long time ago, and Eric would have let him return to the apartment he rented in the city, but Reid had chosen to stay in Shiftertown. He'd also quit his job as a police detective to do security work for Diego and Xavier. The reason Reid stayed was Peigi—one of the Shifter women Reid had helped Diego and Cassidy rescue.

Peigi had suffered some very bad shit and was nowhere near interested in mating yet, but Reid was smitten. He was gently helping Peigi readjust, and Eric knew that sooner or later, the two would be standing before Eric for their sun and their full moon mating ceremonies.

Eric had made Reid one of his trackers, and Reid had been among those who'd found the mysterious compound in the desert. Reid couldn't shift, but he had one talent that no one else did. He could teleport.

"Reid," Eric said, acknowledging Peigi by putting his hand on her shoulder. "I need to borrow you."

CHAPTER FOURTEEN

Eric had only teleported with Reid a couple of times, and both instances had made him sick. This time was no different. When they arrived at their destination, Eric spent a moment with hands on knees, trying not to retch.

Reid had landed them about a half mile from the compound, probably to give Eric time to recover. Nice of him.

They hiked along the ridgeline Eric and Iona had run down in the dark. Reid and Eric kept themselves below the lip of the hill so they wouldn't be silhouetted against the bright morning sky.

The compound didn't look that much different in daylight. Prefab buildings lined up within the rectangle of the fence, and two guards strolled around. No sound, no activity, and again, no distinctive smell.

Reid had brought binoculars, but Eric relied on his own vision. He scanned the quiet grounds and the desert beyond, again wondering what the hell was inside those buildings.

Reid tapped Eric and pointed. "Got him," he whispered.

Eric looked and saw the faintest second shadow under a tall creosote bush on the other side of the compound. A snow leopard. Jace.

"Good. Now I kill him."

Jace must have seen them, because he ever so carefully slunk out from under the bush and slid into a nearby dry wash.

"Want me to teleport us down there?"

Eric suppressed a shudder. "I'll use my feet. Will you carry my clothes?"

Reid agreed though he looked a little annoyed to be designated clothes caretaker.

Eric didn't take long to shift, then he ran down the ridge and around a sweep of rocks to the edge of the deep wash Jace had used. Jace was climbing out of the wash, about a mile from the compound, when Eric caught up to him.

Eric growled and swatted Jace with a big paw. Jace shifted, rising to his six foot seven height, scowling, hands on hips. Eric shifted and rose to meet him.

"You checking up on me now, Dad?"

Eric barely contained his rage. "What the hell are you doing coming out here alone? You decided danger doesn't apply to you?"

"What the fuck?" Jace looked at him in amazement. "I do solo jobs for you all the time. I thought you trusted my judgment."

"Not with something this weird," Eric's words ended with a growl. "Not with Graham threatening us. Your orders were to watch Iona's house last night, then come back and help me protect her."

"So I took initiative. I didn't have the chance to ask your permission. You've been hard to track down lately, if you hadn't noticed, and distracted when you are. I'm glad you've met someone, Dad, but your brain is warping."

Fathers were supposed to be proud when cubs struck back. That meant the father had raised the cub to be strong.

Eric's hand sprouted claws, and he snarled. Jace looked surprised, then he snarled too, his eyes going flat.

Reid popped in right next to them, displacing air. "You might want to keep it down," he said. "Sound carries."

Eric forced his claws to recede, but his anger didn't diminish. Jace took a step back, but the move was in no way submissive.

"Don't you want to know what I saw?" Jace asked, his voice quieter.

"*I* do," Reid said before Eric could answer.

Jace let out a breath. "They did absolutely nothing until about five thirty this morning. No lights, no one moving around, just the guards smoking and talking. Then, jeeps, five of them. They came straight across the desert from the north." Jace pointed to where coarse sand stretched, empty and white to the hills. "The guards opened the gates like they were expecting the jeeps. Each jeep had a driver and a passenger. They all got out and started unloading—one big cage from each one. Not mesh cages, but ones that looked like dog carriers, only much bigger."

Eric grew colder as he listened. "What was in the cages?"

"Nothing. They were empty. I couldn't smell anything but the men. They put the cages into the first building, then they all got back into the jeeps and drove away."

Eric thought about the layout of the place, the tidy rows of buildings with the air conditioners on the top. "We need a look inside there."

"Want me to teleport in?" Reid asked. "I could have a quick look around."

Reid could only teleport to a place he'd seen or been to, or so he'd said. He'd come out here with the trackers to have a look before, which is why he could teleport Eric so close, but he'd have to get a look inside one of the buildings before he could will himself into one.

"Not yet," Eric told him. "We don't need a guard to see you. I don't want them alerted that anyone knows about them until we find out more."

Diego and Xav's research had drawn a blank so far on the compound and what was in it, they'd told Eric. They'd found the place via satellite photo but couldn't zoom in close enough to have a good look, and they couldn't find plans or building permissions for the compound. Xavier had promised to look for something more covert, but so far, he'd turned up nothing.

Reid shrugged. "It might have nothing to do with Shifters."

"True," Eric said.

But the mention of cages bugged him. Sure, the people here could be out to capture mountain lions, maybe for some zoology professors to study. But mountain lions were few and far between, and it was unlikely they'd need to be prepped for five of them.

Not good. Not good.

"We'll keep an eye out," Eric said. "And have Diego and Xavier keep looking for info. If it has nothing to do with us, then it has nothing to do with us, but I want to know."

"You're welcome," Jace said. "I'm going back to Shifter-town to get some sleep."

Jace turned his back and walked away, sun strong on his bare back. He'd gotten a tattoo in stages this year, across his shoulder blades, a prowling leopard in full color. Eric watched him go, proud that his son was so strong and upright, and still as worried about him as he'd been when Jace was the cute little cub who liked to chew on Cassidy's shoes.

Then Eric grimaced. "Wait, Son. I need to ride back with you. Teleporting makes me sick."

Jace kept walking. "Suck it up, Dad," he said, then he shifted, jumped back down into the wash, and was gone.

I ona spent the day helping people move. The bulk of the Shifters from Graham McNeil's Shiftertown would start arriving the next day, and houses had to be cleared for them.

Iona had called her mother after breakfast. Penny hadn't been happy that Iona had let Eric take her to Shiftertown, but she agreed to wait and see what happened. Iona heard tears in her mother's voice when they hung up, and her heart burned.

She worked off her anger by lugging boxes. She, Cassidy, and Diego carried boxes and pieces of furniture from porches to Iona's truck, and then to the porches of the houses that the Shifters were moving into. Cassidy, as pregnant as she was, carried plenty, though Diego was after her to rest a lot.

Iona offered to carry the boxes all the way into the houses, but her offer was declined by their owners—politely but firmly. She was to set everything on the porch and come no farther inside.

"Why?" she asked Cassidy when they took a breather. "You'd think they'd welcome the help."

"Shifter secrets," Cassidy said between sips from the bottle of water Diego had brought her. "If you were just visiting, that would be one thing. But they're clearing out their houses from top to bottom, and want no one outside their clan to enter until they're settled."

"You're talking about the underground spaces Eric wants my company to build in the new houses, aren't you? And the Shifters don't want me to see what's in them."

"They don't want me to see either, or Diego. Every pride, pack, and clan has its own space, and even the Shiftertown leader doesn't get invited in. We have to keep something of ourselves totally private."

"I understand." Iona was curious, but she'd respect their wishes.

The Shifters they helped, though, didn't seem to worry about invading Iona's privacy. They asked about her family and who her Shifter parent was, gave her frank and assessing stares, and openly sniffed her. No one was aggressive, only curious, but very much so. She admitted her father's name after some initial reluctance, but no one had heard of Ross McRae.

The sniffing bothered her though. The Shifters would lean close to her and inhale, then give her another grave stare and nod.

They were checking her scent, Cassidy told her, because Eric had scent-marked and mate-claimed Iona. They were acknowledging that Iona belonged to him.

"I don't belong to anyone," Iona said irritably.

"Doesn't matter. They still know to keep their hands off."

Luckily—or maybe it was planned—they never saw Graham or the few Lupines who'd come down from Elko with him.

By the time Iona drove the last load and returned home with Cassidy and Diego, it was late afternoon. Eric was there, with Jace and Shane, who were both giving him advice about tonight's fight.

Eric listened to them while he sat on the edge of the couch, arms on knees. Listening, not arguing.

When Iona walked in, Eric was off the sofa in one fluid motion, moving to her side. He pulled her close, nuzzling her hair. "I missed you," he said.

She'd missed him, she realized. More than she really should have.

Iona turned her head, and Eric covered her mouth in a warm kiss. The others in the room kept talking together, as though they didn't notice.

Diego and Cassidy fixed another magnificent meal, and they ate in the living room, sitting around on couches, chairs, and the floor, in Jace's case. Jace filled in Cassidy about what they'd found out at the compound, and then Shane and Jace turned the conversation back to the fight.

"The rules are simple," Shane said. "You can fight in any form you want—human, animal, or between—but no weapons allowed. No one can enter the ring to help you once the fight starts, and when the referees declare the fight over, it's over. That's about it."

Eric nodded, taking it in as he ate Diego's fabulous pollo en mole verde. "As long as Graham follows the rules, we're fine."

"That's why you have seconds," Shane said, "to make sure both sides follow all the rules. We have to make sure you do too, Eric."

"I get that. I asked Diego to be my other second—humans are allowed to be, right?"

"Sure," Shane answered. "Humans go to these things all the time. They can be seconds, even refs, but they can't fight. Way too dangerous."

"Dad," Jace said from where he sat on the floor, his empty plate on his lap. "I thought I'd be your second."

Eric shook his head. "I don't want to give Graham any excuse to get near you, or to blame you if the fight goes wrong. I don't even want you there tonight, but I have a feeling you won't bother obeying that order either."

"No, because I don't like Graham anywhere near *you*. He'll try to take you out, Dad. If not in the ring, then afterward in the parking lot. I'm not letting you go unprotected."

"How about if I ask you to stay here and keep watch over Iona?"

"Forget that," Iona said. "I'm going with you."

Eric growled. "Do none of you understand how dangerous McNeil is?"

"We're all going," Cassidy said. "Get over it, Eric."

Eric growled some more, but said nothing. Iona sensed his uneasiness, his conflict over what to do. She understood why he wanted his family out of harm's reach, but on the other hand, he wanted them close where he could watch over them, and where they could all protect each other. It had to be hell being so paranoid.

"About time to go, then," Diego said, ever practical. "I'll grab Xavier on the way. I'll try to talk my mother out of coming, but I can't guarantee she'll listen."

E ric's blood was hot by the time they reached the location of the fight club.

He'd always known where it was, tucked deep inside an old casino resort, about thirty miles outside of town, that had closed years ago, too remote and expensive for anyone to buy or redevelop. The advantage was that the road to it wound around manmade hills that screened the abundance of vehicles and milling Shifters from any cop passing on the highway.

Eric had never attended the fights, wanting his Shifters to be able to work off steam without worrying about hierarchy or what their leader would think. Eric pretended not to notice the majority of his Shifters disappearing any given night, and they pretended to think he didn't know. He trusted his people to keep themselves in line and not get caught. He also trusted his trackers, like Brody and Jace, to keep everyone relatively safe.

The dark parking lot was already packed with vehicles by the time Eric and his party arrived. Iona drove Eric and Shane in her truck, the right half of the little pickup listing from Shane's bulk in the passenger's seat.

Eric followed Shane through the hordes of cars and people to the other side of the resort, where a wide space on what had been a golf course had been cleared down to the dirt. Circles were marked here, five of them, so more than one fight could occur at once. The darkness was broken by fires flickering in trash cans, and in fire pits or grills people had brought with them. Some had brought lantern flashlights or battery-powered work lights—in short, anything portable that didn't need to be plugged in.

The crowd of Shifters and humans parted under the mismatched glare as Eric approached, with Shane and Diego. Iona came right behind them with Jace, Cassidy, Xav, Brody, Nell, and Diego's tiny mom, Juanita. All weapons had to be left at the entrance, so Eric didn't have to worry about Nell helping things along with a shotgun.

The Shiftertown's Guardian, Neal, was already here, the hilt of his huge sword rising over his left shoulder. The Guardian's sword would dispatch a dying Shifter to the Summerland, rendering the Shifter a pile of dust, his soul freed. Neal was a necessity, but the other Shifters gave him a wide berth.

Graham was already waiting near the center ring. By tacit consent, no other fights would go on while the two Shiftertown leaders battled, so the other rings were empty.

Graham's seconds came forward to meet Diego and Shane. One of Graham's seconds was the nephew, Dougal, whom Eric had smacked down for attacking Shane. The other was called Chisholm, a young Lupine from the second-highest-ranking pack in Graham's Shiftertown. Eric had made it his business to know the lineage of every single wolf Graham was bringing with him from Elko.

Chisholm spoke first, addressing Shane. "Your fighter understands the rules?"

"He does," Shane rumbled. "Yours?"

"He's made himself familiar with them."

"No interference," Shane said.

"No interference." Chisholm nodded.

Chisholm and Dougal were wary of the huge Shane, but Eric watched the two try to best Diego with a stare down. Diego, however, didn't flinch, and the wolves backed down first.

To Graham's credit, he didn't even look in Iona's direction as they waited for the fight to begin. Graham was respecting the Challenge. The warriors would concentrate on the fight, and the one who remained standing would then claim the female. She was off-limits to the Challenger until he won. At least Graham knew how to follow Shifter rules.

Diego turned to Eric. "Ready?"

"Let's get this done," Eric said.

His followers started an immediate volley of advice and encouragement behind him. "Kick his ass, Eric," Nell said.

"I'll tell you what I used to tell my boys," Juanita Escobar said. "Fight dirty if you have to, but come out looking good. Don't just win the fight, win respect."

Cassidy gave Eric a warm hug. "You'll do it, Eric."

Iona remained apart, her dark hair stirred by the wind that had sprung up over the desert, her light blue eyes gleaming in the odd light.

Damn the Challenge, and damn the humans who'd decided Graham should be moved to his Shiftertown. Eric could be holed up with Iona somewhere right now, teaching her not to be afraid of her mating need. Instead he was standing here in a crowd of excited and smelly Shifters, waiting to battle an asshole in a stupid posturing fight.

Eric put his hands on Iona's shoulders, caressing with his thumbs. "Don't worry. I'll finish here, and we'll go out for pizza."

Hunger flared in Iona's eyes. "Don't talk about pizza." Her arms stole around his waist. "Seriously, Eric, be careful. Like you said, he's tricky."

"Yeah, but so am I."

"No kidding." Iona pressed a quick kiss to his lips. "I hate everything about this, but . . . Nell's right. Kick his ass."

Eric grinned, gave her another kiss, straightened up, and strode to the ring, where he stripped off his clothes. It was time.

CHAPTER FIFTEEN

As unhappy as Iona was about this fight, the woman in her appreciated the sight of Eric's honed, naked body as he walked toward the ring. His back was straight, shoulders broad, waist tapering to firm buttocks, unashamedly bare.

He moved as calmly as ever, even though he was about to fight, maybe to the death. Iona had come to realize that Eric's nonchalant stance, like his casual sprawl on the sofa, hid a man sharply aware of everything around him. He was poised to spring even now as he stood waiting for the fight to begin.

The referees entered the ring first, three Shifters and a human. Iona wondered how they'd been chosen—who organized these fights anyway?

Graham had stripped down, the man as big as Eric, and even more broad of shoulder. The hair on his head was buzzed short, but he had thick wiry hair on his chest. Red and black fire tatts wound down his arms, more wild than the neat jagged black pattern down Eric's right arm. Graham's eyes were white gray, stark in the dim light.

The cold knot in Iona's stomach tightened as the refs stepped back and Graham and Eric entered the ring.

As soon as the refs signaled the start of the fight, the noise around her became insane. All Shifertown must be there, the Shifters shouting, yelling, screaming, or roaring and growling.

Diego's diminutive mother had made Xavier find her a box to stand on so she could see. She and Nell were hollering, hands around mouths. Cassidy shouted as much as they did, the other Shifters and Xav not drowning her out.

Iona couldn't make a sound. She watched from the edge of the ring as Graham and Eric circled each other in silence, each assessing the other, each waiting for an opening.

As the crowd's noise escalated, Graham finally attacked.

He remained human but dove at Eric, rage in his eyes. His Collar sparked, but Graham totally ignored it to slam himself into Eric.

Eric shifted as the man came down, and rammed all four wildcat paws into Graham.

Who became a wolf. Graham's wolf was huge and black, his red mouth open to show gigantic teeth. Eric's leopard snarl reached even over the crowd noise as he let himself fight.

The refs circled, but what went on in the center of the ring was too fast to follow. Cat and wolf fought with whirlwind madness, paws striking, teeth tearing, dust billowing. Blood flowed, both on Eric's white fur and Graham's black sides.

Graham's Collar kept arcing snakes of blue, the thing never letting up, but it didn't slow him down for a second. Eric's Collar remained silent, which no one but Iona seemed to notice.

As the fight continued, something started happening inside Iona. The hunger that was driving her crazy didn't abate, but a new sensation rose to match it.

Fury.

Eric was fighting for his life, fighting for *her*. Graham was pounding him, the wolf larger than the wildcat, though the leopard was plenty fast.

Another alpha was beating up her mate, and here was Iona, stuck on the sidelines, unable to go to his defense because of the stupid rules of the fight club.

What would they do if she ran in there? Simply stop the fight? Declare Graham the winner? Didn't matter, because Iona wasn't about to become Graham's mate, regardless of how the battle turned out.

The Challenge was more symbolic, Eric had tried to explain—he was out here to put Graham in his place.

The wildcat inside Iona didn't give a shit. She saw Eric battling, and the need to get in there and save his ass surged within her until her vision filled with red haze.

Her body started to change to the panther, never mind that she'd rip her clothes to shreds, and a long growl came out of her throat.

Cassidy glanced at her. "Iona?" She leaned to her. "You okay?"

Iona couldn't answer. The Shifter in her was taking over, and she had no Collar to stop her. She could kill Graham and, as Eric had said, go out for pizza.

She took a step forward, but Cassidy grabbed her with a strong hand. "I know," Cass said in Iona's ear. "I know how it feels. But you can't."

Iona shook her off. In the ring, the wolf and wildcat were tearing each other apart, bodies rolling around in a tight ball, the refs circling them, trying to decide what was happening.

The refs would never be able to pull them apart in time. One of those Shifters was going to die, and if Iona had anything to say about it, it wouldn't be Eric.

The need to defend him rose like a black tide. She snarled as she ran forward—and came up against the bulk of Shane.

"No," Shane shouted at her. "He'll have to forfeit if you put one toe in the ring."

Iona switched her rage-filled gaze to Shane, who took a startled step back. Iona pinned him with her glare, willing him to get out of her way, promising silently that she'd rip him open if he didn't.

A wildcat scream sounded from the ring. Iona shot past Shane, the sound of Eric in pain propelling her.

Graham, still a huge black wolf, scrambled back from Eric, blinking and breathing hard. Eric was on the ground, his Collar silent, but he writhed in agony. Blood coated his fur, but Iona knew that wounds weren't causing the pain.

Eric had moaned in the same kind of agony last night in his bed. Unexplained pain was again twisting his body, his wildcat snarling and rolling to try to stop it.

Graham's Collar was going off like crazy. The wolf rose

on its hind legs, shifting on the way, until the human Graham stood up, hands on hips, panting, Collar still sparking.

"It's over!" Graham, gray-faced with his own pain, yelled at the refs. "He's done. I've won."

Iona ducked away from Shane's outstretched hand and leapt into the ring. She was half changing, her limbs becoming the cat's, but her feet still propelling her like a human.

Dimly she realized this half state had never happened to her before, but she didn't care. She turned a snarl on Graham that made him blink.

"This isn't you," she shouted, her voice coming out guttural and strange. "You didn't do this."

Graham glared at the refs. "Get this bitch out of the ring."

One of the refs started forward, but when Iona swung on him, he slunk back. Iona ran the final steps to Eric's side and dropped to him, lifting the leopard and cradling him against her.

She smelled another scent similar to Eric's and saw Jace land next to her. "She's right," Jace said to the refs. "This isn't because of the fight. I've seen this before. Collar malfunction."

"Which means I win," Graham said. "The alpha is down."

Iona flowed back to her full human self, still holding Eric's wildcat. Her shirt was torn, her black lace bra visible in the wide gap, and she couldn't be bothered to care.

"Eric, I'm here." Iona stroked his fur, never minding the blood. His wiry coat covered a heavily muscled body, which was hot but trembling all over.

As she smoothed his fur, Eric's shaking calmed a little, though his moans of pain didn't cease. Iona felt him start to shift, this one difficult for him.

He took a long time to change to human, and when the wildcat vanished, Eric was curled up, fetal position, half in Iona's lap, skin covered with dirt and blood.

Graham stood next to them, his massively muscular legs also covered in blood. "I win the Challenge," he declared. "The mate-claim is mine."

Iona looked up at him, meeting his alpha stare. "You didn't win, you asshole. He's hurting from something else. He was beating you!"

The flash in Graham's gray eyes told Iona she was right about that and he knew it. "All I see is Warden on the ground, and me standing over him. I've won you, bitch. Get it through your head."

The refs closed into a knot with each other a few yards away, talking rapidly. The rest of the crowd alternated between concern for Eric, anger at the refs, and yelling for Graham's blood. Diego, Shane, and Xavier positioned themselves around Eric, Jace, and Iona, the solid barrier of their legs comforting.

One of the refs broke from the other three. He addressed the crowd, keeping his colleagues between himself and Graham. "The fight's a draw. No winner."

The crowd screamed its approval, though shouts for Eric to rip open Graham continued. Graham snarled, but the man had the good sense not to dispute in a crowd that clearly hated him.

"Then the Challenge stands," Graham said in a loud voice, cutting over the noise. "Another time and place, Warden. I'll win her."

Eric's eyes were still closed, his breathing labored. Iona gently moved him to Jace's lap, then she stood up.

Graham didn't move as Iona stepped toe-to-toe with him and looked up at his tall bulk. Graham's gaze swept over her open shirt and bra, but Iona didn't have time to worry about it.

"Eric," she said in a clear, loud voice, still looking at Graham. "I reject your mate-claim."

"What?" Jace bellowed, and the crowd's shouting diminished into startled murmurs.

"I said, I reject Eric's mate-claim," Iona said, holding Graham with her gaze. "Cass, does that mean that Graham's mate-claim is good, and the Challenge is no longer necessary?" Cassidy had been teaching her about Shifter rules all day. Archaic, Iona found them, but she was starting to understand how they worked.

"Yes," Cassidy said with reluctance.

Graham smiled down at Iona, his teeth still pointed like his wolf's. "Yes," he said in triumph.

"Good." Iona smiled too, hers so full of malice that Graham's faded. "In that case, Graham McNeil, in front of witnesses, I reject your mate-claim."

The Shifters roared with laughter and appreciation. Some applauded. Graham's snarl returned. "You fucking—"

"Eric told me you hate Felines," Iona interrupted him. "You don't want me as mate, you only want to take me away from Eric. So stop this bullshit and make your fights about what really matters."

Graham's eyes were flat with rage, but something else glimmered in there—approval? Maybe even respect? No, couldn't be.

Graham motioned for his seconds, who came forward with his clothes. "You really are a bitch, you know? Warden can have you. That means, when I take him down, you go with him. The leader and his alpha mate burn together."

"I'm not his mate," Iona said, never taking her eyes from Graham's. "I just rejected his claim—weren't you listening?"

"Oh, you're his mate, sugar," Graham said, sliding a T-shirt over the drying blood on his torso. "You are *so* his mate. The blessings of the Goddess be upon you."

Giving Iona a final sneer, Graham turned his back on her and walked away, grabbing the rest of his clothes as he went. The crowd, as much as they'd chanted for Graham's blood, parted to let him through.

You are so his mate. Graham had said the words derisively but with conviction. Iona thought of the black fury that had risen in her at the sight of Graham ripping into Eric, and watched the wolf go in stunned silence.

"Iona." Eric's voice was weak, and Iona's fear returned. She knelt next to him again, touching him, her pulse speeding.

"Iona, mate of my heart," Eric rasped. "Please, get me the fuck out of here."

Graham went home to the house in Shiftertown he'd commandeered on arrival, and showered off the blood and grime of the fight. He hurt like a son of a bitch, his chest gouged by Eric's wide claws, a piece of his shoulder ripped by the wildcat's teeth.

In the mirror, he studied the bruising on his neck caused by his Collar that had continuously shocked him during the fight. Shifters down here went to that fight place for fun? They had to be seriously crazy.

Admittedly, it had been good to get his adrenaline going, to work off his frustration on his biggest obstacle—Warden. Fighting him had given Graham a new appreciation for Eric's strength. The man wasn't leader by chance. Eric would be tough to beat.

Strange that Eric's Collar hadn't gone off at all, even though the man had gone down, writhing in pain, and not because of anything Graham had done. Eric's cub had claimed that a Collar malfunction had taken Eric down, but Graham doubted that. Something was going on, and Graham would find out what.

He'd lathered off with the new soaps his nephews had been buying at the nearby grocery store. They smelled girly, but they got him cleaner than he'd been in a long time. The supplies up in his old Shiftertown had been meager.

Graham's energy was still high when he emerged from the steamy bathroom, despite his wounds and Collar fatigue. He could either walk around Shiftertown and listen to people crowing that Graham had lost the fight—which was bullshit—or get out of here for a while.

Dougal and Chisholm had talked about a bar called Coolers, which admitted Shifters, so Graham went there to see what the place was like.

Full of Shifter groupies, Graham saw when he walked in. He wrinkled his nose at their rank scent.

Shifter groupies admired and copied all things Shifter—many wore fake Collars, and some made up their faces to resemble wildcats or wolves, complete with whiskers and fake ears. The groupies, both male and female, for some reason loved to hang out around Shifters, talking to them, having sex with them, or just being near them.

A few groupies had hung around Graham's Shiftertown in northern Nevada, but not many. A person had to be dedicated to drive out to the middle of nowhere in hopes of seeing a Shifter.

Not many Shifters were here tonight, Graham noticed as the bartender shoved a foaming mug of beer at him. They were either still at the fight club, which was having more fights that evening, or back in Shiftertown supporting Eric.

That Iona woman was a feisty bitch. Graham had barely contained his amazement when she'd got in his face and told him, basically, to fuck off.

He had to chuckle, even through his anger. She'd been feeling the female's need to protect her mate, the instinct that overrode every ounce of common sense and turned females into furious balls of sparking crazy. Eric was going to have his hands full with her.

It was too bad Eric would have to slap a Collar on her. They were obviously pretending Iona was human for now, but word would get out to the humans that an un-Collared Shifter was hanging out in Shiftertown, and the humans—especially those like that dickwad, Kellerman—would be all over her. Eric had better have some kind of plan in place for that.

"You a Shifter?" The question jolted Graham out of his thoughts.

A human woman was sitting on the barstool next to him. Her question wasn't eager—she sounded almost bored.

Graham looked her over. The young woman had dark brown hair pulled back into a sleek braid, a sexily plump little body, shown off by a silky, sleeveless dress, and assessing brown eyes. She studied Graham without fear but without much interest either.

"Yeah, I'm a Shifter," Graham said, after looking her over a moment. "You a Shifter groupie?"

The woman gave a delicate snort. "Not me. My friends are. They dragged me here tonight. Said it would be fun."

"You're not enjoying yourself?" Graham asked.

"Neither are you. You're as bored as I am. Picking up Shifter groupies not your thing?"

"Don't know. Never tried to pick one up before."

Her gaze roved him again. "You okay? You look . . . beaten up."

"Fight."

"You lost, right?"

Graham started to bristle, but it was hard to work up anger at this little morsel of a female.

He wasn't a good judge of human age, but he put hers about thirty, older than the college kids who flocked here, and old enough to have acquired a cynical outlook on life. She'd already learned that the world wasn't always a happy place.

Graham took a sip of his beer. "Fight was a draw. We were working off steam."

Again the assessment. "Must have been a lot of steam."

Graham let out a laugh. "Yeah, it was."

"I thought Shifters couldn't fight. They have Collars."

"That's true." Graham wasn't about to tell a stranger that he'd learned to fight through the pain—most Shifters had. How Eric had learned to suppress his Collar like that, Graham wasn't sure, but he'd find out.

"So how'd you fight tonight?" she asked.

"Carefully."

She laughed, the sound somehow soothing. "I'll bet. I'm Misty, by the way."

"Misty?" Graham stared down at her. "What kind of fucked-up human name is that?"

She didn't look offended. "It's what my mother calls me. My real name is Melissa, but I couldn't pronounce it when I was little. They tried to call me Missy, but I kept saying Misty. So my mother decided that would be my nickname."

"My name's Graham. Everyone calls me Graham."

She grinned. "So, what kind of fucked-up Shifter name is that?"

Graham held back a laugh. "It's Scottish. My family comes from Scotland."

"A Scottish Shifter? What do you turn into, the Loch Ness monster? Or maybe a sheep?"

Snarky little human female. Graham could take her out with one blow. Then again, her brown eyes were sparkling, her scent was nice, and she was more interesting than anyone else in this place.

"Wolf," Graham said. He bared his teeth. "Big, bad wolf, sweetheart."

"Sure." Misty's gaze moved to his tattoos. "Don't get the idea that I'm going to let you pick me up, Graham. I don't like Shifters, and I don't like guys with tatts."

"What's wrong with tatts?" He stretched out his arms, now scratched and bruised, and displayed the tattoos on his muscular forearms. "A true artist made these."

They were flames, red and yellow and orange, outlined in black. The lines were delicate, finely drawn, each flame different from the others. The tatts had taken a long time and much patience from both Graham and the artist.

"Yours are kind of pretty, I admit. But I can't imagine anyone painting on me with needles. It's painful, right?" Misty displayed her bare arms, which were delicate and pale but not too thin. Graham didn't like skinny women.

"Not as painful as a wildcat biting off half your shoulder," he said.

"Is that what happened to you tonight?"

"Yes."

"Ow." Her gaze went to his shoulder under his T-shirt. "You okay?"

Graham stopped. Her voice held concern. She was worried that the fight might have hurt him, that he might even now be sitting here in pain.

No one spoke to Graham McNeil like that; no one had in years. No one asked about his well-being—to ask might force Graham to admit a weakness. A pack leader, clan leader, and Shiftertown leader could never show his pain.

He thought about Eric's people closing in around him to help him and take him home. Eric would be no less their leader tomorrow, even though his sister, son, mate-to-be, and even his human in-laws had converged on him to take care of him.

Graham never had been able to risk showing weakness. His wolves didn't so much have his back as were waiting to take him out the first chance they could. He understood—they'd lived on the edge of feral for so long, they didn't know how to behave any other way.

"I'll be all right," he said gruffly.

Misty put her hand on his shoulder, and Graham winced a little. The bite did hurt. Eric had sharp teeth and knew how to use them.

"I hope so," she said.

Her touch, her concern, her voice loosened something inside

him. Graham's worry, anger, and frustration didn't go away, but they eased the slightest bit.

Because a human woman had touched him, had spoken to him like she cared.

Shit.

Misty glanced behind her and grimaced. "I have to go. It looks like my friends have given this place up as a bust tonight. I guess I'm the only one who got a Shifter." She laughed and patted Graham's arm, right on the tattoo. "See you, Graham. Nice to meet you."

"Likewise," Graham said. He lifted his beer in a silent toast as she slipped off the stool and made her way through the crowd to meet two women wearing fake cat's ears. Misty's legs weren't long, but the mile-high shoes she wore made them strong and sexy.

"Misty," he said, trying out the word. He liked it.

A human. Interesting.

CHAPTER SIXTEEN

Eric leaned back in his tiled shower, hot water washing away the blood. He was weak and sick, doubly so because Iona had rejected the mate-claim.

Water cascaded over the deep scratches and gouges in Eric's body, cleansing him, but unable to ease his pain.

He knew why Iona had done what she'd done. Smart move. She'd shut out Graham and made him admit that he didn't want her in the first place—in front of the entire Shiftertown. A bold stroke by a female, one that hadn't been done before. Eric was proud of her.

Proud and bereft. Once he got his strength back, though, he'd convince Iona that she needed to stay with him. Eric didn't trust Graham not to find another way to use her, or hurt her, plus the other Shifters now knew she was technically free of Eric, making her fair game again.

She couldn't leave. Eric wouldn't let her.

The bathroom door opened, steam swirling like fog in wind. Iona closed the door, undressed, and walked into the shower stall.

Eric remained against the wall, the cool tiles at his back. Iona came against him, cupped his face in her hands, and kissed him.

A slow kiss that opened in him all he was trying to shut down. Eric's arms went around her, and he scooped her slick, warm body to his.

He was falling in love with everything about this woman. Her scent, her touch, the way she knew when he needed her. Iona was afraid of being Shifter, and of her mating hunger, and of losing the life she'd made for herself. And yet, she'd come to him.

"Better?" she whispered.

For answer, Eric turned around with her and pressed her into the wall. The shower poured over them, soaking Iona's black hair, beading on her skin. Eric licked the water from her breasts, loving how full and round they were, how dark her nipples grew under his touch.

Eric ran his tongue around her breast before drawing the nipple into his mouth. Something eased inside him. She tasted like sunshine.

Iona sucked in a breath, her hands smoothing his wet hair. Eric widened his mouth, wanting more of her, her breast heavy on his tongue. Her body moved, a slow rising to him as he suckled.

He finished feasting on one nipple and took the other, giving it as much attention as the first.

His pain ebbed as he sucked on her. *The touch of the mate*, Eric had told her. It calms and heals.

Whether she'd rejected the mate-claim or not didn't matter, he told himself. Mate-claims, Challenges, and the rituals to finalize the mating were trappings Shifters had invented to keep themselves from going feral.

Shifters used rites to formally acknowledge the mating, but a true mate—one who shared the mate bond—was a magical, unexplainable joy. The mate bond sealed mates to each other, ritual or no ritual.

Iona was the mate of his heart. Eric knew it like he knew the sound of his son's voice. Iona knew it too, though she might not admit it.

But her body knew it.

Eric licked the warm space between her breasts and took kisses down to her navel. He let his tongue play there, enjoying how she jumped with laughter as he tickled her. He got to his knees and kissed the wiry hair between her legs.

The mating hunger in her responded instantly. She was wet
there, not just from the shower, the scent of her honey filling
Eric's senses.

Eric knew she'd never been with a man—he could smell
that. She'd probably been too cautious to take a human to her
bed. She wouldn't know how not to reveal the Shifter in the
wildness of sex.

But Iona's body knew what it wanted. Eric slid his tongue
over her clit, licking the little berry to life. Iona rose on her
tiptoes, moving her hips to press herself to his mouth. She
made a noise of pleasure, a woman learning what it was like
to have her sexual places touched.

She tasted of salt and musk, and beautiful female. Eric
clasped her hips, leaned into her, and drank.

Iona's legs slid apart, wet feet moving to let Eric take more.
Eric slid his mouth over her opening and let the goodness of
her fill him.

Iona alternately groaned and whimpered, her strong body
pressing at him, wanting more. She wanted all of him, he
knew, his cock filling her up, the Shifter female craving the
male's seed.

That would come. For now Eric assuaged his weakness by
tasting her, letting himself drown in her scent and her heat.

"Eric." Her voice filled the tiny room, echoing from the
tiles. Iona shivered, though the hot water coated her skin.

Eric slid his tongue inside her in slow thrusts. He tasted the
depths of her, savoring her heat on his tongue. She tasted of
nectar and incredible sweetness, smelled glorious.

Iona's fingers bit into his shoulders. When Eric looked up,
it was to see her head rocking back, her mouth opening with
her cries, the ends of her drenched black hair curling on her
breasts.

The hair he licked was as black, her petals wet with her
honey. Eric drank her, his hands cupping her buttocks, and
Iona went into shudder after shudder of pleasure.

Eric plied his tongue faster, liking how she responded. She
was coming beautifully, her cries blending with the patter of
the water. He drank her, lapping her goodness like a greedy
thing, then he rose, rinsed his face in the shower's stream, and
kissed her.

Iona responded hungrily, tongue tangling his, lips bruising, mouth opening to take him. Her fingers caught on his Collar, and for a moment, she tugged at it, as though desperate to unfuse it from his skin.

Someday.

Iona's roving hands found his erection, which stood out straight and hard from his body. As she had in the back hall of her house, Iona closed her hand around him and began to stroke.

Eric broke the kiss to pull her close. She'd learned well, squeezing and pulling, the crazed ecstasy of it almost unbearable. Eric's hips moved as he thrust into her hand.

"That's it, my Iona," he said softly. "You're beautiful. So beautiful."

Iona sped her strokes, her tongue busy on his chest and neck, her teeth latching onto his throat. Eric would have more love bites for his family to tease him about, not that he minded.

They were locked together, Eric's arms tight around her, Iona in the curve of his body. Eric felt the need for her deep within him, the urge to mate and mate and never stop.

He braced his hand against the wall as he thrust into her fist, the squeezing almost as good as being inside her would be. Almost.

"Iona. *Damn.*"

His release shot out of him, right into her hands. Eric dragged her close, thrusting and coming, fucking her hand like he wanted to do to her. Iona smiled up at him, her blue eyes soft.

The beauty of her, coupled with the erotic joy gripping his body, took away all pain, all thought except the joy of being with her.

Eric knew he could never let her go. He'd never be whole again without her. Iona completed him like no other person had since Kirsten—he'd not felt this at peace since his mate had passed at Jace's birth. So many years with emptiness inside, and now . . . Iona.

Eric kissed her, slowing now, his pain gone.

Iona leaned him into the wall, strength in her slim body, and pressed openmouthed kisses to his face, his neck. "Eric, I want . . ."

"I know, sweetheart."

"Now. Why can't it be now? I need you."

The feral beast in Eric, so close to the surface, agreed. Take her now, to hell if they drowned, and do her for days. Graham and his wolves, the human world—everything else—didn't matter, as long as Eric could bury himself inside this beautiful woman.

"I don't want to drop a cub on you," Eric said rapidly, his body crying out in protest. *Like your father did to your mother.* "Not until we're joined under sun and moon. Join with me, love, and then we'll slake the mating frenzy—I don't care if it takes a month or a year of nonstop screwing."

She didn't laugh. "Live forever in Shiftertown?" She shook her head. "I don't know, Eric. I just don't know."

"Shh." Eric pulled her close, his body and hers warm with their release. "I'm keeping you near me, no matter what, love. I need to protect you, and I need you to ease this pain, whatever it is."

Iona's fear turned to concern. "Are you all right? I was so scared."

"Fine now."

She ran her hands down his chest. "What is happening to you?"

"I wish I knew. There's a couple of people I need to talk to, who might have some answers."

"You told me you'd felt something like it before, when you took the Collar, but you never finished explaining."

Eric went quiet. He didn't like to think about the dark days of their initial confinement, when the Collar first fused to his neck, when he had to fight the humans every day to keep his family together and unharmed.

He pulled Iona closer, letting the warmth of her body comfort him. "When Shifters were rounded up, some of us were experimented on. The humans wanted to know how we did what we did, how much physical stress we could stand, things like that." He shuddered, involuntarily, remembering. "They wanted to use Jace. He was young enough to stand the experiments, they said, but old enough to be a good test subject. I refused to let them take him, so they took me in his place."

Iona rubbed his chest again, her instinct to comfort. "That's awful. What did they do to you?"

"A lot of things. Pumped me full of adrenaline, tortured me to see how much pain I could take, filled me with tranqs to see how many I could stand. They provoked my fighting instinct so it set off my Collar—again and again and again. They did that, they said, so they could adjust the Collars. I spent a year in a cage, mostly in pain, until a Shifter rights group got the experiments declared inhumane, and we were released."

Iona leaned into him and closed her eyes. "I'm so sorry."

"I got through it. This pain now is like some I suffered in the experiments, but I don't know what's triggering it, or why."

"Your Collar?"

"Don't know. Which is why I'm talking to some Shifters who might."

Iona kissed his chest. "You were suffering like that all those years ago, while I was hiding in my mother's house, pretending to be human. That makes me feel bad . . . weak and scared."

He rubbed her cheek. "You were a cub, a half Shifter. I don't like to think what they would have done to you if they'd found you. I'm glad you were safe."

He truly was. Iona might feel guilty, but Eric had no anger at all that she'd escaped the attention of the humans too curious about Shifters.

Eric kissed her again, enjoying the hint of afterglow. As he pulled back from the kiss, savoring her taste, he reached over and shut off the water.

"Let's go to bed," he said. "We've used all the hot water, and Cassidy's going to kill us."

Iona woke when sun came pouring through Eric's high window. Eric slept next to her, spooned into her side. His face was relaxed, his sleep, peaceful.

As Iona lay back, trying not to think about what she'd have to face today and the decisions she'd have to make, she wondered why Eric, the big, bad Shiftertown leader, had what must be the smallest bedroom in Shiftertown.

The room was wide enough for Eric's bed and a night-stand, and that was about it. A corner closet had been built into the wall, not a very big one. The rest of the walls were blank, long and narrow.

Iona thought about the way Eric wanted her to alter the plans for the new houses, and she studied the walls around her with interest.

Eric stirred beside her, coming awake. His body was warm, his cock plenty stiff against her thigh. For a night *not* filled with sex, it certainly had been sensual.

"Morning, love," Eric murmured. He pressed a kiss to her bare shoulder.

What would it be like to have him say that to her every morning for the rest of her life? Heady.

"Your room doesn't match the house," she said, to distract herself.

"Mmm?"

"Your room doesn't fit. There's too much space between it and the bathroom. It doesn't match the footage in the hall."

"That's true."

"Why squeeze yourself in here like this?"

Eric shrugged, his body moving in a good way. "Diego and Cass need the biggest room, especially with a cub on the way. I like Jace in the front room, where he can come and go as he pleases. He's restless. I don't need much space."

"And these are false walls, aren't they? You sleep in here to guard whatever's behind them."

"I knew you were smart the moment I met you." Eric drew a fingertip between her breasts, but Iona refused to let him divert her attention.

"It's not too hard to figure out," she said. "What's back there?"

Eric swung himself out of bed. The sunlight fell on his naked body, bronzed from the strong Nevada sun.

Regrettably, he pulled on jeans before he turned to the closet in the corner. He opened the door, revealing hanging shirts, pants, and a couple of jackets, then he reached up for a catch and pulled the whole closet away from the wall.

Iona stared in astonishment as the closet moved aside to reveal a solidly beamed doorframe in whitewashed brick. The

brick passage led to shadows, but Eric reached around the
corner and flicked on a light switch.

"Come on," he said.

Iona scrambled out of bed, pulled on her jeans and a
shirt—one of Eric's—and followed him.

The lit passage ran five steps beyond the opening and
ended in a stair going down. Eric flicked on another light,
which illuminated the staircase and a door at the bottom.
Everything was dry, dust-free, and very, very clean.

"Careful," Eric said, leading the way.

Iona followed him on bare feet, the stone steps cool. The
lights in the ceiling were nice canister spots, not bare bulbs,
the walls finished and painted.

At the bottom, Eric punched a code into an electronic pad
on the wall, and the door—which had no knob—clicked open.

"In the old days, we used elaborate locks that needed three
keys in the right sequence," Eric said. "Modern technology is
so much faster."

He pushed the door all the way open and ushered her
inside.

Lights came on, flooding the large room Iona found inside.
Correction—rooms.

The floor opened out into an area as big as, or maybe bigger than, the house upstairs. A small kitchen had been tucked
into a corner, and other doors led to more rooms. Most of the
doors were ordinary hardwood six-panel doors, but one was a
slab of steel with no lock or handle that she could see.

The main area was a living room with comfortable furniture, a big flat-screen television, a computer workstation, and
beyond a room divider, a pool table. A soft rug covered the
ceramic tile floor.

Iona looked around in astonishment. "But . . . where did
all this come from?"

Eric shrugged. "We pick it up here and there, over the
years. Cassidy likes to remodel from time to time, and Jace
likes gadgets."

"Without anyone knowing?"

"We're discreet."

Iona walked slowly through the main room, noting that the
oversized couch and matching chair were made of finest

leather, the rug cashmere, the television a high-end model that cost thousands. "What?" she asked, marveling. "No wet bar?"

Eric didn't laugh. "We mostly drink beer, and we only need a refrigerator for that."

She turned in a circle, taking it in. "Do all Shifters have this under their houses?"

"Almost all. If a family is large enough to spill to several houses, they might have the underground area in only one house, where the whole pack or pride gathers. Cassidy likes to call this a man cave, but she's got plenty of stuff down here too. Who do you think insisted on the pool table?"

"But . . ." High-end penthouse suites in the best hotels on the Strip weren't this nice. "Why do you live like you do upstairs, if you can have all this?"

"Keeps the humans happy. If the dangerous Shifters live in near poverty, the humans think we're under control." Eric's grin at her astonishment vanished. "These places are secret, Iona. Deadly secret. Only members of the pride or clan see them, no one else."

"Then why are you showing me?"

Eric rested his warm hands on her shoulders. "I want you to see this, so you'll understand exactly what we need from you." He brushed his thumbs along her collarbone. "And because I've decided to trust you."

"Trust me with this?" Iona asked.

"More than that. I'm going to trust you with *this*." Eric took her hand and led her to the blank door at the end of the hall.

CHAPTER SEVENTEEN

As they passed one of the six-paneled doors, it opened, and Jace filled the doorway, half-asleep and alarmed at the same time.

With his hair tousled, his green eyes, and his hastily pulled-on clothes, Iona marveled at how much he looked like Eric. At the same time he looked different from him; the shape of his face and set of his body had come from his mother's Shifter family.

She wondered how he'd gotten down here—Jace had been in the living room when she and Eric had exited the bathroom and gone to bed last night. She would have woken if he'd come through Eric's room.

"Dad?" Jace asked. "What the hell are you doing?"

"Showing Iona the vault," Eric said calmly.

Jace rubbed sleep from his eyes and bolted in front of him. "Are you crazy?"

"She needs to see it."

"Yeah, but, you haven't been thinking too straight lately. Cass know about this?"

"She will."

Jace stepped in front of them again, putting his back to the steel door. "Only mates of the pride, Dad. Only *mates*. Or did you have a full sun ceremony without telling me?"

"Jace."

Eric's voice took on a note of patience, a patience so old that Iona for the first time was struck with how long Eric already had lived. He'd lost his parents and his mate, had raised his sister and then his son on his own, had fought covertly in a war to help humans escape atrocities, had made the decision to move his family here and let humans put Collars on them, had prevented humans from torturing his son by taking on that torture himself.

The laid-back Eric, who lounged barefoot in his house or kissed Iona so sensually in the dark while he fed her chocolates, was a man of complexities and hurt so deep, she'd never understand it.

"We need her to see this, Jace," Eric said. "She needs to understand how to help us."

"Cass should be here, then."

"Cass needs to rest for her cub. Leave her be."

Father and son faced each other. Jace had the impatience of youth, Eric the calm of experience, but Iona sensed that otherwise, they were evenly matched. She wondered if Jace would ever decide it was time to take over from his father, and what he'd do then.

She saw, in Eric's eyes, that he knew that time would come. But not today.

"Open it up for me, Son."

Jace sighed, took a small, round disk from his pocket, and touched it to a blank space in the door. The disk, Iona saw, had a Celtic knot design on it, but she couldn't discern any place on the door the disk fit. To her, the door looked like an unbroken surface.

A ponderous sound like gears grinding filled the little hall, and the door slowly slid back into the wall. Beyond it was, indeed, a vault.

Eric led the way inside, flicking on lights as he went. The vault was long and narrow, taking up the rest of the space under the house and heading toward Nell's side yard.

The room was lined with shelves and niches, though, unlike in a bank, only one had a door with a lock. The rest of the shelves were open and held boxes and small glass cases, with no organization that Iona could see.

Eric gestured for Iona to look around. Jace waited unhappily at the entrance, arms folded, as Iona strolled through in curiosity.

The collection looked like a jumble. Iona took one box off a shelf and found inside a clump of little plastic dolls with large eyes and tufts of long purple hair. She started to laugh. "Trolls. I used to play with these when I was little."

"Cass liked them," Eric said.

Iona put the box back, wondering why on earth they'd been stored in a vault.

The next box she pulled out was lined with velvet and held about two dozen uncut diamonds.

Iona nearly dropped the box. "*Eric*. Where did you get these?"

"I forget. When was that, Jace?"

"Eighteen eighty-two. From Africa. Grandfather traded for them—he never went there."

"Traded with who?" Iona asked.

"Some lion Shifters," Eric said. "They needed resources more than diamonds, and a safer place to live. My family helped them out, and they gave us a handful of stones."

Iona quickly set the box back into its niche. "What *is* all this?" she asked, waving at the shelves in general.

Eric stood in the middle of the room, as nonchalant as ever. "Things our pride and clan have acquired over the years. Some have sentimental value, others more."

Iona browsed another niche and found an egg decorated with jewels and gold filigree set in a delicate gold holder. *Holy crap.* "Do the other Shifters know you have this down here?"

Jace answered. "All Shifter families have a vault. Their pack's or clan's most prized possessions are stored there, kept secret from humans. *Secret*," he repeated with a severe look at his father.

"She needs to know exactly what her construction company needs to do for us," Eric said. "I want her to understand why it's necessary."

Iona looked around in still more wonder. "You're saying Graham and his Shifters have this kind of stuff too."

"We all do," Eric said. "Shifters live a long time. We watch the world change and see that the value of most things evaporates. But some things endure."

"And some of this," Jace interrupted, "is from clan wars."

"Clan wars? You have clan wars?"

Jace snorted with laughter at her amazement, and Eric answered. "We used to. After the Fae-Shifter war, when we found ourselves free of being fighting slaves for the Fae, our dominance fights began. Shifters being Shifters, we couldn't help but battle it out to see who'd be in charge."

"Fights between species, and between clans," Jace finished. "Bad fights, over which clan would dominate the others. We stole from each other, killed each other. In quieter times, we traded with each other, but there weren't many of those."

"But . . ." Iona looked around, bewildered. "If you have loose diamonds hanging around in a box, why do you say Shifters were starving and dying in the wild? Why let humans put you into Shiftertowns?"

"It's complicated," Jace said.

"It is," Eric broke in. "Jace is the clan historian and our keeper. He knows all the nuances. The simple explanation is—it's hard to buy bread with an uncut diamond. If humans knew we had something like that, they wouldn't stop until all Shifters were eliminated, and *they* had the diamonds."

"Not to mention the Fabergé egg," Iona said.

Eric nodded. "Not to mention the Fabergé egg."

"Given to you by Fabergé?" Iona asked, joking.

"Yes," Eric said, perfectly serious. "What you're looking at are long-term solutions. We were starving and dying because we were fighting each other and turning feral, mates were scarce, cub birthrates were low. We came to Shiftertown to save ourselves. For now. We keep these things for what comes next."

Iona remembered what Cassidy had said to her the other day—that Shifters saw their stint in Shiftertown as a short blip in their history. They'd use their stay in Shiftertowns to right themselves, then they'd go on.

"No wonder Graham is so cranky about having to move here," Iona said. "That's got to be tough, to require all his

Shifters transport things like this, without the humans being the wiser."

"Exactly," Eric said. "It's why he doesn't want to double up with my Shifters. We could share *houses* in a pinch, but never vaults. The secrets of each pack, pride, and clan need to remain hidden."

But members of families and clans could move in with each other, already knowing what the clan as a whole had stored, Iona realized.

"That's why no one wanted me to take the boxes all the way into the houses," she said. "I thought one woman was going to claw me when I suggested helping her unpack. I thought she just didn't like half Shifters."

"She was protecting her family secrets." Eric gestured to the contents of the vault. "This is what I need you to understand."

To protect Shifters that weren't even under his command, Eric was telling her, he was willing to trust Iona, to make her understand how to help them. He needed her. Hell, *Graham* needed her.

"Is this why Graham wanted to mate-claim me?" she asked. "For my expertise on house construction?"

"Probably part of it," Eric said. "He wants to control you. Mostly, he's a shithead who's looking for any leverage over me he can get."

"Including whatever is causing your debilitating pain."

Eric's humor left him. "Yes."

"We have to find out what it is and how to cure you," Iona said.

Eric came to her. "You're an amazing woman, Iona."

He was amazing. Iona couldn't help moving closer to his warmth, his heat and scent so *right*. "I'm practical. I don't want Graham to beat you. And I don't like to see you in pain."

"Good," he said softly.

Eric no longer looked ancient and wise as he studied her with hot green eyes. He looked hungry for her.

Jace was no longer there. The smell of something delicious from the kitchen drifted down the stairs, and Iona's stomach rumbled, her insatiable hunger raising its head again.

Eric cupped the nape of her neck, his hand strong. Iona

didn't resist as he leaned down and kissed her, his mouth a place of heat. Iona sought him, needy, hungry, a growl in her throat. His kiss opened her, his hands stroking down her back, promising sin.

"Eric!" Cassidy's voice rang down to them.

The word was steady, almost calm, but even Iona recognized the tone that said, *Get up here now—something's wrong.*

Eric had Iona out of the vault in two seconds, pulling the door securely behind him. He did nothing to lock it, but she heard the mechanism grate back into place.

She saw how Jace had descended without her knowing about it, because there was a second door in the wall that led to another staircase, which spilled them out into Jace's bedroom. Eric kept his hand firmly around Iona's as he led her out of Jace's bedroom and through the now empty kitchen.

Graham stood on Eric's back porch. He was accompanied by two Shifters Iona hadn't seen before, all three carefully watched by Diego, Jace, and Cassidy, and by Shane, Brody, and Nell in the yard behind Graham.

Graham's glare was only for Eric. "Warden!" he bellowed as soon as Eric made it to the back door. "What the fuck have you done with my wolves?"

CHAPTER EIGHTEEN

Graham was furious, his eyes Shifter white, voice filled with rage.

Eric kept calm, though everything in him came alert. He was aware of the exact placement of everyone around him, including Iona, standing unafraid by his side. "What the hell are you talking about?" he asked.

"My wolves. They started coming in last night and today, but about twenty of them are missing. *Where are they?*"

Graham's scent of panic overlaid his anger, his fear triggering Eric's own uneasiness. "It's a long drive from Elko, McNeil. Maybe some took it slower than others."

"They all came together, asshole. In trucks and buses provided by the humans. Two hundred Shifters left my Shiftertown. One hundred and eighty arrived. Some of the missing are cubs. What the hell did you do with them?"

Eric's uneasiness increased. "Are you sure?"

"Of course I'm sure! When a couple of my wolves say they put their mates and cubs on the humans' bus, but when the bus rolled into this Shiftertown, the mates and cubs were gone—that makes me sure. Bus arrived, they didn't."

Iona broke in. "How could Eric possibly have had anything to do with that?"

Eric understood why Graham was lashing out at him. Eric was the closest enemy, and Graham's instinct to protect his people, especially cubs, was strong. He wasn't bothered by Graham's rage—what bothered him was the missing Shifters.

"You'd do anything to weaken me," Graham was snarling. "Did you make some kind of deal with Kellerman?"

Eric made his voice hard to cut through Graham's fury. "I wouldn't kick your ass by abducting cubs, no matter how much you irritate me. Who is missing? Give me specifics, names and ages."

"Why? What do you know?"

Eric thought about the line of buildings in the desert, surrounded by barbed wire—empty buildings—coupled with Jace's report about the cages. "I'm not sure yet."

"I'll kill you, Warden."

"This has nothing to do with me, idiot. We need to get those Shifters back."

"I might just kill you for the hell of it."

Graham could. He was enraged enough to take out Eric with one blow. Then Iona, Cassidy, and Jace would be on him, and Diego might just shoot him. Graham's seconds would attack *them*, and so it would begin.

"Don't kill me until we find your wolves," Eric said. "Give me a list of who we're looking for, and I'll get my trackers. The cubs are more important than our battle."

Graham stopped, and Eric watched him rearrange his ideas. "You do know something."

"There's a place we found, out in the desert. My trackers and I could never get close enough to see what was going on. I'll take you there."

"Tell me where it is, and *my* trackers will rip it open."

Eric fixed Graham with a steely gaze. "No. We track, we find, we get them out. My trackers and yours. The humans guarding it have high-powered rifles. If we go in fighting, they'll best us with bullets, and then every Shifter in Shiftertown could be rounded up and killed."

Eric saw the acknowledgment in Graham's eyes. Graham didn't like it—the man was a fighter, and he hated humans. But they needed stealth right now, not claws.

The human Kellerman might have nothing to do with this, but Eric would find out whether he did. Kellerman was always too cool when dealing with Shifters, as though he had some kind of hold over them that kept his fear at bay. Eric needed to discover what that hold was.

"Round up your trackers and meet me back here," Eric said. "And we'll get them."

He deliberately turned his back, catching Iona's eye as he went into the house. She followed him.

Iona had never seen Eric like this. She'd seen the seductive lover, the vicious fighter, the man suffering, and the protector. She'd never watched him be leader.

Anything laid-back about him was gone. Eric didn't stand any straighter than usual, but his air of command was unmistakable. Even Graham had stopped arguing and quietly departed to do what Eric told him to.

Iona found that she too was ready to follow his commands, to her surprise. "What do you want me to do?" she asked. "Come with you to the compound?"

"No." The word was sharp. "I don't want to risk any humans finding out you're Shifter."

"But I might be able to help with the women and kids. If they've been captured, they'll be scared. They won't know you."

"I'll take some Lupine females with me for that. These Shifters aren't used to Felines, and they might not trust you. What you could do . . ." Eric's eyes were intensely green as he looked down at her. "Can you or your mother get Kellerman to your office? Ask him to come to talk about the house plans or something? I'd like to corner him somewhere away from his pristine office suite and his toadies."

"Kellerman the Shifter liaison?" Iona asked in surprise. "What does he have to do with the buildings in the desert?"

"Maybe nothing. He might just be an asshole. Set the appointment for this afternoon. I want a look at the compound first."

"Eric, if humans have taken the Shifters there, and you steal them back . . ."

Eric put his hands on her shoulders. "They'll retaliate? Not this time, love. Humans put a lot of rules on us, but one we make *them* obey is: Don't touch the cubs."

"Good," Iona said.

Eric leaned to her. "Stay away from Graham's Shifters while I'm gone. They'll smell you're half Shifter, and if they see you're un-Collared, I don't know what they'll do. And you're still fair game. Best thing you can do is go back to your office, like it's a normal Monday."

A normal Monday. Right.

Eric started to release her, then pulled her close again and gave her a swift, hard kiss. "Be careful," he said. "Come home to me."

Iona wanted to say the same to him. Instead, she sent him a cocky look. "And if I decide—to heck with Shiftertown?"

Eric's grip tightened to one she knew she could never break. "I'll come and fetch you back."

Iona believed him, and the thought of that chase suddenly excited her.

She saw her excitement reflected in his eyes. "Run as much as you want, Iona. The pleasure will be mine when I catch you."

Iona didn't trust herself to answer. Eric gave her one final kiss, and then she had to watch him walk away.

Strange, when Eric had first informed her he wanted her to stay in Shiftertown, Iona had rebelled. Now that Eric thought she'd be temporarily safer in the human world, Iona was reluctant to leave.

Cassidy came to stand next to her. "I know," she said. "It's tough to watch them walk into danger. I feel that way every morning that Diego leaves for work. Our need to protect the mate is strong."

"I'm not Eric's mate," Iona said automatically.

"Has Eric told you about the mate bond? Some say—and I believe this—that it's a magical binding between true mates. Your heart knows it even if you haven't done the mating ceremonies." Cassidy looked down at her. "I'm seeing the mate bond now in Eric's eyes, and I'm seeing it in yours. Especially when you look at him."

Iona didn't answer, unsure how to respond. Cassidy studied her with an alpha stare, so like Eric's.

Iona didn't quite understand what Cassidy was talking about, but she couldn't deny the pull she felt to Eric as she watched him walk off now with Jace, or the violent urge to protect him she'd had at the fight. When Eric had showered last night, Iona hadn't been able to stop herself going to him, knowing he was suffering, and wanting to ease his pain.

"Ooh." Cassidy flinched and put her hand to her abdomen, then she smiled. "She's feisty. And wanting to come out and play." She caressed her full stomach. "Not long now, love," she crooned.

She looked so delighted, and also a little scared, that Iona couldn't help squeezing Cassidy's hand before she went back to Eric's room to grab her shoes and head off to her red pickup.

Graham met Eric and Shane as they exited Nell's house. Graham had brought his tracker Chisholm with him but said that his second-in-command, who'd arrived this morning, would remain in Shiftertown, since Eric's second-in-command would too. Eric didn't bother arguing with him.

At least Graham had found out who the missing twenty wolves were—mostly females and cubs, but a few grown males as well. All had disappeared from one bus, and the others on the bus had arrived groggy, as though they'd been drugged.

Somewhere on the long roads between here and Elko, the wolves had been spirited away.

"I don't guarantee they're at this compound," Eric said as they made for their motorcycles. "But something not good is going on in that place."

"If Kellerman has anything to do with this," Graham said, "I'll have his balls for breakfast."

"Get in line." Eric started his bike, waited for Jace to mount behind him, and they rode out.

Traffic heading north out of town was sparse, this being a workday. No one bothered a cluster of Harleys heading up the highway. It was cold enough to wear jackets that hid their Collars, Eric's leather one keeping him warm.

Eric led the way to the county roads that cut through the desert, then to the trail that led to the ridge above the compound. He killed his bike and advised they shift or hike as humans for the next few miles.

Stuart Reid waited for them near the foot of the trail. He'd teleported, disliking riding double on a motorcycle as much as Eric hated teleporting.

"I've been up to have a look," Reid said as they shut down the bikes. "Seems quiet."

Graham dismounted and thunked his helmet onto the back of his bike. "What did you bring the Fae for, Warden? He creeps me out."

"*Dokk alfar*," Reid said, eyeing him steadily. Reid was no submissive. "Not Fae."

"Whatever," Graham growled.

"Learn the difference," Reid said. "Someday your life might depend on it."

Graham leaned belligerently to Reid as Graham passed him. "Whatever."

"Let's move," Eric said sternly.

Jace, Shane, Chisholm, two other Felines, and wolves who'd ridden up chose to shift, but Eric walked. He'd shift closer to the compound if he needed to. Graham did the same, walking right behind Eric.

From the top of the ridge, the small compound crouching in the desert looked quiet, as Reid had said it would be. Eric didn't see the guards this time—no movement at all in the shadows of the buildings.

Though the November air was cool, the sun was high and strong, the blue sky unbroken. Eric could see for miles from up here, but nothing showed beyond the compound but pale sands, creosote, grasses, and blank rock.

"That's *it*?" Graham muttered as he hunkered behind a large slab of boulder and stared down at the buildings. "That's nothing."

Eric tested the air. He couldn't scent as well in human form, but he'd honed the sense over years. This time, when a gust of wind turned their direction, he caught the whiff of fear. Pure, stark fear, the stink of it unmistakable.

Graham caught it too. The scent was faint but enough to have Graham halfway to his feet, snarling in rage.

"Wait," Eric said. "Let the trackers and Reid get closer."

Graham nodded reluctantly, and motioned for his wolves to go ahead with Eric's trackers. The animals slunk down the hill, bodies fluid, hardly visible against the shadows. The wildlife went quiet, sensing the predators.

Reid was the only one easily seen darting down the hill. He had the lithe body of a runner, and he was fast. He made it to the fence before the others and then popped out of existence.

"What the fuck?" Graham asked, staring at the spot from which Reid had vanished.

"He can teleport," Eric said. "He's useful."

"Shit."

The Shifters circled the compound, keeping well out of sight. Shane was the most visible, but he wisely kept to the large boulders clumped to the west of the compound, his grizzled fur blending with the sun-dappled rocks.

Then Reid walked out from between two buildings and to the fence. He looked up the ridge toward Eric and shook his head. A second later, Reid disappeared, then reappeared next to Eric in a rush of air.

"No one there," Reid said.

Graham bellowed and leapt aside, then he came back, teeth bared, claws out. "Never do that again, Fae. I'll take your head off."

Reid gave him a look of contempt. "Whatever."

"Fucking Fae."

Reid turned back to Eric. "I teleported in between the buildings, but they're all locked up. No guards, and I heard nothing from inside anywhere. It looks deserted."

Eric stared down at the compound for a moment, contemplating. The place was a mystery, but he'd not mistaken that scent of fear.

He quietly unfolded to his feet. "Let's check it out."

Graham emitted a wolf growl and started down the hill after Eric. They picked their way along, stones rolling out from under their feet, dust rising in the still air. They met Chisholm and Jace near the gate, both of them waiting, looking grim. They'd scented the fear too.

Graham reached for the large padlock, ready to break it, but Eric stepped in front of him. "Reid."

"What's he going to do?" Graham asked. "Fae magic it open?"

Reid pulled a flat pouch from his back pocket, unzipped it in silence, and removed lock picks. With the rest of them watching, Reid calmly worked the picks into the lock. In a few seconds, the padlock clicked open.

"All right, so he's useful," Graham said grudgingly.

"I don't want anyone to know we got in," Eric said. "Stealth first, fighting later."

"Wuss," Graham said.

Shane's grizzly growl sounded right behind Graham—a long rumble that went on and on and on. Graham gave him a scowl and strode past Eric through the gate.

"Shane," Eric said, and the growl stopped. "Search," he said to all the Shifters and Reid. "Let's be quick."

The compound was as simple as it looked from above, three long buildings with doors and no windows. The air-conditioning units were silent, and none of the lights above the doors were on.

Eric chose a door in the middle of the quiet compound, one that wouldn't be seen from the surrounding desert. Reid obligingly picked the lock.

Eric wondered where Reid had obtained the skill, but he didn't want to pry too much. Inside Faerie, Reid was able to make iron do whatever he wanted—making the metal change shape or form, or obey his will—which scared the hell out of the high Fae, who were weakened by iron. Reid couldn't use his talent in the human world for some reason, but maybe it helped him manipulate locks and other things made of metal.

The door opened. Graham grabbed it and shoved himself inside without waiting for Eric. Eric followed him in closely, his senses straining, the beast in him ready to fight.

They found themselves in a room about twenty feet long and ten wide, with no windows but with doors on either end. The room was dark, but Eric's Shifter sight took it in—two beds shoved lengthwise against the back wall, sinks next to each door, an island in the middle of the room holding another sink and cabinets.

Everything was white except the island, which was black with wooden cabinet doors. The pervasive odor was of antiseptic.

Eric flashed back to another white room, where he'd lain flat on his back on a hard bed, cuffs around his wrists, chains wrapping his lower limbs. Machines on the wall beeped with his vital signs, and six different tubes snaked into his arm.

People with nothing on their faces but mild curiosity stared down at him, not even bothering to take notes. All the while, Eric screamed.

Sudden pain cramped his body. He hugged his arm over his abdomen, letting out a grunt that sounded loud in the silence.

Graham swung around. "What is it?"

"Bad memories," Eric said through clenched teeth.

Graham's eyes narrowed. "Malfunctioning Collar, my ass. You're weakening. How about if I take you out right now and put you out of your misery?"

Eric couldn't answer, being caught in a spasm of pain.

Reid stepped to Graham and wound one long-fingered hand around Graham's bicep. "How about if I teleport us to the top of the tallest building in town and then drop you?"

Graham stared at Reid for a time, reassessing him. "*Dokk alfar?* Okay, Warden, so now I know why you let him hang out with you. You all right? Or are you going to pass out on me?"

The pain receded a bit, and Eric straightened. "I'm fine."

"You've been in a place like this before," Graham said, giving him a shrewd look.

"Worse than this." There weren't nearly as many machines here, or the smell of as many chemicals.

Graham looked around the room, then back at Eric. "Fucking humans." He walked to the door on the left wall and waited for Reid to unlock it for him.

Eric knew they should check every building and figure out what was going on here, even after they found the wolves, but he didn't relish the thought. The ghost of pain past was still haunting him, and he wanted out of here as soon as he could.

When Eric caught up to Graham and Reid, they'd entered the next room, which was identical to the one they'd left except that a large cage stood against the wall. The fear smell from the cage overpowered the antiseptic smell that tried to cover it—sweat, blood, a hint of urine. Eric remembered Jace's report of the empty cages being brought into the compound by jeeps—they must have used these to transport the Shifters here once they'd taken them off the buses.

Graham's scent betrayed raw anger. "They were here," he said. "My wolves."

Reid looked around. "They couldn't have put twenty of them in here. Probably used rooms up and down this row. But there's no one here now."

Graham swept his strong arm across the center counter. The curved faucet of the sink broke and clattered to the floor. No water came out of the broken tap—the water must have been shut off as well.

"Where are they?" Graham roared. "Where the hell are they?"

"Alive," Eric said.

Graham rounded on him. "How do you know that?"

"No smell of death. They were here, they were scared, but they were taken away again. Not killed."

"Taken away *where*? And why are the cages still here?"

"Fuck if I know. But we'll find them."

Eric tried to keep his voice calm, but he wanted to rage as much as Graham did. Experiments on Shifters were forbidden now, and no one, *no one* touched the cubs. Didn't matter that they were Graham's Shifters, or Lupine Shifters. Eric tasted the need to find and slaughter whoever had frightened those cubs.

Graham's Collar started to spark. He was about to go on a rampage. Eric shared the urge, but if they tore up the place, humans would figure out that they'd been there, and the Goddess knew what they'd do—to the Shifters they'd already taken, to Shifters in general.

Before he could tell Graham to take his ass back outside, Eric's cell phone vibrated. He yanked it out of its holder.

"Brody. What?"

Eric listened to Brody's excited and garbled words, then said, "Fine. We're coming," and hung up.

He looked up to find Graham an inch away, the man fully in his space, Graham's breath fanning Eric's face.

"Got them," Eric said. "Brody's found them—on a highway not far from here. We need to get there. Reid?"

Eric hated what would come with the teleport back to the motorcycles—the dizziness, the nausea—but as Reid grabbed Graham first, Eric had the satisfaction of watching Graham's eyes widen in sudden, pure terror.

CHAPTER NINETEEN

Eric slowed his motorcycle when he saw the bus canted off on the side of the road and surrounded by Shifters, both Eric's and Graham's. He also recognized the large pickup in front of the bus that belonged to Xavier Escobar.

Graham pulled up alongside Eric and killed his Harley's engine. Eric didn't stop Graham leaping off his bike and running to the bus's open door.

"Tell me what happened," Eric said to Brody, who came forward to meet him.

"We didn't do this," Brody said, indicating the bus that was half-sunk into the road's soft shoulder. Brody looked much like Shane, with black and brown hair and dark eyes, but Brody, a little younger, wasn't as restless as his older brother. Brody was Eric's tracker, but Shane worked for Nell, his mother, though Nell lent Shane to Eric much of the time. "Not on purpose, anyway," Brody went on. "When the driver saw us following him, he panicked and ran off the road. I decided to hold him here and wait for you."

"Good thinking. Where did the bus come from?"

"We were driving around the area, like you said, and I just happened to see it pull out of an unmarked dirt road and onto the highway. Another few minutes, and we'd have missed it."

"The Lupines are all there?"

"Think so," Brody said. "I guess McNeil will know."

"Thanks, Brody. You did great."

Brody did his best to look modest, but grizzlies were bad at not looking smug. Eric patted his shoulder and went to the bus.

The human driver was still in his seat, looking terrified. Nell sat behind him, thankfully minus her shotgun, and she was twirling a set of keys that likely had come out of the ignition.

Xavier sat on a jump seat next to the driver, armed with a Glock, but the gun was holstered. Eric wondered whether the driver realized that Xavier was protecting him from the Shifters.

Xav nodded to Eric as Eric climbed past him. Shifter women and kids slumped in the seats, most of them asleep, others glassy-eyed and staring. Graham was halfway down the aisle, and an older Shifter woman in the seat he bent over was clinging to his arm and crying. The woman looked groggy, her face flushed as though she'd just woken.

"Everyone accounted for?" Eric asked Graham, moving past him.

"Not sure yet." Graham's voice was gentler than Eric had ever heard it. The man was trying to be calm, reassuring, so his Lupines wouldn't panic.

Eric walked on through the long bus, the same size as a tour bus, and checked all the seats. Women, fast asleep, had arms protectively around their cubs. A few males were there, sitting alone, all sleeping or half awake, staring unseeing as Eric went by.

In the back, he found two cubs, alone. The two wolves were very young, and in wolf form. Curled up around each other, they were all ears, big paws, and long tails, with noses too large for their little faces.

Eric, as a Feline, had an instinctive dislike for Lupines, but these two cubs were just so darned *cute*. He found himself smiling as he leaned over them, but at the same time, he felt a chill. They were alone—where was their mother?

"Hey, little guys," he said. Their faces didn't tell him their gender, but their scent did.

One of the wolf cubs opened his eyes. He stared at Eric in a puzzled way, then he growled. It was a tiny growl, the little body rumbling. His brother woke and blinked at Eric as well.

Their confused frowns only made the wolf cubs cuter. Eric was careful not to reach for them though, as much as he wanted to. They were waking up to a strange Feline, and if Eric put a hand toward them, he'd soon have a hand shredded by tiny claws and teeth.

"That's Kyle and Matt," Graham said, a note of relief in his voice. "Youngest in my Shiftertown. Thank the Goddess."

The cubs, recognizing Graham, their alpha, went crazy with glee. Their tails wagged so hard their little bodies moved, and when Graham reached down and scooped up the two cubs, they began climbing him enthusiastically. Graham stayed very still while the cubs scampered up his tattooed arms, one perching on his shoulder, the other climbing to the top of his head.

The belligerent, angry Graham looked very different with a fuzzy little wolf on his head, Graham keeping his movements slow so as not to startle them.

"Where's their mother?" Eric asked, looking back down the bus's aisle.

"Lost her," Graham said. "When they were born. Their dad before, in a car accident."

Eric didn't like hearing that. "Goddess go with them."

"Yeah, it sucked. They're being fostered. The foster mom made it to Shiftertown, and is about crazy with worry."

"Are all the missing here?" Eric asked.

Kyle or Matt—the one on his shoulder—busily licked Graham's ear. "All twenty," Graham said. "The question is, why?"

"Let's go ask someone who might know."

Graham agreed. He steadied the cubs with his big hands as Eric led the way back down the aisle.

Nell was speaking to the driver. Her voice was pitched too low for Eric to hear the words, but whatever she was saying, the driver looked terrified.

When Eric and Graham stopped to tower over him, the guy said, "Please, don't let her touch me."

Nell sat back, an innocent look on her face. Then her

expression changed, and she reached for one of the wolf cubs.
"Aw, now, who's a sweetie-pie?"

The cub held back a little, smelling bear, but when Nell's
strong hands closed around him, the cub recognized the
maternal touch and relaxed against her. The second cub clung
to Graham's head and made little growling noises.

Xavier leaned back in the jump seat and looked at the
driver. "Now how could you do bad things to these adorable
little guys?" he asked.

"I didn't do anything to them." The driver had reddish
curly hair cut short at his neck, reddish razor stubble, and
wide blue eyes lined with pale lashes. "I swear to God. I was
told to drive them to Shiftertown in Las Vegas. That's it."

"Who told you?" Eric crouched next to the driver's seat,
which put his head lower than the driver's. There was something about looking up with full confidence at a person you
wanted to interrogate. Height wasn't always an advantage.

"My boss. He called me early this morning, told me to
come in, get my bus, pick up a bunch of Shifters, and take
them to the Shiftertown."

"Where did you pick up these Shifters?"

"At a place out in the middle of the desert. I don't know
what it was—a military outpost or temporary housing, or
something. I drove out, the people there loaded the Shifters
on, and I drove away."

"Early this morning." Graham grunted, choosing to tower
over his victim. "It's after ten now. What took you so long?"

"Finding the place, first," the driver said. "It took for-
fucking ever to drive out there—there's no good roads, and
this bus isn't high clearance. I thought I was going to get stuck
lots of times. Then it took a long time for them to get the
Shifters in here, because they were all like that." He jabbed
his thumb at the back, where most of the wolves were still
slumped in sleep.

"Tranqed," Eric said. "Then what?"

"I drove back out. I finally made it to the highway, thank
God, but then I was surrounded by bikers. I see some of them
wearing Collars, and I know they're Shifters. I thought they
were going to kill me." He looked at Xavier. "You're human."

Xavier showed white teeth in a smile. "Yep. But these Shifters are my friends."

"Are you going to kill me?" the driver asked, looking fearfully up at Graham. "I have a wife, and two little girls . . ."

Nell patted his shoulder. "Don't worry. You'll go home to them."

"Maybe," Graham rumbled.

"Who's your boss?" Eric asked. The driver's attention swiveled back to him.

"I work for Sun Valley Transportation. It says so on the side of the bus."

"Yes, but who hired your company? These aren't the buses that brought the rest of the Shifters in this morning, are they, McNeil?"

"Nope," Graham said. "Those were government crapmobiles."

"Find out," Eric said to the driver.

"What?"

"Find out who hired the bus. Tell me, and no one else, and life will be good for you."

The driver stared. "Find out? I won't be able to, will I? I'll lose my job over this."

"No, you won't." Eric laid a strong hand on the man's trembling shoulder. "You'll deliver the Shifters to Shiftertown as requested, and then you'll go turn in your bus, wash it off, whatever you do. As soon as you can, find out who asked for this special service, and call me. Where's your cell phone?"

Xavier was the one who took a phone out of his own pocket and handed it over. Of course, Xavier would have relieved the man of any kind of communication ability first thing. The bus's radio was dead as well.

Eric punched his phone number into the driver's top-of-the-line smartphone. He was willing to bet that the phone had been a gift from one of the driver's kids, and that the driver probably had never figured out how to use all its functions.

"That's me, E. W.," Eric said, handing the phone back. "Now we'll get you out of this little ditch and on your way. I'll ride with you to make sure nothing else goes wrong."

"And me," Graham said. Little Matt or Kyle must have

understood that Graham was staying with them, because his tail wagged faster, and he leaned down to start working on Graham's ear with his tongue.

"And me," Nell said. "We can have a nice chat on the way back, and I'll look after these little guys."

"You're not a wolf," Graham said.

"Maybe not." Nell reached up for the second cub, who wriggled his hindquarters and then took a leap into her outstretched hands. "But I raised two grizzlies on my own, and these kiddos could never be anywhere near the trouble Shane and Brody were. Still are."

Eric smiled at the driver, letting his teeth get a little pointed, and his fingers sprout a claw or two. "See? You do what we say, and everything will be just fine."

Iona didn't have any trouble getting Frank Kellerman to agree to come to her office.

Kellerman said that, yes, it would be a good idea to go over some details, and he'd make the trip to her construction company to talk to her and her mother that afternoon. Iona was surprised he didn't ask her to come to *his* office, but Kellerman half explained by saying he wanted to see their setup, their construction company in action.

Iona spent the rest of the morning trying to get work done and giving up. Eric was out running around the desert with Graham McNeil, going to that compound that she knew was dangerous. She wished he'd call and tell her all was well, but her phones remained silent.

She felt strange wearing her office clothes—dressy pants, sleeveless knit top, blazer, and high-heeled pumps. In the two short days she'd been in Shiftertown, she'd gotten used to casual jeans and T-shirts, or Cassidy's loose skirt and top—clothes that could be quickly removed for shifting.

It was also strange for Iona to have to rein in her Shifter side again, to be careful not to growl or make sure her eyes weren't changing. She couldn't stop using her scent ability now, and smells came to her nonstop—her mother's soap, the foreman's habitual cloying cologne, the sweat and dirt on guys who'd come in for paychecks. Iona had to stop herself closing her eyes to sort out all the scents as they flooded past her.

Her hunger was driving her nuts as well. She'd downed two and a half cheeseburgers at her desk at lunch before she realized that her mother and the foreman were giving her strange looks.

Damn it, Eric. *Call.*

Kellerman showed up at two, a little early—Iona had set the appointment for two thirty. Nothing yet from Eric.

Iona pasted on her best customer service smile when she greeted Mr. Kellerman. Kellerman was on the tall side for a human, and looked like any successful businessman—he kept himself in shape but not buff, wore a suit of lightweight cashmere, and had neatly trimmed dark hair going gray but didn't try to hide his bald spot. He smiled back at Iona when she shook his hand, but the smile never reached his eyes.

Kellerman's position on the Shifter liaison council was voluntary, a successful man trying to look like he cared about the community. He'd made his money in retail, not hotels and casinos, and by owning land that he sold at the right time to hungry developers.

Iona had looked all this up about him, knowing she might have to carry the conversation before Eric arrived—if Eric arrived at all.

Penny put on a more genuine smile as she came around her desk to say hello. As far as Iona's mother was concerned, Kellerman, cold and calculating or not, was giving them a lot of business.

"So good to see what you ladies have going here," Kellerman said.

Instead of bristling, Penny smiled at him. She'd gotten used to the condescending attitudes of men who found themselves dealing with a woman-run business, especially a traditionally masculine business like construction.

"The surveys are going well," Penny said. "I don't think there will be much trouble. Ground breaking will start soon."

The Shifter council expected Duncan Construction to build the houses almost overnight, but there were permissions, inspections, and the involvement of the county and city, plus the power and water companies to slow things down.

Because this was about Shifters, state and federal segments had to sign off on things too.

At least Penny and Kellerman had plenty to talk about while Iona sat at her desk and fidgeted.

"Why don't we take a trip out to Shiftertown?" Kellerman suggested. "Walk over the site? A couple of reporters are following the story—maybe they can join us."

A photo op. Iona nearly snapped her pen in half. *He's turning this into a photo op.*

"Mr. Warden was hoping to join us here," Iona said quickly. "He wants to discuss a few things. Can't think what's keeping him."

Was it her imagination, or did Kellerman look alarmed? "We can speak to him in Shiftertown," he said. "Where else would we find him?"

His words were too slick, too glib. Iona fell silent. If Kellerman and her mother went to Shiftertown, she couldn't go with them. There'd be too much danger a Shifter might spill to Kellerman—accidentally or on purpose—that she was only half-human.

Her mother, thankfully, understood that. "Not sure we can spare the time for the trip today," she said.

"Ah, well. Oh." Kellerman glanced out the window at the same time Iona heard the throb of Eric's motorcycle. "Here he is."

Iona went weak with relief. And then wound up with worry again. Had Eric found the missing Shifters? Or was he here to beat their whereabouts out of Kellerman?

Not one Harley pulled up, she saw as she rose from her desk, but two. The second Shifter was Graham.

The two Shifters removed helmets and walked to the office side by side. Not in comradeship, but each not wanting to let the other lead.

Iona went to the door and opened it herself to prevent a power struggle over who got to knock. Eric gave her a warm look, then masked it as he climbed the steps to the office.

The Shifters seemed to fill up the space in the small office and left little room for Iona, Kellerman, and Penny. Iona smelled the rage on Graham, and the same rage, more controlled, but maybe even greater, on Eric.

"We were just talking about coming out to the site," Kellerman said, extending a hand to Eric. "To look around, perhaps let a few of the local rags get a photo or two . . ."

Eric looked at Kellerman's hand, then back up into his eyes. "Small problem today," he said. "Twenty of the Elko Shifters came in on a bus they didn't get on in Elko. They were missing for twelve hours. Know anything about that?"

Penny gasped. Iona clutched the lip of the desk she leaned on. They'd found them. Thank God, they'd found them.

"Missing?" Kellerman looked concerned. "What do you mean, missing?"

"He's lying," Graham said to Eric. "He stinks of lies."

Kellerman raised his hands. "Boys."

"What happened to them?" Eric asked. "Where were they taken? What was done to them?"

"I swear to you, Mr. Warden, I have no idea what you're talking about."

"Then find out." Eric didn't move, didn't approach, but he might as well have picked up Kellerman by the lapels and slammed him into the nearest wall. "I want to know who did it, what was done, and why."

"Don't give me ultimatums, Mr. Warden. You're Shifter-town leader by our sufferance."

Eric's eyes narrowed. "The deal is, we put on Collars and follow your rules. In return, you let our kids grow up safe, and *you don't mess with them*."

Kellerman met Eric's stare with one of his own. The man wasn't afraid, but not because he was brave, Iona decided. She guessed he'd lived so long without anyone challenging him that he considered himself invulnerable. Not very smart.

"Fine, I'll find out," Kellerman said. "But it was probably nothing. The bus must have broken down."

"Broken down, my ass," Graham said. "Moving here wasn't my choice, but you and your little council promised me safe passage for the females and cubs. Anything happens to them, and you'll find out how pissed off I can truly get."

Kellerman reddened. "Are you threatening me, McNeil?"

"Sounds like a threat, doesn't it?"

"I can have you arrested for even speaking to me like that."

"Humans. When you have to call on your warriors every

time you're in the least bit of danger, you know what happens?" Graham leaned to Kellerman. "You get weak."

Kellerman at last showed uneasiness, but he didn't step back. Graham grinned in his face, then turned his back on him.

Eric remained where he was, like a solid pillar, unmoving. Her hunger for him flared.

I need him . . .

"I'm sorry you're taking this stance, Mr. Warden," Kellerman said with the air of someone unjustly insulted. "I will look into the matter, but I can guarantee it was nothing dangerous. You've wasted a very good opportunity today to show the world that Shifters and humans are working together. You need a lot of good PR on your side if you want to be fully accepted into human society."

Graham turned around at this and opened his mouth, but Iona glared at him. The Lupine actually gave her an acknowledging nod and kept quiet.

"Catch you next time," Eric said to Kellerman.

"There might not be a next time." Kellerman turned his attention to Penny and Iona. "I'm sorry that you had to witness this, ladies. Why don't we go, gentlemen, and leave them in peace?"

So, Kellerman saw himself as protecting Iona and her mother from the Shifters. That was rich.

"Agreed," Eric said. He gestured at the door. "After you."

Graham looked meanly delighted. Cassidy had explained to Iona that Shifters considered having the strongest Shifter going first through a door the right thing to do—the Shifter made sure all was safe on the other side for the weaker members of the party. A dominant Shifter sending someone else out first was an insult, implying that the Shifter didn't think the person worth protecting. Kellerman would assume Eric was deferring to him, when in reality, Eric was spitting in Kellerman's face.

Kellerman gave Eric a gracious nod. "Warden."

Eric walked out right after him, not saying good-bye to Iona or Penny. He wasn't being rude, Iona knew, but keeping Kellerman from knowing that Iona and her mother were important to him.

Graham, on the other hand, faced both of them full-on as the door closed behind Eric.

"So you're her mum," he said to Penny. "The human lady who couldn't resist a Shifter. I get that."

Penny flushed, and Iona made an exasperated noise. "Your ego is the size of a city, did you know that?" Iona said

Graham gave her a grin that wasn't friendly. "That's not the only thing super-sized, sweetheart. You should have found that out when you had the chance."

"Are you talking about your ass or your head?"

Graham growled. "I was right—you are a mouthy bitch. Warden can have the joy of you. See you in Shiftertown, babe."

He started to leave again, but Iona said, "Wait. Are they safe? The missing Shifters. They're back?"

Graham's sarcasm left him. "All of them. They'd been tranqed. I think they'll be all right, but we won't really know until they wake up."

"The Goddess go with them," Iona said, repeating what she'd heard the other Shifters say.

Graham looked surprised at the blessing then gave her another nod. "Thanks," he said, and then he went.

CHAPTER TWENTY

In the darkness of the night, Eric sat at the foot of his bed and touched the match to the last candle on the small table in front of him. The glow of candles surrounded the framed photograph of Kirsten, Eric's mate.

The photo had been taken more than thirty years ago, before digital cameras. The image was slightly yellowed, the paper shiny and stiff.

Eric and Kirsten had been walking along a loch on a rare sunny day in northern Scotland. She'd turned, laughing, and Eric had snapped her picture. Not long after that, Kirsten had discovered she was carrying her first cub, Jace.

In the photo, the wind and sun played in Kirsten's golden hair, her smile as warm as when Eric had first seen it. They'd both been excited and eager for life—by the time the photo had been taken, they'd started giving up on ever having young. The weekend by the loch had been a magical time.

The other thing on the table was a tiny stuffed leopard, black and gold, like Kirsten.

Eric dropped the spent match into an ashtray, rested his hands on his knees, and drew a long breath. Meditation and prayer were supposed to calm him, but Eric searched in vain for calmness.

He'd spent the bulk of the afternoon and evening helping Graham settle the new wolves. The ones that had been kidnapped had woken groggy, scared, and cranky. They hadn't wanted to see Eric, a Feline, in their midst, but he'd waded in, with Cassidy and Jace, and tried to soothe their fears.

Graham, Eric had seen, was a good leader. He knew how to get his Shifters to do what was needed without bullying them. He had crude strength but common sense, and his wolves followed him willingly. They didn't mindlessly obey but looked to him for guidance.

Eric wasn't about to bow out and relinquish Shiftertown to him, but he admitted that Graham knew what he was doing. Leading wasn't just about dominating everything in your path, and Graham appeared to know that.

At least the Lupines were settling down in their temporary quarters together, unpacking, beginning the adjustment. Eric had sent all his Felines home, gulped down a meal Diego and Jace put together, and retreated here.

To think.

His thoughts roiled and spun, the hunger in him uncontrollable.

He knew Iona had rejected his mate-claim only to stay ahead of Graham in the Shifter game—she hadn't seen it as an emotional decision, but one to expedite things. Hell, Eric had told her that the mate-claim was a convenience, to protect her from other Shifters while Eric decided what to do.

What a liar he was.

But Iona's rejection had kicked the Shifter in him in the gut. The beast wanted Eric to go after Iona and carry her home by the scruff of her neck, or roar in an onslaught of pain. The big, bad Shifter leader had been brought down by a half-human Shifter with eyes the color of a deep Scottish loch.

He traced the outline of Kirsten's face. "I miss you."

Eric knew what he had to do, and he wanted Kirsten, somehow, to know.

She smiled, understanding.

The door opened so softly Eric barely heard it. Cassidy sat down next to him on the foot of the bed, her warm weight rolling against him. She looked at the photo of Kirsten, touched the little stuffed leopard, and breathed a prayer of her own.

"She would have liked Iona," Cassidy said.

Eric nodded and didn't answer.

"I think it's the right thing to do," Cass went on.

Eric let out a faint laugh. "I told Iona that I wanted to bring her in for her own protection, to keep her safe until she learned how to be Shifter. That's total bullshit, isn't it?"

"Yeah." His sister nodded. "You saw her, you said, *Goddess, she's hot*, and you tried to figure out how to get her into your bed."

Eric flicked his fingers over the nape of his neck. "Somewhere in the back of my brain."

"I'd say it was pretty much in the front of your brain. You haven't consummated anything yet though, no matter that she's spent the night in here a couple times. I'd know. No wonder you're twitchy."

"Mmph. Shifters don't understand the meaning of *privacy*, do they?"

"Not in this family." Cassidy ran her fingers through Eric's short hair and kissed him above his ear. "Go, Eric. You deserve a little happiness. Goddess knows you've given up so much of it for the rest of us. Jace thinks so too." She smiled. "Well, what he said was: *When is Dad going to bring Iona home for good and get this done? He's driving us all crazy.*"

"Sounds like Jace." Eric rested his hand on Cassidy's knee. "I didn't want to go without saying good-bye."

Cassidy knew he didn't mean to her or Jace. "It's never good-bye when you had the mate bond. She'll still always be a part of us."

She would. Eric touched Kirsten's face again, then he and Cassidy blew out the candles.

The hunger was controlling her now. Iona paced the downstairs rooms of her house, shaking, sweating, and hoping like hell she could hold herself together.

She'd done pretty well at the office while her mother demanded Iona tell her everything that had happened over the last few days. Her mother had listened, both alarmed and angry.

"So what are you going to do?" Penny had asked.

"I don't know." Iona's hunger had started to flare, and she'd known she needed to get out of that office and home where she wouldn't hurt anyone. "I can't keep it secret that I'm Shifter forever. Eric says he can fix the records to show I've always been Shifter, always been part of Shiftertown. I didn't believe him before, but now that I've been there, and I've seen . . ."

She'd closed her mouth, knowing she couldn't betray the Shifters' secret places under their houses and what they kept there, not even to her mother. Not yet.

"I think they can do it," Iona finished.

Penny's eyes filled. "I just don't want to lose you."

"You won't." Iona put her arms around the smaller woman. "No matter what, you won't."

Penny's hugs had always been able to comfort her. Not today. Iona was restless and worried, feeling trapped. She hadn't been this way in Shiftertown—her hungers had been somewhat abated there.

What had Eric done to her? Addicted her to Shifters?

But, no, this restlessness had begun before she'd met Eric, starting with what she now knew was called her Transition. She'd survived that only to have her frenzies flare again with mating hunger. If Eric hadn't found her that night in Coolers, she'd by now either be a puddle of quivering goo, or else out in the woods as a panther, unable to remember how to be human.

Iona had gone home after that, eaten everything in her refrigerator, and started on what was in the freezer. She stared at the low-calorie frozen meals she'd bought a few weeks ago, thinking herself virtuous. She couldn't believe her stupidity.

Snarling, Iona hauled all the boxes out of the freezer and threw them into the garbage.

No, wait. The spaghetti ones were pretty good. She grabbed all the spaghetti and tomato sauce dinner boxes back out of the trash, ripped them open, scraped them all into a bowl, and popped the bowl in the microwave. She waited impatiently for the stuff to heat up, then she gulped down the entire bowl of pasta, the red sauce sliding down to ruin her pristine white shirt.

Not enough. Iona tossed the empty bowl—which she'd licked clean—into the sink, tore off her sauce-stained clothes, showered, brushed her teeth, and dressed again in sweats and a tank top.

There. Civilized.

And still starving. Iona walked back through the dark house, not bothering with the lights. She could order pizza again, but she worried about what she'd do to the guy who brought it, in the state she was in.

She called Eric. He didn't answer. She knew he'd walked out of the office without saying good-bye because he was protecting her from Kellerman. He didn't want Kellerman to know Iona was anything to him, that he even noticed her in the room. Iona knew that, and still felt empty.

Iona threw the phone down. She shivered, so hungry. She had to *get out*.

And then he was there. Eric came out of the shadows of her back hall while Iona was reaching for her keys. She didn't bother wondering how he'd gotten in. Eric always found a way.

Without a word, Eric took the keys from her fingers and dropped them on the table, then he flowed against her, and their mouths met.

Eric twined his fingers through hers, lifting their hands out to their sides, and turned slowly with her as though they danced. All the while he kissed her in silence, his mouth a place of heat.

Their bodies fused, her sweatpants thin enough that she could feel his hardness in his jeans. She loved the ridge of it against her, remembered the feel of it in her hand, wanted it inside her.

"Eric," she whispered.

He caught the word on his lips. He opened her mouth and explored it in long, sultry strokes of his tongue, licking, then nipping. He still wore his leather coat, the scent of it mixing with his musk and his taste.

Eric drew their twined hands up between them, releasing her mouth to transfer hot, slow kisses to her fingers.

"Be my mate," he said. "Sun and moon. Say yes." He sucked the tip of her middle finger into his mouth. "I'm dying for you, Iona."

She was dying for him. "You want me to be Shifter."

"You *are* Shifter. Experience it with me, at my side."

"I want . . ." Heat and frustration warred within in her. "I don't know what I want."

"It doesn't matter. I need you." Eric touched his face to hers. "It's killing me."

"Yes." Iona let out a breath. "Eric, I'm so *hungry*."

Her frustration came out as a growl. Eric growled in response. He took a step back, shed his jacket, and stripped off his shirt.

"Feast on me," he said.

Iona just looked at him at first, letting his beauty fill her senses. The faint glow from the kitchen touched his body, his muscles a play of light and shadow, his eyes jade green in the darkness.

Looking wasn't enough. Iona's hands went to his bare torso, firm muscle under her fingertips. Hard pectorals, strong shoulders, tight biceps. She traced his tattoo, her mouth watering with the desire to lick it.

The world took on a slightly reddish tint, the walls around them concave, and she knew her eyes had become the Shifter's. She growled again, the beast's snarl in her throat.

Iona didn't want to hurt him. She started to lift her hands away, fearing they'd sprout claws and gouge him, but Eric grabbed her wrists and pulled her hands back to him. His own eyes turned Shifter, with cat slits, his animal growl echoing hers.

Feast on me.

Iona bent her head, his hands still around her wrists, and washed the lines of his tatt with her tongue. His skin tasted salty, the ink lines smooth. She wound her way up the painted lines, across his bicep to his shoulder.

Now she wanted to bite. Iona moved her mouth to the skin between Eric's shoulder and neck, and sucked a fold between her teeth.

He made a raw sound in his throat. Iona started to pull back, fearing she'd hurt him, but Eric slid his hand to her neck and pulled her to him again. "Slake the hunger. That's why I'm here."

Iona let out a sigh of need and suckled harder. He tasted good, so good. Iona felt her fingers become the cat's claws, and her teeth sharpened.

Hungry. Mate. Mine.

"Iona . . ." It was a whisper, his hand strong on the nape of her neck. She felt him rock his head back, heard his intake of breath. "Goddess, you are good to me."

His hard-on was rigid against her sweatpants, making Iona's blood sear. She drew her hands down his chest, seeing that she'd already scratched him with her claws, and ripped open his belt.

Within seconds she had his jeans unbuttoned and the zipper down. Iona pushed his underwear out of the way and happily closed her hands around his cock.

The weight of it in her hands, the warm hardness, made her hungrier than ever. Iona squeezed both fists around his cock while she licked the bite marks she'd left on his shoulder.

Eric undid the drawstring of her sweats and thrust his hands inside, making a noise of satisfaction when he found she hadn't bothered with underwear. He dipped one hand between her legs, fingers sinking into her heat.

Iona hummed in delight while she continued licking, biting, suckling his neck, the metallic taste of the Collar blending with the heat of his skin. She closed her eyes when he slid a finger inside her, the slim but firm thrust making her arch against him.

She had to have him. No more playing. Iona opened her eyes and raised her head, the Shifter in her in no way dismayed to see the line of red bruises she'd left from his shoulder to neck, even with the few dots of blood.

My mark. He's mine.

Eric's eyes were half-closed in pleasure. His hand went again to the nape of her neck, holding her in place while he pressed a second finger inside her.

Iona ripped herself away from him. He stared in surprise, then gave her a slow smile as he raised his fingers to his lips and licked them clean.

Iona's informal family room was only a few steps from the

hall, the high-backed leather sofa that faced the fireplace only a few paces more. Iona pushed Eric backward to it. He kicked out of the jeans and underwear pooling around his feet and caught Iona's shirt at the same time, lifting it off over her head.

Iona hadn't bothered with a bra either, finding the band too itchy and confining. Cool air caressed her skin but couldn't stop the burning.

She pushed Eric again. "On the back."

Eric waited a beat, as though wondering what she meant, then he gave her a savage smile and swung one leg over the high back of the sofa. His knee bent, strong foot resting on the sofa cushions, the other leg tight where he braced himself against the floor.

Iona shivered in delight. Eric was naked, liquid gold skin slick with sweat, his cock hard and tight, against the leather of her sofa. Iona slid off her sweatpants, now as naked as he. She held Eric's shoulders to steady herself and swung up to strad-dle the sofa's back, facing him.

Eric's grin set his green eyes sparkling. "I'm glad I taught you how to ride on the back of my bike."

This would be even sexier on his motorcycle, the sudden thought flashed through Iona's head. *Next time.*

She clutched his shoulders, hands turning to claws again. "Tell me what to do."

Eric's smile vanished. "You sure? I'm big."

"I'm not small—for a human. I want you, Eric. I need you."

"Lift up a little," he said.

Iona rocked forward, and Eric slid his hands under her thighs. He leaned back, strong body bracing, until his cock stood up between them. He scooted her forward, still holding her, until she was poised above him.

Then he let her go. Iona stood on tiptoe on one side, her foot feeling the pull, her other foot comfortable on the sofa's cushions. Eric's tip brushed the opening between her legs, her wetness there making her dizzy with heat.

"Join with me," Eric whispered, urgent.

He didn't reach for her. He braced one hand on the sofa cushion, the other on his thigh. He'd let Iona do this herself.

Because he was afraid of hurting her. The tenderness of that made Iona want him all the more.

Iona closed her eyes as she lowered herself the last inch separating them.

The sound that came out of her mouth as Eric's cock flowed inside her was primal. She'd never felt anything like it—hot, large, pushing her, spreading her, opening her.

Eric's groan was loud in the silence, and she opened her eyes. "That's it, sweetheart," he whispered. "Just like that." His jaw went tight as his head rocked back. "Just. Like. That."

Iona had no awareness of anything but him solidly inside her, the point where her existence began. She rocked her hips, which drove him another inch deeper and dragged another groan from him.

"Goddess."

It didn't hurt. Iona had thought it would hurt, though in her frenzy, she hadn't cared. But, no, this wasn't pain. It was freedom, Eric penetrated her, opening and stretching. She felt full, ecstatic, and she shuddered.

The wild burning in her skin that had made her so itchy lessened, draining downward to where they joined. The heat was incandescent there, a hard ache. Sweat filmed her skin, the night air finally cooling her.

Eric smiled up at her, his teeth pointed like his leopard's, but his eyes warm. "You are beautiful, my Iona."

Her sexy, naked Shifter, laid out for her pleasure. His Collar gleamed in the moonlight through the windows, the band of silver and black the only thing he wore.

Iona skimmed hands over his body, her tongue swiping her lips. "Hungry," she whispered.

"I know, sweetheart."

The snarling in her stomach turned to a different kind of hunger. Eric was all the way inside her, but Iona wanted him deeper. She wanted all of him, everything he had to give her.

She *needed* it. Iona rocked her hips, pushing down. Eric steadied her, showing her how to move. This, *this* . . .

The rhythm began, and Iona's thoughts dissolved. The panther in her gave a satisfied growl, the female happy finally to have a mate.

And *what* a mate. Eric was a beautiful man—strong, powerful, gentle, and protective. The perfect catch.

Eric's body balanced effortlessly on the sofa as he held her steady. His mouth twisted with his pleasure, his eyes half-closed to watch her.

Iona's rhythm rocked her on him, the ache inside her unbearable. At the same time, she never wanted it to stop. Never stop, never stop . . .

Eric's thoughts had ceased being coherent as soon as she'd slid down onto him. He felt her heat close around him—*perfect*. He was exactly where he belonged, inside this woman, his mate.

It had been so long since he'd found this kind of completeness. Hell, since he'd felt this good about anything.

Her rocking motion made her breasts sway, the nipples dark little points. She squeezed without realizing she did it, drawing him farther into her. Deeper, deeper. They were one, joined, bonded, to hell with ceremonies.

Iona. Love. Keep me inside you, forever.

Her fingers were firm points against his chest. Her claws had receded, but her fingertips were strong. He loved that she wasn't afraid of him, was ready to take anything he gave her.

Eric's hips rose with her rhythm, the cool back of the couch an exciting contrast to the absolute, tight heat inside her. He liked the way her waist curved in a bit, belly a little soft above her rounded hips, a woman lush enough to take him.

And strong enough. Iona was no weak human. She was a beautiful Shifter woman, and she was winding up Eric's frenzy at the same time as she was relieving it.

Eric wanted her now, and he wanted her always. It would never be enough.

His body burned, the hottest part where he pushed inside her. Iona rocked down, down, and Eric pressed up. He was shuddering now, sweat coating his body, his hands locked around Iona's wrists.

His cock reached higher into her, as high as it could, trapped by her wet, slick, tight sheath. He moved in slow, gentle thrusts, liking the way her face softened. Then he moved faster, his cock so hard it hurt. The wiry curls around her opening tickled, sweet contrast to the need to pump and pump and never stop.

Eric arched back, his naked body slick against the sofa. She made soft, female noises, mixed with wildcat growls, as she rode him, her breasts swinging, her hair snaking down to tangle around her nipples.

A shout tore from his lips as Eric's seed shot into her, her cry echoing his. He closed hands around her hips, holding them together, his instinctive need to fill his mate making him thrust and thrust again.

Iona cried his name, her voice ringing through the night, laughing with tears running down her face.

Warm tendrils wound through Eric's heart, trapping him with unbearable strength. Tears wet his own eyes as he held her, their intense frenzy spiraling down to easy little thrusts.

Eric knew he was bonded to her in more ways than one, body and soul, and there was nothing he could do about it.

CHAPTER TWENTY-ONE

"**D**amn, I'm still hungry."

Eric wanted to laugh as he stroked Iona's hair. They'd fallen together onto the sofa's seat—nearly onto the floor before Eric had stopped their wild roll. Eric lay on his back now on the leather, Iona stretched on top of him.

There was nowhere in the world Eric wanted to be but right here, with her.

"Still as bad?" Eric asked.

"No." Iona drew a long breath. "Eric, I've been eating so much food. How can I do that without getting sick? I'm not a teenager anymore. I won't burn it off."

She looked annoyed with herself. Eric cuddled her closer and kissed the bridge of her nose. "Shifter metabolism is much faster than a human's. You can take it."

"But why? I didn't even want this much food when I did the Transition thing."

"Mating instinct," Eric said lazily. "Hunger so you'll eat for strength, mating frenzy so you'll drag down a male and have him land a cub on you."

"That sounds so . . ."

"Animal-like? Would be, wouldn't it?" Eric slid his hands along her warm sides, her skin silk under his fingertips. "The

Fae weren't wrong when they called us little better than animals." He smiled a little. "Fucking Fae bastards."

Iona moved against him, restless. "I still want to run around too."

"Mmm, I must be getting old. I want nothing more than to lie here, with you, the sexiest woman in the world, on top of me."

Iona smiled. "I'm not sexy."

"Sexy, hot, erotic, cute, beautiful as hell, and I want to make love to you all day and all night."

"I see." She sounded pleased. "We wouldn't get much else done."

"Who gives a flying fuck? What's more important?"

Iona rested her crossed arms on Eric's chest, her chin on her forearms, which put her a breath from his face. He liked her there. "Running Shiftertown?" she suggested.

"Let Cassidy do it. And Jace. I'm busy."

"And Graham will keep fussing about the houses."

"He can kiss my ass." Eric growled. "I'm with my mate."

"And those poor Shifters who were abducted."

Eric's humor evaporated. "Yeah, we'll have to deal with that."

Iona pressed a kiss to the hollow of his throat, a feather touch. "Kellerman was lying when he said he didn't know anything about it."

"I know. I'll get the truth out of him."

"At least the cubs are all right," Iona said. "Aren't they?"

"They are. Thank the Goddess."

Iona touched his Collar. "I'll have to wear one of these eventually, won't I?"

Eric gently lifted her hand from his Collar, then he brushed his fingertips across her bare neck. "Maybe not."

"You'll have me keep passing as human? The other Shifters know now, and you said they might say something . . ."

Eric stilled her words. "A different solution. Collars that look like Collars but aren't."

"Fake Collars? How can that work? Won't that be obvious?"

"I don't know how they work, but they do. Some of the Shifters already have them, but that's not common knowledge. The Shifters in Austin, the Morrisseys, they've figured out how to make these Collars, and they've offered to share."

Iona frowned. "Let me see if I understand. You'll have me wear a Collar that doesn't work, and you'll have the databases or whatever changed to make it look like I've lived in your Shiftertown all my life."

"That's it."

"Won't my friends and family notice? And the people I've worked with for years?"

"I guess you'll have to learn who you can trust. The records will show the humans that you've always been Shifter, no matter what anyone says."

"No blowback on my sister or mother?"

Eric covered her hands with his. "I'll do my damnedest to prevent that. You have my word."

"It's my whole life, Eric."

"I know. I'm sorry." He looked into her eyes, which were blue and anguished. "Spend that life with me."

"Do I have a choice?"

Eric swallowed, his throat tight. "You do. You don't have to pick me. You don't have to pick anyone. Live in Shiftertown, and I'll keep you safe, like I do the rest of my Shifters. It'll be tough for me to keep all those males off you, but I'll do it. You'll be under my protection. It's your choice, Iona."

She watched him with a stunned look. She'd expected him, he knew, to throw her over his shoulder and drag her home, to sex her until she admitted she was his true mate.

Which sounded very appealing, but Shifters weren't feral anymore. As much as it killed him, Eric had to let Iona choose.

Iona let out her breath. "I still want a run. A nice long one."

Eric's excitement kicked in again. A chase. *Yes.* "You and your mom have a cabin up in the mountains, right? Is it off the beaten track?"

Iona nodded. "Nice and isolated. We love it."

The excitement escalated. Eric rose with it, lifting Iona and setting her on her feet at the same time he came to his. "Then let's go."

Iona ran. Her panther stretched and flowed, paws pounding through the soft pine needles, the sharp chill drying her sweat.

Eric came behind her, his leopard's breath loud in the still air. They ran under soaring trees, leaping over frozen streams and snowbanks that cut through the woods.

Iona always marveled how different the world was up here. They were only short miles from the desert floor, but the mountain climate was alpine—cool summers, snowbound winters, vast pine forests that opened into surprising meadows of flowers in the springtime.

Iona's family's cabin was a little way from the clusters of cabins that filled Mount Charleston and the surrounding area. She loved it up here, where she could shift and run, run, run.

Now she was being chased. Eric sprinted behind her, running flat out, and Iona stretched to keep ahead of him.

He would catch her. She sensed his determination, felt the earth trembling under his stride.

Eric would catch her, and then . . . Iona shivered and increased her speed.

The air was thin at this altitude, Mount Charleston reaching about twelve thousand feet at its peak. But Iona had more or less grown up here, spending her summers at the cabin to escape the heat, part of her winters up here skiing. She knew every nuance of this mountain, every cranny and place to hide.

But she couldn't ditch Eric. He'd driven them up here in her pickup, Iona still too frenzied to get behind the wheel. She'd cuddled next to him in the front seat, and he'd held her with his arm around her as he drove, like they were in love.

Once inside the cabin, while Eric laid a fire in the big stone fireplace, Iona had given him an impish grin, thrown off her clothes, and dashed outside. The minute or so it had taken her to shift lost her the advantage though, and she'd had to run fast to get ahead of Eric.

Now he closed in on her. She heard his growls, felt his paws swat at her back feet. His breath touched her tail, and she flicked it out of his reach.

Iona doubled her speed. Her long panther legs should have been able to outdistance Eric's compact leopard body, but Eric was fast, and he was strong.

Eric leapt, pushing off with his powerful hind legs, and landed on Iona's back.

Iona went down with a snarl and an explosion of pine needles in the dark. Eric's leopard was on her, his Collar shining in the moonlight, his big paws pinning her down.

Iona writhed and struggled, but Eric fastened his teeth around her throat, not enough to penetrate the skin, but enough to make her still. Growling, he rolled her panther over onto her belly and covered her body with his.

The panther went still with shock when the leopard entered her. Eric rumbled softly, teeth gentle in her furry neck. Then Iona's wildcat brain took over, and Iona the human ceased to think.

The panther in her both fought Eric's domination and reveled in it. *This* is what Shifters were for—to fight, to mate, to breed. The leopard was strong, the best of his clan, perfect for cubs. The panther had made him chase her and catch her, exactly as planned. She made a little yowling sound and turned her head to lick his paw.

The leopard held her down, his wildness crazy as he loved her. At last he backed away, flipped the panther over onto her back again, and shifted into his human form.

The panther held Eric against her furry body for a moment, then Iona slowly shifted to human.

She lay, panting, on her back, Eric pinning her hands and smiling into her face.

"How do you shift so fast?" she asked, still trying to catch her breath. "It's not fair."

"Keep it simple. Think of the form you want to be, then be it."

Sure. Simple. "I want to be this one, right now."

"I want you to be this one too."

Eric kissed her lips, his mouth hot, his eyes still Shifter white. He licked her neck, pausing to give her a love bite.

"Mmm," Iona said, arching her head back. "I know why you like it when I do that to you."

"You don't have a Collar," Eric said, licking where the band would go. "I rejoiced in that the first time I saw you. I still do."

Iona touched the Celtic knot gleaming against his throat. "I wish this could be off *you*."

"Someday. We're working on it."

Her caresses on his chest became firm presses. "Damn you, Eric. I still want you."

He laughed softly. "Mating frenzy."

He locked his legs around hers and rolled over. She rolled with him, landing on top of him.

"What are you doing?" she asked, half laughing.

"You want leaves and pine needles poking you in the back?"

Iona hadn't noticed them, not with Eric's heavy warmth on her. Eric took her hands and raised her to a sitting position, her knees on either side of his torso.

"Wait," she gasped. "We're in the woods."

"In the dark, a long way from anywhere, love. You want to walk back to the cabin first?"

She didn't. Iona's excitement was still high, her blood hot. She held Eric's strong hands while she rose over him and, as she had on the couch, slid herself down onto him.

This second time was easier than the first, but no less incredible. Iona moaned as his cock entered her, his hardness penetrating and opening her. Eric sucked in a breath as she settled on him, pressing his hips upward as she came down.

He fit into her tightly, every long inch of him. Iona knew she'd been made for this joining, to feel Eric pushing high inside her. He opened her wide, her female places so wet that he thrust up and in without any barrier.

She started riding him, knees and toes burrowing into the wet earth. Eric slid his hands beneath her breasts, his hands so warm, his thumbs teasing her nipples. The tingle of his touch spiraled down to join the tight, hard need where she rocked his cock deep inside her.

The scent of their lovemaking, sweet, heavy, and exciting, blended with the scent of pine and old leaves. The night air brushed frigid fingers over them, but Iona was toasty warm with Eric inside her.

She wanted this to go on and on, she forever locked with him in the splendid silence of the night woods. Moonlight filtered through the trees to touch them like a gentle embrace.

But their bodies wanted mating, the basic need to procreate

driving them on. A wave of black pleasure washed over Iona,
beginning where Eric joined with her and rippling through
every inch of her body.

Eric! I love you!

Iona cried out as the thought tore through her, and she
nearly fell, but Eric held her upright, his hands rock steady.
He groaned low in his throat, and she felt his seed scalding
her, filling her up, heady heat and pleasure.

The sensation sent her over the top. Iona's cries rang out
into the night, blending with Eric's as they sealed themselves
together. Mating.

Iona collapsed on top of him, laughing again, so happy to
be gathered into his arms. She was warm, safe, well.

I love you, Eric, the voice whispered inside her, and Iona
shook.

They shifted to run back to the cabin, this time side by side.
Eric's leopard's shoulder bumped Iona's as they negoti-
ated narrow parts of the trails.

Their breaths steamed, the November night cold and clear.
The rivulets of snow that ran through the woods were hard
packed, their paws making no indentations in it.

Eric flowed back to his human form when they reached the
cabin porch, and he turned, watching her expectantly.

Think of the form you want to be, then be it.

Iona pictured herself as her human, tallish and bare, with
thick dark hair and eyes of icy blue. She took a step forward,
visualizing herself easing into human form as quickly as
Eric had.

Her limbs distorted and changed as slowly as ever, her
muscles protesting as they moved from long-legged panther to
a woman with hips more curved than she wanted them to be.

"Ow," she said, when her mouth became human.

Eric shook his head. "You'll get it."

"What are you laughing at, hot-ass?"

"Not laughing. Enjoying."

Eric shoved open the door and let himself into the cabin
first. This let Iona stand back to observe his oh-so-nice butt.
Tight and smooth, it was fine indeed.

Iona followed Eric into the high-ceilinged front room, enjoying watching him bend down to touch a long-handled lighter to start the fire he'd laid.

"You don't have to bother with that," she said. "I'm not cold."

"Me either." Eric set the lighter back on its shelf. "The mating frenzy makes you forget about hot and cold, and sleep, food, and safety. You can die from not paying attention."

With warmth and need wrapping around her, Iona couldn't quite grasp that. "You've been in the mating frenzy before."

Eric looked up at her, his eyes quiet. "Yes."

"With Kirsten."

"Yes."

Iona touched her hands together. "You must have loved her very much."

Eric nodded. "Yes. Very much."

"Then why do you want another mate?"

Eric pushed himself from the fireplace and came to her, the first flickers of fire shadowing his tall, naked body. He skimmed warm hands down her arms.

"Because I saw you."

Words stuck in Iona's throat. The heat of his hands made her realize that she truly was cold, and she shivered.

Eric's eyes darkened. He cupped Iona's face in his hands and drew her up to kiss her.

His mouth was as warm as his skin. Eric kissed her with slow seduction, the frenzy slightly abated from all their love-making, but not by much. His lips sought, touched, warmed. Iona slid her arms around him as he kissed her, and pulled him close.

The surging fire began to grow, the only light, filling the room with a rosy glow. In it, Eric lifted Iona and carried her to the thick rug in front of the hearth.

On this rug, where Iona had played as a child, cuddled with her mother as a preteen, and daydreamed with her little sister as a teenager, Eric laid her down and made slow, sweet love to her. With his warm weight on her, his jade green eyes watching her, Iona knew she wanted to be no other place.

"Iona," he said, his voice rasping. "Say you'll be my mate. Sun and moon. *Please*."

The *please* had so much emptiness in it, so many years of loneliness, that it wrenched Iona's heart. "All right," she whispered.

They spent the rest of the night making love, first on the hearth rug, then in the large bedroom on the first floor. Eric said very little after her acceptance, but he kept looking at her with such triumph in his eyes that he made her nervous.

Iona's nerves wound up even more in the morning when they banked the fires, locked up the cabin, and headed back to Shiftertown.

CHAPTER TWENTY-TWO

Iona noticed a change in the Shifters when she returned to Eric's house, and not just the smirks that told her that everyone knew how much sex she and Eric had enjoyed last night. The Shifters seemed to know, without being told, that she'd agreed to be Eric's mate.

Shane, who'd entered the kitchen to talk to Diego, snapped his head around to look at Iona as she and Eric came in the front door. Then Shane took a deliberate step back, as though acknowledging he should stay away from her.

Cassidy rushed to Iona and hugged her hard, kissing her on the cheek. "Welcome to the clan," she said.

Jace's embrace, coming a second later, was as warm and heartfelt. "Thanks, Iona," he said in her ear. "Dad needs you."

Diego laughed and grabbed Iona for another hug, this one Diego-and-Cassidy scented. "It's not so bad here once you get used to it," he said, with a slow wink at Cassidy. "Eric, you need to build on to your house. You can't stuff Iona into that shoebox-sized room of yours."

"I'll vacate my room and sleep downstairs," Jace said, sounding unworried. "I'd rather, with all the mating that will be going on up here. I'll need the quiet. The babies can have

Dad's room, until they get big enough to start screaming for their own space."

"You're very thoughtful, Son," Eric said, deadpan.

"He just wants the man cave to himself," Cassidy said. "Diego and I might have to join him down there if Eric gets too loud. He is clan leader, after all." She laughed and then slid her hand to her abdomen. "Ooh, she's ready to fight her way out soon."

"You don't know it's a she, *chiquita.*" Diego leaned to Cassidy's ear and licked it. "We've never had an ultrasound."

Cassidy shrugged. "I just know."

Iona believed her. Shifters knew things, especially about cubs, just as Iona had scented that her sister was pregnant before Nicole even acknowledged the possibility.

Eric put his hands on Iona's shoulders. "Don't scare her, and get her whatever she needs, all right?"

"Sure, boss," Shane said. "You ever feel like booting him out, Iona, you know where I live." He sent Eric an evil grin and departed out the back door, already yelling the news to his brother and mom.

"What do I do now?" Iona asked. "I feel like I'm supposed to do something, but I don't know what."

"Nothing." Eric kissed the top of her head, lips gentle. "You're part of the family now. We'll have the full sun ceremony as soon as I bring in someone to do it, and then the full moon as soon as there's a full moon. A few nights from now, I think."

"Who? A priest or priestess?" Iona was still a bit fuzzy on Shifter religion. So much to learn.

"A clan leader or Shiftertown leader," Eric said. "I'm both, but I can't mate bless myself. Graham's the equivalent rank for now, but I don't want him doing it, so I'll have to bring in outside help. For now . . ." Eric kissed her again and released her. "Do whatever, but stay near Cass, Diego, Jace, or Nell. They'll protect you when I'm not here. I hate to leave, but I need to see Graham and talk to some of the wolves that were abducted."

Yes, he needed to figure out what had happened. Eric was leader, which meant, despite his statements last night that he

would rather mate with Iona than anything else, he had plenty
to take care of.

"*Do whatever,*" Cassidy repeated, shaking her head at her
brother. "You're such a male, Eric. Iona has tons to do. We need
to move her in here, bring stuff from her house, move Jace's
stuff downstairs, redecorate Jace's room, and introduce her to
all the other females in Shiftertown, since she'll be their alpha
now—"

"Wait, what?" Iona stared at her. "Why will I be their
alpha? You're Eric's sister—his second-in-command, right?"

"Second in the clan, but you're top female, and all the
other females will respect that," Cassidy said. "Don't worry,
you'll catch on."

Iona hoped so. It was difficult though—she was surprised
how difficult it was—to kiss Eric good-bye and watch him
walk away between the houses in his nonchalant stroll to
return to the business of being leader.

Eric spent his morning talking to the Shifters who'd been
abducted. Graham insisted on accompanying him to
every interview, stating that the wolves wouldn't let a strange
Feline ask the questions, Shiftertown leader or no. Eric knew
the truth of this, so he let Graham precede him and introduce him.

The new Shifters lived in houses vacated by Felines,
Lupines, and bears of this Shiftertown as late as yesterday. Most of the new wolves didn't want Eric inside their
homes, indicating with body language, scowls, or outright
declarations to Graham that they'd talk to Eric—maybe—but
only outside.

The wolves who'd been abducted could tell Eric very little,
but one female whose son was in his teenage years did remember some of it.

"The bus pulled off the highway," the woman said, while
her lanky son stood behind her, hands on her shoulders. "It
was very late, and most of us were asleep, but I looked out the
window, thinking we'd stopped for gas or at a rest area. I was
hoping I'd be able to get out and stretch my legs.

"But some men got on the bus—humans. They walked down the row, stopping at every seat. I wasn't sure at first what they were doing, then I realized they were sticking needles into every Shifter, tranquilizing them. Most of them were already groggy—I think they put something in the water bottles they provided, but I hadn't drunk from mine. I tried to fight when they came for me—I screamed, but they jabbed my son, and then they got the needle into my neck."

Her son rubbed her shoulders, his distress scent nearly overwhelming hers. Graham put a hand on the boy's and nodded for the woman to go on.

"They must not have gotten enough into me, because I came to when they were taking me out of a cage in a hospital room or clinic somewhere," she said. "They strapped me down to a bed, and I was too weak and sleepy to fight them.

"Then some doctors came. At least, they wore white coats, surgical masks, and sterile caps. I almost peed myself, I was so scared they were going to kill me, but all they did was draw a little blood and scrape some skin into a tube. Then they left me alone. I thought they were prepping me for something, but I was too exhausted to stay awake. I passed out again, and when I woke up, we were on another bus, and *he* was there." She pointed at Eric. "But my son was back with me, and everything was fine. Well, as fine as it could be."

Her son leaned down to embrace her, shutting out Eric and even Graham, his worry and emotion pouring from him.

"They were human, these doctors?" Eric asked.

The woman nodded around her son's shoulder. "They all smelled human. No Shifter or half Fae or . . ." She shrugged. "Nothing but human."

"Dead humans if I find them," Graham rumbled.

Eric didn't disagree. He touched both the female and her son on their shoulders. "Thank you," he said. "We'll let you rest now." He gentled his voice as he said a Goddess blessing, and the two Lupines looked startled but grateful.

"We know Kellerman hired the bus to take the Shifters out there," Eric said to Graham as they left the house. Across the street, the Shiftertown fence had come down, and surveyors were marking the ground with stakes for the new houses. The bus driver had gotten it out of his boss that Kellerman had asked for the bus. The boss had almost bragged that someone so prominent in town had wanted their services.

"But we don't know why," Graham said. "I really, *really* want to find out."

"We've already put Kellerman on the defensive. But I'm thinking someone else on the Shifter council might be easier to crack. Kellerman is the only one not afraid of us. The others are scared witless."

Graham twined his fingers together and stretched his arms, knuckles cracking. "Let me do it."

Eric eyed him. "All right."

"What?" Graham looked surprised. "Just like that? No *I can do it better because I'm the badass Shiftertown leader?*"

"I think you'll scare the piss out of them, which is exactly what we need. Just don't kill anyone."

"How about maiming? I'm in the mood for a good maiming."

"Only if it doesn't show," Eric said.

Graham laughed. "You have balls, Warden. For a Feline. I also know you're sending me in your place because you don't want to leave your mate. Yeah, I heard she caved and agreed to your new mate-claim, poor woman."

"About that." Eric lowered his voice, one eye on the humans working across the street. "Keep your Shifters from spilling that she's Shifter for now." He held Graham's gaze. "I'm asking you as one leader to another."

Graham looked offended. "You think I'd tell on her and let the humans torture her? I don't give up Shifters to humans, Warden, and neither do my wolves."

His outrage that Eric would think so was so strong that Eric believed him. "Good."

"Now, you, I'd like to see run away whimpering with your tail between your legs. But I won't betray your mate. Coax her away from you, sure, beat your face in for the fun of it, yeah, but tell humans our secrets? I don't do that shit."

On that last word, Graham turned his back on Eric and walked away. The back-turning was another insult, but Eric

felt a twinge of relief. Graham's Shifters wouldn't disobey
him. Iona would be safe.

Graham did like scaring the piss out of humans. The two
he faced over a table at the county courthouse later that
morning stank of fear.

They were the weakest on the council, he'd figured from
their former meetings, and asked to meet with them. He
implied that Kellerman would be there, knowing they'd never
come alone, and he also implied that they were being asked
because Kellerman trusted them the most. Humans so easily
fell for flattery. When they arrived, he fed them the bull that
Kellerman had been delayed but knew these two could handle
the meeting alone.

They had no idea, Graham thought as he eyed the two
humans—a thin man in his fifties and a woman ten years
younger in a coal black business suit—how easily Graham
could kill them. They thought that because he had a Collar
and they were in a public building, within shouting distance
of a security guard, they were fine.

They were wrong. And some instinct inside them knew it,
because their fear smell had Graham nearly gagging.

"When you took my wolves to your facility in the desert,"
Graham said, as though the adventure was common knowledge, "did you remember to immunize your humans? If they
were messing with Shifter blood, Goddess knows what they
might catch."

The man and woman exchanged an uneasy glance.

"Everything was sterile," the man said. "Checked. No
harm to the Shifters or the human staff."

God and Goddess, they believed him. Their correct
response should have been: *What facility? Shifter blood? We
have no idea what you're talking about.*

"You'd better double-check," Graham said. "One of my
wolves said she saw a bunch of test tubes just sitting around.
Hope they didn't leave them out there."

"No, no," the woman said. "The samples were transferred
to the lab, all properly. Wait, how do you know all this?"

Graham gave her an easy smile, making sure he showed a

lot of teeth. "Kellerman told me. I wanted to check, for your sake. I hope the tests are a success."

The woman pressed her lips together as if deciding, belatedly, to clam up.

The man didn't look as worried. "You'll know the results in due time. Shifters will have to participate eventually."

In what? But both council members looked prim and their fear smell receded a little.

They'd been afraid, he realized, that Graham knew the entire truth, and Graham had somehow just revealed he didn't. The secret, he understood now, was not that the Shifters had been taken, but what would be done with the blood and tissue samples.

Damn it.

But at least he'd gotten that much out of them. He stood up. "Kiss Kellerman for me," he said. "Or tell him he's a dickhead. Your choice."

The woman actually smiled, probably having wanted to tell Kellerman that for years. Her fear came back, though, when Graham winked at her.

He walked out before the two could rise and leave, striding back through the courthouse to the garage where he'd left his bike.

"Oh, hey, Shifter."

Graham looked around as he came out of the garage stairwell and saw the young woman he'd met at the Shifter bar waiting for the elevator to go down. She wore a fairly plain dress today with low-heeled shoes, had combed her hair into a straight ponytail, and wasn't wearing much makeup. A far cry from her sexy look the other night—tight shimmering dress and spike heels—but her smile was still the same.

"Remember me?" she said. "I'm Misty. From the bar the other night?"

"Yeah." Graham leaned against the stone wall next to her. "Yeah, I remember you."

He looked her up and down, and she glanced self-consciously at her dress. "I have a meeting. Best I look like a Plain Jane for it. In legal-land, girls who wear anything cute are considered trashy."

"You a lawyer?"

Misty laughed. "No. I run a flower shop. There, it's good to wear cute clothes. And knowing a lot about flowers doesn't hurt either. Which I do."

She liked to jabber. Graham had never admired that in a woman, but in Misty, it seemed . . . sweet.

"You recover from the fight?" she asked, moving her brown-eyed gaze to his shoulder.

"Shifters heal fast," he said.

"Lucky you. That's probably why it didn't hurt you to have all those tatts. You made me start thinking about getting one, though. What do you think I should do?"

A flower, was his instant thought. A little red rose, on her buttocks. And a heart right at the small of her back, something he could lick when he got behind her . . .

Shit. What was he thinking? She was *human*.

"A flower," he said. "You know, because you have a flower shop." Graham pushed himself from the wall, took her hand, and turned it palm up. "Right here on your wrist. A rosebud."

He skimmed his fingertips over her skin. She shivered, and the scent that came to him was one of arousal. Graham felt himself growing hard in response, and he lifted his hand away.

Misty traced her wrist where Graham had touched her. Her scent, her caressing fingers, that smoky voice . . .

Time to go.

He didn't move.

"A rosebud," she said. "What a great idea. Maybe when I work up the courage, you could go with me?"

Yes. "Thought you didn't like Shifters."

"For some reason I thought Shifters would be like in the movies. You know. Half man, half beast, bad breath. I'm glad I found out wrong."

"That's because you've never met my uncle."

She laughed, which made her eyes flash and her voice go sultry. "You're funny too. I didn't know Shifters would have a sense of humor. I'm glad I met you, Graham. Slapped my ideas right in the face."

The elevator doors opened. Misty pressed the call button so it would stay there, but she didn't get on. "Guess I'd better go. If I'm late to that meeting—well, let's just say it won't be good."

"You decide to get the tatt, come to Shiftertown and ask for me. I'll have my friend do yours."

"Is he another Shifter?"

"He's a wolf. Best tatt artist I've ever met."

"Huh, I'll have to think about that. See you, Graham."

Graham lifted his hand in a silent good-bye. Misty smiled at him, a warm, genuine smile, no fear in her eyes, and stepped onto the elevator. She waved at him as the doors closed, and then she was gone.

Graham stared at the closed doors of the elevator for a long time, unnerving feelings stirring inside him, before he finally turned away and sought his Harley.

"**M**elissa Granger?"

Misty pulled herself out of the daze her second encounter with the Shifter called Graham had sent her into, and looked at the man speaking to her.

He had a balding head and wore a business suit, one that must have cost him a lot of money. A lawyer of some kind. Probably a prosecutor with that expensive suit. Defenders were notoriously underpaid.

She stopped her walk across the courthouse lobby. "Yes?"

He stuck out a well-cared-for hand. "My name's Kellerman. Frank Kellerman. Are you a friend of Mr. McNeil?"

"Of who?" She'd never heard of Kellerman, or McNeil. Nothing to do with her.

"The Shifter you were talking to in the garage. Graham McNeil."

He'd seen them? They'd been on the top floor of the parking garage, and Misty could have sworn no one else had been up there. Creepy.

"Oh, him," she said. "I barely know him. Met him once or twice, that's all."

Kellerman smiled. He put an arm around Misty's shoulders and started walking her toward a quiet corner. *Very* creepy.

"How would you like to do something for me?" Kellerman asked. "Something worth your while?"

Misty pulled away. "This might be a courthouse, but I'm not a prostitute on my way to a hearing. I've come to meet with my brother's lawyers."

"I know who you are, Ms. Granger." Kellerman laughed a little, like she'd made a good joke. "What I'd like you to do is not illegal. I want you to get to know Mr. McNeil—Graham—a little better. And then tell me everything about him."

Misty took a step back. "Make friends with him to spy on him? Why would I do that?"

"McNeil is a Shifter, and not a trustworthy one. He's new around here, and I want to find out all about him."

"Then ask him yourself."

"I don't think you quite understand, Ms. Granger." Kellerman put his arm around her again, this time sinking his grip into her shoulder so she couldn't pull away. "I know about your brother. I know about what he's going through in prison. And I know members of the parole board, with whom I have much influence."

Misty stopped, icy fingers touching her heart. "That's . . ." She looked up into his cold face. "You're evil."

"Your brother committed a crime, for which he needs to pay," Kellerman said in a matter-of-fact voice. "McNeil is dangerous and needs to be watched. You be my eyes and ears, and your brother might be released early. He can come home where he won't be beat up every day."

Misty found it difficult to breathe. She knew enough of the ways of the world to know she couldn't readily trust him. If she said yes, if she helped this Kellerman, there was no guarantee he'd do what he promised for her little brother.

Kellerman was too slick, too sure of himself. He'd not bend over backward for a young man who'd made one stupid mistake at eighteen and was paying for it with an unfairly long sentence. She and Paul hadn't been able to afford a good lawyer.

On the other hand, if Misty said no, a guy like Kellerman might make sure that Paul never got out of prison again. He'd have to stay in that place where gangs beat up on him every day, and no one did anything about it.

"Fine," she snapped, ducking out from under his hand. "I'll do it. Now, if you'll excuse me, I have to go."

Kellerman took a thin card from his inside breast pocket. "Here's my number. Call me when you have something to tell me. Make it soon."

Misty snatched the card from his hand, jammed it into her purse, and clicked her way down the hall to the room at the end. She thought about Graham, the tall biker-looking Shifter, she thought about her gentle little brother Paul, and her heart hammered until she thought she'd be sick.

CHAPTER TWENTY-THREE

"But they didn't spill what Shifters would be participating *in?*" Eric asked Graham that night.

"I told you six times. They didn't seem worried about me finding out about the compound in the desert. Seemed happy when they realized I didn't know what they were up to beyond that."

Eric moved restlessly. He and Graham stood on Eric's back porch in the cold darkness, the house lit behind him. Cassidy's and Iona's laughter drifted out, the two of them and Jace busy helping Jace move his stuff downstairs.

My mate, my mate, my mate. The words hummed through Eric's head, drowning out Graham's voice.

Eric still craved Iona with an intensity he hadn't felt in many, many years. He wanted to be nowhere but curled up with her, buried inside her, surrounded by her warmth. Graham with his grating voice and Lupine scent was poor compensation.

"Damn it," Eric said, heartfelt. "We're going to have to search that compound again."

"They were long gone this morning."

"I know, but they might have left *something* behind." Eric broke off and rubbed his temples.

"You okay, Warden?"

He shrugged. "No sleep."

Graham barked a laugh. "That's what happens when you chase a mate. You want to fuck all the time, no stopping for anything else. I loved it."

Eric had found out everything he could on Graham, so he'd known that Graham had once had a mate. The information in the Guardian's database had said that Graham's mate had died trying to bring in his cub, and the cub had died as well.

Eric made a quick sign of blessing. "The Goddess go with them," he said. "I'm sorry."

"Yeah, well." Graham's voice went quiet.

Sudden, terrible worry clutched Eric. Kirsten had gone bringing in Jace. Graham's mate had died in childbirth. Iona was half-human, not even as robust as female Shifters.

Exactly why we agreed to live in Shiftertowns, Eric told himself. Better medical care, better nutrition, better chance of females surviving with their cubs. There hadn't been many deaths in childbirth since they'd moved to Shiftertown. Things were different now.

Even so, the fear gripped him so hard that pain followed. A spark shot from his Collar. *Oh no.*

"Warden? What is wrong with you?"

Eric straightened up from where he'd sagged, but another spasm wracked his body, snakes of pain whipping through him.

"Get out of here," he said to Graham.

"What the hell is up? You dying of something? Might as well concede leadership to me now, save yourself the trouble."

Eric managed to remain upright and take two steps to reach Graham. "Get the fuck away from me. Stay away from my Shifters, my family, my mate. This is *my* Shiftertown, and I'll never give it to you."

Spittle came out with his words, landing on Graham's biker vest. Eric's finger slammed into Graham's chest. "Do you understand? You will never win. I'll kill you if you try."

Eric's Collar sparked a few more times, then went silent, controlled. But Eric couldn't control the pain. Every muscle locked as agony raked through him. Eric fought it, jaw clenched, fists balled, making himself stay on his feet.

"You're dying right in front of me," Graham said.

"Fuck you. I'll kill you." Eric's eyes went Shifter, the world taking on a red hue, his awareness stretching to every corner of it. "I'll kill you now."

He felt his body half shift, his teeth and claws emerging, his snarls filling the night. Graham's Shifter reacted, his own claws bared, warning growls long and low. Eric knew Graham would never back down from him, not without a long and bloody fight.

Fine. Eric would kill him. Rip his body open and feast on his entrails. Eric could taste the hot blood pouring into his mouth, wanted it now. He snarled and launched himself at Graham's throat.

He heard screams, his sister's voice, then the harsher, human one of her mate. Then the note of fear in his son, his cub.

Eric had to protect his cub. He hadn't been able to protect Kirsten. He'd failed. He had to protect this Shiftertown, everyone in it, all the cubs and the females, to make up for the fact that he'd let Kirsten die. Graham would never take that away from him. The wolf deserved to be torn apart.

"Eric."

He felt the touch of his mate, her scent surrounding him, Iona fresh and clean like mountain heather.

"Eric, stop." Her hands moved to his chest covered with leopard fur, which had split open his shirt. Her fingers stroked, soothed.

Eric's Collar remained silent but the pain ground on, so much pain. It was killing him.

Graham was right—he was dying, but Eric would kill him first. He'd not leave his family at the mercy of Graham. The first thing the Lupine would do would be to kill off Eric's pride, especially his son, so that son didn't challenge for leadership.

"Eric."

Iona had her arms all the way around him. Cassidy and Jace stood to either side of him. Eric sensed and smelled them, though he couldn't turn to look at them.

Graham had backed all the way off to the middle of the open yard. Shifters were coming out of houses to see what was going on—the bears from next door, the wildcat Shifters on the other side.

They sensed a dominance battle. Eric felt their curious excitement, the underlying tension that could explode into war at any excuse.

Graham, though, had his hands up. "Not the time and place. Let your mate take you inside. We figure out this human thing first, then we fight. All right?"

Eric lunged at him. Cassidy, Jace, and Iona tried to hold him back, but Eric topped all three in strength, even in this kind of pain. He threw them off and charged Graham.

Every inch of body language Graham threw out told Eric he didn't want to fight right now, but too bad. Graham was finished.

Eric heard a muffled shot and then he couldn't feel his leg. He stumbled as the rest of his body went numb, then a blackness rushed through him.

He looked over his shoulder to see Diego Escobar regarding him sternly over the barrel of a tranquilizer rifle.

"Sorry, Eric," Diego said.

The world went dark as Eric hit the ground.

"Do you know what's wrong with him?" Iona's voice cut through the darkness a long time later.

Iona's beautiful, dusky voice. Eric swam toward it, his need for her scattering the pain.

"Well, I'm no medic, lass. He told me he thinks it's to do with the Collars, but I can't be certain. I could dissect him and find out, but that would be a bit of an inconvenience for him, eh?"

Eric knew the voice—he'd met the Shifter a few times, but for the moment, the name wouldn't come. No one from this Shiftertown. The man smelled Feline, lion probably. He was very strong, a clan leader at the least.

"No dissecting," Iona said in a hard voice.

"I'm teasing you, lass. Sorry."

"He does that," another voice came, the crisp, clear one of a human woman. "He tries to be funny at all times."

"It eases the tension," the Irish voice said.

Irish. Eric remembered now. The Austin Shiftertown was run by a family of Irishmen. Their last name still swam out of his memory, but he recalled the brothers, one the Shiftertown leader, the other their Guardian.

"Liam," he croaked.

"Ah, he's still with us, is he? How're you feeling, lad?"

Eric tried to wet his lips and found no moisture in his mouth. "What are you doing here?"

"You sent for me, didn't you? Said you had a ceremony to perform, and oh, by the way, having a bit of trouble with your Collar."

Eric pried open his eyes and looked into the very blue ones of the dark-haired Liam Morrissey. Liam wore a smile, as he often did, and his eyes held humor. But behind the man's bonhomie lay a sharp mind and a powerful will.

Eric seemed to be lying in bed in Jace's bedroom—what had been Jace's bedroom. Covers were bunched over him and bright sunlight poured through the window, not helping his headache.

A phone call Eric had made this morning—no, yesterday morning—came back to him. Eric rubbed a weak hand through his hair. "I remember now."

His entire being relaxed as Iona climbed onto the bed with him and sat cross-legged by Eric's side. He reached for her hand, and she held his between hers.

Liam touched Eric's Collar. "Looks intact. You try to take it off?"

"Take it off?" Iona asked at the same time Eric shook his head. "The Collars come off?"

"Carefully, slowly, painfully, and sometimes, disastrously," Liam said. "Trust me on this. And that information goes no further than this room."

"She's my mate," Eric said.

"I'm seeing that. You're going to trust her with all things, are you?"

"I've already started." Eric showing Iona their strong room was the first step. "She'll be leader's mate. I have to."

"Aye, I know what you mean."

The crisp female voice came again. "Leader's mates are better at keeping secrets than any Shifters I know."

"Iona," Liam said. "This is Kim. The love of my life."

"We met in the hall," Iona said.

Eric remembered meeting Liam's mate the last time he'd gone out to Austin, the short young human woman with the dark hair and no-nonsense attitude. Kim had been a defense lawyer, and now she ran a law firm that specialized in helping Shifters.

"No, I didn't try to take off my Collar," Eric said, strength beginning to return. "I've been able to keep it from going off when I fight, but not for long, and that's about it."

"And these attacks come when?"

"Seem to be all over the place. After I fight, yes, but other times too. Last night, on the porch with Graham. He wasn't being aggressive, just his usual shithead self."

"But he's a threat," Liam said. "To you, to Shiftertown, to Iona."

"Yes."

"What happened before the other attacks? Maybe not right before—say within the few hours before?"

"Whenever I fight," Eric said, thinking back. But then, he'd had a huge attack after he'd gone to Iona's house and seen her dancing at her sister's bachelorette party. He'd taken Iona into her back hall and done many pleasant things. He told Liam this, omitting the glorious details. "The night after Graham Challenged for Iona as well," he went on. "When I was remembering experiments done on me, I had a small attack, but it went away quickly."

"Hmm," Liam said. The man sat comfortably on the armchair Cassidy had brought into Jace's bedroom, leaning back with his feet on the bed like he owned the place. Kim perched on the chair's arm. "Seems to me like every attack came after an adrenaline spike. Fighting triggers it, sure, but when Graham Challenged, I bet the spike was a big one. And then when you thought about being experimented on, that had to be full of bad images."

Iona broke in. "What about when he came to my house during the party? We were just kissing." She flushed.

Eric's smile was slow. From the twinkle in Liam's eyes, the man guessed how much more they'd been doing.

"Ye said you saw her dancing with a male stripper," Liam

said. "I'm thinking that would raise the ire of a Shifter watching his mate."

"You got that right," Eric said. "I didn't like it at all."

"Stripper?" Kim asked in a bright voice. "What did he do? Did it all come off?"

"Most of it," Iona said. "He came as a fireman. He got all the way down to his bright red thong."

"Mmm. Did he have a hose?"

"A very long one," Iona answered, and both women laughed.

"Tell me you took pictures," Kim said.

"Oh yeah."

Eric felt it immediately—the red rage of his possessiveness. He saw the same flare in Liam's eyes.

"Ladies," Liam said. "You want to get yourselves sequestered, do you?"

"Only if you bring us pizza," Iona said.

"And dress as a fireman," Kim added. She sent Iona a sly look. "With a big hose."

"I think our mates don't know their danger," Liam said to Eric.

"They know," Eric answered, feeling stronger by the minute. "But they don't care."

Liam growled at Kim. "Wait 'til I get you home, love."

"Promises, promises." Kim smiled.

"Adrenaline," Eric said loudly. He pushed himself into a sitting position, the sheets bunching around his bare waist. He seemed to be naked under the covers, and sincerely hoped Iona had undressed him, not Diego. "Adrenaline is supposed to trigger the Collar. Maybe it's triggering pain directly, bypassing the Collar?"

"Possibly," Liam said. "When I stave off the Collar, I pay for it pretty bad later, but you've been suffering from triggers that wouldn't necessarily have set off the Collar at all."

"Which leaves me where?"

"I don't know." Liam frowned. "I'll have to ponder."

Outside the room came a loud cry, a child's voice. A cub. Kim quickly slid off the arm of the chair. "I'd better go get Katy before she takes over your house, or the entire Shiftertown."

"Katy?" Iona asked.

Liam answered. "Katriona Sinead Niamh Morrissey. Our firstborn cub."

"He's so proud," Kim said. "Like he did it all himself." She leaned down and gave Liam a fond kiss on the forehead, then went for the door. "Come and meet her, Iona."

Iona scrambled up and followed Kim with only one glance back for Eric. The door closed, and Eric looked around for some clothes within reach.

"The ladies like the babies," Liam said.

"And you don't? Right." Eric leaned to the chair on the other side of the bed and snagged his jeans. "Why didn't you bring your cub in with you? She might have cheered me up. Cubs are good things."

"Bring my only daughter into a room with a crazed, maybe feral Shifter? No, thanks."

"Feral." Eric paused. "You think that's what happening?"

"I don't know, my friend. I sincerely hope not. I know from experience it's not a pleasant thing. Thank the Goddess for my mate sticking with me when it happened to me, or I'd not be here talking to you now."

"I know how you feel," Eric said, and slid out of bed to get dressed.

"You narrowed it down to three?" Eric asked Xavier several hours later.

Xavier Escobar tapped his laptop where it sat on his crossed legs and nodded. "Yep. Three Ross McRaes of seemingly the right age living in the northern Nevada, or western California, western Oregon, or southern Idaho areas at the time in question. Two of them definitely human, because I found pictures of them, and they've aged like humans. The third—don't know, because I haven't found him. He's the one from western California, residence listed as Grass Valley. Locals still there from that time say he was a loner, came and went, and they haven't seen him in thirty or so years."

"Hmm," Eric said. "I think we have a Shifter."

CHAPTER TWENTY-FOUR

"Could be," Xavier agreed.

"You're good, Xav. Neal?"

Neal Ingram was a big man, a Lupine, and the Shiftertown's Guardian. Often the Shiftertown's Guardian came from the leader's family, but the Guardian most closely related to Eric had died years ago. Eric, to keep the peace, had requested that Neal, the Guardian for his clan, be made Guardian for the entire Shiftertown.

Guardians were another thing the humans had almost fucked up. Each clan had its own—the Shifter male whose Fae-made sword would send dead Shifters' souls into the afterlife—but the humans insisted on only one for each Shiftertown.

They just didn't want too many guys with big swords running around, Eric supposed. So each clan's Guardians had to hide their swords and submit to the one Shiftertown Guardian. Eric appointing Neal, the next-highest Guardian in the dominance order, instead of holding a choosing for the Guardian to be picked from Eric's own clan, told the other clans that Eric wasn't going to insist his clan dominated everything. Now Eric's clan had no Guardian at all—they used Neal.

Eric had an ulterior motive that he figured his Shifters understood. When a Guardian died, tradition dictated that all eligible-aged members of the clan gathered for a choosing. The Goddess herself picked the next Guardian—so legend said.

Jace had been about the right age to qualify, and Eric had no desire at all for Jace to become a Guardian. Guardians lived a lonely life. Females avoided them, and while Shifters respected them, they were also uneasy around them. Guardians dealt in death. Everyone knew the last person they'd see in life was their Guardian arriving with his sword to send their bodies to dust.

Neal was unmated, fairly young for a Shifter at age one hundred, a gray wolf, and the silent type. He lived with his brother and several nephews, but didn't get out much or say much for himself.

However, the man was a genius at computers. Most Guardians were.

"I'll check the Guardian network," Neal said in his deep voice. "If he did take the Collar, I'll find him."

"And then I'll have a talk with him," Eric said.

"You have a ceremony," Neal said in his quiet way.

"After. You'll come with me."

Neal inclined his head.

Xavier, who'd watched the exchange with undisguised curiosity, tapped a little more on his keyboard. "About the other name you wanted me to look up. I might have found him too. Dr. Peter Murdock?"

Neal's gaze snapped back to Eric. "Him? Why?"

"I have questions he might be able to answer," Eric said calmly, though his pulse sped up at the thought of facing the man again. He kept those thoughts at bay, not wanting to trigger another attack. Not today.

"Who is he?" Xavier asked.

"A bastard who used to stick needles and probes into Shifters," Neal said. Neal had been a victim of the experiments too, the humans wondering what a Guardian had inside him that made him a Guardian.

Murdock had been part of the team of scientists studying Shifters, but he'd seemed a bit more ashamed than the others that he was torturing live specimens. Not that he stopped it, or protested, or anything. And he'd still called them *specimens*.

"Sounds like a real nice guy," Xavier said. "And successful. Full professor at UCLA, but now retired back in good old Vegas."

"After the ceremony," Eric said, looking at Neal again. "A long time after."

He didn't want bad memories to destroy this time with Iona, no matter how much he needed to get to the truth.

E ric looked much better when he stood next to Iona at the mating ceremony that afternoon—the mating under full sun.

Iona wore a garland of flowers, woven by Cassidy and her friend, a Feline called Lindsay. The two women had helped Iona pick out clothes they said were very Shifter—a loose brown skirt and a sleeveless white top with a high collar. Iona's hair hung unbound, and the day had warmed enough for bare legs and sandals. Winter on the desert floor sometimes took its time.

Eric was dressed up—for Eric—in a button-down shirt, black jeans, and square-toed black boots. His slicked-back short hair was still damp from a shower.

He smiled down at Iona next to him, a look of heat in his green eyes. But she sensed the tension in him, no matter how nonchalant he tried to appear. He was wound up, ready to get this over with.

Iona's mother had come for the ceremony, though Nicole was still in Hawaii on her honeymoon. Iona had talked to Nicole earlier on the phone, explaining to her sister that she was about to mate officially—in Shifter terms—with a Shifter.

Nicole had been stunned, then hopeful, then sounded relieved. Nicole had always known, she said, that Iona would have difficulty in a relationship with a human, but had been uncertain that Iona finding a Shifter was a good solution either. But because Iona sounded happy, Nicole would be happy. When she met Eric, though, she would make sure he was good enough for her big sister.

They'd both cried, Nicole sorry that she couldn't be there

for the day. But there'd be a full moon ceremony, Iona had been told, and Nicole might be back in time for that.

Penny stood a little behind Iona as Cassidy had instructed her. Her mother was a bit nervous to be among all these Shifters, still uncertain that she wanted to lose Iona to one. But, like Nicole, she seemed relieved she no longer had to worry about Iona finding a companion for life. And, like Nicole, she'd make sure Eric made her happy.

Jace stood behind his father, Cassidy and Diego on the other side of Jace. Xavier had come, and he stood with Lindsay, talking and laughing with her. Diego's mother stood next to Diego, talking like mad to Cassidy.

The other Shifters began forming circles around the group in the middle, an inner ring of close friends, an outer ring of everyone else, including Graham and his Lupine Shifters. Each circle moved in a stately dance in opposite directions, the Shifters holding hands as they moved around the ring. The whole thing was informal, with everyone smiling, laughing, talking, calling out to each other.

Silence fell when Liam stepped into the middle of the double circle, Kim at his side carrying little Katriona.

Liam, grinning, his Irish blue eyes warm, placed one hand on Eric's shoulder and one on Iona's.

"This is a simple ceremony, Iona," Liam said. "I call for the blessing of the God, and it's done." He leaned to both of them. "You two be happy now. It's a fine thing, another mating."

Eric moved closer to Iona when Liam stepped back, Eric's body heat touching her. Liam took both their hands, raised them up, and clasped them together. Eric's hand was warm, strong, and Iona swore a spark leapt between his fingers and hers.

Liam declared in a loud voice, "The blessings of the God be on Eric and Iona. Under full sun, the Father God, I declare them mated!"

The circles of Shifters whooped, then everyone went crazy. Music sprang up from of one of the houses, old-fashioned rock and roll. Dancing started right away, but first, Iona was jerked into a hug by Jace, who swung her off her feet.

"Thank you, Iona," he said. "Thank you. He needs you—bad."

"Don't squash her," Eric yelled at him, but then he was pulled into embraces by Cassidy, Diego, and a crushing one by Nell.

Cassidy's strong arms went around Iona, her cub inside her pressing Iona's abdomen. "I'm so happy you're my sister now."

Iona's eyes were wet when Cassidy released her and so were Cassidy's. Cassidy immediately turned to Penny and hugged her as well. "Mother of my sister, you're an honorary member of our clan now."

Penny looked a little bewildered but hugged Cassidy back. When Penny came to Iona, she broke down. "I'm so happy for you, sweetheart. I was worried, but I see how he looks at you. And how you look at him. I know that feeling."

"Thanks, Mom."

"Be happy, darling. And don't worry about the business. I can handle it. I took care of it the whole time I was raising you, remember."

"I'll still come to work, Mom. I haven't abandoned you."

"We'll see," Penny said, tears in her eyes.

Iona was stolen away then, for hugs with Diego, Xavier, and Juanita, their mother, then instantly claimed by Shane and Brody, who gave her, well, bear hugs.

"Leave her be," Nell said, coming for her share. "My house is always here for you, honey. I'll kick out these two louts, and we can talk about anything that troubles you."

"Thanks, Nell. Everyone's being so nice to me."

"To the mate of the alpha?" Nell's eyes widened. "You betcha. You've got the full trust of the dominant Shifter, and everyone's going to want to get next to you. Take some advice—show that you're neutral to everyone and favor only your family. Trust me on this. But the offer of a haven is there if you want it."

"Thank you," Iona said sincerely. She had the feeling she'd be asking for advice from both Cassidy and Nell a lot.

"Hey." Graham stopped next to Iona, his tattoos sharp in the bright sunlight. He opened his arms. "I question your taste, but the blessings of the God and Goddess go with you, Iona."

Iona let Graham hug her, aware that Eric was breathing down Graham's neck from the other side.

Instead of giving Iona a perfunctory hug and releasing her, Graham wrapped her in a powerful embrace that lifted her from her feet.

"And I'm not just sucking up to you because you're the leader's mate," Graham said as he held her. "You have balls, Iona. Good thing for Eric that you do."

Graham finally thumped her back to the ground, and Eric shouldered his way between them, a low growl in his throat.

Iona grabbed Eric's hand to draw him away. Eric left with her, but only after he and Graham had exchanged long gazes promising violence.

Iona and Eric were pulled into the circles of dancing Shifters, finding themselves in the midst of laughing, shouting— and growling and howling—males and females of all three Shifter species, in both human and Shifter form. Bears, wolves, and wildcats surrounded her, but Iona was with Eric, his hand on hers like a secure tether, and she wasn't afraid.

She let herself be swept up in the celebration, very aware of Eric's hard body by her side, and of her rising mating frenzy.

Misty found Graham sitting by himself on top of a picnic table in the middle of Shiftertown, a little way from the uproar that was filling the place.

She'd arrived to find the streets beyond the gates deserted but heard the commotion behind the houses. She'd parked her large black pickup on a quiet side street, then walked the rest of the way to see what was going on.

She'd found what looked like a free-for-all bacchanalia— wild animals writhing around each other and with tall humans, some of the humans clothed, others naked, men and women alike. Music blared up and down the yards. Misty had realized, after the first few freaked-out moments, that they were *dancing*.

Graham had been easy to spot sitting on the table, surveying everyone like a god, a bottle of beer held loosely in his hands. Though the other Shifters pretty much ignored her,

Graham saw Misty coming—she felt his gaze on her all the way across the revelry.

Misty hopped up and sat next to him, for the first time nervous about being near him. Too bad, because she liked him. Graham was a big, tough guy with bad-boy appeal, but when she looked into his strong face and winter gray eyes, she saw a man who had to make hard decisions and hid his emotions behind harsh words.

There were two kinds of leaders, Misty had learned—the bullies that pumped themselves up by belittling others and those who were men good at command. The first were weak, the second strong. Graham, she sensed, was the second type. Misty's instincts about this were good, honed by growing up in neighborhoods where it was survival to tell the difference.

Graham McNeil had power. His large body exuded it, his huge muscles solid—no sagging flesh on this man.

"Hey," she said when he didn't say anything to her. "Am I crashing a party?"

"A mate blessing."

He watched her in quiet contemplation, his stare not letting her go.

"Mate blessing? What's that?"

"Male and female Shifter joining," Graham said. "Like human marriage, only better. The male in this case is the asshole Feline who beat me so bad the other night."

"And you came to his wedding?"

Graham made an indifferent gesture with his beer bottle. "It's a Shifter thing. We fight, we agree to hate each other, we move on. Everyone has a place, everyone knows what it is."

"That's good. I guess. Better than having to fight your way out your door every morning."

His gaze fixed on her even harder. "You're talking from experience."

"Grew up in a bad neighborhood in Los Angeles. This is better. Las Vegas is Sin City to some, but for me, it was a fresh start."

Graham listened, all his awareness on her. When she fell silent again, he said, "What are you doing here? In Shiftertown? Today?"

She shrugged, doing her best to be offhand. "I was talking

about getting a tattoo. Remember—you suggested I come to Shiftertown and find you when I made up my mind? You'd take me to the best artist, you said. I'd like your opinion on the design too."

Graham finally looked away from her. He moved his gaze to the couple in the center of the crowd, a tall man who knew how to move his body in the dance, and a black-haired woman with a garland of flowers on her head. Red gerbera daisies and white roses, woven with a red ribbon. Good choice.

When Graham spoke again, his words were clear. "The thing about Shifters, sweetheart, is that we're very good at knowing when people are lying." His gaze switched to her again, skewering her all the way through. "And you, sweet baby, stink of lies."

CHAPTER TWENTY-FIVE

Fear licked down Misty's spine, a primal terror felt by small animals when a huge wolf had them in his sights.

He can't hurt you, she told herself. *Shifters wear Collars to keep them under control.* Sure. Graham looked like that Collar totally controlled him. And he'd told her he'd been in a fight with the thing on him.

"You're right," Misty said, her throat dry. "I suck at lying. A guy called Kellerman is blackmailing me to spy on you. You heard of him?"

"You know I have."

"Actually, I don't know anything at all. I'd never met him before, or any Shifters before you either. He thinks you're up to something and need to be watched."

"He's right about that." Graham fixed her with unblinking gray eyes. "He shouldn't trust me. He's doing something underhanded, and I'm going to find out what and stop him."

"I don't want to be in the middle of this."

"You're already in the middle of it, sweetie. This is what happens when humans talk to Shifters."

Graham took one of her hands between his. His hands were gigantic, Misty's swallowed in them, but his touch was incredibly gentle.

"How did he convince you to come here?" Graham asked. "By the look on your face, you didn't decide he was wonderful and wise and deserved your obedience."

"No way in hell. My brother is in prison and up for parole. Kellerman said he'd block Paul's chances if I didn't help him."

"Dickhead. Why is your brother in prison?"

Misty didn't like talking about it, but under Graham's stare, her tongue loosened, and the words came out.

"When Paul was eighteen, he and his friends stole a car. To go joyriding, that's all. They were drunk and out to have fun. They got into an accident, and the people in the other car were killed. Paul was tried for grand theft and manslaughter and given twenty years."

"Is that a lot for a human?"

"More than the situation called for. Paul wasn't driving. He was in the backseat, and he didn't break into the car either. His friends did that. The kid who was driving was killed too, and the prosecutor came down hard on Paul and the friend that survived. The people in the other car were rich and prominent, and their family had a lot of influence. The judge decided to make an example of Paul. One stupid mistake, and Paul pays with twenty years of his life. But he's up for parole and maybe early release. Kellerman says he has influence, and that if I don't help him, he'll make sure Paul stays there for the whole sentence. So here I am. I can't jeopardize my brother's chance to get away from the gangs who beat him up every day. He needs to come home."

Graham listened without moving. No change of expression, no nodding. It was like talking to a statue, except for his watchful eyes.

When Misty finished, Graham said, "Don't worry about Kellerman. When Eric and I are done with him, he won't be able to influence a traffic light. But here's what you do: You run back to Kellerman and tell him some good dirt on me. We'll make something up. And then *you* tell *me* everything you can about Kellerman."

"Be a double agent, you mean?" That sounded dangerous but preferable to Kellerman having a hold over her.

"Sure." Graham ran his thumb over the inside of her wrist, a tickle of heat on her skin. "And I'll help you pick out a tatt."

"I'm so sorry about this," Misty said. "When I saw you at the bar, this is not what I meant to happen. I just wanted to talk to you."

Graham's callused thumb moved across her wrist again. "Why did you?"

"You looked interesting. And in pain. And lonely."

Graham stared down at her, and Misty again tried to read what was in his face. A powerful man might take what she'd just said as an insult.

Graham cupped Misty's cheek, turned her face up to his, and kissed her.

It was a slow, strong kiss that promised a multitude of pleasure. His lips were firm, opening hers without concern. He tasted faintly of the beer he'd drunk and more of himself, the bite of maleness Misty hadn't experienced in a long, long time.

When he released her, Misty struggled for breath. "What was that for?"

"You look interesting," he said, his face straight. "And in pain. And lonely."

"I am. The last two."

"Then sit here with me awhile," Graham said.

She shouldn't. Misty needed to get back to the shop and help her employees fill orders, talk to the wedding party for Saturday, make sure they were stocked with emergency bridal bouquets—this was Las Vegas, after all.

"Yes, all right," she said.

Misty gazed across the yards to where the woman danced, twirled by another Shifter, while the man laughed. Yes, she was surrounded by crazed animals and naked people, but they didn't take away from how the man and woman gazed at each other. That was what happiness looked like.

Graham's body was warm beside her, his hand strong over hers. Misty wasn't sure where this would go, but for now, she'd enjoy it. Snatch happiness where it's found, she'd learned. Happiness dissolved all too soon.

"I thought the mating ceremony would make my mating frenzy go away," Iona said as the music slowed. "But I'm still hungry."

Eric wrapped his arms around her and swayed into her warmth. "The mating ceremony increases it, love. There's only one way to conquer the frenzy."

He read the heat in her eyes. "Too bad all these people are here."

"They're busy." Eric scooped Iona up into his arms, her loose skirt fluttering.

"Eric, wait . . ."

Iona trailed off as the Shifters started to cheer. They knew exactly where Eric was taking her and what they'd do when they got there.

The cheer grew as Eric carried Iona from the circle and back to his house. The Shifters broke into laughter, applause, louder music, and more raucous shouting as Eric and Iona disappeared inside.

Eric took Iona to Jace's bedroom, laid her on the bed, and closed the blind against the bright afternoon and the crowd outside.

"I'm barely keeping it in, love," he said, ripping off his boots.

Iona lay back, so sweetly waiting for him, his dark-haired beauty, her clothes mussed and hair tousled. The garland of daisies and roses had fallen halfway over one blue eye.

Eric fumbled with the buttons of his shirt, fingers shaking. To hell with it. He ripped the shirt open, buttons pinging to the floor, while Iona laughed at him. He peeled off the shirt and T-shirt underneath, then got out of his jeans.

He liked how Iona's gaze went to him as the underwear came off, her eyes taking in his cock standing straight out, dark and hard. Her eyes changed to her Shifter's as she got to her knees, reaching across the bed for him.

Oh, yes. Iona's hot hands closed around his cock, tugging him closer. Eric lifted the garland gently from her head and tossed it to the nightstand, then he ran his hand through her silken black hair. He tugged open the catches of her shirt, spreading it apart.

She wore a bra underneath, a white slash of lace. Eric sprang the hook, and Iona heaved a sigh of relief.

"I hate wearing bras anymore," she said. "They chafe. They never used to."

Iona had to release Eric's cock so he could pull the lace from her warm breasts. He didn't mind, because he could catch the weight of her breasts in his hands. Her skin was so smooth, like the finest satin.

"Your panther doesn't want to be fettered," he said.

"I suppose in the wild, you always went naked?"

"No way in hell. Scottish winters were cold."

"Winters here are warm," she pointed out.

"Doesn't mean we can't cuddle up."

Eric undid the button on Iona's skirt as he pushed her backward to the mattress. He tugged off the skirt, then the panties, and then she was bare for him.

He wanted to pause to look at her, taking in Iona's beautiful nudity against the sheets, her full breasts, flat belly, her twist of hair between her thighs. He wanted to look his fill of her half-closed blue eyes, her sultry smile, the black hair spread across his pillow.

But his need called to him. He craved her, needed to fill his mouth with her taste. Eric hooked her knees over his arms, spread her legs, and lowered himself to drink of her.

Iona groaned with pleasure as he licked and drank the honey between her thighs. The scent and heat and taste of her stirred the frenzy higher, and Eric let the madness come.

He filled his himself with her goodness, teasing her tight berry until she was squirming, lifting her hips from the bed. He licked some more, washing the sensitive skin with his tongue, then Eric lifted himself up, slid up the length of her, and entered her in one stroke.

Wildness spiraled through him as he thrust once, twice, and again, and again. Iona's hot sheath squeezed him, wet and tight, the sensation erotic as hell.

This time, at least, he was loving her in a soft bed, not on the back of a couch, the floor, or a mat of pine needles. The leopard in him remembered the satisfaction of being with her panther in the stark cold of the woods. The clouded memory sent excitement through him, and he thrust that excitement into her.

"Eric."

The moaned word made him crazy. Eric increased his speed, holding her down, loving how her legs twined his and urged him on.

Forever, my Iona. Forever.

He heard snarls come from his throat and her answering cries. He saw the feral beast in her eyes and felt his in himself. Collars couldn't tame him, and would never tame her. They'd go wild together.

Iona's claws were in his back, tearing his skin. He growled at her, and she made a snarling noise in return. She was losing control, and right now, Eric didn't care.

Being inside her erased every worry he had, every empty space, every fear, every doubt. There was only Iona, and this room, and the heat between them. He would love her until they couldn't move, and then they'd sleep, then they'd love again.

The afternoon sun had reached its highest point by the time Eric hit his climax, spilling his seed in her while Iona bit and licked his shoulder. His back would be a mess, but so what? Shifters healed quickly.

Eric rolled over, pulling Iona on top of him, and they slept for a short time. They woke when the sun started to sink, and Iona smiled down at Eric before she wriggled herself onto his cock.

He held her there while she rode him, the lovemaking less frenzied this time. Iona's eyes closed to slits, her smile sexy as hell. Sweat slid between them, and the round of her breasts moved sweetly against his hands.

Iona lay down on him when they finished and fell asleep with him still inside her.

When they woke again, it was fully dark. The party outside still raged—Shifters loved a good party.

Eric and Iona pulled on a few clothes and crept out to the kitchen, where they raided the refrigerator and carried the food back to the bedroom to satisfy their hunger.

Energy restored, the frenzy returned. Eric shoved the plates and boxes off the bed, flipped Iona facedown on it, and pulled her hips back toward him. The leopard in him liked this—*the natural way*—as he entered her from behind. Eric the human only felt Iona around him, heard her cries of delight, felt her move on him as she squirmed against the bed.

They ended up with Iona flat on the mattress, Eric on her back, his whole body covering her.

They loved like that until they fell asleep again. When they woke the next time, Eric rolled over with her, and started loving her once more.

The mating frenzy, a cool voice said in the back of his brain. *Nature's way of ensuring the continuance of the species.*

Shut up, Eric responded, then heard nothing but Iona's cries and his own, as their loving went on into the night.

In the first light of morning, Iona peeled open her eyes to find Eric facedown next to her. He lay on top of the covers, his face relaxed in sleep.

Eric was a beautiful man. Liquid bronze skin covered a body of sculpted muscle, his waist tapering to a tight, bare backside. The tattoo that covered his shoulder and trailed down his arm invited her tongue, the scratches on his back testimony to her frenzy last night.

She moved to stretch and stifled a groan. Every muscle was sore, her mouth raw from Eric's wild kisses.

Life with a Shifter. Exhausting.

And yet, something within Iona had relaxed, a tightness dissolving. She'd spent her life up to this point knowing she was different and would never fit in, no matter what she did. She'd learned to pretend, to act human enough that she made it through school and college, enough so she didn't concern her mother and sister.

Then Eric had come into her life. He'd told her bluntly that she was denying her Shifter side, and he'd been right.

This man wanted her to explore that forbidden part of her—all of it. Iona had been terrified at first, but she knew that she was perfectly safe learning about her Shifter self, because Eric was with her to guide and protect her.

She could do any Shifter thing she wanted, while Eric watched, ready to catch her if she started to fall.

Iona ran her hand down Eric's back to his firm buttocks, his skin smooth. If learning to be Shifter involved touching his naked body, she'd just have to live with that.

She snuggled down a little closer to him as he went on sleeping. Her fingers drifted over his fine ass and back to his tattoo, lightly tracing the lines. She let her eyes close, as close to contentment as she'd ever been in her life.

Iona jumped awake to someone pounding on the bedroom door. The sun was high now, hours having gone by. Eric was up and on his feet.

"What?" he called irritably.

"Dad, it's Cass." Jace's voice was agitated and breathless. "The cub is coming, and Cass wants Iona."

CHAPTER TWENTY-SIX

The cub is coming.

Iona dressed in record time, Eric right behind her. Iona charged out to find Cass in the kitchen in sweatpants and T-shirt, hanging on to the breakfast bar while she leaned over it, her breath coming in slow gasps.

Diego wasn't there, having already departed for his office, Jace said, but he was on his way back.

"Iona," Cassidy panted.

"I'm here." Iona put her hands on Cassidy's shoulders and nearly jerked away. Cassidy's skin was roasting hot through the shirt. "You okay?"

"Except for being about to drop a cub in the kitchen? Fine."

"You're hot."

"Supposed to be." She looked up, her eyes full of both fear and excitement. "Say you'll come, Iona. I need someone with me besides a bunch of males."

"Hear the gratitude," Jace said.

Eric was already out of the house, starting up Iona's pickup.

"Time to go," Jace said. "Diego will have to meet you at the clinic."

"Probably a good idea," Cassidy said, her voice nearly a whisper. "Iona?"

Iona thought about how Nicole had looked both glad and apprehensive when she'd confirmed that Iona had been right about her pregnancy. Cassidy's scent conveyed the same kind of happy worry—and that this cub was on its way.

Iona kissed Cassidy's burning cheek. "Of course I'll come. I've got you."

Cassidy looked relieved that Iona walked out with her, though Iona was uncertain how effective her help would be. Iona had been very young when Nicole had come along, and she was certainly no expert on children—let alone Shifter cubs.

But she could be a friendly face and a hand to hold. Iona slid into the middle of the truck's cab next to Eric, and Jace helped Cassidy wedge herself into the seat. Jace leapt gracefully into the truck bed behind them, and Eric gunned the pickup into the street.

"Where are we going?" Iona asked.

"Clinic," Eric said, as they shot down the road. Other Shifters seemed to figure out what was up, because they came out of houses, waving and looking excited. Eric acknowledged them with a return wave as they raced through Shiftertown and out the gates.

"A clinic?" Iona prompted.

"One that will help Shifters," Eric said. "Not state-of-the-art, but better than nothing. We'll have doctors and nurses standing by in case anything goes wrong."

"I hate doctors," Cassidy muttered.

"So do I," Eric said, "but they can help if we need them to, and they have antibiotics and things."

"And epidurals," Iona said.

"It doesn't hurt that much," Cassidy said. "Except I want to shift, *so bad*."

"Don't," Eric said. "Your cub will come out human, so stay human."

"Why will her cub come out human?" Iona asked.

Cassidy answered, her words breathy. "Pure Shifters are born animal and learn to shift later. Half-human Shifters are born human. Mixed species come out whichever species happens to have the dominant gene."

"What will my cubs come out as?" Iona asked. "He or she will be three-quarters Shifter."

"Hell if I know," Eric said. "But I guess we'll find out." He sounded smug.

"You won't have long to wait," Cassidy said with a laugh, "the way you two were going at it last night."

Iona's face went hot. "It's too soon to tell, isn't it?"

Cassidy glanced at her with the same knowledge in her eyes Iona knew she'd had when she'd sensed Nicole's baby. "It's not. This time next year, we'll have two cubs in the house."

Iona realized she was right. Too many distractions—and maybe a little denial—had prevented her from acknowledging what her panther knew to be true. "Crap," Iona whispered.

Eric laughed. "Yes!" he shouted. He stomped on the accelerator, and they shot through the streets to his whoops of joy.

The clinic, only a few miles away, was so ordinary that Iona had to ask if they were in the right place. Jace grabbed someone with a wheelchair in the front, and he wheeled Cassidy inside a fairly generic clinic full of staff in scrubs or neat uniforms.

Shane and Brody walked in, followed closely by a wild-eyed Diego and his brother, as well as Neal the Guardian with his broadsword strapped to his back. Iona understood why Cassidy had begged her to be there. A Shifter birth was an Event, apparently, and everyone attending was male.

The staff of the clinic seemed to be used to the entourage that accompanied a Shifter mother about to bring in a cub, because they let the group into a large room upstairs in the back without question.

This was a delivery room, Iona saw when Jace wheeled Cassidy in. A delivery table waited in the exact center of the room, leaving plenty of space for family and friends to surround the mother. The walls were lined with counters and cabinets, one with a large sink. A sagging vinyl sofa had been shoved under the one window, the only seat.

Iona started for the delivery bed to make sure Cassidy would be comfortable, but Eric's hand on her shoulder stopped her. The Shifters hung back, waiting for Neal to approach the bed first.

Neal drew the Sword of the Guardian, touched it to the mattress, and said, "Goddess, mother of all, attend our sister as she brings strength to her pride."

The other Shifters responded: "We give our sister into the hands of the Goddess."

Not the most reassuring of prayers. But Iona thought about Eric's and Cassidy's tales of how Shifter women often didn't survive childbirth. In the past, they must have believed that all they could do was let the Goddess decide whether she lived or died.

Eric squeezed Iona's shoulder. Iona would be in this room herself sooner or later, if Cassidy was right. Next year, they'd be saying the prayer for her.

Iona went to Cassidy's side as Diego lifted her onto the bed. "If the pain gets too bad," Iona said, "swear at all the men. My mother said that helps."

Cassidy laughed weakly. "Sure thing."

Diego held Cassidy's hand after he settled her, not looking happy at all the Shifters around them. He didn't argue, but he obviously didn't like it.

Iona understood further why when the males, including Xavier, formed a ring around Cassidy, then, as one, turned their backs to her, standing like sentinels around her.

"What are they doing?" Iona asked.

"Guarding me." Cassidy winced and touched her abdomen. "All the males of the clan form a ring around the female when she's giving birth, to keep predators away, which includes other Shifters who might try to steal the woman and the cub. These days the pride plus friends of the family guard the female."

"You expect predators in the clinic?" Iona asked Eric's back.

"It's tradition," he said without turning around.

"Or Cassidy might want to be alone with her husband. I mean, her mate."

Cassidy gave Iona a wan smile. "Give up. The ritual has

been going on for centuries. They'll stand there until this cub comes, whether I like it or not."

"Or I could always tase them," Diego growled.

Iona left Cassidy to walk around Eric. She looked up at the stubborn light in his green eyes and understood that he participated in the ritual from instinctive fear, his need to protect his sister.

"Eric, how much power do I have in Shiftertown now, as your mate?"

His gaze shifted slightly. "A lot."

"Enough to speak for all the females in Shiftertown?"

"The ones who want you to, sure," he said guardedly.

"Then on their behalf . . ." She rose on tiptoe and kissed Eric lightly on the lips. "Stand the guards outside the doors and let Cassidy have a little peace."

"Hmm," Eric said. "Not have my trackers in the room?"

"Diego's here, and he's pretty good at guarding. I'll stay, if Cass wants me to, and she might concede to have you here too. There are two doors into this room, both of which can be defended from the outside, can't they?"

Eric relaxed his stance and looked almost amused. "It will be a scandal, love. The old-guard Shifters will pass out when they learn my sister didn't have a ring of protectors two feet away when she dropped her cub."

"We can throw cold water on them," Iona said. "Please, Eric?"

Eric studied her, and Iona looked straight back at him.

"Shane, Neal, guard outside the rear door," Eric said. "Brody, Jace, Xav, the front. I'll stay in here and liaise."

Iona mouthed, *Thank you.* Eric returned her light kiss. "You're a radical."

"I hope so."

Eric gave her a deeper kiss, then went out the front door. The other Shifters, looking surprised but a bit relieved not to have to be in the actual birthing room, left as well. Xav paused to kiss Cassidy's cheek and clap his brother on the shoulder. "Good luck," he said to Diego.

"This is why I want you here," Cassidy said to Iona as Xav followed the others out. "The female voice of reason. That

and I just feel better with you around." She stopped and
sucked in a loud breath. "Oh, not long now."

I ona still felt a bit intrusive as the morning wore on, but Cassidy seemed relaxed and happy with her there. Cassidy had
nowhere to lie but the table, but she didn't appear to mind.
Diego pulled up a chair next to her, and their clasped hands
rested on her belly as they talked to each other in low voices.

Eric returned. He held Iona in the circle of his arms on the
vinyl sofa under the window, the two of them cuddling while
they waited.

"Is it always like this?" Iona whispered to him. "Why
won't they at least let her have a bed until it's time?"

"Shifters are allowed this room, no others," Eric said. "I've
attended many births here—which is a good thing, love."

"I'll be fine," Cassidy said from across the room. Iona still
wasn't used to Shifter hearing, which could pick up a whispered word at a hundred feet. "Eric and you are here, Diego's
with me, and I have guards outside the door. The cub will
come, and we'll go home and have another party."

"After you rest," Diego said sternly.

"Hey, I'm robust."

"Have you picked out a name?" Iona broke in.

"Amanda Kirsten," Cassidy said promptly.

"If it's a girl," Diego said. "If it's a boy, Carlos Robert,
after my father and hers."

"Nice," Iona said.

"It's a girl," Cassidy said with conviction. "But I guess
we're going to find out." She sucked in another deep breath,
then let out a wail.

Iona was on her feet. Cassidy pushed Diego's hand away
and fought to get up and turn over on her hands and knees.
She wailed again.

"Call the doctor," Iona said frantically to Eric.

"No," Cassidy said. "No doctor. Not unless something's
wrong."

"I'd be happier, Cass . . ." Diego began, his face damp with
nervous perspiration.

"We've been over this, Diego. I do it myself. Eric."

"I've got you. Iona, help her undress. Diego, stand over here with me. We guard, and the females do the work."

Cassidy managed a laugh. "Isn't that typical? It's all right, Iona. I know what to do. I'll tell you, and you'll help me."

Diego did not want to leave her side. He scowled until Eric came to him, took him by the shoulders, and pulled him across the room to face the front door.

"Our job is to guard," Eric said to him. "We don't let anyone near her. You start protecting your cub *now*."

"The males say they turn their backs because that's the tradition," Cassidy said to Iona. "Really, it's because they're squeamish."

Iona didn't smile as she helped Cassidy out of her pants, top, and underwear. Naked, Cassidy climbed to her hands and knees again.

"Everything you need is over there," Cassidy said, gesturing at the longest of the counters.

Iona followed her direction and found a large basin, towels, and some scary-looking surgical instruments. She put everything on a cart and wheeled it over to Cassidy, feeling ineffectual.

"You really should have a doctor or a midwife," Iona said.

"I *am* a midwife. I've assisted in quite a few Shifter births. Now, hold me steady and don't let me fall. It's going to be tough. I wish I could shift."

"Hang in there, Cass," Eric said without turning around.

Iona took a deep breath and put her arm around Cassidy's bare back. "It's all right. I'll help." Iona knew, as soon as she said it, that she could.

"Thanks." Cassidy's smile was laced with pain. "You'll make a good alpha."

Iona gave Cassidy the barest squeeze. That remained to be seen.

Cassidy groaned again, the groan ending on another sharp cry. "I think she's coming."

Iona skimmed her hand down Cassidy's back. Cassidy had dilated quite a bit, though Iona saw nothing on its way.

"Help me," Cassidy moaned. "This stupid table is for humans, damn it."

Iona helped Cassidy spread her knees, making sure she

didn't fall off the narrow table. Iona then got towels ready and hoped she didn't have to touch the gleaming instruments.

If anything went wrong enough for Iona to have to even *think* about grabbing an instrument, she was getting a doctor, to hell with Shifter tradition. Iona would not let Cassidy or her cub die on her watch.

Iona rubbed Cassidy's back and hips. "You're doing good, Cass."

"Hope so."

"I'm right here. Not going anywhere."

"Thank you."

The whisper ended in another cry of pain. Cassidy rocked her hips, her body shuddering, then suddenly, her skin became a leopard pelt, her hands, claws.

"No!" Iona shouted. "Cassidy, don't shift."

"Keep it together, Cass," Eric called, and Iona heard Diego swearing in Spanish.

Cassidy shuddered again, and then she was human. "She's coming!"

This time, Iona saw it, the head of a child coming from Cassidy's birth canal. Iona had never seen a baby be born, and she'd feared she'd freak out and run when Cassidy's cub actually started coming. But when Iona saw the top of the baby's head, something inside her changed.

A new life, a new beginning, a cub struggling to take its place in the world. That cub needed help, and Iona wasn't about to run away and abandon it.

"Come on, little one," she said. "You can do it."

"Do you see her?" Cassidy asked, excited.

"Yes, she's on her way." Iona wanted to cheer, to urge the cub on. *Come on, girl!*

Cassidy wailed again, the sound winding into a shriek. Iona spread the towels and reached for the cub as her head slid out. For some reason, Iona knew exactly what to do—not the human in her, but the Shifter.

"One more, Cass. You can do it."

Cassidy screamed. Diego cried, "Fuck this!" and Iona heard his harried footfalls as he ran back to the table.

At the same time the cub, a human baby, slid into Iona's hands.

Diego's face nearly blotted out the baby Iona struggled to hold as he looked with great shock at his daughter. Then Eric was there, clearing the infant's nose. The little one inhaled her first breath and blared her unhappiness to the world.

Cassidy turned, the cord still stretching from her to the cub. "Amanda," she said.

She sounded so sure. "Yep," Iona said in a choked voice. "It's a little girl."

"See?" Cassidy said to Diego, whose dark eyes streamed tears as he touched Amanda's face. "I knew it was a girl." And Cassidy reached to gather her into her arms.

Diego came over all fierce as soon as little Amanda was cleaned up, Cassidy nursing her, and went out to bully the staff into giving Cassidy a bedroom where she could rest. Cassidy protested that she was fine to go home, but when Diego and Eric got her to the back bedroom the clinic finally allowed them to use, she drooped.

Iona and Eric left Diego and Cass to be alone with their child, and went to celebrate with the other Shifters who waited in the lobby. Jace, all smiles, kept breaking into a gyrating dance. Because he was as handsome as his father at thirty years old, the nurses at the front desk enjoyed feasting their eyes on him.

Iona's eyes were filled with tears. "That was so wonderful."

Eric held her close, kissing the top of her head. Shane and Brody fell into teasing each other and laughing, loudly, the bear brothers excited. Bringing in a cub—successfully, with mother and cub alive and well—was a cause for great celebration.

Diego came down after a time to report that Cassidy and the baby were sleeping. He looked wrung out, triumphant, radiantly happy, and exhausted. Xavier put an arm around him and declared that Diego could use a drink.

Cassidy had asked for Iona before she'd fallen asleep, and Iona gladly went back upstairs. Shane, Brody, and Jace stayed as honorary guards, while Eric said it was his task to go back to Shiftertown and spread the glad news. Neal went with him, his usually taciturn face bathed in smiles, the Guardian happily not needed today.

Upstairs, the nurses had rolled a baby bed next to Cassidy's so Cass could be near Amanda while they slept. Iona lay in an armchair, her feet over one of its arms, drowsing in the warmth of the room, the curtains pulled closed against the sunshine.

Iona didn't mean to sleep, but she jumped awake into sudden silence, knowing someone had entered the room.

Her Shifter nose told her it wasn't Diego or Eric or even another Shifter. She began to swing up from the chair, ready to fight.

Her hand contacted a human man hovering over her in the dim light, but though the man grunted in pain, Iona felt the prick of a needle in her skin, and her limbs suddenly stopped working.

Iona tried to shout to Cassidy, but the floor rushed up to her, and blackness closed in. The last thing Iona saw was a man in a white mask bending over Cassidy and Amanda, and then nothing.

CHAPTER TWENTY-SEVEN

Iona drifted to wakefulness, stiff, sore, and angry, though she didn't remember why she was angry. She also didn't remember the beds in Eric's house being so uncomfortable.

No, she seemed to be on a chair. Had she fallen asleep in the living room? But even those chairs weren't as uncomfortable as this one.

Then Iona remembered—she was at the clinic with Cassidy. She'd dozed off in an armchair while Cassidy and baby Amanda snoozed across the room. Then someone had come in . . .

The panther in her came wide awake, though Iona kept her eyes closed. The memory of the wrong scent, the human bending over her, then the prick of a needle had her Shifter as alert as a predator spotting elusive prey.

Iona stretched her other senses without opening her eyes, not wanting to alert whoever had attacked her that she was awake again.

The scent of this room was different from Cassidy's room in the clinic. That one had borne the overlapping hospital scents of antiseptic, people, and the faint, faraway odor of urine. This room was dusty and dry, and the tickle of rust spores touched her nose.

Iona also scented Cassidy lying nearby and heard her breathing. That was a relief.

What she did not scent was the powdery, new-baby smell of Amanda.

Iona sensed no one else—not human or Shifter—and she risked opening her eyes a crack.

The only light came from a window high in the wall that showed a patch of twilit sky. The dim light revealed that she was in another hospital room, but one that looked as though it hadn't been used in a long time.

Cassidy lay on what looked like a gurney, her arms and legs unnaturally stiff. Iona saw why as her Shifter sight adjusted to the light—Cassidy's wrists and ankles were locked down with metal cuffs. A bag of clear liquid hung on a stand next to Cassidy, an IV drip snaking into her arm. Iona definitely didn't like that.

No one else seemed to be in the room or even outside it. Iona strained to listen, but her Shifter hearing picked up nothing beyond the door. Either the hallway was deserted, or the room was well soundproofed.

Iona had been tied to the metal and plastic chair on which she sat, but with ordinary rope. The rope was cheap, its prickly, synthetic fibers chafing her wrists, but it was strong.

Not strong enough for a Shifter, however.

They still think I'm human. A normal human might not be able to extricate herself from the bonds, but a Shifter easily could.

The panther within her urged caution. If their captors believed Iona to be human, of minimal danger to them, she needed to let them keep on thinking that.

Iona scanned the room for webcams or other cameras or listening devices. She saw nothing, but that didn't mean they weren't cleverly hidden.

The room grew darker, night coming quickly in the winter desert. Iona contained her impatience and waited as the sun continued its descent.

No lights came on when the last of the sunlight winked out. Iona waited another five minutes, making herself count every second, until at last she sat in full darkness.

Think of the form you want to be, then be it.

Iona pictured her limbs becoming those of her panther, slender and strong. She suppressed the growl in her throat as her arms and legs changed, black fur emerging over flesh.

She spread her front paws. The plastic ropes stretched, then slackened enough for Iona to easily slip out. Her dainty panther paws also slid quickly out of the ropes that bound her feet.

Iona closed her eyes again and willed herself back to human. Leaning over, she slipped her shoes on and leveraged herself silently from the chair.

She had three goals—wake and free Cassidy, find Amanda, and contact Eric. Eric would already be coming, once he and Diego discovered the abduction. She had no doubts that the two men would tear apart the town trying to find them. They'd have an easier time if Iona could figure out where she and Cassidy were and let Eric know.

A quick check told her that their captors had taken the small purse Iona had snatched up when going with Cassidy to the clinic. That meant they had her phone and wallet with her driver's license and all her credit cards. Oh well, more proof that she was human.

The room had no phones, not that Iona had expected one. She couldn't spot any outlets for phone lines, which was unusual in a building that looked as though it had been constructed at least in the eighties, maybe earlier.

Iona made her way to Cassidy and, without bothering to figure out what was in the drip bag, untaped the needle in Cassidy's arm and tugged it out. Whatever they were feeding her, it couldn't be good.

Cassidy drew a long breath, then her eyes opened, and she jumped, her limbs still tethered to the table.

"Shh." Iona touched her shoulder. "Be quiet. They might be listening."

Cassidy drew another breath, which broke on a sob. "They took Amanda. I couldn't stop them before they tranqed me. They took my cub." Tears trickled from her eyes.

"We'll find her, I swear to you. Are you all right?"

"I will be, once I kill the humans who took my cub."

Iona patted her shoulder. "Sounds like you're all right,

then." She touched the metal cuff on Cassidy's wrist. "Can you shift and slide out of that?"

"It's tight."

Cassidy closed her eyes and, as Iona had, let her hands and feet change to those of her wildcat. The cuffs, however, were small enough to clamp down on her slender cat's limbs, and too strong for Cassidy or Iona to break them.

Cassidy changed back to human, letting out a sigh. "They must be designed to contain Shifters. They knew what they were doing."

Iona figured out how to turn off the drip from the bag, then she laid the needle under the crook of Cassidy's arm. "Stay still and pretend to be unconscious. I'm going to look for Amanda."

Cassidy's eyes shone with fear in the darkness "Goddess, Iona. I can't just lie here."

Iona leaned over her, putting her hands on Cassidy's shoulders. How did Eric do it, soothe away fears when he was afraid himself? Iona gently caressed her new sister-in-law, meeting Cassidy's terrified gaze.

"I promise you, I won't stop until I've found her. And I'll find a way to contact Eric. We'll get out of this and go home. All of us."

Cassidy looked no less afraid, but she gave Iona a faint smile. "You don't have to try to reassure me."

"I'm not reassuring you. I'm telling you. I will find Amanda and call Eric. If someone comes back, tell them I managed to get out of my ropes, but you don't know how. Or just pretend to be so groggy you don't know what's going on. Promise me, Cass."

Cassidy's eyes widened, but she seemed to strengthen under Iona's gaze. "I'm just not used to being the one who has to be rescued."

Iona kissed her forehead. "Consider it a chance to rest. I'll be back for you."

Cassidy didn't answer, but she looked grateful.

Iona studied the ropes still around the chair she'd vacated, changed one of her hands to her panther's paw, and used razor-sharp claws to slice through the bonds. With luck, their captors would think Iona had managed to cut her way out with a knife they'd overlooked. Then Iona took off her clothes and hid them.

She said another quiet good-bye to Cassidy and tried the handle of the one door to the room. It was locked, of course.

The door looked fairly new compared to the dinginess of the rest of the room. The door handle, likewise, was new and stout, locked with a key. A human being, unless very strong, probably couldn't do anything with that door.

Iona thought about her half-shifted self, which she hadn't liked becoming, because her Shifter mind and human mind had warred within her too much. She swallowed, willing herself to stay calm, and let herself become the half-human beast.

As soon as she flowed into that form, she wanted to stay in it. *Strong, I am so strong. Let those humans get in front of me, I dare them.*

She wanted to charge through the halls of wherever they were, find someone—anyone—and choke them until they told her where Amanda was. The cub was her niece, a child of her pride. Anyone who'd touched her would pay.

Iona grabbed the door handle with her half hand, half paw and twisted until the handle broke. She thrust her fingers into the resulting hole and pushed the lock mechanism with all her strength. The lock gave way, and the door silently opened.

Iona sniffed and listened to the hall beyond, but she heard nothing, smelled no one near. She crept out and closed the door, making sure the outer handle fitted back on so the door would appear, at first glance, to still be locked.

The panther was better for stealth, but Iona had a hard time convincing her in-between beast to change to it. She felt so powerful and clever in this state.

At last, the half beast conceded to flow into the panther. Iona was surprised how easy that shift was once she made up her mind, but she'd have to think about these things later. For now, she prowled the hall on silent feet, trying to figure out where she was.

She and Cassidy might have been taken to the compound in the desert that Iona and Eric had viewed from the ridge, the one to which Eric said they'd taken all the wolf Shifters. But this building looked larger and more solid, with a corridor running between rows of rooms. Iona might be in a regular hospital, albeit an old and disused one.

The only light came from windows in open rooms, where the moon was waxing to the full. Those windows were high in the walls, as was the one in Cassidy's room, which could indicate that they were in a basement.

Not necessarily, she knew. Older buildings in Las Vegas had used small windows under the eaves to protect against the summer heat. The junior high and high school Iona had attended hadn't had any windows at all.

At the end of the hall, she came upon what looked like an old nurses' station. If the station had ever had any phones, they were gone now. Iona would have to hunt down the humans who'd taken her cell phone and beat it out of them. That thought appealed to the beast.

First, she needed to find Amanda. The panther put her nose to work.

Iona found nothing alive on this floor but herself, Cassidy, a few nests of field mice, and some scuttling roaches. At least it was too cold for snakes and scorpions right now. In summer, this place was probably infested.

The vision of baby Amanda with insects crawling all over her spurred her on. Infants were fragile, and Amanda would need warmth, protection, food. Were their captors giving her that? Or was it already too late?

Iona forced such thoughts away. Focus. Find her.

Eric, please come. We need you.

Even thinking about Eric made Iona feel better. His name twined around her heart, giving her strength and comfort.

At the end of a hall was a door, unlocked, which led to a stairwell. Iona shifted to her in-between beast to open it, then stayed the half beast as she ducked inside and tested the stairwell's scents.

The stairs led down at least three floors, Iona thought, maybe more, and upward, maybe two or three. Iona stood there a long time in the darkness, trying to decide which direction was best. Upstairs might lead to light and a way out. Or she already might be on an upper floor, and upward would only take her to a roof.

At least she'd see where she was if she found the roof, she

reasoned, but another sniff made her change her mind. From the lower floors, she scented life, and it smelled fetid.

Rescuing Amanda was the first priority. Iona remained her half beast and moved quietly down the stairs.

She found that there were a total of five floors below her. The first level down was pitch-dark, and she smelled nothing there. Nothing on the next floor either, though the scent grew stronger, and she realized that it was coming from the bottom of the stairs.

Iona continued down, opening the last door on the stair-well very softly. As soon as she was through, she flowed back to her panther and moved in silence.

No lights shone down here, and the smell from the walls was more earthy—definitely underground. The corridor off the stairwell was short and ended in a door that opened, unlocked, into a wide space.

Iona couldn't see what was in that space as she slipped inside, opening the door only enough for her wildcat to slither through. She stopped, waiting to let her panther's eyes adjust.

Gradually, she saw the dim forms of square pillars, as though people had removed walls down here but left support-ing posts. Or perhaps this had once been a loading dock, garage, or storage area. It was empty now, the silence and cold vast.

The scent came from about halfway down the room. Iona slunk that way, her hackles up, paws making no noise on the cement floor. Against the wall, she found the cages.

She remembered Jace explaining how he'd seen jeeps tak-ing cages to the desert compound. Whether these were the same cages, Iona had no way of knowing, and Eric said he hadn't found them all when he'd gone in to rescue the wolves.

These cages were about five feet tall and three wide, a few of them six or so feet high. Large enough to contain Shifters, but even these cages would make for tight fits, especially to the larger Shifters, like bears or the bigger wildcats.

But what better way to keep a Shifter penned than give him or her barely enough room to turn around?

Or, Iona thought, a chill stealing through her, they were for smaller Shifters. The young.

She counted more than twenty cages stretching in front of her. She went down the line, the scent of animal growing stronger as she walked.

Each cage Iona passed was empty, until she came to the cage at the end.

This was one was about seven feet high, had thicker walls. The bars that closed it were at least six inches in diameter. Behind those bars was a snarl and a smell.

Iona backed away, her fur standing straight up, growls coming from her throat. She wanted to lie flat on her belly in a stalking-cat slink, teeth ready to rip out the throat of whatever was behind those bars.

The beast inside the cage growled in return. Iona saw eyes in the darkness, yellow with rage. The Shifter smell was strong but not quite right.

Iona forced her panther to calm. Whoever was in the cage was a Shifter, trapped, taken against its will. She should help it, not fear it.

But the waves of emotion that emanated from the cage had Iona's defensive instincts roaring. She shifted back to her in-between beast, the shift a little slower and more painful this time.

"It's all right," she said, her voice the guttural one of the beast. "Who are you? I can help you."

Another snarl of pure, aggressive rage. The yellow eyes flashed red and a body slammed into the bars of the cage.

Iona jumped back, but the cage held, which seemed to enrage the creature even more. It pressed its face to the bars and glared out at her.

Tiger.

Iona stared at the animal in surprise. Feline Shifters could be any wildcat or a combination of wildcats, each family tending toward the traits of one more than the others. Iona's father obviously had a lot of panther in him; Eric's family, snow leopard.

While in Shiftertown, Iona had met Felines whose wildcats resembled lions, lynxes, pumas, and one family of cheetahs, but no tigers. Cassidy sometimes looked after an orphaned cub who was a white tiger, but he was the only one.

This Shifter was a Bengal, orange and black striped, and gigantic. His scent was overwhelmingly male. No Collar gleamed around the tiger's neck, and his eyes held madness.

He'd gone feral.

Iona stared at him in horror, finally realizing what Eric had been trying to tell her would happen to her if she didn't control the beast within her. This was what he meant.

Crazed, furious, out of control, dangerous to herself and everyone around her.

Looking at the feral tiger in the cage, the untamed beast inside Iona tasted a tang of his madness and liked it.

Iona quickly shifted fully to human. "Who are you?" she asked again. "Did they capture you? Why don't you have a Collar?"

The tiger's face distorted, nose receding, eyes growing more human, but the Shifter settled into his half man, half beast form. "Let me out."

The pheromone scent that came to her was loud and clear. Crap. He was an uncontrolled Shifter male facing a female who'd recently entered her mating years and was a bit wild with the mating heat. He wanted her.

Iona took a few steps back. "And have you jump my bones? No, thank you. I smell what you want to do."

"I smell it on *you*. You want to mate. You want cubs."

"I have a mate. He's the leader of the Shifters. He'll help you."

"No one can help me." The words were matter-of-fact.

"Where's your Collar?" Iona asked.

The yellow eyes narrowed. "What collar?"

Interesting answer. "How long have you been in there?"

Surprise flickered in his eyes, as though he'd never considered it. "Always."

"Who captured you?"

"I was never captured," the tiger said. "I have always been here."

The chill in Iona's blood grew. "Where are the humans who run this place? They took a cub. I need to find her."

"A cub." The voice became sharp, more alert, more enraged. "Don't let them have the cub."

"I'm trying not to. Tell me how to find them."

The tiger went silent a moment, claws scratching the floor. "Let me out. I'll show you."

"How about you just tell me? I'll find the cub, and my mate, and he'll help you. Promise."

"No promises. Promises are lies."

Iona took one bold step toward the cage. She couldn't show fear. She had to calm him, to make him understand.

The dominance game, she understood with sudden clarity, wasn't about fighting. It was about making the challenger know what would happen if things came to a fight. Iona might be smaller than the tiger, but she had to prove that she was fast and strong, and smart enough to win.

"I'm not one of the humans who put you in here. I'll find the cub, with or without your help, and I'll come back for you. That's how it will be."

The tiger fixed her gaze with his crazed red one. Iona didn't flinch.

Staring him down was harder than staring down Shane or even Graham. But not tougher than facing Eric.

Eric, as calm and laid-back as he pretended to be, had dominance down to an art form. He didn't need to challenge anyone, because he knew he'd already won before the game even started.

Defiance in the face of Eric's will was almost impossible, but Iona had managed it. And she knew that if she could withstand Eric, she could withstand Tiger Man.

The battle took a long time though. Whoever this Shifter was, wherever he'd come from, he was a dominant.

The tiger didn't lower his gaze or turn away, but finally Iona sensed a minute change in his stance.

"They do experiments on the top floor," he said. "When they don't do them down here. But they wouldn't bring a cub down here with me."

Top floor it was, then. Iona hoped he wasn't sending her into a trap, but he didn't smell of lies.

"I'll make sure you get out too," Iona said. "What's your name?"

He hesitated for a long time, then finally said, "Twenty-three."

"That's not a name." Iona glanced back down the row of

empty cages. "What happened to numbers one through twenty-two?"

"They died. Now it's just me."

Iona met his gaze again, her fear of him changing to sympathy. "I'll come back for you," she repeated.

As though the conversation had become too much for him, the tiger shifted back into his huge wildcat, snarling breathily in his throat.

Iona became her panther again, finding it easier this time, and slunk back into the darkness.

CHAPTER TWENTY-EIGHT

"Tell me you've got a fix," Eric said for about the tenth time.

Xavier tapped keys on the keyboard in the offices of DX Security. "Getting there. A little quiet would help."

Diego was pacing the long room, his fingers fondling the handle of his Glock. He paced, Eric knew, to keep himself from ripping the computer out of Xavier's hands and trying to pull up the GPS data from Iona's cell phone himself.

Eric contented himself with standing over Xavier and breathing down his neck.

Shane had summoned Eric back to the clinic in a state of panic. Iona and Cassidy had disappeared, Shane said, little Amanda with them. Shane and Brody had scoured the clinic and bullied the staff, but the three were nowhere to be found. Jace had already headed out to the compound in the desert to search for them there.

Eric had been about to call Diego and break the news, when he and Xavier had returned from a restaurant near the clinic, where the brothers had celebrated Amanda's birth with beers and burgers.

Shane had been about to shit himself. He'd always had a thing for Cassidy, and now he blamed himself for losing her,

her baby, and Iona. He should have checked on them more often, he said. He'd let them down. He deserved to have Eric and Diego kick his grizzly ass.

Eric had interrupted this self-flagellation by saying in clipped tones that if Iona had her phone with her, they could track her through its GPS chip. Even if Iona couldn't use the phone, they could still find her, and Xavier knew how to get to that data.

"Won't help if they threw her phone away," Xavier had said glumly.

Eric answered, "Even finding out where they threw it away gives us a place to start."

"Here we go," Xavier said now from his computer. "Iona's phone is at these coordinates, which is roughly . . ." He brought up a map and entered the data. "Here." A red dot blossomed on the map in the middle of nothing.

Eric leaned to look and felt Diego crowding behind him. The dot was in empty desert, not at the compound they'd found, but farther north and west.

"That's Area Fifty-one," Diego said. "What the hell are they doing in Area Fifty-one?"

"Experiments," Eric said, his rage burning cold. "That's where they did the experiments on Shifters twenty years ago."

"The fuck they're going to experiment on Cassidy and my daughter."

"Or my mate," Eric said.

Xav broke in. "Diego, you can't take a posse up there. There's gates and guards and people with guns to shoot your ass as soon as they see it."

"They can't take my daughter hostage. I'll get every law enforcement official in the state of Nevada to make them let us in."

"No," Eric said, his eyes on the map. "I'll go in myself."

"To a top secret government facility?" Xavier asked, incredulous. "They have security cameras and guards happy to shoot you as soon as they see you. What does *authorized use of deadly force* mean to you? Trust me, I've studied their security—I study everyone's security—it's my job."

"You drop me off here." Eric pointed to a spot on Highway 95. "I'll go through the desert. It's dark now, and I'm very good at navigating terrain without being seen."

"It's a long way, and it's rough," Xavier said. "Mountains, canyons, dry lakes, you name it."

"Norway wasn't easy either, and this time I don't have bombs strapped to me."

Diego interrupted. "Fine for you getting in. But how are you going to get Iona and Cassidy out safely, with my daughter?"

"Reid."

Diego relaxed a little, but only a little. "Reid can only teleport to someplace he's seen."

"Which is why you're giving me a satellite phone and a camera and a way to send you photos with your state-of-the-art surveillance equipment. Show the photos to Reid, and he can get there." Eric hoped.

"Eric, this is my mate and daughter . . ."

"And when I need a helicopter and machine guns, I'll call you. There's no way you can keep up with me through the desert, no way you can sneak into wherever they are like I can. If you want to drive around to the front gate and create a distraction, be my guest. But I need someone to get the photos to Reid as soon as I send them."

"Diego, he's right," Xavier said. "It would take you too long to cross that country on foot, and any vehicle will be seen. Let him go. I'll take care of alerting Reid."

Diego's face was hard, but he gave Eric a nod. "Fine." He fingered his pistol again. "If you want a distraction, I'll give you a distraction."

"It's still a long way," Xavier said to Eric. "Straight through desert, no water. You sure you'll be okay?"

"I'll be just fine," Eric said.

The mate bond would pull him on. It was already urging him out the door, to run, run, run to Iona's side.

"Get me the equipment and let's go," Eric said. Every minute could be a minute too late.

"You got it," Xavier said. He managed a grin. "Say hi to the aliens for me."

U p, up, and up. Iona climbed eight floors, panting by the time she reached the top. She opened the door a crack, and finally found people.

Not many. She hadn't scented them in the stairwell—she'd smelled them only when she opened the door, which meant the doorway must be airtight. To keep germs out, she reasoned as she slunk inside.

This floor was a laboratory. While she'd found the lower floors to be old and cluttered, the lab here had state-of-the-art technology.

Rows of sealed, glassed-in cooling units marched down the room, each containing racks and racks of test tubes. Lab tables held glass-fronted exhaust hoods with gloves extending into them so people wouldn't have to put their bare hands onto whatever was inside. At the far end of the room, two people wearing white clean-room suits and surgical caps studied large flat-screen computer monitors.

Iona was bringing her panther germs and the dirt from the floors below into their pristine lab. Aw, wasn't that too bad?

Being a black cat against all this white was a decided disadvantage. Iona slunk from bench to bench, keeping low. The lab workers, fascinated by whatever was on their screens, never looked up and never saw her.

As Iona paused to decide what to do—rip into their bodies until they talked or question them calmly?—she heard Amanda cry.

The sound was faint, very weak, and would have been inaudible to a human. But Iona, Shifter and now a member of the cub's pride, heard her loud and clear.

Iona couldn't smell Amanda, which meant they had her sealed in someplace, like the hoods on the lab tables. She'd kill them.

The thought formed and grew, delighting the half-Shifter beast and panther. Even Iona the human wasn't alarmed. Killing these researchers for hurting Amanda sounded like a good idea.

Iona picked her way forward as far as she could as a panther, then silently rose into her human form—effortlessly this time. She took a small acetylene torch from a holder on one of the lab benches and walked forward on bare feet.

As she drew closer, she saw that the large computer screens nearly hid a small glass window behind them. The two researchers fixed their attention not on the window, but on the screens, which showed electronic scans of a baby. Amanda.

Amanda lay beyond the glass in a room where she was being X-rayed or MRI'd or whatever, and she was crying.

Iona turned on the acetylene torch, stepped forward, and aimed the stream of fire at one of the computer screens. It melted.

The researchers, a man and a woman, swung around. The woman screamed. The man said in shock, "What the hell?"

Neither looked like they were going to grab for her, so Iona melted the second computer monitor. Both were now nicely warped, useless hunks of plastic.

"Open up that room and take her out of there," Iona commanded.

"How did you escape?" the man asked, still staring. "Where are your clothes?" His gaze swiveled to Iona's breasts, his mouth dropping open. Some researcher he was.

"Robbie," the woman wailed.

"Don't worry," Robbie said. "She's not a Shifter. Call security."

Iona snarled. She morphed into her half-Shifter beast, swung the acetylene torch's canister, and smacked Robbie on the side of the head with it. Robbie's eyes rolled back, and he fell to the linoleum in a boneless heap.

The woman screamed again and dove for the red fire alarm on the wall. Iona got there before she did, smacked the woman out of the way, and slammed her fist against the base of the woman's skull. The woman slid silently downward, joining Robbie on the floor.

Iona set down the torch and fumbled to open the door imprisoning Amanda, praying it wasn't sealed by an electronic lock opened by the computers she'd just melted. But, no, the researchers were at least wise enough to have a door with an ordinary handle, which Iona nearly broke when she wrenched open the door.

She rushed inside the little booth, which had scanners surrounding the tiny baby on the table. Amanda's body was nearly covered with sticky nodes that attached multiple wires to her skin. She too was being fed an IV drip, the needle huge in the tiny arm into which it had been shoved.

Amanda was crying fretfully, a child alone, scared, and unhappy. Iona peeled the disks from the baby's skin and gently tugged the needle out of her arm. Amanda began to cry more strongly, and Iona swept her up.

Iona was still her half beast, but Amanda quickly snuggled against her soft fur. Her little mouth sought Iona's breasts, small in this between state, and Iona shook her head as she cuddled Amanda close.

"Sorry, little one, I don't have anything for you. But I'll take you to your mommy, all right?"

Amanda seemed to understand that things were looking up. She cried harder, but in irritation now, not in her too faint whimper of fear.

Iona could move faster as a panther, but she had to worry about carrying Amanda. She needed to make it to Cassidy quickly though, in case these two woke up and sounded the alarm, or in case their unconscious bodies were found by more researchers.

She glanced around for some kind of sash in which to sling Amanda. She found no handy towels or blankets—everything here was plastic or flimsy paper towels. She looked down at the woman in her clean suit and smiled in satisfaction.

Iona tore the woman's suit in half with her beast strength and pulled it away from her body. The woman wore shorts and a T-shirt beneath, the T-shirt with a glittering, sexy neckline, maybe to entice the breast-liking Robbie.

"You can do better than him, sweetie," Iona said, fashioning the pieces of the clean suit into a sling.

She wound the sling around her body and used it to hold Amanda securely against her belly. Iona cradled Amanda as she made her way out of the room, but she stopped when she noticed a niche near a dark window that held a familiar-looking purse and cell phone.

Iona snatched up her phone and began punching numbers. Then she made a noise of irritation when the phone gave a desultory beep. *No service.*

"You have got to be kidding me." Iona glared at the phone. "I am *so* changing my service provider."

She dropped the phone into her purse and wedged the

purse into the sling alongside Amanda. Iona checked the stairwell, heard nothing, and shifted back to her panther, Amanda hanging snugly beneath her.

Iona hurried down the stairs on swift panther feet, changed to her beast to open the door on the floor where Cassidy waited, and ran on through without shifting again. She touched Amanda's face, the half Shifter surprisingly gentle, but all was well. The little cub was still, her breathing deep and even.

Iona quietly opened the door to the room where Cassidy lay, but the broken door handle clanked, the sound echoing in the deserted hall. Iona halted for a frozen moment, her heart pounding furiously, but she heard nothing, saw no one.

She slipped inside and shut the door, changing back to human as she approached Cassidy on the bed. Cassidy's hands were still strapped down with the metal cuffs, but Cass was wide awake.

Cassidy gave a cry of joy to see Amanda, then started to cry because she couldn't reach for her. Iona unwound the sling, set Amanda on Cassidy's chest, and carefully retied the fabric around Cassidy, holding Amanda in place against Cassidy's bare breasts.

"There. Now she'll be fine," Iona said, trying to sound reassuring. "And that's a clean suit, so she's germ free." She smiled, but Cassidy didn't relax

"Iona, we have to get out of here. And then I'm going to kill everyone in this building."

"I already whacked a couple of them. It felt good. But I agree. We'll go."

Iona checked Cassidy's cuffs again, metal and tight, bolted down, no latch to break. Even Iona's Shifter beast wasn't strong enough to break them. A couple of Shifters together might, but Cassidy couldn't help.

However, there was a Shifter in this building who might be strong enough. Iona looked at Amanda, who'd happily found sustenance at her mother's breast. Amanda and Cassidy would be sitting ducks for someone like the tiger Shifter in the basement.

On the other hand, there were no other Shifters in sight,

and Iona had no way of knowing how long it would be before Eric would find them, or if he even could. She had to use the resources she had on hand.

Right now her resources consisted of one of the strongest females in Shiftertown secured to a bed, a half-crazed Shifter with no name in the basement, a building full of old equipment, and a baby.

If Iona could handle the tiger until she freed Cassidy, then Cassidy would be able to help them all get out of there. Including the tiger. Iona had made a promise to him, and she'd keep it.

"Cass, I'll be right back," she said.

"Why? What are you going to do?"

"Find a way to get you out of here. Don't go running off now, all right?"

Again, Cassidy didn't smile. She'd relaxed from her insane worry about Amanda, but her attention was now entirely on her baby.

Iona kissed Cassidy's forehead, touched Amanda's cheek, changed to her half-Shifter beast, and left the room again.

Eric sensed something moving in the dark desert with him. Diego had driven him up the 95 toward Indian Springs, where they'd stopped at a roadside bar. Diego had headed on to the 375 to Area 51's front gate, while Eric had walked quietly around the building, holding his breath against the noisome garbage in the back, and faded into the night.

He'd stripped when he was well away from the bar, hiding his clothes in a plastic bag under some rocks. He'd fastened the pack that contained everything he needed tightly around his torso, shifted to his wildcat under the moonlight and clear sky, then loped off east and north.

Now someone else moved in the dark with him, and that someone wasn't human. Eric sniffed the wind, then stopped to wait for the large black wolf to trot down from the shadow of the nearest ridge.

Eric said in body language, *What the fuck are you doing?*

The wolf answered in his own body language with plenty

of expletives, basically conveying the message, *You need me, asshole.*

Eric didn't have time to shift and swear at him, so he growled again, moved off into the darkness, and let Graham follow.

CHAPTER TWENTY-NINE

The tiger Shifter who called himself Twenty-three was surprised when Iona returned. She could tell the surprise only through his scent, however, because he glared in fury through the bars and didn't change expression when he saw her.

"I need your help," Iona said to him. "You help me free my friend, and I'll take you out of here."

"You said you'd take me out if I told you where the cub was."

"And I will. But I have to take my friend too, and the cub. And you have to promise not to touch them."

The noise that came back to her was a feral snarl, and she worried again.

"Hold it together," Iona said. "Tell me about yourself. What did you mean when you said you've always been here? Were you brought here as a baby? A cub, I mean?"

"No. I have always been here."

"Born here?" The tiger looked full-grown, about the same age as Jace perhaps. "Your mother was captured?"

"I don't know. I never knew the female they made me from."

"*Made* you? You mean like artificial insemination?"

"I don't know."

"Holy crap on a crutch," Iona muttered.

Humans *breeding* Shifters? Iona thought about what she'd seen up in the laboratory—dozens of test tubes in the glass cabinets, Amanda, a half-human Shifter baby, being scanned every which way, the data flowing across the computer screens.

Humans had stolen Graham's wolves from a bus and taken them to the facility in the desert to harvest blood and skin samples. Iona bet the Shifters had been scanned and studied there too, while they'd been tranqed.

She looked at the cages again, all empty except this one. Tiger Shifter was number twenty-three. Numbers one through twenty-two were all dead.

"Why?" she asked in horror.

"To fight for them."

"But Shifters aren't allowed to . . ."

Collared Shifters, Shifters acknowledged by humans, weren't allowed to be in the military or law enforcement, the human government reasoning that dangerous Shifters couldn't be trusted with weapons. Shifters might turn the guns on their human masters.

But Shifters bred in secret, in this building in the middle of who knew where, un-Collared and allowed to go feral . . . Were humans trying to create Shifters they could control to fight for them, the same reason the Fae had bred them long, long ago?

Shifters they could control without Collars . . . Iona thought about what Eric had told her about the experiments done on him twenty years ago, and the pain he was experiencing now. Liam and Eric had surmised that Eric's adrenaline spikes were causing the pain, as though the Collar was doing its job without actually going off.

Iona went cold. Had the experiments on Eric been a precursor to this? If the humans had been trying to develop Shifters to fight, they'd have to be un-Collared so they could battle without restriction. But the humans would need another way to control the Shifters when they wanted to—had they been trying to find a way with Eric? And now, twenty years later, whatever they'd done to him was biting him in the ass.

And how long had the humans been doing this? Experiments had been forbidden on Shifters, but if Tiger Man was Jace's age, apparently they'd gone on all these years in secret.

The experiments couldn't be going well though. Not with the first twenty-two Shifters dead. Was that why they'd wanted the wolves' blood and DNA? To try again? What if it hadn't been just blood and skin that the researchers had taken, but eggs and sperm?

"Oh, Goddess." Iona had never thought about the pagan deities much, but right now, the Goddess, with her moon shining high above them, was the only thing available to give her comfort and strength. "I'm taking you out of here."

The lock on the tiger's cage was thick and electronic, and opened with a magnetic key card. Of course. They'd need to make sure Twenty-three was securely confined. If Iona broke the lock without swiping the electronic key through it, the cage door still might not open.

Iona heaved a sigh. "I'll be right back."

She shifted to her panther again as Tiger growled, not believing her. She sprinted to the stairwell, then through the door and up all the damn stairs again.

Iona peeked into the lab at the top before she went in, to find the two researchers sprawled on the floor where she'd left them. She wondered, as she went to the niche where she'd found her purse, whether she'd hit them hard enough to keep them out awhile, or so hard they'd never wake up again.

She broke the lock of the cabinet next to the niche and found the researchers' personal belongings. They had phones, which she took, and keys, which she also took, and felt grim satisfaction when one of the key rings had an electronic key card attached to it.

She stayed human this time to run back down the stairs carrying all the goodies. Iona set everything out of harm's reach and approached the cage with the key card.

"Let's hope," she said, and swiped the card through the reader.

The lock's light went green, and the cage door clicked open. At the same time, Tiger Man slammed himself against the bars, his eyes red and enraged. He barreled out of the cage, straight for Iona.

I n their trek through the desert, Eric and Graham had passed several guard posts containing men in SUVs with high-powered rifles, and signs posted everywhere warning people to stay out or expect to be shot for their pains. Eric and Graham had moved like ghosts in the night, flowing against the black desert, never spotted.

They now looked down from the top of the knifelike hill they'd crested to the heart of Area 51 spread out before them.

A long runway stretched north toward the huge dry bed of Groom Lake, the lake bed stark white in the moonlight. A few planes were on the airstrip running in the night, lights blinking. Hangers clustered in tight formation near the end of the runway, illuminated, work going on even now. Other buildings filled the spaces to the west of the runway, but Eric was fixed on one a little way away from them.

The humans hadn't bothered to put fences around the building to which Xavier's directions had brought Eric. He studied it—a military rectangular block a few stories high with antennas on top, one narrow door, which was guarded, and few windows. The windows Eric could see were narrow and set high in the walls, all too small for a man or large leopard to squeeze through.

Eric shifted to human in the darkness, and Graham rose into his man shape next to him.

Without speaking, Eric moved on down the hill toward where he knew Iona to be, Graham right behind him. Never mind Xavier's GPS coordinates, Eric knew Iona was there. He felt the pull of the mate bond leading him straight to her.

The mate bond told him now that she was in deep trouble.

Eric halted again to crouch in the darkness a few yards from the building. "You sure?" Graham whispered to him.

"Yes." Eric took the camera phone he'd worn on a pack around his waist and snapped a few pictures.

"Brilliant ideas on how we get in?" Graham said, lips nearly touching Eric's ear.

Eric scanned the building, which didn't seem to be as

heavily guarded as the hangers and the airstrip, though it did have one guard, standing upright and alert, at the front door. No cars were parked around it, though the other buildings had plenty of vehicles in their parking lots. This building looked deserted, ignored by the humans, which meant something pretty bad must be going on in there.

"Roof," Eric said. He looked at Graham. Eric knew he could scale the wall—he was a cat after all—but could a big wolf?

"I'm right behind you," Graham said.

"Don't get caught."

Eric put away the camera, morphed back into his leopard, slunk forward, and moved stealthily to the building. He hoped no humans had come up with the idea to put land mines around it, but too late to worry about that now.

He made it to the building, found a dark corner, crouched down as far as he could, and sprang upward. He caught bricks and window ledges with his paws, and when he got high enough, a fire escape. At one point he found a CCTV camera, which he smashed.

Eric reached the top and pulled himself up, hearing Graham panting and climbing behind him. Graham made it over the lip of the roof, and Eric saw that he'd chosen to climb in his wolf-beast form.

In silence they searched the rooftop for a door that would take them inside. Then they'd scour the entire building for Iona, Cassidy, and the cub, and pray they found them alive.

Tiger Man's half-Shifter beast grabbed Iona by the throat, madness in his eyes. Iona gasped for breath and found none. His fingers bit into her windpipe, starting to crush, points of pain. He was strong, enraged, crazed.

Iona fought him in watery terror; then that terror snapped something inside her. Iona's control dissolved as blackness filled her vision.

She shifted to her half beast without realizing she'd done it, her neck muscles hardening under the Tiger's hands, until his fingers could no longer crush her. Iona brought her hands up between his and snapped apart his hold on her.

Tiger let her go, but he took one step back, flowed into his pure tiger form, and attacked. The tiger's eyes were bloodshot and feral, and the feral inside Iona responded.

Never mind Eric's lessons in control, or Iona's worry that she'd succumb to the wild thing inside her. She no longer cared. This animal was attacking her and needed to be subdued

Iona had a cub of the pride to protect. Iona was a dominant, never mind how big the guy was, and she'd teach him to obey her.

She changed all the way to panther and ripped into Tiger Man, her wildcat enraged. The tiger was huge, his paws the size of Iona's head, but she was fast. They fought close, snapping, snarling, tearing. biting.

Blood flowed hot down Iona's fur, pain bit into her side, but she kept on fighting. She'd defeat him, rule him, bend him to her will.

Tiger Man had no intention of bending to anyone's will. He'd been the only experiment to survive—all these cages were now empty except his. He'd thrived, which meant he was very strong.

He used that strength to raise Iona into the air and slam her to the cement floor. Iona's breath crashed out of her, but she rolled and regained her feet, the panther quick.

She was hurt, gasping for breath, but she would not let him defeat her. To lose would give the tiger control over her, and she could not afford to do that.

Tiger didn't wait for her to recover. He was on her even as she stood, his weight dragging her back to the floor. He rained down blows, but Iona fought back, ripping claws across his belly and drawing blood. Tiger roared his pain and smacked his paw across her head, making the world spin.

He drew back for another blow but something streamed across the room with terrible swiftness, and landed with all four feet against Tiger Man's side. Iona saw a flash of white and black, then Eric was fighting the tiger, his leopard teeth and claws moving faster than Iona could see. Eric's Collar sparked once, then went silent.

A human arm covered with flame tattoos reached down to

help Iona to her feet. Iona shifted from her beast to her human form and let Graham help her up. She stood with her hands on hips, breathing heavily, her side bleeding, the claw wounds hurting like fury.

In the middle of the room, Eric and the tiger fought in a flurry of fur, claws, teeth, and snarls.

"Eric, don't kill him!" Iona shouted.

"Are you crazy?" Graham asked. "That's a feral—what's he doing here?"

"I'm not sure. I think . . . I think humans created him."

Graham stared at her, his gray white eyes luminous in the darkness. "*Created* him? What the fuck?"

"I don't know." Iona dragged in a breath. "We need to keep him alive and get him out of here. I promised him."

Graham rolled his eyes. "Felines." He shifted to his black wolf form and loped into the fight.

Graham at first tried to pull apart the two snarling balls of wildcat, but he got knocked into a wall for his trouble. His wolf howled, then he sprang into the fight again, swatting and biting both leopard and tiger.

A harsh scream rose from the tangle of Shifters, but it wasn't the tiger. Iona heard the sound with her heart. The agony came from Eric, and she knew in that moment, without doubt, that her mate was going to die.

Iona shifted back to panther and raced across the room, her own pain forgotten. She grabbed the tiger with her claws, and Tiger Man fought her, completely wild now.

Graham went for Tiger Man's throat and missed, the tiger landing Graham a spinning blow on the side of his head. Graham staggered, and Tiger Man went after him. But the distraction gave Iona enough time to drag Eric out of the middle of the fight.

Eric's leopard was in deep pain, his lips pulled back from his teeth in silent agony. His Collar was dormant, but Iona knew the pain came from inside himself.

The humans here had been breeding Shifters to fight for them, Tiger Man had said. No Collars to stop them. But twenty years ago, they'd tried, with Eric, to find a way to control a Shifter with pain.

Iona wasn't sure if the researchers would consider Eric a

success or a failure, but she didn't care. She knew only that her mate was in pain, and that she'd die if she lost him.

Iona, as her panther, lay down over Eric, desperately trying to warm him with her body. Eric's eyes had clouded over, and she knew he couldn't see or hear her. His fur was stifling hot and his heartbeat was way too fast.

A band of iron squeezed Iona's heart, pain beyond anything she'd felt in her life. If Eric died, she'd die too. She knew that with every breath she took.

No.

She rose, her limbs stiff with fury. Tiger Man was beating down Graham, Graham's wolf fighting desperately, his black fur covered in blood.

No.

This was what it had been like in the wild, long ago, when Shifters had fought each other to the death for territory, mates, dominance. They'd also fought tooth and claw to protect each other.

Eric was her *mate*. That meant Iona met any threat to him with violence, and didn't stop fighting until that threat was dead.

Tiger Man saw that in her eyes. Iona saw in his that he'd been bred to fight until every enemy in his path was slain.

So be it, then. Iona attacked him. Tiger Man met her onslaught, as ready to kill as she was.

Iona would drink of his blood and feast on his bones. She'd scatter his remains throughout her territory as a reminder to all who crossed it what she did to those who threatened the ones she loved.

Iona fought, ripped, bit, pounded. She would kill, and it would feel so good.

"Iona!"

The voice was Graham's, his harsh, hated wolf's voice.

Graham would be next. He'd threatened Eric's leadership, he'd hurt Eric, and he needed to be eliminated. Iona would finish with the tiger, then tear off Graham's head and lap up his blood.

"Iona, stop!" Graham shouted. "Eric needs you."

Iona hesitated a split second, and in that second, the tiger got in a blow that stunned her. Iona's rage returned, and she shifted into her half-human, half-panther form. Kill these males first, help her mate second.

"He's going to die." Graham grabbed for her, but Iona spun out of reach. "He needs the touch of a mate. *Shit*."

Graham took two rapid steps backward as Iona fixed him with her enraged stare, ready to kill. Then she spun around and drove her claws into the tiger.

"You're going feral, woman!" Graham yelled at her. "Fight it!"

No. Iona wanted to be wild. Free.

No humans Collaring her, no Shifters telling her what to do. No following rituals and their rules—she'd kill everyone here and race away, no ties to any of them.

Except Eric. She'd take him with her and cure him, and then he'd be hers. No one else would ever touch him again. She'd sequester him in a cave somewhere and have him all to herself. She was an alpha female, and no one and nothing would come between her and her mate and her freedom.

"Holy Goddess, Iona."

Graham's voice was like the buzz of an annoying mosquito. She'd swat it down when she was done with the tiger.

Tiger was proving difficult to defeat, but she'd do it in the end. After that, Graham would be nothing.

She heard, dimly, Eric get to his feet. She didn't have time to rejoice that he was able to do so. Fight first.

Blood. Kill. Defeat.

"Iona."

Eric's human voice was weak and full of pain. The pull of it made Iona turn to him, even as the Tiger drew back to strike her down.

Iona saw Eric's green eyes looking at her down the barrel of a tranq rifle. Before Iona could blink, the rifle popped, and a dart thunked into her chest.

Iona stared at her mate, bewildered, the betrayal hurting more than the pinprick of the dart. "Eric," she whispered, and then she collapsed.

CHAPTER THIRTY

Eric reloaded the tranq gun Graham had found as fast as he'd ever done anything, and shot the next dart straight into the tiger. The tiger roared and collapsed to the floor, but he didn't fall unconscious.

The tiger shifted instead into a large man, with an immensity that rivaled even Shane's. He had a strong face covered with unshaved whiskers, eyes that remained golden yellow, and hair, while matted with blood, showing the orange and black streaks of a tiger.

Eric stared at him a moment before another wash of pain cramped him. The tranq gun slid from his slack grasp, but Graham grabbed it, loaded another dart, and pointed the rifle at the tiger.

"Who the fuck are you?" Graham demanded.

The tiger remained slumped on the floor, watching them with angry eyes. "Twenty-three. I told her."

"She said humans . . . *created* you?"

"Yes."

"How? How is that possible?"

"I don't know."

Eric barely heard them. He crawled to Iona, who'd reverted

to human form in her slumber, her beautiful limbs tangled on the floor and covered with claw and bite marks.

He'd seen her eyes before he'd shot her. Feral. His beautiful Iona. Eric had feared so much that her beast would take over, and now it had. Because she'd been fighting to protect him.

He lay down beside her and gathered her into his arms, burying his face in her neck.

Help me, love.

The mate bond warmed him, and the pain receded the slightest bit. The touch of a mate, her scent, that's what healed.

He loved her, a love he'd fought and denied. Eric had told himself his craving for her was his mating hunger, or his loneliness, but he knew now that it was all *her.*

He'd fallen in love with Iona the moment he'd seen her months ago, she sitting in the corner of Coolers in that sexy blue dress, impatiently tapping her straw into her slushy drink. Her lovely face, her lush black hair, and most of all her clear blue eyes had wrapped around him and stolen his heart.

If Iona had taught him anything over the months, it was that true love wasn't selfish. Iona had loved her mother and sister enough to hide her Shifter nature so they'd be safe from it. She'd fought her craving for Eric for *them.*

When Eric had more or less forced Iona to accept entry into Shiftertown, she'd embraced his family without hesitation. She could have hated them, fought them, derided them for being what she didn't want to become.

But Iona had viewed them as individual beings and accepted them each for themselves. She'd loved his sister and his son, formed a camaraderie with Diego and Xav, and had willingly helped bring Cassidy's daughter into the world.

Iona had stood up to Graham, she'd protected Eric, and she'd been down here fighting like a demon in this strange human place. Fighting, protecting—not cowering in a corner in terror, as she had every right to.

Eric loved her for all that, and also for her laughter, her quiet sense of humor, and her strength.

He stroked her hair. "I love you, mate of my heart."

Iona's eyes cracked open, the lovely blue untarnished by any feral red. "Eric?"

"Love." Eric laid his body over hers, trying to pour the warmth she'd given him back into her. He kissed her, her warm lips parting for his.

"Eric." Iona's eyes widened in alarm. "Cassidy. She's upstairs with Amanda. We have to help Twenty-three. The humans are doing some weird experiments, stealing DNA and things. We have to . . ."

"Hush now." Eric kissed her again, silencing her.

"You shot me," she said, a spark of anger in her eyes.

"I had to, love. You were going feral."

Anger fled, and concern returned. "Are you all right? Is the pain still there?"

Iona touched him as though searching him for hurts, even though her own body was bloody with claw wounds. But her touch stilled the throbbing pain inside Eric and, at the same time, brought one interested part of him to life.

"I'm better," he whispered.

"Are we going to get the hell out of here anytime soon?" Graham asked from where he still trained the gun on the tiger.

Iona struggled to sit up, pushing her long hair back from her face. "We have to take him with us. I promised."

The Tiger Man, still awake, regarded her with groggy eyes. His body was scored with dozens of deep gouges, but still he looked like he'd be willing to go another ten rounds.

"You want to take *him*?" Graham asked. "What the fuck is he?"

Iona got to her feet. Eric decided that watching her long legs unfolding in front of him, all the way to her fine, tight ass, was a wonderful thing. "He doesn't deserve to stay here and be experimented on," she said. "I came down here to free him, and I guess getting free triggered his fight-or-flight instinct."

"You think?" Graham growled.

"She's right." Eric sat up, not minding being right next to Iona's fine legs. "No Shifter deserves to be a guinea pig. He comes with us. Tranq him if he gets unruly."

"But what are you going to do with him? Take him to Shiftertown to steal our females and threaten our cubs?"

"We'll figure it out," Eric said. "Have faith, Graham. Leaders need that."

Graham kept the tranq rifle firmly aimed at the tiger. "I swear to the Goddess, Warden, you are a piece of work."

"Argue later. Find Cassidy now. Where is she?"

Iona reached down for him. "Upstairs. I'll show you."

Eric's heart lightened as he put his hand in hers and let her pull him to his feet. *Mated*. They'd help each other, always.

"Bring him," Eric said to Graham, the strength of command returning to his voice.

"Whatever." Graham scowled at the tiger. "We need to find some clothes to cover that semitruck between his legs."

The tiger growled as he got to his feet, but he was finished attacking, Eric saw in his eyes.

Eric walked up to him. The tiger made another soft snarl, but Eric didn't flinch. "We'll help you, my friend. But you obey *me*."

The tiger looked down at him, as tall as any bear Shifter, a glint of defiance in his eyes. He pointed at Iona, never taking his gaze from Eric. "I follow *her*."

Eric felt momentary surprise, but then, it wasn't so surprising. Iona had been seriously kicking his ass, she had promised to free him, and Tiger had heard Iona insist on making good on that promise. Small wonder this lone Feline would consider Iona his alpha.

"Works for me," Eric said lightly. "Iona, lead the way."

"And I follow *you*," Graham said from behind the tiger. "With this." He gave the tranq rifle a loving stroke.

Tiger eyed him not in fear but irritation, and turned to let Iona lead them out.

The building remained quiet as they followed Iona up the stairs. It was the middle of the night, yes, but the humans hadn't stationed any guards on this building apart from the one outside the front door. The walls were thick, the basement deep, and apparently no sounds of their battle had reached the guard.

Eric wondered. When he'd been brought to Area 51 for experiments, he'd not been in this building, but a smaller one, with plenty of humans and military guards swarming it. This was an old building that looked as though it hadn't been used in a few decades, one guard, no backup, silence.

Iona told them about the lab upstairs and the people she'd knocked out. She calculated about twenty-five minutes had passed since she'd done that.

"How about we go up and tranq them?" Graham suggested. "Give us another hour or so?"

"We get Cassidy first," Eric said, a little distracted by the fine shape of Iona's backside as she led them upward. "If Reid can take us all out of here quick enough, we might not have to worry about them."

Iona shot Eric a curious glance over her shoulder, not yet knowing about Reid's gift. She said nothing, however, as she led them out of the stairwell into a deserted corridor. They reached a door with a broken handle, which Iona opened into a hospital room.

Eric's blood boiled hot when he saw his sister stretched out on a bed, her hands and feet shackled in place. A mound of clean suit on her chest emitted a little coo.

"Eric!" Cassidy cried in relief, then her voice strengthened. "Let me out of here so I can kill whatever humans touched my cub."

Eric went quickly to her, leaning to embrace her in joy and relief. His embrace encompassed Amanda, who opened her infant eyes and burped.

Cassidy relaxed under Eric's touch, then she looked past him and stiffened. "What is *that*?"

She lifted her head to study the tiger, who stood uncertainly halfway inside the room, Graham still fixing the rifle on him. Tiger Man's gaze went to Amanda, and he drew a long, shuddering breath.

"Cub," he said, then his voice filled with sorrow. "They took mine."

"You had a cub?" Iona asked, shocked.

The tiger nodded. "He died." His gaze moved hungrily to Amanda again. "Can I see?"

Graham's hand tightened on the rifle. "Careful, Iona. Why did you bring him in here anyway?"

"Because I think he can help break the bonds that hold Cassidy. Have you noticed how strong he is? He's like a super Shifter."

"Come over here," Eric told the tiger, who still looked at

Amanda. "Stay sane, or Graham gives you two shots. Easier on me if you're asleep."

The tiger man nodded. He came forward slowly, moving like a Shifter trying not to startle anyone. His golden-eyed gaze remained on Amanda, the sorrow on his face heartbreaking.

Cassidy watched him come, expression guarded, but she was letting him. Iona followed, her fingertips on her lips, the compassion in her warring with her protectiveness. Eric knew that as much as Iona felt sorry for the tiger, if Tiger made one wrong move toward Amanda or Cass, Iona would be on him, probably even faster than Eric was.

Tiger Man reached the table, stretched out one blunt finger, and touched Amanda's downy hair. He swallowed, his eyes softening.

"Can you break these?" Eric asked, touching a cuff.

The tiger studied them, then he hooked his fingers under the metal and tore upward. Cassidy cried out in pain, then the cuff broke from its bolts and clanked to the floor. Cassidy snatched her hand away and shook it hard.

"Thank you," she breathed.

She clenched her teeth while the tiger broke the other cuff, then the ones on her ankles. Cassidy sat up, cradling Amanda, anger making her strong.

Eric put his arms around Cassidy again, lending whatever strength he could, then he kissed her, took up the equipment Xavier had given him, and started taking photos of the room.

Both Iona and the tiger watched, mystified, as Eric hooked the camera to the sat phone the way Xavier had shown him and dialed the number.

"Xav," he said when the man answered. "Send these to Reid and tell him to get his *dokk alfar* ass out here."

"Xavier's there?" Cassidy asked, leaping down from the table. "Where's Diego?"

Iona picked up one of the phones she must have stolen from the researchers, smiled when she got a signal, and handed it to her. Cassidy punched in a number with one thumb and eagerly lifted the phone to her ear.

Eric heard Diego's voice loud and clear. "Who is this?"

"Diego?" Cassidy said.

"Cassidy." His voice flooded with relief. "Fuck." He flowed into a long string of Spanish, while Cassidy laughed, tears in her eyes.

Then air displaced with a little bang, and Stuart Reid stood in the room. Iona let out a startled scream, and the tiger snarled.

Iona blew out her breath, hand on her heart. "I didn't know he could do that. *How* did he do that?"

"Diego?" Cassidy yelled into the phone. "I'm coming home. With Amanda. You'll be there, right?"

"I'm on my way, *amorcita*," Diego said and clicked off.

Reid studied the roomful of Shifters, all naked except Cassidy in her hospital gown. His dark Fae eyes narrowed at the sight of the tiger. "Is that a Shifter?"

"Long story," Eric said. "Time to go."

"I can't take you all at once," Reid said. "One at a time, maybe two with the kid."

"Start with Cassidy and Amanda, then. Make sure they're okay and get back here."

Reid went to Cassidy and put his slender arms around her, touching Amanda as well. "This place gives me the creeps."

Eric grunted a laugh. "This from a man who can make iron bars turn to raining bullets."

"That's natural. Area Fifty-one is just weird."

He flashed a look around, then light flared, and Reid, Cassidy, and Amanda were gone.

"I hope he hurries," Graham said, while Iona and the tiger stared at the empty space in amazement.

"Before he does," Eric said, "I want to find out everything I can about this place and exactly what they're doing here. You." Eric walked to the tiger, feeling his strength return, the pain nearly gone. "You are going to tell me everything you know, starting from the moment you first were aware of being here, and leaving nothing out."

Iona dressed herself while Tiger Man leaned against the table Cassidy had vacated and told his story.

There wasn't much to it, but Iona listened in dismay and sympathy. Tiger Man had lived in his cage most of his life, let out only when humans wanted to watch him shift or run around, or when they carried him off to other rooms to put needles and probes in him. They'd lock him into glass-windowed rooms sometimes to watch what he'd do.

Tiger remembered only bits and pieces of his life, which, if Iona judged aright, was about forty years. He remembered his Transition, the pain of it, during which time they'd given him a female they'd made for him to mate with.

He remembered only flashes of that, then they showed him the cub she'd brought forth, but the female had died having it, they'd said. The tiger had touched the cub only once before it was taken away from him. Later, when he'd asked, a human had told him that the cub had died.

There had been more Shifters here, Tiger said. When he'd been young, the facility had been full of people working—the place had teemed with them. What they'd meant to accomplish, he didn't know. He'd stopped wondering the why of things a long time ago.

For the last about ten years, the place had been quiet. Most of the humans had gone away, the bodies of the dead Shifters gone, and the tiger had been left alone. Fed and watered, and that was it.

Then, about six months ago, some humans had come back and started poking at him again. Tiger hadn't seen any other Shifters, but he'd been taken from time to time to the top floor and put through different scanners, tranqed, scanned, and probed again.

When Tiger finished his story, Iona folded her arms, shivering. Even Graham was quiet, his usual bluster replaced by angry sympathy. Eric watched Tiger with a stillness Iona had come to know masked deep rage.

"If he's about forty," Iona said, "then that means humans were doing the experiments *before* the existence of Shifters was revealed. The Shifters were outed only a little over twenty years ago."

"I thought of that," Eric said grimly. "The experiments they did on me weren't here, but in a similar place. The humans that studied me knew nothing about us, were trying to figure out what Shifters could do."

"So a different set of scientists?" Graham asked. "Doing Goddess knows what?"

"The people here were trying to make their own Shifters," Iona said. "But they didn't work. I bet when the Shifters started dying, not being viable, the program got its funding cut."

"And started back up again?" Eric looked around at the old room. "This doesn't look like a refurbished facility."

Iona shrugged. "Maybe whoever started it again wasn't forthcoming about exactly what he was doing in here. Told the government it was for weapons or something and then went back to trying to create Shifters."

"Kellerman," Eric said.

"I was just thinking that," Graham said. "He's up to something, that's for certain. I'm betting even if he didn't do this himself, he knows who did. He damn well knew my wolves had gone missing and why."

"How about if we ask him?" Eric said, rage making his eyes hard green. "We have phones."

Iona broke in. "If you tell him you've found this place, won't he just call more guards out here to raid the building?"

"Possibly," Graham said. "I was thinking about using a sneakier method. Make him need to come out here and see for himself."

"How are you going to do that?" Iona asked in puzzlement.

"Give me the sat phone, and I'll show you."

Eric handed over the big phone. Graham took it and started punching in numbers. After a few seconds of ringing, Iona heard a sleepy human female voice on the other end say, "Hello?"

"Misty. Sweetheart. This is Graham. I need you to do something for me. Call Kellerman—no, I don't care if it's the middle of the night—and tell him you heard me saying something about checking out his place in Area Fifty-one. Yep, I said Area Fifty-one. Tell him you're not sure, but I seemed excited about something. Got it? Thank you, sweetie. Drinks are on me."

CHAPTER THIRTY-ONE

Graham said good-bye and hung up to find Iona and Eric, and even the tiger, staring at him. "She's a friend," Graham said. He might actually be blushing.

"So we wait," Iona said.

Reid interrupted by reappearing. Iona suppressed another startled scream and jammed her hand to her pounding heart.

"Who's next?" Reid asked.

"Iona," Eric said. "Then come back, but we're going to look around here for a while. We might need you."

"No," Iona said. "If you're staying, I am."

"Iona, I want you safe."

"Not if you're running around here in danger, especially with your pain attacks. I can't pull you out of them if I'm not here."

"And you started to go feral downstairs," Eric growled, green eyes hard. "You can't risk that. I might lose you for good."

"I'll more likely go feral if I'm forced to sit at home and worry about you. I'll be tearing my way back here, not caring who gets in my way." The wild need stirred as Iona spoke, the instinct to protect her mate, no matter what.

"Reid," Eric snapped.

Reid lifted his hands and stepped away from Iona. "I'm not

getting into an argument between Shifters. No transporting against her will."

Eric didn't look happy, but at least he stopped arguing. Iona went to him and put her hand in his, liking the warmth of him, his scent telling her he wanted her there despite the danger.

She still saw the pain in his eyes, though, and it worried her. She knew right then that she'd rather risk going feral, or going insane from her mating heat, or being caught as a Shifter, than watch him go through that pain again.

Eric sent Reid to the roof to keep an eye out for activity while they waited for Kellerman, having Reid report via the phones Iona had taken from the researchers. Reid's first call said that no guards were rushing to the place, and the humans he did see ignored the building.

His observations supported Eric's idea that no one really knew what the researchers were doing in here, nor did they care. He suspected that no one took Kellerman's research seriously, or else he'd offered to pay a lot of money to use the run-down facility.

The two researchers on the top floor were just coming around when Eric knelt next to them. Iona had hit them hard in her half-feral state, to which their bruises attested. But they were recovering. The woman wore shorts and a T-shirt with a spangled neckline; the man was still in a clean suit. Both opened their eyes now to find a naked Eric grinning into their faces.

"Hello," he said. "I'm a Shifter. I'm about to destroy this lab and everything in it, so you might want to leave."

The man blinked at him. "What?"

"I said . . ."

Iona leaned down next to him, her lovely face bearing a sweet smile. "You kidnapped me, my sister-in-law, and a new-born baby. You took my niece from her mother and stuck needles into her and wires all over her. I'd say you need to leave."

"We weren't hurting her," the woman said quickly. "Just trying to figure out her gene sequence."

"So you could clone her?" Iona's voice continued to be deceptively pleasant.

"We only want to know how Shifters work. They could be the best weapons—"

"Shut up," the man said quickly.

Eric said, "Is this how you got the government to fund you? Said you were creating secret weapons? You see him?" He pointed to the tiger, who was standing next to Graham, his yellow eyes pinning the researchers. "That Shifter was the only one who survived. The 'experiments' were a failure."

"But we have new—" The woman broke off again when the man elbowed her.

"Shut *up*."

"New DNA samples from the Lupine Shifters you abducted," Eric supplied. "You thought you could revive the experiments, succeed where the previous ones failed. I have news. It can't be done."

Both researchers, the woman with her pale, lined face, and the man, younger and angry looking, said nothing.

"But we're *nice* Shifters," Eric said. "At least I am. My mate here wants to disembowel you for touching our niece. The tiger over there wants to gut you for what humans have done to him over the last forty years. The wolf just wants to shoot you because he can."

Graham's laughter rumbled. "And it would be fun."

The woman flinched, but the man looked more angry.

"But I'm going to let Reid take you out of here before we get destructive," Eric said. "Because I've learned how to be kind to stupid creatures."

Eric unfolded himself and summoned Reid from the roof. The man and woman looked more perplexed than afraid as Reid approached. Lanky Reid in jeans, shirt, and jacket against the winter cold looked innocuous and obviously not Shifter.

"He'll have to take you one at a time," Eric said. "The male first, I think."

"Where do you want me to leave them?" Reid asked, expression neutral.

"I'll let you decide."

Reid thought a moment, then he grinned. A *dokk alfar* was a frightening thing when he smiled, especially when his midnight eyes began to gleam. "I have just the place."

Reid put his hands on the man's shoulders, then both he and the man vanished.

The woman screamed. She tried to scramble away from them, but Iona put a strong foot on the woman's leg and stopped her.

Reid slammed back in a few seconds later and reached for the woman.

"Where did you take him?" Iona asked.

"Las Vegas Police Department," Reid said. "Processing cell." He closed his hands on the woman's shoulders, and then they were gone.

"Huh," Graham said. "Good sense of humor, for a Fae." He looked around the room. "So they brought the blood and tissue samples from my wolves here?"

"Maybe egg and sperm samples too," Iona said. "If they're trying to breed Shifters."

"Shit."

Graham strode to the cooling cabinets, ripped one open, and started throwing the test tubes to the floor. They shattered, whatever agar preserved the samples oozing out and mixing with the broken glass.

The tiger Shifter watched Graham a moment, then he walked to the next glass cabinet and tipped it over, without bothering to open it. The resounding crash was satisfying, and Graham gave triumphant cheer.

"You all right?" Iona came back to Eric, her hands warm on his arms, her blue eyes soft with worry.

"Much better. The mate bond is helping."

"The mate bond," she said. "Cassidy told me about that. She said it was magic."

Eric cradled Iona's face in his hands, thumbs brushing her cheekbones. "Whatever it comes from, it's filling me. It's making me know I love you."

He saw the hunger in her eyes. "I love *you*." She touched his face. "I never knew—I never thought I could love like this."

"The Goddess must have known. I'm glad she did."

Around them, crashes sounded, along with the satisfied growls of two Shifters enjoying themselves. Eric slid his arms around Iona. "I love you. I'm going to keep saying that because I like hearing it. I love you. I love you. I love you."

Iona smiled as she leaned into the warm curve of his body. "I wish we were home."

"Soon, love. And then, we won't come out for *days*."

Graham looked around at them. "Will you two take it out of here? Your pheromones are making me crazy."

He'd strapped the tranq rifle across his back while he found and broke things. The tiger ignored them all while he swept his arms over the lab benches and punched the glass out of the hoods. He finally looked happy.

"Watch him," Eric said to Graham.

"Don't worry. I'm on it."

Eric craved Iona with his entire body, but he knew that would have to wait. "We need to search the rest of the floors."

"Yes," Iona said. "Unfortunately."

But later, when he had her home . . .

Eric fixed what they needed into a pack around his waist, then they walked together, hand in hand, to the stairwell, where Eric had the pleasure of watching Iona remove her clothes again. Then they shifted to their wildcats and descended to see what they could find.

An hour later, Reid, back on the roof, alerted Eric that Kellerman had arrived.

Eric and Iona had found little downstairs—the rooms hadn't been used for years. Fortunately they found no more victims of the researchers' experiments, no more captive Shifters. The researchers had used the top floor, the lowest basement, and Cassidy's room, and that was it.

Reid's message was to the point. "He's here."

"Go down and tell Graham." Eric flipped the phone closed, his heart beating in rage and anticipation. He looked at Iona, who returned the look with the same anger in her eyes. "Let's go meet him."

Kellerman headed up, not down when he walked into the building. He took the one working elevator to the top floor and emerged, a semiautomatic in his hand.

Eric's half-leopard beast twisted the pistol away.

Kellerman's eyes widened, and he tried to leap back into the elevator, but Eric grabbed him by the collar and jerked him forward as the elevator doors closed. Iona stepped behind Kellerman and checked his pockets for more weapons, relieving him of his phone and a magazine of bullets.

Iona had resumed her clothes upon arriving on the top floor, but Eric and Graham had left theirs far away in the desert. Kellerman gave them a contemptuous look.

"I have backup coming," he said. He tried to sound unworried, but he couldn't conceal the tremor in his voice as he took in the ruined lab, the floor a river of broken glass.

"We'll be long gone before they get here," Eric said.

Graham aimed the tranq rifle at Kellerman. "I have backup too. Except I don't know his name." He whistled, and Tiger Man stepped from behind the pile of wreckage that used to be a lab table.

Kellerman's face drained of color. "You let him *out*?"

"He looked unhappy," Iona said. "So I opened the cage."

"But he's dangerous. He could kill us all."

"Why?" Iona asked. "He's only a Shifter."

"No, he isn't." Kellerman wet his lips. "He's a *programmed* Shifter. He's been coded to kill. To fight the enemy and not stop until that enemy is destroyed."

"Oh." Iona looked ill. "So you didn't only breed him, you also messed with his DNA?"

"*I* didn't," Kellerman said. "The people who ran this facility before me did. They were brilliant. They blended genetics from animals, humans, and other Shifters to create the perfect Shifters, but ones obedient to human wills. The perfect fighting machines. Military weapons. They imagined whole armies of them."

"So, what happened?" Eric asked. "I don't see any armies of Shifters."

Kellerman shook his head. "The prototypes didn't last. Too unstable. The project got cut because they didn't produce results fast enough." Derision entered his voice. "The government was too shortsighted."

"How do you know about what went on here?" Iona asked. "You were wandering through Area Fifty-one and stumbled across it?"

"No, I stumbled across it researching Shifters," Kellerman said with a touch of his usual arrogance. "When I was put in charge of the Shifter council a few years ago, I did my homework on them. I found a file on this project, parts of it declassified because it was forty years old. I looked into it. I had ideas for how to make the project actually work, so I put together a team and got permission to research what people had done here. They had good ideas back then, but not the technology to implement them."

"And when you had to combine Shiftertowns," Eric finished, "you saw an opportunity to take fresh DNA and other samples without anyone being the wiser. So you thought. Graham was going to notice when some of his Shifters went missing—why did you think he wouldn't?"

"They took too long," Kellerman said impatiently. "The whole transfer and tissue harvesting was supposed to take only an hour or so. I'm surrounded by idiots."

"Tough break," Eric said. He understood why Kellerman used the compound in the desert for the blood taking—it was closer to Shiftertown, and he'd never have gotten permission to haul twenty cages of Shifters into Area 51. He'd have his researchers take all the samples there then transport them to this facility later.

"How did you get that other compound built?" Eric asked. "Without anyone being the wiser? No one noticed?"

"I didn't have to build it. It was already there. Researching the effect of radiation from the nuclear testing sites, or something like that. Another project that got defunded, and the buildings left there for me to find in another file. *Temporary* buildings just means they get left until someone remembers to take them down. I appropriated the place for my purpose."

"But you didn't get enough?" Eric asked, letting his voice go deceptively soft. "So you thought taking my sister and her newborn was a good idea?"

"Again, I'm surrounded by idiots," Kellerman snapped. "I have a nurse on staff at that clinic who supplies me with samples from time to time. She called my researchers. They decided they couldn't pass up the opportunity to study a Shifter baby, especially one that was half-human. So she drugged them and had them sent here. And once more, they took too long. They should have had them back to you by now. Scientists are like children with ADD. They get fixed into their experiments and forget what time it is. They wouldn't change their socks if no one was there to tell them."

As he finished, Eric took the magazine out of Kellerman's gun and crushed it in his strong, half-shifted hand. Bullets rained harmlessly to the floor, most of them bent. Eric then twisted the pistol in two in front of Kellerman's face.

Eric dropped the broken pieces of pistol. "Well, my friend, you won't have to worry about your pet scientists anymore. We're closing you down."

"You don't have that much power, Warden," Kellerman said, still too confident. "You'll be arrested for abducting me, probably executed. And everyone in this room with you. Except Ms. Duncan. She'll go to prison for aiding you, and her mother will likely lose her nice business."

"*I'm* not a Shifter," Reid said quietly.

Kellerman jumped. The Fae had remained in the shadows, and now he leaned against the elevator's doorframe. "I used to be a cop before I resigned," Reid said. "Believe it or not, abducting Shifters is against the law, and experimenting on them is too."

"I wasn't experimenting on them," Kellerman said quickly.

"No, you were harvesting from them," Eric said, anger in his voice. "To make a new species of Shifter. It didn't work before. Why did you think it would work now?"

"I told you. Technology has improved in the last forty years."

"Doesn't matter," Reid said. "Shifters were never bred by men in the first place. They were created by the Fae, in Faerie. The Fae used genetic engineering and technology, sure, but also a good dose of magic. *That*, you don't have, and you never will, thank the Goddess. That kind of magic doesn't work outside Faerie anyway."

"Fairies?" Kellerman laughed. "What the hell are you talking about?"

"Fae," Reid corrected. "Or *hoch alfar*, as my people called them. Evil bastards. It's interesting to me that, no matter how bad you are, you'll never be as evil as the high Fae. You're too petty and full of yourself."

"My backup should be here any minute," Kellerman said angrily. "You are the overconfident ones. You're going down. Fae, my ass."

"Why don't you demonstrate, Reid?" Graham suggested, sounding eager. "Show him a little Fae magic."

Reid shrugged. "Nah. Waste of energy."

"Aw," Graham said. "You're no fun."

Kellerman looked Reid up and down, then back at Eric, his fear not as great as it should have been. "The fact that you stand around without clothes and don't notice proves you're animals. No one cares what happens to you, in the long run. Remember that."

And there were many Shifters, Eric though silently, who didn't care what happened to humans. Humans walked a knife-edge, and they didn't even know it.

"What do you think?" Eric asked Graham. "Burn the place to the ground before we go?"

"Sounds good to me. Lots of acetylene and gas around here. Make a nice little inferno."

Kellerman looked at the faces surrounding him. Eric saw him realize that they weren't joking—Eric, for one, did not intend to let this building or anything in it remain.

"You fucking bastards," Kellerman said hotly. "This is years of work. Science. And money. *My* money."

"Can we stop talking?" Graham asked. "And start torching?"

"Wait." Iona stepped forward. "What about Eric? What did your files on Shifter research tell you was done to him?"

"I'm not a scientist," Kellerman said testily. "I don't have all the details. But he was part of this—he and some others. They were messing around with chemical cocktails, bioengineering, trying to see if they could turn regular Shifters into killing machines, but under their direct control. Those experiments didn't work." He gave Eric a small smile. "They said you were too old. Their notes said they were annoyed that they had to work on you, not your son."

Eric went cold. Twenty years ago, Jace had been a true cub, a little over ten years old, and scared about the move to Shiftertown and taking the Collar. And these people had wanted to change Jace into something like Tiger Man, who was standing motionlessly behind Kellerman, the rage in his eyes mirroring what Eric felt.

"And then they were ordered to cease," Kellerman went on, oblivious of his danger.

He was counting too much on his backup, who were taking their time. Eric remembered Diego's grim enthusiasm about causing a diversion at the front gate if necessary, and he wondered if Diego was taking care of that.

"I imagined it pissed them off," Eric said. "But not as much as it pissed *me* off."

Something in Eric's voice made Kellerman take a step back. Iona growled, with her panther's anger, and Kellerman's eyes widened suddenly. "Son of a bitch. You're one of them! Ms. Duncan, you're a Shifter."

Instinctively, Eric stepped in front of Iona. "A fact that you'll forget."

"The hell I will." Kellerman looked both disgusted and gleeful. "You're going down, woman. You've been Collarless all this time, which is against about fifteen laws. Your pretty little mom is going down too, for not reporting that a Shifter got her pregnant—or is she a Shifter too? What about your sister?"

Iona tried to get around Eric. "You leave them the hell alone."

"Control her, asshole," Kellerman snarled.

His words were drowned by a long, low growl, one of terrible menace that rattled the broken glass all over the room.

Tiger Man had come to life, the big man's stance radiating that he did not like Kellerman threatening Iona. At all.

Kellerman blanched. He came out of his daze and tried to get to Graham, reaching for the tranq rifle Graham still held.

Graham back-stepped out of the way, but before he could bring the rifle around to shoot Kellerman with it, Tiger, with a roar that filled the room, slammed himself into Kellerman.

"Graham!" Eric shouted.

Graham aimed the rifle, but the tiger had Kellerman pinned beneath him, Kellerman screaming as they grappled. Tiger shifted to his cat, a Bengal twice the size of a regular tiger. He'd been bred to be stronger than other Shifters—a killer, Kellerman had said.

Eric changed to his half beast and sprang into the fray—he saw Graham shove the tranq gun at Iona and shift to half wolf.

He and Graham tried to pull the tiger off Kellerman, but the tiger was far gone in rage, taking out his long life of fear, pain, and loneliness on Kellerman. Tiger fought for himself, for his dead cub, and for Iona, the first person to try to give him his freedom.

Kellerman screamed as claws ripped into him, peeling flesh from his bones and bloodying the floor. The tiger slashed in hard, rapid strokes, then dove to latch his teeth around Kellerman's throat.

Eric heard the *thunk* of the tranq rifle, and Tiger Man shuddered. He let go of Kellerman, and Kellerman fell in a limp heap, his head bloody and lolling.

Iona stood over them, holding the tranq rifle ready. Eric and Graham together grabbed the tiger and hauled him off Kellerman. The tiger landed on his side, still awake, his black and orange sides heaving.

Kellerman was a mess. The smug face that Eric had often wanted to punch was now a bloody pulp, the man's breath coming in bubbling gasps.

"I can get him to an emergency room," Reid said.

Eric nodded and moved aside to let him, but Kellerman raised his head and glared at Eric. "Fucking Shifter bastards," he whispered, then the life went out of his eyes, and he slumped back to the floor.

"Shit," Graham said.

Eric studied Kellerman, the Shifter in him feeling glee, the man in him relieved that Kellerman would not now be able to expose Iona. He reached down and closed Kellerman's eyes.

"The Goddess go with you," he said quietly.

From outside, they heard the wail of sirens, security police, Kellerman's backup finally arriving.

CHAPTER THIRTY-TWO

"This can blow up on us, Warden," Graham said.

Eric got to his feet. He took the rifle from Iona, who still stood where she'd fired the bolt into the tiger, her face too pale.

"Get that fire we were talking about going," Eric said. "Reid, take Iona and everything we brought and meet us at the roadhouse where Diego dropped me off. We'll come cross-country. My clothes are there, and I don't want them left around for police to find. Graham, *everything* here has to go. No DNA from any of our Shifters, nothing left of the experiments. Got it? No, Iona, don't argue with me."

Reid was already gathering up the sat phone and Xavier's equipment, the researchers' phones, and anything they'd left behind. He piled everything into Iona's numb arms.

Iona glared at Eric as he bent to kiss her. "Don't you dare blow yourself up, get caught, or get shot." She melted into the kiss then, her look saying everything. "Come home to me."

"Don't worry, love. I've done this before."

Iona smiled a crooked smile. "And I want to hear all about it."

Eric dropped another kiss to her lips and stepped back. Reid folded his arms around her, and then they were gone.

Sabotage. Eric had gotten good at it during the last World War. It was amazing what a Shifter could do with a little gasoline, fabric, and matches. Shifters were good at getting away quickly and silently as well. The Nazis hadn't known what hit them.

No gasoline here, but plenty of natural gas lines and tanks of oxygen and acetylene. Eric got the tiger Shifter up and shifted back to his human form to help them build piles of debris and make them so explosive they would bring down the building.

Eric took more tanks of acetylene and oxygen and went down into the basement with the tiger, setting the canisters leaking at strategic support points.

They raced back up the stairs and out onto the roof as Graham finished on the top floor. When Graham joined them, Eric dialed the cell phone he'd left down in the basement to set everything off.

They heard a distant boom that rocked the building. Tiger Shifter stood up in the dark and spit onto the roof. "It is finished," he said.

Graham lit an alcohol burner he'd brought upstairs with the lighter he'd found, and threw it hard into the stairwell. The three of them sprinted for the fire escape, flowing over and down it as the windows blew.

Orange fire lit the dark as the building belched flame. The three Shifters, in their animal forms, leapt from the fire escape to the ground two floors below and sprinted into the darkness.

Behind them, the building exploded, lighting the sky. A giant ball of fire arced toward the runway. Security police and a fire truck raced toward the runway, more worried about whatever planes were there than a building that housed iffy experiments.

The tiger was running, following Graham, and Eric came right behind them as they headed west through the desert.

Reid and Iona popped back into existence in what looked like a dark parking lot full of pickups and Harleys. At least, Iona thought she saw that before dizziness spun her around, and she started to fall. Reid caught her in surprisingly strong arms and held her upright.

"That was weird," she said breathlessly.

"Not what I said the first time *I* did it," Reid said. "I didn't know I knew that many swear words."

"Where the hell are we?"

"The roadhouse on the Ninety-five. There's Shane."

Shane was running out to them, his big bulk made even bulkier by the heavy jacket he wore against the November cold. "Iona. Thank the Goddess."

He caught Iona in a large hug that stole the rest of her breath. "Mom drove me up here. I take it Eric's on his way back?"

"Running across the desert as we speak," Reid said. "With Graham and . . . another Shifter. Hope your mom brought the big truck."

Nell had, and by the time she pulled her F-250 around to them, Eric came walking out of the desert, fully dressed, Graham at his side, flanked by the tiger Shifter—in his tiger form now. Eric didn't stop until he reached Iona, who shivered in the darkness, and pulled her straight into his arms.

"What do we do with him?" Iona asked Eric the next morning.

She sat in the circle of Eric's arms on the edge of the back porch, the sun streaming warmth but the air cool. Cassidy lounged next to them on her favorite Adirondack chair with baby Amanda in her arms. She'd liked the sling Iona had fashioned that kept Amanda against her, but Nell had found her one that was soft and pretty. Diego sat on the arm of the chair, his touch never far from his mate and cub.

Graham was out making sure his Shifters were safe, while Reid was here, having decided to keep an eye on Tiger Man. The tiger Shifter was dressed now in sweatpants and T-shirt that Shane provided, the man as big as the grizzlies. Reid sat next to him on a picnic bench in the yard, Jace on his other side.

Kellerman had been reported dead this morning in a fire

on a military base—news reporters never said which base. He'd gone into a deserted building alone, according to the guard that had been stationed in front of it, and the building had blown up not long later. No survivors.

The Shifter council said the appropriate things, such as, "He will be missed," made noises about appointing a new head, and got on with it. The council people Graham had spoken to resigned. Tomorrow, the human council would come for the ground-breaking ceremony for the new Shifter houses. Life in Shiftertown would move on.

Liam Morrissey had set out lawn chairs for himself and Kim, the pair of them sitting together, baby Katriona on Kim's lap. Liam took a sip of coffee that Iona had seen him spike with something in a flask.

"Well, now, I thought I'd take him home with me," Liam said in answer to Iona's question. "There's room in my Shiftertown, and he needs somewhere to go. I'm also good with introducing Collars."

"Will he have to wear a Collar?" Iona asked in trepidation.

The tiger Shifter was calm enough this morning, sunlight glistening on his tiger-striped hair. He'd showered and learned how to shave, courtesy of Eric, and Iona was struck with how handsome he was. Whatever unfortunate Shifters and humans had donated DNA to make him, they'd been fine-looking people.

"I think he'd better wear one," Liam said. "They help keep us from going feral, and he's going to need help. I hate to do it, but 'tis temporary."

"The Goddess go with him," Cassidy said softly. Diego, sitting on the wide arm of her chair, leaned down and kissed the top of her head.

"He needs a name," Iona said. "We can't call him Twenty-three or Tiger Man."

"What name do ye want, lad?" Liam called to him.

The tiger Shifter looked up, but Iona had no doubt that he'd heard every word of the low-voiced conversation.

"I don't know yet," the tiger said.

Now that he'd had a chance to sleep and eat in a place he

didn't have to be driven by rage, the harsh throatiness of his speech had calmed somewhat.

"Don't be in a hurry," Iona said. "The perfect name will come to you."

"She's a generous lady," Eric said.

Tiger Man, watching Iona, didn't respond.

Eric still looked tired after the fight, his struggle with pain, and the charge back across the desert, but he kissed Iona with as much skill as ever. He'd been able to make love to her fairly robustly early this morning as well.

"And you," Liam said. "We need to be fixing your pain problem."

"About that." Eric looked through the open patio door into the house, where Xavier sat at the kitchen table with Neal the Guardian, both of them taking advantage of another of Diego's hearty breakfasts. "Xav, did you track down Murdock?"

"He's standing by," Xavier called, not looking up from his chilaquiles.

"Neal, what about that other thing?"

"Got it," Neal said.

Iona gave Eric a questioning look. Eric leaned back on his elbows, his body as relaxed as ever, but something eager sparkled in his eyes.

"Can I know what that's all about?" Iona asked him.

Eric closed his eyes and tilted his face to the sun. "Not yet."

"Eric."

Eric's green eyes were warm when he finally looked at her. He touched her cheek, the slow caress heating her blood. "I have a couple of things to take care of before the full moon ceremony tonight. Then I'll tell you everything."

Iona wasn't the least bit content with that, but Eric traced her lips, and Iona kissed his fingers. She liked the way heat flared in his eyes when she ever so gently bit his fingertip.

D r. Murdock was retired, living in a small house in Boulder City, the only town in Nevada that didn't allow gambling. Eric arrived at his house, accompanied by Xavier and Neal, and scared the man half to death.

Eric interrogated him for a couple of hours, until he knew everything he needed to know. Then he went to an airstrip out in the desert, well hidden from the humans, and asked the pilot called Marlo, who owned the place, to fly him to Idaho.

In a Shiftertown near Sandpoint, Neal led Eric to the house where one Ross McRae lived. The Shifter was unmated with no family, but he shared a crowded little house with another pride of Felines.

Eric talked to him for a time, then he helped the Shifter pack up his meager belongings. Eric met with the leader of the Shiftertown—a Lupine from Alaska—explained the situation, and got the leader's blessing to take McRae with him back for a visit to Las Vegas.

Marlo, the thin man as cheerful as ever, flew them back the long way south, getting them home in plenty of time for the full moon to rise.

The full moon ceremony, Iona saw, was even more of a celebration than the full sun one had been. The entire Shiftertown was there, Iona once more wearing a flower garland and standing with Eric in the backyard.

Graham now stood in the front circle, which was reserved for family and friends of the pride. He'd brought a date, a human woman with dark brown hair. He had his arm draped over her shoulders and glared defiantly at anyone who dared give him a surprised look. Graham, who'd claimed he wasn't interested in any females but Lupines—interesting. The woman gave him wide smiles, obviously seeing something in Graham past the blustering anger.

Iona had seen more to him too, as he'd helped Eric out in Area 51. Graham was aggressive and didn't hold back his opinions, but he was smart, decisive, and knew how to take care of people. His Lupines trusted him, the little ones running readily to him without fear. He and Eric still needed to work things out, but Iona had stopped doubting they'd be able to.

Tiger Man was there too, he who still didn't have a name. Liam would take him home with him tomorrow before the construction crews came. In Austin, maybe Tiger could start a new life.

Tiger Man looked uncertain, standing among so many Shifters, but the constant feral rage had gone from his eyes, to be replaced by a hope that maybe he could find more in life than mere survival.

The circles closed around Eric and Iona in the cool, white moonlight. Liam and Kim performed the ceremony, blessing Eric and Iona under the sight of the Mother Goddess. Her presence was here, Liam said, and the mating was now complete.

The party that followed was manic. Shifters danced, shouted, and howled in human form, between beast, and Shifter. A full moon mating, even more than a full sun ceremony, tended to raise the mating frenzy in others. There'd be much sex in Shiftertown tonight.

"Warden." Graham stopped next to Eric and Iona, interrupting their slow kiss. He was still with the young woman, who peered at them interestedly. "I've decided not to challenge you for leadership. At least not right away."

Eric regarded Graham with his usual dispassion. "Nice to know you'll honor my full moon blessing by not trying to kill me."

"You're not as incompetent as I first thought you were. I'll let you keep your Shiftertown, as long as you don't undermine my authority over my wolves. I rule them, you rule your Shifters. Got it?"

"You're talking about joint leadership," Eric said. "It's never been done."

"Not so much joint as you don't step on my toes, I don't step on yours. I'm leader over my Lupine clans, and you don't mess with that. And I won't tell your Shifters what to do. I don't want to have to deal with a bunch of fucking Felines and crazy-ass bears anyway."

He trailed off into growls, and Eric stuck out his hand. "Done."

"Done."

Graham shook his hand in the human way, but their hands remained clasped, sinews working as each tried to out-crush the other.

Iona stopped herself rolling her eyes and smiled at the young woman. "I'm Iona. Shifter males are rude. I'll never know your name if you don't tell me."

"Misty. Misty Granger. It's Melissa, but everyone calls me Misty. Do you like the garland? Graham said I should do it for you—I own a flower shop on Flamingo."

"Yes." Iona touched it. "It's beautiful." The garland had been delivered to the front door that afternoon, but Iona and Cassidy had been so busy getting ready for the ceremony that Iona hadn't noticed where it had come from.

"I thought white roses and baby's breath, since it was a moon ceremony." Misty studied it critically. "Came out well, I think."

Eric and Graham finally let go of each other's hands, the testosterone contest ending in a draw. Eric slid his arm around Iona's waist.

"It is beautiful," Eric said, giving Misty one of his warm smiles. "Thank you. Now, I have another surprise for my mate."

Eric led Iona away from Graham, who showed all his teeth in a grin as he watched them go.

Eric walked with her toward the largest bonfire built in the center of the yards, but before they reached it, Iona saw her mother break away from Diego, Cassidy, and Amanda, and walk, her body taut, to a Shifter male who stood a little outside the circle of firelight.

The Shifter was as tall as Eric but not so bulked. He had jet-black hair that was just going gray at the temples and a hard face that softened as he watched Penny approach him. Her mother kept moving to him, bewildered. When Penny stopped in front of him, the Shifter looked down at her for a long moment, then his face crumpled, and he pressed his hands over it. Penny gently took the man's hands, lowered them from his face, and raised them to her lips.

Iona's mouth dropped open in astonishment. "Eric, who is . . ."

Eric took her hand and started to walk her toward him. "I found your dad, Iona. Well, Xav and my Guardian did."

Iona stumbled. Eric's strong grip kept her upright, encouraging her along until they reached the Shifter and Penny.

The Shifter turned and looked at Iona, stunned. His eyes, Iona saw, were the same blue as hers, and in them she read pain, fear, loneliness, and shame. "I'm sorry, lass," the man said, his Highland Scots accent thick. "Iona, my daughter, I am so sorry."

"He didn't know about you," Eric said, his voice a warm rumble. "He was one of the first Shifters rounded up, and has been living in a Shiftertown in Idaho ever since."

"You could have tried to find me," Penny said, tears in her voice. "You knew who I was. You could have tried."

"You were married, lass," Ross McRae said. "You married the man you truly loved, and were happy. How could I take that from you?"

"But he died," Penny said. "And I was alone." She still had his hands, holding them as though she never wanted to let go.

"And I was a Shifter with a Collar. Life with a Shifter is hard, and I couldn't force you to live it. And I had no idea that one of your bairns was mine."

"I didn't know how to find you to tell you."

Iona's eyes burned as she listened to them. With a moan that wrenched from her heart, she pushed past her mother and flung her arms around her father.

Ross McRae's face streamed with tears as he swept Iona up into a tight hug. He held her there, shaking, while Eric's strong hand on Iona's back warmed her through.

"You can start making it up now, I think," Eric said. "I've put the procedures in motion to move you to this Shiftertown, if that's what you want."

Ross lifted his head, his cheeks wet. "Do you want that, Pen?"

Penny nodded. "I think so."

Ross wrapped one arm around Penny while keeping Iona within the embrace of the other. "Thank you, Eric Warden," he said.

"My pleasure. Welcome to the family, Ross McRae. I love your daughter with all my heart. Hope you don't mind."

"Not at all, lad," Ross said, trying to smile.

The look Eric bent on Iona had her heart speeding. "And now, if you don't mind," he said, "it's our full moon ceremony. Which means we have lots to do."

Ross relinquished Iona to him with a bit of reluctance. Eric instantly slid his arm around Iona as though he intended to be touching her in some way the rest of their lives.

Iona looked back as they started for the house. Her mother and Ross had turned to each other again, Ross enclosing Penny's hands in his.

"How did you do that?" Iona asked. "Find him for us?"

"The Guardian Network. Don't ask—I don't understand it all myself. Guardians are the keepers of information, and once Neal had a place to start, he found Ross fairly quickly. I think he's here to stay."

"Thank you," Iona said, heartfelt. "Thank you so much, Eric."

They'd reached the house. Eric pulled Iona inside its stuffy darkness and warmed her lips with his kiss. "I'm your mate. I do everything for you now."

Eric's hard body came against hers, his wanting obvious. Their kiss was quiet, the solitude of the house a soothing contrast to the wildness outside. Eric's firm, hot hands slid down Iona's back, and she scented his frenzy rising.

"Wait," she whispered. "Be careful. What if the pain comes?"

"It won't." Eric nipped her neck. "Not as long as I'm with you."

"What did you find out about it? That was why you went to see this Murdock, didn't you? Cassidy told me who he was."

"Come with me." Eric took Iona's hands and tugged her down the hall to Jace's bedroom—which was now theirs—but instead of making for the bed, he opened the secret door that led downstairs.

Eric took her into the stairwell and locked the door behind her, then led her down, not bothering with the lights, both of them seeing fine in the darkness.

He took her to one of the bedrooms in the hall, next to the one Jace had been using. This was a luxurious contrast to the rooms upstairs—a four-poster bed draped with airy hangings, a cavernous bathroom with a marble sunken bathtub, and a rug whose softness she felt under her sandals.

Eric lifted Iona to the edge of the bed and started unbuttoning her blouse. "Dr. Murdock was the one researcher twenty years ago who actually felt sorry for me as he stuck needles into me and shocked me almost to death. Which made him, in that place, a nice guy. I did see him today, and he confirmed what was wrong with me. I told him he needed to cure me, and in return, I'd let him live. He agreed."

Iona's Shifter felt a twinge of satisfaction at Eric's casual threat of violence. She'd grown enraged when Cassidy had told her that Dr. Murdock had been one of the researchers who'd experimented on Eric. Iona had been ready to run after Eric and claw the man herself. These people who treated Shifters like lab animals—as they'd done to Tiger and had started to do to Amanda—deserved to be a little scared.

"And what did he say was wrong with you?" she asked.

Eric finished unbuttoning Iona's blouse and pulled it open. She wasn't wearing a bra, and the cool air of the underground room touched her bare skin as Eric's gaze slid to it. He didn't ogle, he admired, warmed.

He slid the blouse off her and started on her skirt. "You were right, and Kellerman was right, that what was done to me was part of humans trying to make a super Shifter, like the tiger. Only, they started with a full-grown Shifter in my case. They planned to take off the Collar but keep me programmed with the pain if I turned violent, but only if I turned violent on *them*. They were thinking that with a series of remotes and implants they would control me with pain when they wanted to, or let me kill for them when they pointed me at their enemies."

Iona listened in anger and revulsion. "How could they do that?"

Eric shrugged. "They were humans who didn't know what to think when they discovered that shapeshifters were real. What do humans always do when they find a new species of animal? Capture it, study it, tag it. Or kill it and hang its head on a wall."

"But what they did to you didn't work, did it? They stopped the experiments, obviously."

Eric pushed the loosened skirt down, and Iona wriggled her way out of it. She sat bare, in panties only, and reached for the buttons on Eric's shirt. "They stopped the experiments because Shifters' rights activists started to raise hell. I told Murdock that what they were trying to do wouldn't ever work. The Collars are partly magic, not just technology—a half Fae shithead designed them. Murdock and his colleagues were trying to recreate the effect with biotechnology—just like the humans in Area Fifty-one were trying to recreate Shifters themselves with biotech. They put an implant in me all right, one so tiny I never knew I had it. The implant was supposed to trigger a chemical reaction whenever I turned violent, but they never got the reaction right, and my Collar always went off before it did. Then they were forced to stop the experiments and let me go, so they never could fine-tune the implant."

Iona opened all Eric's buttons and skimmed her hands inside his shirt. "But why did the pain go away for twenty years and then come back now?"

"Because I started learning how to control my Collar," Eric said. "When Jace began teaching me the meditation techniques to keep my Collar from reacting to my adrenaline, the little implant woke up. They'd never taken it out—either they forgot or hoped they could get around the new rules sooner or later and begin work on it again. Then the implant started malfunctioning—or maybe making up for lost time—who the hell knows? *Any* adrenaline spike set it off, even small ones that wouldn't necessarily have triggered my Collar."

"I'm so sorry." Iona rubbed his warm, bare chest, hating how the pain had torn at him. "But Dr. Murdock is going to help you?"

"He started today." Eric shrugged the shirt off and turned to show her the deep gouge in his right shoulder blade, the wound already closed and scarring. "I told him to get his scalpel and dig the damned implant out of me. It was so tiny, like a dot. I couldn't believe something that small caused me that much pain."

"What did you do with it? You didn't let him keep it, did you?"

Eric's smile was feral. "I crushed it while he watched, appalled that I'd destroy something that unique and expensive. Then I told him to dredge through his memory for any other Shifter he'd done this to, and find them, tell them, and fix them."

"Good," Iona said, her anger rising. "Good."

"He needs to give me a few injections, he said, to put my adrenaline balance back the way it should be," Eric said. "But it's a start. I already feel better."

Iona slid her fingers along the puckered skin of the gouge. "Are you sure there was only one implant?"

"He says so. I told him that if I discovered I had more, I'd come back and break his neck, so I'm pretty sure he told me the truth."

"Good," Iona said again.

Eric turned to face her again, stepping between her parted thighs, hands sliding up her arms. "But I would have died without your touch."

Iona caressed his chest, not liking that he'd gone through so much. "Are you sure you're all right?"

"Like I said, as long as I'm with you, I'll be fine. The touch of the mate, *your* touch, is what kept me from going insane, no matter how close I came." His breath warmed her cheek. "The Goddess sent you right when I needed you. I can talk all I want about the science, but you're what keeps me alive. You always will be."

She leaned forward and kissed his chest, feeling the heat of his body, the pound of his heart under her lips. "Then I'll be here. I'll be here always."

"That was the plan." Eric's voice rumbled pleasantly around her. "Love you, Iona."

"Love you too." She slanted him a smile. "If you're feeling better, then I can do this . . ." She let her fingers become claws and lightly scratched him down his chest. "And this." She rocked up, scraping his throat with her teeth, giving him another love bite.

"Mmm. You can do anything you want, love. It's not mating that hurt me, it was anger, and the need to protect you." He licked her cheek. "*Mating* just makes me a little wild."

Iona slanted a smile up at him. "Are these walls soundproof?"

His eyes flicked to Shifter. "Why do you think I brought you down here?"

Eric pushed her back to the bed, tearing her panties off her as she went down. He unbuckled, unzipped, and got out of his pants, then climbed over her, naked, trapping her wrists above her head.

"I think we started this way," Iona said, her excitement rising.

"I held back," Eric said, a growl in his voice. "I didn't want to hurt you. I might have if I took you fully before you were my true mate." He came down to her. "Which you are now."

"And I always will be."

Eric's smile blazed, and the last vestiges of loneliness she'd seen in him vanished.

"And I'll always be yours, Iona." He nuzzled her. "Mate of my heart."

Iona's smile grew wicked. "Mate of my heart," she whispered. "With the best ass." She drew her foot up the back of his leg. "Don't hold back now."

Eric's smile vanished. His weight pressed her down, his kiss hot and raw. He growled as he moved his mouth to her neck, nipping and biting, his cock hard against her abdomen.

Iona twined her leg around his, urging him. Eric pulled her upright, still on his knees, and holding her hips, he slid her down onto him. She groaned in pleasure as he filled her, her fingers turning to claws to dig into his shoulders. Eric widened her, filling her, winding up her mating frenzy until she wanted to scream with it.

His growls continued, the male Shifter finding his pleasure in his mate. He held her hard against him, Eric kneeling back, their bodies entwined, face-to-face. Eric nipped and kissed her, his cock high and hard inside her.

Then the joining grew wild. Iona never knew exactly what happened, but they were grappling with each other, licking, biting, laughing, shouting. The mate bond twined around Iona's heart as their frenzy grew, changing her mating hunger into pure bliss.

"I love you." Iona was never sure if she yelled it or whispered it.

Eric's leopard eyes shone hot and green. "I love *you*, Iona. Mate of my heart."

She was on her back now, with her mate on top of her, his

warm weight making her rejoice. Her mating frenzy floated into the darkness as the mate bond grew, binding her forever to this man, this leader, this protector she loved with all her heart.

The panther inside Iona smiled and gave a little rumble of satisfaction.

Turn the page for a special preview of the next
Shifters Unbound novel by Jennifer Ashley

TIGER MAGIC

Coming June 2013 from Berkley Sensation!

"No, no, no, no, not *today*. You can't do this to me today!"
But the car died anyway.

It throbbed onto the shoulder of the empty highway, bucked twice, and gurgled to silence.

"Aw, damn it." Carly's four-inch heels emerged from the car, followed by tanned legs and a tight white sheath dress. She glared down at the vehicle, the Texas wind tugging her light brown hair out of its careful French braid.

She'd have to be wearing white. Carly jammed her hands on her hips and skewered the Corvette with her enraged stare.

Take the 'Vette, her fiancé Ethan had said. *It's a big day. You want to make an entrance.* He'd been in a hurry to get Carly out of the house, so he'd pressed the keys into her hand and pushed her out the door.

Carly had agreed with him—the artist they were showcasing liked classic cars, and he was doing an exclusive with their gallery. Buyers were already lined up. Carly's commission would be enormous.

If she could get there. Carly kicked one of the tires in rage, then danced back. Her shoes were substantial but that still hurt.

Perfect. Ethan could be generous—and he had the filthy

richness to do it—but he also forgot little details like making sure cars got tuned up.

"His lazy highness can just come and get me then." Carly went around to the passenger side of the car and leaned in through the open window to grab her cell phone from her purse.

Today. This had to happen, *today*. Still bent into the car, she punched numbers with her thumb, but the phone made the beeping noise that indicated it was out of range.

"No effing way." Carly backed out of the car and raised the phone high. "Come on. Find me a signal."

And then she saw him.

The man stood about ten feet from the car, not on the road, but in the tall Texas grass beside it. Being late spring, that grass was full of blue, yellow, and white flowers, and this being Hill Country, the grass was a nice vivid green.

It wasn't every day a girl saw a tall hunk of a man, shoulders broad under a black and red SoCo Novelties T-shirt standing by the side of the road. Watching her.

Really watching her. His eyes were fixed on her, not in the dazed way of a transient wandering around in an alcoholic haze, but looking at her like no human being had looked at her before.

He wasn't scruffy like a transient either. His face was shaved, his body and clothes clean, jeans mud-free despite him having walked through the field. And he must have walked through the field, because she sure hadn't seen him on the road.

His hair . . . Carly blinked as the strong sunshine caressed sleek hair that was orange and black. Not dyed orange and black—dye tended to make hair matte and stark. This looked entirely natural, sunlight picking up highlights of red orange and blue black.

She knew she should be afraid. A strange guy with tiger-striped hair popping out of nowhere, staring at her like that should terrify her. But he didn't.

He hadn't been there when Carly had first stopped the car and climbed out. He must have arrived when she'd bent over to get the phone, which meant he'd seen every bit of her round backside hugged by her skintight white dress.

This stretch of road was deserted. Eerily so. The streets in Austin were always packed, but once in Hill Country, it was possible to find roads empty of traffic, such as the one she drove to get to the art gallery every day.

There was no one out here, no one speeding down the straight road to rescue her. No one out here but herself in now-rumpled white and the tall man staring at her from the grass.

"Hey!" Carly shouted at him. "You know how to fix a car?"

He didn't have a name. He didn't have a clan. He'd had a mate, and a cub, but they'd died and the humans who'd held him captive for forty years had taken them away. They hadn't let him say good-bye, hadn't let him grieve.

Now he lived among other Shifters, brought to this place of humidity, heat, and colorful hills. He only felt completely well when he was running in his tiger form, way out in the back country where no one would see him. He usually ran at night, but today, he hadn't been able to stay in the confines of the house, or Shiftertown. So he'd gone.

He'd left his clothes hidden behind a little hill at the side of this road. Connor was supposed to pick him up, but not for a couple more hours, and Connor was often late. Tiger didn't mind. He liked being out here.

He'd dressed, walked around the hill to the road . . . and saw a fine backside sticking out of a bright red car. The backside was covered in thin white fabric, showing him faintly pink panties beneath.

Below the nice buttocks were shapely legs, not too long, tanned by Texas sun. Heels that rose about half a mile made those legs even shapelier.

The woman had hair the color of winter-gold grass. She had a cell phone in her hand, but she waited, the other hand on her shapely hip, for him to answer her question.

Tiger climbed the slope from the grass to the road. She watched him come, unafraid, her sunglasses trained on him.

Tiger wanted to see her eyes. If she was going to be his mate, he wanted to see everything about her.

And this woman would be his mate. No doubt about that. The scent that kicked into his nostrils, the way his heartbeat slowed to powerful strokes, the way his body filled with heat, told him that.

Connor had tried to explain that mating didn't happen like that for Shifters. A Shifter male got to know a female a little bit before he chose, and then he mate-claimed her. The mate bond could rear its head anytime before or after that, but it didn't always on first glance.

Tiger had listened to this wisdom without arguing, but he knew better. He wasn't an ordinary Shifter. And this female, hand on one curved hip, wasn't an ordinary woman.

"Can you put the hood up?" Tiger asked her.

"I don't know," she said, frustrated. "This car is different from anything I usually drive. Hang on, let me check."

Her voice was a sweet little Texas drawl, not too heavy. A light touch, enough to make the heat crawl through Tiger's veins and go straight to his cock.

The woman found a catch and worked the hood open, then dusted off her hands and peered at the inner workings without comprehension.

"Classic car, my ass." She scowled at it. "*Classic* just means *old*."

Tiger looked inside. The layout was much different from the pickup he and Connor had been tinkering with all spring, but Connor had been teaching him a lot about vehicles. "Got a socket wrench?"

When he looked up at the woman, he saw her staring at him from behind the sunglasses. "Your eyes," she said. "They're . . ."

"Yellow."

Tiger turned away before her scent convinced him to press her back against the side of the car. This was his mate, and he didn't want to hurt her. She wasn't a female someone had tossed into his cage to trigger his mating frenzy.

He wanted to take this slow, woo her a little. Maybe with something involving food. Shifter males around here liked to cook for their mates, and Tiger liked the rituals.

She opened the back of the car and found a toolbox, which did have a set of socket wrenches. Tiger took one and reached inside the car, letting himself look for the silence in him that would lead him to the problem. He seemed to be able to sense what was wrong with engines, and how to coax them back to life. He couldn't explain how he did it—he just knew that cars and trucks didn't watch him, or fear him.

As he worked, the neck of his T-shirt slid down, baring the silver and black Collar that ran around his throat. The woman bent over to him, the top of her dress dangerously open, the warmth of her breath touching his cheek.

"Holy shit," she said. "You're a Shifter."

"I know."

She lifted her sunglasses and stared at him. Her eyes were clear green, flecked with a little gray. She stared at him frankly, in open curiosity, and without fear.

Of course she wasn't afraid of him. She was going to be his mate.

Tiger met her gaze, unblinking, binding her to him. Her eyes widened the slightest bit, as though she realized something had happened between them, but she didn't know what.

She restored her sunglasses and straightened up. "I've never seen a Shifter before. I didn't know y'all were allowed out of Shiftertown."

Tiger picked up the wrench with one hand and moved the other to the timing belt chain, which had come loose from the gear. "We're allowed."

The repair needed both delicacy and strength, but Tiger finished quickly, leaning all the way inside and letting his fingers know what to do. He backed out and closed the toolbox. "Start it now."

The woman eagerly rushed to the car, slid inside, and cranked it to life. She emerged again, leaving the car running, while Tiger scanned a few more things. "The timing belt will hold for now, but the whole shaft is worn and needs to be replaced. Take the car home and don't use it again until it's fixed."

"Terrific. Armand is going to kill me."

Tiger didn't know who Armand was and didn't much care. He carried the toolbox to the back for her and closed the small trunk, then came back to close the hood.

He found her smiling at him on the other side of the hood as it came down. "You're kind of amazing, you know that?"

she asked. "So what were you doing out in that field? Were you running around as a . . . Let me guess. Tiger?"

"What gave it away?" he asked dryly.

"Very funny. I've never met a man with striped hair and yellow eyes. Call it a clue. Anyway, you're a lifesaver. I'm Carly, by the way." She stuck out her hand then pulled it back from his now-greasy one. "Hang on. I think there's some wipes in here."

Carly leaned in through the passenger window again. Tiger stood still and enjoyed watching her, and when she came out, she had no doubt he'd been looking. "Like what you see?" she asked, her voice holding challenge.

Tiger saw no reason to lie. "Yes," he said.

"You sweet-talker." Carly pulled out two damp wipes for him.

Tiger took them and wiped off his hands. Wet wipes were familiar at least. Connor's aunt always made him clean up with them when he'd been working on the truck, before she'd let them back into the house.

"You need a ride to town?" Carly asked. "I'm going to have to go back and get another car. Serves me right for letting Ethan talk me into making an impression. Like I said, Armand's going to kill me, but I'm so late now, it's not going to matter."

"Yes."

Carly leaned toward him. "Yes, you want a ride? Or are you just being polite while I ramble?"

"The ride."

"Man of few words. I like it. Ethan, my fiancé, can talk on and on and on about his family, his business, his day, his life, Ethan—his favorite topic."

Tiger stopped. "Fiancé."

"Do Shifters have fiancés? It's what humans call the man they're going to marry."

Tiger wadded up the now-dirty wipes in his big hands. "I didn't know you'd have a fiancé."

Carly opened the door of the running car as though she hadn't heard him. "Get in. Ethan's house is on the water—I know that's a long way from Shiftertown, but I can always get you a taxi, or one of Ethan's many lackeys can run you home."

"Why are you marrying him?"

Carly shrugged. "Girl's got to marry someone, mostly so her mother stops mentioning it every five minutes. Ethan's a good catch." She smiled. "Besides, I'm in love with him."

No, she wasn't. The slight motion in her throat, the scent of nervousness as she replied gave the lie. She didn't love him. Tiger felt something like triumph.

He got into the car as Carly slid into the driver's seat inches away from him. Her fingers ran over the steering wheel as she made a competent u-turn on the still-empty road, and she drove, somewhat slowly, back toward the city.

Carly tried to talk to him. She liked to chatter, this female. Tiger was fine with sitting back and listening to her, scenting her, watching her.

As they neared town and the road started getting busier, Carly lifted her cell phone and called the man named Armand. She explained she'd be late then held the phone from her ear while a male voice on the other end yelled for a long time. Carly rolled her eyes at Tiger and smiled, unworried.

"Bark's worse than his bite," she said, clicking off the phone.

"I know some wolves like that."

Carly laughed, her red mouth opening. Tiger leaned in closer to her, not hard to do in this coffin of a car, and exhaled his scent onto her.

She glanced at him, again with the puzzlement of knowing something had happened, but not sure what. "It's dangerous to give strange men rides. I wonder why I'm not worried with you."

Because you're my mate. "Because I'd never hurt you."

She gave him another smile. "Well, you can't, can you? Shifters are dangerous, but that's why you wear the Collar. Keeps you tame. You can't be violent with it."

Tiger could. This Collar was fake. It didn't have the technology or Fae magic that would send shocks through his system if he started to attack.

They'd tried to put a real Collar on him, and Tiger had nearly gone insane. Thank God the females and cubs hadn't been allowed to watch. Tiger might have gone for them, sensing their weakness. They concluded that Tiger should wear a fake Collar—not that the humans realized it was fake—and proceed from there.

This Collar would not stop Tiger from scooping up Carly and running off with her if he wanted to. He could sequester her, mate with her, soothe his need for her until they both collapsed in exhaustion.

Or he could be kind and wait for her to get used to him.

Carly kept up the conversation all the way up into the hills along the river. She pulled into a drive that arced in front of an enormous house, the mansion white with black shutters and black trim. Carly parked the car and emerged, and Tiger got out with her.

Gates on either side of the house led to the backyard, and Carly opened one, beckoning Tiger to follow. Tiger got in front of her and went through the gate first, his Shifter instinct urging him to make sure the way was safe for her.

The backyard overlooked the river and the hills opposite it, where similar houses had a view of this one. A stair ran down the side of the hill to a private dock, where two boats bobbed.

A row of glass windows lined the back of the house, but the glare of the sun and tint of the windows kept Tiger from seeing inside. A man with pruning shears looked up from a bush at the corner of the house, then stood up in alarm as Carly reached for the handle of one of the glass doors.

"Ms. Randal, you don't want to go in there."

Carly turned to him, startled. Tiger tried to get around her to enter the house first, but Carly was too quick. She was opening the door and walking inside before he could stop her, and he had to settle for following a step behind her.

What Tiger smelled inside the house wasn't danger, however. It was sex.

He saw why when he and Carly rounded a wall behind which stretched a huge kitchen. Cabinetry in a fine golden wood filled the walls, the long counters shiny granite. It was clean in here, no dishes cluttering the counters, no one cooking something that smelled good, no chatter and laughter as a meal was prepared.

A woman sat on top of the counter with her blouse open, her skirt up around her hips. A man with his pants around his ankles was thrusting hard into her, holding her bare legs around his thighs. Both humans were grunting and panting, and neither noticed Carly or Tiger.

Tiger stepped in front of Carly, trying to put his huge body between her and the scene. Carly stopped, her purse falling from nerveless fingers to the floor. "Ethan," she said in shock.

The man turned around. Tiger was growling, feeling the anguish of his mate in waves, the animal in him wanting nothing more than to kill the person who'd upset her.

The man jumped, his mouth dropping open, then he stumbled over his pants and had to catch himself on the counter.

"Carly, what the *fuck* are you doing here?" His gaze went to Tiger, whose fingers were sprouting the long, razor-sharp claws of the Bengal. "And who the hell is *he*?"